"A SPLENDIDLY SOPHISTICATED KARATE CHOP TO THE GROIN . . .

Richard Condon has tapped the most awesome power source of them all—SEX!"

—*Los Angeles Times*

"A WILD, FAR-OUT BLITZ, IN CONDON'S BEST WHOOP-IT-UP, PUT-IT-DOWN STYLE . . . The cast includes a political candidate called 'Funky Dunc,' his nymphomaniac mother-in-law and her 70-year-old lover, a Democratic leader known as 'Captain Pedernales,' a hirsute homosexual who slavers in anticipation of a jail sentence, assorted hippies, yippies, teeny-boppers and nuts of all shapes and sizes."

—*Saturday Review*

"CONDON ZEROES IN ON THE UNITED STATES WITH THE CROSS HAIRS OF A BOMB SIGHT . . .

Presidential campaigns: POW! The Mafia: POW! The Government: TRIPLE POW! Organized Religion: BOOM! Drugs, legal and illegal: WHAMMO! Militant homosexuality, pornography, Women's Lib, the arms trade: WHOOSH! *The Vertical Smile* is OUTRAGEOUS, BITTER, SAVAGE AND WILDLY FUNNY!"

—*Detroit Free Press*

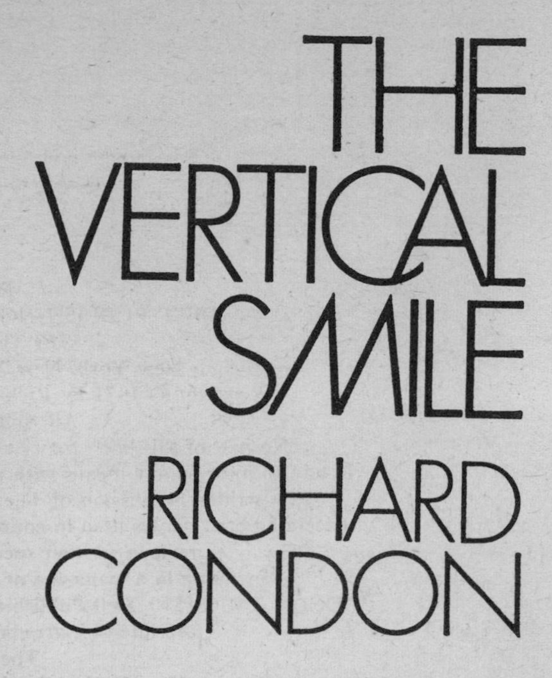

THE VERTICAL SMILE

RICHARD CONDON

A DELL BOOK

For Jemma and Nito, this book
and—Aiiee!—this world

Published by
DELL PUBLISHING CO., INC.
750 Third Avenue
New York, New York 10017

Dell ® TM 681510, Dell Publishing Co., Inc.
Reprinted by arrangement with
The Dial Press
New York, New York 10017
Printed in the United States of America
First Dell printing—August 1972

"The
human
comedy
begins
with
a
vertical
smile."

1

On a lovely late-March evening she strolled along Park Avenue wearing a palomino mink car coat and a beaded bag which a beautiful man (who turned out to have acne on his back) had given her in Paris when her husband had been alive. The beautiful man's wife had bought forty-three beaded bags before he could stop her.

She was thinking about Dunc Mulligan, her son-in-law, who would be nominated to the United States Senate at the state convention in April; a shoo-in because he was the Attorney General's candidate. All she had ever been able to say in favor of her son-in-law was that he had a beautiful set of caps on his teeth. If they could run him on a combined Republican-Conservative-Democrat ticket, the Panthers would sweep the elections.

She was a small-boned woman with good posture to make her chest look nice. She wore dainty white gloves and virgin's tear pearls. Her hair was blacker than the ravens' wings in Victorian poems; not dyed. It had been the hair of a healthy young vegetarian who had cleaned fish for a living in the heart of the low-rent district in downtown Fuchow. It would have cost six hundred and seventy dollars plus tax if she had not bought it through a doorman whose brother-in-law was a shoplifter.

As she reached the corner of Fifty-fourth Street she glanced to her left and saw the red, double-decker bus which Jemma's had imported from London to take diners across town to the theatres. She loved double-decker buses. She had kept in touch with one friend who lived on Washington Heights because in those days she could take a green double-decker to visit him while her husband Arthur was downtown winning the money. She would sit in the last row on top of the bus, reading the Gulden's Mustard signs which were screwed into the backs of the seats, sailing right through Harlem with her hair flying while nobody, but nobody, fired a gun or threw a rock at her. Then after a marvelous afternoon under Al, who worked nights as a heat maintenance engineer at Hearn's, she would ride downtown on a Number 5, bowling along Riverside Drive opposite the Spry sign on the crowded Jersey shore.

For old time's sake she turned into Fifty-fourth Street, smiling at the red bus because double-deckers still made her feel sexy, entered the revolving door of Jemma's, kept pushing it, made a complete circle without entering the restaurant, debouched upon the pavement and entered the bus. A young man with sensual teeth said something to her but she smiled at him, gestured over her shoulder, and kept going. She climbed the narrow steps to the upper deck slowly. There was nothing to rush about and she had a trick knee.

There were dozens of empty seats on the upper deck but four feet away, all alone, she saw a hauntingly familiar face hovering wistfully above an ectomorphic body which took expensive tweed like paint. Always favor the ectomorphs had been one of the most successful rules of her life. They could go all night, standing up if necessary. She approached him intently, trying to place him before she sat down, thinking how pitiable it was that they didn't nominate a magnificent-looking man like this for the Senate instead of Duncan Mulligan. She sat down with supreme control, reminding herself of another of her successful rules: if you don't ask you don't get. He was pretending he did not know she had sat beside him: hilarious. He seemed to be counting bricks in a building wall. With the confidence she had every right to have in her forty-three-dollar-an-ounce perfume, she slipped her right hand out of its glove and let it rest on her knee to show the six-carat penoloque emerald which Arthur had finally been able to buy from the estate of the woman who had been intensely interested in *chemin-de-fer* but who, no matter how much she lost or how rough things got, no matter how often Arthur approached her with cash, would never, until did death part, give up the ring. If the perfume didn't break him down the emerald would. If they didn't work then she would have to remember his name. She knew she had met him. He was not just one of those people making a fortune on television commercials who drive the public crazy trying to figure out who they are when they go walking around. Maybe she didn't always remember a man's name instantly because maybe she didn't always get fussy and formal and ask their names. Because you have a wonderful meal in some place like Lorand-Barre you don't necessarily go rushing out across Brittany stopping people to demand that they tell you the name of the chef.

The mind was a river. She floated inland from Brittany to Angers. She was drifting back to a long time ago, to the time of Arthur's induction into his fourth wine society.

Arthur had refused to be inducted into wine societies in New York because he said it was snobbish. "In my wine societies in France, Australia, Italy, Chile, Germany and Yugoslavia," he would say, "you are at the headquarters where the wine brains are. Where the region is right under the fingernails of the top wine people." Arthur had given the impression that if he could have carried all of his huge, nine-color wine certificates with him into restaurants that head waiters would begin to show some respect. (Arthur hated to tip.)

She became surer and surer that the man sitting next to her must be one of Arthur's fellow Chevaliers. Angers, the *Confrèrie des Chevaliers du Sacavin,* the oldest wine society in France? The town with the tapestries; not easy to get to—but what was?

They had been invited to stay at a château which had long, high, freezing corridors like a girl's school in an old German movie. There had been no loo in the room. She had lain awake on that bed at about two o'clock in the morning, absorbing water from the air around her. Arthur was snoring D7 chords. She had to pee. She kept putting it off and putting it off until the suffering of getting up got to be less than the suffering of staying in bed. She had finally thrown back the two feather quilts, put on Arthur's robe over her robe and had waddled rapidly out of the room, down the long, gelid hall, as full as a pelican. Nothing could awaken Arthur (who never peed) except sunshine.

As she started back through the darkness of the eighty-meter course, as she passed a doorway, she heard a man's voice whisper to her. She went closer to it to hear what it was selling and the man grabbed her and kissed her in an ingenious way, causing her vagina to whirl like a pinwheel. She pushed him back into the room, that is, well back, onto the bed. He was like the Masked Marvel of Sex with the stamina of a Dominican diplomat and the technical virtuosity of a certain employee at a certain Italian ski resort. But when it was over she had forgotten to ask who he was and it had been too dark inside that room to see his face.

To keep her place at the château at Angers, she folded over a corner of time on the right-hand page of her memory just to spend a little time re-savoring the Dominican diplomat from the summer she and Arthur had attended an *arroz con pollo* tasting in Havana. Arthur knew a man named Klarnet who was always setting up junkets to have something tasted and they always had to travel at least a thousand miles to taste whatever it was. The Dominican diplomat had a secret which any one of Arthur's pharmaceutical companies would have bottled and sold if it had been anything a woman could have told her husband about.

She had met the Dominican diplomat at the craps table at Sans Souci. He had been very diplomatic and they had arranged to meet at his place the next afternoon while Arthur was off being made an *Amigo de Arroz con Pollo de los Antilles*. What a spectacular certificate those Cubans could turn out!

All over the Dominican diplomat's four-story house, which had a regulation-sized boxing ring on its top floor, were round crystal pitchers carefully covered with cheesecloth to keep the flies out. Each pitcher held a supply of Japanese Mushroom Tea: a jar of Instant Erections infinitely marinated and sustained. But when she and Arthur got back to New York she must have bought the wrong mushrooms—or maybe it was the local water—because the stuff had no effect on Arthur.

She turned back the dog-eared page of time and returned hurriedly to the château and the identity of the man seated beside her.

All right: after a fantastic night in the sack it was the following morning. They all met downstairs for brunch. Out of the six men assembled she had not one clue as to which man it had been, except she knew it hadn't been Arthur. It could have been this man. She undressed him mentally and stretched out under him. The size was right. He was tall, not too heavy. Her mother had always mourned very tall girls because she was convinced they couldn't have orgasms which certainly didn't apply to tall men. To produce his name she closed her eyes lightly and squeezed down hard with her legs as though she had him, perhaps as before, in the grand, old nutcracker position. Nothing identifying recurred. She flashed instantaneously to the Angers town hall and the wine investiture but it had all been in French and his name had been lost in the torrent. But it had to come back to her. If she got lucky and came up with the right name he would be permitted to proceed as required but if she got the wrong name she would need only to pretend to be flustered and try to move to another seat. If he were the gentleman she knew him to be, the man who had run across that freezing room just to get her a towel, he would stop her before she could get away and introduce himself. More and more she felt herself evaluating that he was a tre*men*dously attractive man with a very warm left thigh and calf.

While there was a sudden diversion in the street below —someone's viciously trained guard dog was savaging a passing woman's throat—his name flashed into her mind. She would have to wait until the screams and shouting subsided below because he was fascinated with the activity, but it was as though his name had arisen from an automatic-tickler file. That made her think of the gift-wrapped ticklers, eight for four dollars, which she had bought one Christmas Eve on the Reeperbahn in Hamburg while Arthur was being made a *meister* of the prestigious German potato pancake society. One of the ticklers had been tufted gaily in the shape of Little Bo Beep. Another was a mass of circular, miniature tires as a promotion for the Michelin company's little tire man. The men's room attendant who had sold them to her had carried the crazing smell of Vicks VapoRub with him. It was her personal opinion that Vicks VapoRub had done more for sex than it had done even for the common cold.

"Mr. Noon?" her small, cultivated voice asked. "I think you are just too shy to say hello after all these years so I'm going to be bold and say hello to you."

He turned toward her, away from the blood in the street, to stare at her the way the emu at the Lone Pine Sanctuary outside Brisbane had stared at Arthur just before it had attacked.

"You *are* Osgood Noon, Chevalier du Sacavin?"

He nodded, bemused. If a cobra nods to a mongoose, that was how he was nodding to her.

"It's Ada Clarke?" she said, lilting the end of the sentence like a Texan, as though there were some question about her name as well. "That is—*I* am Ada Clarke?" She used her eyelids like hummingbirds' wings worrying a little if she could be spattering him with mascara. She was shy-seeming, perhaps a little wary. Not wary for her own sake but for his. The way a bacteriological-warfare scientist well back in a laboratory under the Rocky Mountains might feel wary about what people might think of him if they survived.

"We met a long time ago at the Château de Montvictoire?" she said/asked tentatively. "That time you were being—uh—*intronisé* in that—uh—*association bachique* in the Anjou?"

He went colorless. It was as though a silent picture comedian had emptied a sack of flour over his head. From the deep, carbon-monoxide cherry which had suffused his face when she first addressed him, he went to middle-pink then to an iguana-belly shade. She wasn't alarmed by it but she was curious. She leaned across him to open the window slightly to help him to breathe.

"I was with my husband? Arthur Harris?" she said smoothly. "And you were with the Emmets and their teensy-tiny dogs and your wife?" Here was a man who had investigated the lower part of her torso like a mining engineer but who now had become almost faint with embarrassment because she had remembered his name.

Osgood Noon was indeed immobilized, but not from embarrassment. It was as though he were being boarded by a swarm with cutlasses in their teeth led by the most piratically forward woman he had ever met. He was dizzied by yet another impact even though it was happening years later. It would be like trying to waltz with a sex-maddened rhinoceros who saw him as its temporary mate. She offended and terrified him still as she had always been able to do but she had that damnable ability to squirt extraordinary excitement ahead of her, as though the sex act were just about to be invented for human history as she leaped in, tearing open his English trousers and his expensive cambric underwear.

The last time he had seen her (from afar, and she had not known he had seen her) had been seven years ago, aboard the *Reina Gertrudis* of the old Radin Line where he had avoided her with mounting inner hysteria. But now she had found him again in the middle of a trading area of forty-eight million people. He was pinned. He was virtually locked against the wall of the bus and she blocked the only egress. And she was still strong enough to be able to lift that goddam emerald which had gotten caught under him at Montvictoire, costing him a consistent three strokes off his game for the rest of the season. Fate wasn't playing fair. Christ, Computer, Himself, would not be able to figure the odds against their ever meeting again. But here she was, threatening him with her merciless lust. He had set out that evening innocently, on the blandest of bland excursions only in the hope of the most conventional diversion and now this. No!

Time tumbled in upon him like a weakened brick wall in an earthquake. He had been sipping a Clover Club aboard the *Reina Gertrudis* two hundred miles at sea, feeling safer than he had ever been allowed to feel on land, when Skutch, the crooked smoking-room steward who sold the ship's run in advance for twenty-five per cent of the pools (requiring an advanced mathematical mind, extraordinary seamanship and certain inside information), had passed out the printed passenger list for the run. Noon sat there within the ineffable languor which had been brought about by an hour in the ship's baroque Turkish bath, so striking in its authentic Moorish decorations of the seventeenth century with portholes concealed by an elaborately carved Cairo curtain through which the fitful light had seemed to reveal something of the mysterious East. From dado to cornice the room had been completely tiled: warm teak illuminated by suspended bronze Arab lamps. It had relaxed him sublimely. He looked forward with such tremendous zest to the voyage while he waited for his wife to finish abluting and anointing in their stateroom below when, as he read the passenger list, this woman's name(s) had struck his eyes like a fist(s).

Harris, Mrs. Arthur Bainbridge

He had nearly panicked. In retrograde hopelessness he had sent his palsying finger back to the *C*'s to have his dread confirmed:

Clarke, Ada

The abominable *cute*ness of her affectation of two names wherever she went made him smoke with acrid disapproval. He gulped the Clover Club (something he detested doing) for he knew, as Valjean knew Javert, that if she ever discovered that he was aboard she was capable of breaking into his stateroom at night (as she had done on that awful night at Montvictoire) and begin to chew on his parts. It would offend his wife to say the least. Cerce might not have been overly possessive about him—in fact there was an accurate record which showed that she was even somewhat indifferent to him and what might happen to him, but no wife could be expected to behave amiably if this woman were to be allowed to have her aberrant way.

He had spent the days of that voyage running before her like a hunted thing. He would huddle in the ship's library, as safe from her as if he were an Arab in Mecca. But he would lose his nerve and sink from the first-class library to the second-class reading room to the third-class comic-book rack, ever fearful that she would spot him. He bribed the chief steward beyond that man's right to accept such an amount for such a tiny service, to rearrange their dining table far across the salon from the purser's table where she sat kneading and ogling. He could not stand to watch her so he had had them shifted to the first sitting, appalling Cerce who was a figure in the film industry (or had been). He told his wife that the sea air had given him a prodigious appetite, that he could not wait for the second sitting, and then to prove it he had had to gain twelve pounds on the crossing and utterly disgust his fitter in Cork Street a week later.

He would sit on the edge of his bunk with his toes intertwined anxiously, staring at the cabin door, pressing his palms into the sides of his head, acid with self-pity, fearful yet hopeful that she would find him: in a condition of the helplessness of classical masculine sexual timidity.

"How are the Emmets?" the woman asked brightly.

"Why—uh—just fine, I think. He's still with the bank. In charge of the Reykjavik office."

"Does she still have those tiny little dogs?"

"Oh, yes."

"Do you still see them?"

"Oh, yes. At least whenever I'm in Iceland. Which isn't really often. They send me the traditional barrel of herring every Christmas."

"How sweet. And how is your wife?"

He did not answer but that could have been, she thought, because as the bus had started to move away from Jemma's, someone had shot at the guard dog and had missed, winging a child at the elbow. She winced herself remembering how the funny bone could hurt but she persisted with Osgood Noon. "Your wife was *such* a beauty. And I always remember her as being so wondrously amiable."

He did not answer.

"I was transformed when I actually met her—in person. When I was a girl my mother always kept up our subscription to *Film Fun*. Why, even Arthur was thrilled with her and he never read anything but *Drug Age*. He actually asked her for her autograph."

Noon stared out of the bus window at a mugging which was taking place on the far side of Park Avenue. The mugger held the elderly woman's head locked in his arm while he slammed a metal garbage can lid into her face repeatedly with his free hand. People hurried around them or reversed their directions casually.

"Did you divorce?" Ada asked.

"No."

"Is she—?"

"I don't know."

"Arthur died. My husband. Do you remember him?"

Os remembered Arthur as the biggest wine boob he had ever known. The man had carried a pocket wine thermometer and if the stuff in the bottle with the label he could pronounce only by pointing to it were over fifty-five degrees Fahrenheit he would go berserk. For all the years Os had known Arthur, only on the various tasting junkets which Klarnet had organized, Os had never felt he really understood the man because Arthur would be in shock from having memorized a wine and food dictionary and seemed to be able to speak only in the jargon of a *sous-chef*.

"Yes. Oh, yes. Indeed I do. A positive peach."

"Are you surprised that I remembered you?" She laughed with three low musical tones, deliciously, like a dying sailor's memory of a whorehouse doorbell.

"Well, it has been some time since our—our little nocturnal escapade," Os smirked.

A slight malaise passed through her vanity, no more than if it had taken a dozen or so heated spears. "But—you did remember?"

"Oh, I remember."

"You won't mind if I ask? It has bothered me for *so* long. Where was your wife that night?"

"My wife?"

"You went upstairs together when we all did. I mean later on—when I relived the experience—it seemed so—well, so *kinky*. Your wife wasn't somewhere in that pitch-dark room all that time?"

"I don't know where she was," Os answered grimly.

"You don't *know?* Oh, you poor man!"

2

One of the Attorney General's brilliant deputies drove F.M. Heller to the Air Force base where the big jet was waiting to take him into New York. They had meant to put him down at La Guardia but the tower sent them to Teterboro to land. The Everest Bank's helicopter was waiting for him. It flew him to the Wall Street landing pad. A long black Chrysler with an Isotta-Franchini body took him to Wall Street's tallest building. The private chute lofted him to the law offices of Lantz, Lantz, Tolliver & Farr, the great American law firm of which the Attorney General had been a senior partner until his nation had called him up to serve its destiny. A very thin but lusciously pretty receptionist who wore a reinforced, tensile-steel wired C-cup combination dropped everything to lead him directly to the Tanzanian law library of the firm, on the basis of whose codes the firm someday soon hoped to gain the Tanzanian government's legal work in the United States, even as they had been slowly gaining the legal representation for most of the countries of the world, where she left him behind locked doors with Duncan Mulligan who was a sort-of member of the firm for the reason that his wife Celeste Mulligan-Harris was the daughter of the late Arthur Bainbridge Harris and the many Harris foundations.

F.M. Heller was the quaggy board chairman of the Everest National Bank (and its chief executive officer). He was a significant second-generation power in the Eastern establishment. His father, F. Marx Heller, the feisty, fearsome, grand old man of tax-free municipal bonds, had been one of the three all-time puissant Wall Street lawyers.

F.M. Heller *fils* was an exaggeratedly sigmoid man in his late fifties who wore a white beard which had been designed by Alexandre "for optimum allure" and, during the three weeks before Christmas, always wore a bright red beret for its shock effect upon the American financial community. He was precisely all-American America. He personally raised his nation's flag outside his Rockrimmon House on Fifth Avenue ("so marvelously near the zoo") on Flag Day (only). Each Arbor Day he planted one tree on his late father's estate at Dover, New Jersey. When he had been much younger he had tried to create one new American mother each Mother's Day. Entering the library he interrupted Duncan Mulligan's study of J. Fagin-Ryan's *The United States Senate,* a background study themed along the lines that the Senate was the last of the great gentlemen's clubs.

At forty-two, any one of Duncan Mulligan's facial features would have made signals of strength of character but all of them were overemphasized so that the impression he conveyed to the world was that he had bought them from a fence or had stolen them during a fire sale at a plastic surgeon's or was merely minding them for six friends who had lost face in one way or another. Held (almost) together under his pale ivory skin, linked (somehow) with the lower-face mask of his blue-black underbeard, a perpetual and luminescent, seemingly painted shadow upon his face which would forever prevent him from selling a used car to anyone; his features were all wrong. Instead of conveying the resolution of a leader of men with that chin, he seemed merely glum. His overpronounced black eyebrows jutting out beyond his everdarting dark eyes accented their shiftiness and opportunism. Overall, at high tide, such as when all his features were assembled by a television camera, his most immediately startling characteristic, irradicable from any memory, was shallowness.

Throughout his life Duncan had retained a weird preparatory-school accent which made him sound as though he were strangling on false teeth. He spoke slowly, evenly and monotonously; a mechanically deliberate man who had used gray hair dye on his temples and the backs of his hands from the age of fourteen. He had the flair of Stanley Baldwin years after the Prime Minister's death and the attack policy of Montgomery of Alamein who would not budge his troops until eleven and a quarter times the required men and materiel had been assembled and if another strong force was attacking the enemy from the rear.

F.M. Heller shucked off his topcoat and pulled out a chair at the far end of the long highly polished table, facing Duncan, and spoke across the intervening twenty-two feet.

"I come here after twenty-two minutes with the Attorney General in Washington," he boomed, "and I bring news to you beyond all dreams of glory." Words from F.M. Heller were not just thrown together into carelessly enunciated groupings called sentences. Each word was individually waxed and polished then lined up as one more shining bottle of elixir on the shelf of his syntax.

Duncan looked up slowly from the volume of Fagin-Ryan. More slowly his right hand began its measured ascent to grasp the template of his black horn-rimmed glasses to lift them from the bridge of his nose at a deliberate millimeter at a time then to lower them slowly and carefully to the table before he took the risk of responding.

"Good morning, F.M.," he said. "Have you been keeping well?"

"Very well, Duncan. And you?"

"Never fitter, F.M."

"Duncan—listen carefully. The Attorney General has authorized me to tell you that even before you get the nomination to the Senate he has every reason to believe there will be a place for you on the national ticket in seventy-two."

"On what ticket, F.M.?" Few politicians champing to leap into the national arena would have asked that question but Duncan was not a quick mind; however, by the merit of his shallow grasp, Duncan profited because F.M. Heller was exasperated to reveal more than he would have revealed if Duncan had rejoiced, or merely cringed, at his news.

"Duncan. Please listen to me. The Attorney General told me directly that he was going to put you on the national ticket. Do you understand?"

"Do you mean—?" The realization now possessed Duncan. He had not evaluated it but the essence of the attention such a fantastic vaulting could bring to him was forming and growing within his imagination.

"We are going to talk about what I mean and what the Attorney General meant for the rest of the day," F.M. Heller told him, staring at him with heavy significance.

"If called I will respond," Duncan said. "If nominated I will accept. If drafted, I shall run. If elected, I shall serve. And from the ramparts of a just democracy, defending law and order, I will fight Mao, I will fight Castro, I will fight the memory of Ho Chi Minh and I will fight the uppityness of the American Negro."

"First we have to get you elected to the Senate. Even the Attorney General can't help if you aren't elected to the Senate."

"I'm in your hands. But further, it is the Attorney General's will. It seems to me that it's only a matter now of assembling the seven million dollars for the television spots and I will have entered American history."

"Your wife can't be allowed to put up all the money and so far your mother-in-law has shown very little enthusiasm for the campaign."

"Money is no object here, F.M. When the word goes out that the Attorney General has chosen me—F.M.?—if I am assigned to the Appropriations Committee or to Military Affairs does that mean I can order a military jet to take me anywhere I want to go?"

"Appropriations and Military Affairs are House committees, Duncan. You promised to bone up on that."

"God, I'd love to bring back a Civil War regimental-style like the Zuoaves. What magnificent uniforms they wore."

"I think we should talk about your place on the national ticket next year. Out of two hundred and eleven million Americans the Attorney General has chosen you to become—"

"I like the WAVE uniform very much but the WAC uniform is—to me anyway—undistinguished. Of course, Mainbocher designed the WAVE uniform and—to me—Mainbocher will always be the most soigné designer we have."

"That will all come later, Duncan. I sat there this morning about four feet away from the Attorney General and he spoke clearly and slowly—much more slowly and perhaps even a shade more loudly than usual—because to a certain extent he intended to speak in parables yet he wanted to signal that to me and to make sure that I understood all nuances."

"I don't think I understand, F.M."

"Without laying it out in so many direct words which might possibly be turned against even him," F.M. Heller said slowly and perhaps even a shade more loudly than usual, "the Attorney General conveyed to me explicitly that he is displeased with the performance of the President and he will replace the President by bypassing him for the nomination in seventy-two."

"Bypass the President? But as every element of our nation's press has established beyond all doubt, the President is our *leader!*"

"Then he told me he had been conducting scientific searches with the evaluating aid of all Apostle level computers to find an enormously exciting dark horse who could be caused to emerge at the convention to sweep the rank and file of the Republican Party and to be swept into the nomination by acclamation. He very much wants to save face for the President who is, after all, an old and dear friend."

Duncan was unable to take it all in. He seemed disturbed that he had been allowed to be privy to such responsible information. His little eyes were screwed down at the corner with the anxiety of trying to place the information in proper context. "Are you saying you don't know who will be heading the ticket I will be running on for the vice-presidency?" he asked with a good deal of concern.

F.M. Heller remained patient. He knew Duncan and greatly respected his ox-like flair for ratiocinating. "Things have happened fast for you this year, haven't they, Duncan. Well, I appreciate that and so does the Attorney General. Shall we go through it again step-by-step, if that will bring security?"

"Please, yes."

"You are clear about the Attorney General's intention to put you into the Senate if by some wild fluke not on the Republican ticket then as representative of his new gimmick, the Conservative Party."

"I didn't know we had a Conservative Party."

"We will have if you don't get the Republican nomination. Now—as I reported to you—the Attorney General this morning openly stated his intention to put you on the national ticket in seventy-two. Have you absorbed that?"

"I have been deliberating on it. I would like to have forty-eight hours before replying."

"Good. Now we will separate what the Attorney General said to me directly from what he said to me indirectly. At first, when he said he wanted you on the national ticket I assumed he meant the vice-presidency."

"Naturally," Duncan snorted. "There are, after all, only two places on the ticket." He had put a sarcastic edge on his voice.

"Indeed, yes. However, when the Attorney General finished saying what he very much intended to say, it became even more clear that, if and when you were elected to the Senate, that he had chosen you—let me put it this way—he had decided that the party would run you for the presidency of the United States in nineteen hundred seventy-two."

Duncan stared incredulously. He fought to absorb what F.M. Heller had just said. He grew pale but he grew taller, even Lincolnesque, which was an incredible physical illusion for a clean-shaven, five-foot nine-inch politician, as if the office made the man even before the man made the office. It was almost three minutes before he was able to speak. When he spoke his voice was hoarse with ambition.

"Do you mean that I can visit the fleet at will and run any war I choose to declare?"

Heller nodded.

"Do you mean I can divide this country into more manageable segments opposed to each other so that they may be ruled in law and order?"

Heller nodded.

"Are you saying that I can declare myself one-quarter Israeli to hold the Jewish vote and be flown to Bethlehem at Air Force expense to visit my great-grandfather's grave and headstone which had been put down by the CIA two weeks before? That I can fight and win for supersonic transport and against Medicare and a guaranteed annual wage and that I can really do something about keeping niggers and students in their place?"

"Yes, Duncan. God bless you. That is exactly what we mean and thank the good Lord that you understand."

Duncan rose very slowly to his feet. His hands were trembling when he finally made it to his full height but he steadied them by pressing his fingertips to the table. But he could not control the emotion in his voice. He looked out across F.M. Heller and through the walls of the building westward across his America, eyes glittering with ambition, his finest quality. "If drafted I shall run," he said. "If elected, I shall serve."

"There *is* that one important qualifier, Duncan," F.M. Heller said softly.

"What qualifier?" Duncan answered harshly.

"Well—the fact is that you aren't going anywhere if you aren't elected to the Senate."

3

Osgood Noon's wife had been the bafflement of his life from the day he met her. As he sat now beside Ada Harris on the top deck of the red bus all these years after marriage to Cerce, he could not say whether his wife had engineered the argument to allow her to stalk from the room that night out of honest indignation or in order to rendezvous with one of the other men staying at the château. She said she had driven in to stay at an Angers hotel for the night. "Look back in Angers," she had said too wistfully as they had driven out to Geneva the next morning. She had been born as restless as Lawrence of Arabia and just as bent. Beneath the constantly shifting sands of what very well could have been unspeakable ambitions had lurked the determination to get only what she had wanted for herself. She was an exhausting, unrewarding woman. But it rankled him to be called "poor man" by this woman beside him. He sat up stiffly. His face had gradually grown pink again back to the characteristic flamingo color which was not choleric.

"Mrs. Harris," he said testily, "that night my wife and I had an argument concerning the merits of Spanish oranges over California oranges for best use in marmalade. I don't know how it started. She worked herself up until she had to leave or begin to throw things."

Because talking about herself was so much more interesting, Ada said, "Actually, although my legal name is Mrs. Harris, my maiden name was Clarke. My whole maiden name had such personality that Arthur always urged me to use it."

"Yes. I believe I knew that."

"My maiden name was Ada Clarke. I have a brother Severn, a sister Nina, and a younger brother, Tennyson. When we are all together it is like the Dance of the Hours. Is that arch? Mother said she thought of the names because Daddy was just passing the time of day on top of her. We were just hours drifting by to him she said."

For his own personally piercing reason, Os was touched by that family tragedy of names. Ada Clarke. How she must have been mocked at school. How she and her siblings must have come to hate time and the clock. And the silly name, so frivolously imposed, made her seem different and suddenly sympathetic to him. Here was a helpless woman who had been used for someone else's joke. The injustice pressed into him with the force of a runaway ten-ton truck encountering a random cyclist against a building wall.

"My own ghastly name, as you may know," he said, "is Osgood Otto Noon. The name has seven *O*'s. It has more *O*'s than any other name in the Western world."

"You have a *gor*geous name."

"My mother chose those names and brought me up to believe that *O*'s in a name were the big, clear picture windows which would let the world look through at me and see that I was always on the level."

"That was a wonderful mother you must have had."

"I still have to undress in a closet if there is a television set in the room. And what is the justice of having a name which lets the world look right in on you to see whether you are on the level when the whole cultural evolvement enjoyed by everyone else is to be deceptive and dishonest?" His voice shook with indignation. "I have been unfairly handicapped in all my business dealings because my name has convinced me that they would know immediately if I tried to cheat them even a little. The damned name has also made me sexually timid. If on the one hand, one is raised to believe that all sex is dirty, as we Americans are, what is the use of facing a woman with sexual ambitions when she would be able to see one's intent instantly and be put on the defensive by it?" He had become so red and angry that he had to go silent and look away as the bus approached Madison Avenue where a band of students were laying a dynamite charge into the façade of a religious articles shop.

Ada said, "They say dissatisfaction with your name can mean basic unhappiness with yourself."

"Not in my case," Os replied. "I've been all through that with my psychiatrist. My name and I are foreign entities."

"Your name will always be Captain Midnight to me."

His cheeks turned maroon. She began to think of him

as one of those weather meters made out of blotting paper which tell what sort of day it had been the day before. "Thank you," he managed to say.

"Call me Ada and you'll always know what time it is. With me it's always Ada Clarke." She giggled.

He grinned. "And if we meet again I invite you to greet me with 'Hi, Noon.' "

"Wasn't that a wonderful château? Did you know that pâté de foie gras was invented by the original owner's cook and that the French government let him patent it?"

But Os was intent upon vindicating his lust. "You see," he explained, "when I heard the sound of your footsteps in the corridor I thought it must be my wife returning to admit that Spanish oranges make the best marmalade whereupon I opened the door and you grabbed me."

"I grabbed you?" She stared at him as though she had just caught him blowing his nose in a Mother's Day card. Her voice rose. People seated two rows ahead of them turned. Ada pretended to get up, or at least moved to give him the feeling that she was getting up, and Os apologized at once, hating himself for behaving with the same reflexive capitulation which his wife had always expected him to provide.

"How did you know it was me in the pitch-black hall anyway?" she asked, mollified. "There were four other women in the château not counting your wife."

Os stared straight ahead at the gauntlet of tall buildings scarred with explosions or disfigured with painted slogans. "Because," he said.

"Because why?"

"Because you just told me."

"When?" Her voice dropped to a new softness. "Do you mean—after all these years—you never knew it was me?"

"Well, you see, although you knew or could trace whose room it was you had left, I had no idea which room you had come from or to where you had returned. Also, as you said, it was awfully dark." They had been forced into corners. As the female she had not known who he had been that night in France but had had to say that she knew to get new action started. He had known who she was now and who she had been then but for reasons of gallantry, which is to say protective coloration, he had had to deny it.

"But you did *want* to know?"

"Yes."

"Terribly?"

"Well—I—no, not terribly."

"But it was good, wasn't it?"

"Yes."

"In fact, it was great, wasn't it?"

"It was enormously uninhibiting."

"Do you still think about it?"

He shrugged lightly.

"A lot?"

They were diverted as two city policemen caught a small group of Negro youths in a crossfire. As the young people fell in the gutters and on the pavement the crowds in the evening streets suddenly vanished. But Ada was not to be diverted. "Would you like to have a little more?" she asked breathily.

"More?"

"A little more of what we had together at Montvictoire?"

"A little more?"

"It's only an expression. Would you?"

He shrugged again.

"Where were you going when you got into this bus tonight?"

"I—I had sent away for a seat for a musical comedy almost eight months ago. In fact I refused wine with dinner tonight because I wanted to be as alert as a terrier. I—I understand it is a *mar*velous show."

Ada completed a movement not unlike the left-hand crossover in "Chopsticks," reaching across herself under the palomino mink jacket, leaning slightly as if she were craning to see something outside the bus window, and lightly squeezing the contents of his crotch. He froze for an instant; then, as she communicated and he responded, he turned to stare at her in gratitude and amazement. He began to quiver lightly as though she had introduced a tremorgen into his bloodstream; perhaps something even more shaking than penicillium cyclopium. He was trembling but he wasn't trembling to shake himself loose from her hand.

Silently, while he was still capable of thinking about them he wondered, in a conditioned flash, what his sons would think of him if they could see him now. He knew.

He was almost sure he knew. Botolf would rejoice. Gawain simply wouldn't care. Tristram would disapprove on behalf of his mother. Oh, well, Os told himself as he swelled into Ada's grasp, too late for that now.

4

Mid-Day Enterprises' offices in Rockefeller Center occupied one-half of a floor. Their offices in Washington, Chicago, Atlanta and San Francisco were equally large. From his own six-window office facing south upon Manhattan, Tristram Noon, owner of Mid-Day Enterprises with a selected group of American industrial and political leaders, could stare far outward, beyond the great slag of floating garbage from the confluence of rivers, across the democracy.

Mid-Day Enterprises was a direct product of the American culture. It had emerged naturally from life in America from the spontaneous generation of native interest in politics which had begun to happen after World War II. Before that Americans had stirred only to the quadrennial sweet-summer excitement of presidential nominating conventions but had ignored, or found "colorful" or "typical" the sinks of graft and corruption, federal, state and local, because they were enchanted to the levels of their understanding by forty-cent movies and men who hit or threw balls.

They were a long time being prepared for the New Way but only as part of a media circulation promotion and not for reasons of civic improvement, Mr. W.R. Hearst had been running ahead of fat ladies fanning themselves on seaside boardwalks and gamblers fixing heavyweight championship matches, and all stripes of gleeful national violence for the sake of violence at first trying it out with alarms about the Yellow Peril then shifting to the El Dorado lode of anti-Communism. It saved his newspapers for awhile. In fact it was so continuously successful that all the media began to try out and tool up the Great Warnings. Television arrived just a bleep before Senator Joseph McCarthy (R. Wis.). Sniffing the wind J. Edgar Hoover turned away from the Warner Brothers and discovered America. A sweet balance was struck between the safe fear of Communism and ambivalence over the Marshall Plan—or the fear of another war versus the fear of massive ingratitude and, by golly, it sold newspapers and that sold advertising and that sold gadgets and that had become the meaning of America. Not only that but this spate of international political issues was a diversion from the continuous television. After decades people once again had something to talk about. They made it into a rock-throwing game, this exciting new politics, of victims and the rest of us and, at last, the system which was the cultural side of the politics: the comic-book printing presses, the nineteen thousand film palaces, the hundreds and hundreds of thousands of hours of television hosed out each day, the literature of sex and death, the deathless cynicism of the expense account and white-collar crime, the celebration of violence on all sides and at every level, produced the supreme American political act, the assassination of their (young) President when, to the dismay of the world, all the rules were changed. Children barely out of school began to demand that they alone had the right to form American political policy.

Within that unexpected development Tristram Noon found and exploited his great opportunity. On the one hand he knew that the country and perhaps the world would soon enough be ruled by the Children and for the Children if it were not to perish from this earth but until that happened the guilty and elderly who controlled the money and the power and the vast overcommunications could be neatly organized to make the Children the scapegoats so he laid down his lines and presented his plans to the highest councils.

His warm-up was at Watts. He delivered a thorough if essentially unsophisticated riot for clients who wished to "stir up various points of view" in the Los Angeles mayoralty and California gubernatorial campaigns. The partisan results were magical. The effect on the sales of newspapers and on the watchfulness of television programs and their respective advertising rate cards was more than magical, it was great for business. In no time the large industries and the local pols wanted their own managed riots but the establishing coup for Mid-Day Enterprises was the beautifully planned and breathtakingly executed Police versus Child Confrontation at the Democratic convention in Chicago in 1968. His client was "a friendly unit" of American life who "wished to encourage the Republican

Party's return to national politics because change is a good thing." He was given a realistic budget and rehearsal time which meant the best actors and costumes to play the Bad Children and Good Police. The styling Mid-Day created for the TV cameras during that confrontation would influence the Children's fashion world for several years to come. It meant that each camera and crew could be at the right place at the right time with all close and medium-close angles of the action worked out and there were ample supplies of costumed Police and costumed Children and fear and disgrace and bleeding violence and shame—more than enough to sweep the Republicans into office on a law-and-order platform.

Chicago really established Mid-Day Enterprises. All political parties of every degree of political orientation, which in the United States meant all the way from A to B, had held the firm under permanent contract. Industry used Mid-Day for counter-strikes and to prepare the savage, simple-minded people for the new and bottomless opportunity which would be the commercial polarization of hard hat versus egghead, white against black, and the partisan results had been magical. The results, too, from a merchandising of Tristram's organizational interest, because soon every powerful state politician wanted to have his own riot to quell, or their opposition wanted riots created which they felt could not be quelled "properly." But it was with the Chicago convention in 1968 that Mid-Day Enterprises Inc. really knew it had crept into America's heart to stay.

The biggest break, aside from the fact that it was so American to organize anything on an industrial, rather than on an ideological basis, had been the three full months Tris had been given to plan the stagework for the Chicago riots. It meant he could go over the individual "confrontations" on hand-picked sites in Chicago with the network directors of the individual camera crews so that they could be properly positioned to broadcast the best show for the American people.

Tris had never received the credit within the context which he deserved, i.e., the man who had organized all modern riots for all ancient causes but for some very new political reasons within the United States. Through one of his trials, he had become famous across the headlines of the world as "The Minneapolis One," and rich, no doubt about it. He had worked, apparently, for the overthrow of the government under retainer from the government. He had done his part to swing the young away from the restless jaggedness of alcohol to a more useful dependency on the much more passive-making marijuana so that the leaders of the nation might lead in a less restricted manner. Not only that, but he would make them a large buck out of it. He was, for example, enormously helpful in merchandising the marijuana industry which had happened along just in time to take up the slack and the worry about tens of thousands of cigarette-packaging machines in a "possibly-doomed" cigarette industry.

Tris was able to deliver casts of two-to-five thousand on both sides of every issue and could load the presentation to guarantee public opinion for either side. His casts would riot with and against eggs, rocks, paint, machine guns, bombs, gas or troops to whatever degree of protest the client's policy/budget required, and Tris was delivering spectacle on a greater scale and with far more believability than anything ever produced by Cecil B. De Mille. Tris' own identification, no matter which riot for what cause, was "student leader" or "hippie revolutionary." At thirty-seven, he was *the* radical leftist of the new revolution, *the* vaunted fighter for the silent majority and *the* militant centrist of the entire nation. The public, instantly and intuitively, appreciated the economies of configuring all social and political moods into one huge industrial container led by one hero. Tris' affiliations, in the *old* ways of viewing such loyalties, were astonishing. He was a dues-paying Ku-Kluxer and a Maoist. He was a founder Anti-war Coffeehouser who had also led the demonstration under the White House windows urging that the war continue until won. He was a Yippie, a Hippie, a White Vigilante, a Weatherman, an honorary Panther, a Bircher, an Effete Snob and a Mitchell Marcher. With Billy Graham he was the hero of the savage, simpleminded people. He explained to his father who was understandably worried that the boy might suffer a diffusion of purpose because he was serving so many contrasting masters, "Pop, don't worry. I have a very good business going." He pronounced the word as "bid-nizz," a Mafia affectation. "I have no capital investment to speak of," he said, "and a low overhead which is offset by a good income. Our leaders know it's better to deal with just one responsible organization if only for service and billing reasons. They know we deliver what we say we'll deliver. The insurance problems and burial costs and hospitals and all like that are much less and much surer than if the kids or blacks rioted for some cockamamie independent outfit. The FBI doesn't have to waste its budget snooping on us. We guarantee the pigs fall guys when they need them, like in Chicago, always good articulate guys who make the points the owners want made. I never have to change sides, Pop, so how can I get confused? There are no sides. It's a business. It's how America became what it is today. I work for me and only for me and it's the job of the over-communications industry to make it all look different because, after all, their business is entertainment for unit sales, right?"

Tris had been arrested, only for the great causes, two hundred and twelve times, without a conviction. He had been the first American boy to call a judge in an American court of law a "stupid shit" and "you Jew prick" and be widely acclaimed for it by the Children element—thus his continuing reputation as the Minneapolis One. He was appreciated, and most substantially underwritten, by all political parties, all national industry, and most particularly by Harold M. Chase, the grand old man of petroleum, who retained Tris' teams to plan and execute all Mr. Chase's political and private assassination efforts. Tris had appointed Mr. Wallace's chief-of-staff and had given up some of his best people to the crusade by Mr. Eugene McCarthy and he maintained more active friendships and payoffs with more police chiefs and mayors in the United States than any American since Francis Wilson Braden had done patchwork for Ringling Brothers, Barnum and Bailey.

Tristram Noon had developed major talents for action, violence, and leadership to become the true military arm and conscience of church and state in his nation.

His father was very fond of Tris and felt that there were isolated instances when he could understand him, but for all the idolizing by the press and the public adoration Os could not, for the life of him, see how or where either Tris or the Children had changed American life. After thousands of miles of marches and hundreds and hundreds of deaths they hadn't even been able to bring about a citizens' meeting for a real revision of the one-hundred-and-ninety-six-year-old Constitution: the true enemy which perpetuated all the shabby uses of power which they were willing to die to oppose.

5

Although he was hardly alone in the world with the feeling, Osgood Noon had always been on the lookout for something which could change his life. His wife Cerce had changed her life whenever she felt like it: as a member of an Antarctic expedition; as an autogyro pilot ferrying small silver change between Reno and Vegas; any number of drastic changes for *her* life during the years of their marriage while he had slogged on as production manager of his family's hat manufacturing company.

She had left for the final change with the suddenness of a parachutist leaving a plane: gone, he was sure, out of contempt for his ever-questing but unresolved need to change. He must have seemed like water to her.

Cerce had the drive of an Apollo missile. She was militant about everything: amiably militant, always on the prod, dieting too much, drinking too much or abstaining too much, defying authority down to the newest meter maid on the block, undertaking almost any extreme of conduct which could make her appear more irrational to the temperate, which he was.

He had said such things to her as: "I read a new book about parakeets last night and it changed my life." A man should be allowed to say a thing like that to his wife without being scalded by her derision. Newspaper sidebars had been announced as having changed his life. Not shocking or mind-boggling announcements such as that the stock market had come back or Spiro Agnew had been elected but items in astrology columns or perhaps an inspirational interview with a third baseman. More than once Cerce had screamed humiliations at him such as "You're such a lightweight that someday you're going to float away like a goddam toy balloon."

He knew she was wrong about that. He hadn't been able to change, therefore he had had the chance to study his character from a fixed position, resting, as it were, on folds of scarlet velvet in its traditional vitrine. He also knew that she was hopelessly helpless about estimating any character. He knew he was not a lightweight. Any man who could stick out, as he had, the years of his young manhood under a father-employer such as his until he had himself ascended to the presidency of a hat company which had been founded before the Revolutionary War and expected to be run that way, had steel character. Any man who could raise three sons while his wife had, six times, floated away like a toy balloon, and had raised strong-minded *good* boys, had especially strong character because sitters had never been all that easy to find. Any man who, two days after he had taken over the presidency of that ancient hat company (when his father had had to sign over all the stock as prescribed by *his* father's will), could sell all of that stock to strangers so that he could move forward into the business he had always wanted to be in, was not a lightweight. No, sir. And no, madame. Cerce could never have done things like that. Why should he change her? Let her change herself. A real flaw had been, of course, letting her have those three national credit cards.

He wanted to change. He felt he needed to change. But, as he had grown older, he had become sceptical about the power of extraneous forces to change him. Subtly, sometimes he thought they had. The wind and the sea changes the shape of rocks. It would be too futile to say that it had been merely time, changing him by the erosion of hundreds of thousands of invisible daily experiences. To say that would negate his sacred free will, imbedding him in the stasis of time, vain time, sunk in the cornerstones of amusement parks, as meaningless as the Children's concept of politics as existing only beyond government. He had been watching for his own evolution so closely that he had come to feel that he had been more fascinated by what was changing him than whether he was changing.

He still polished his birthright daily, morning and night: his thrusting sense of hope, the mindless optimism which he had lusted wistfully to label as courage. Opposingly, he had hoarded negative positions: the anxiety which drove him about money—that he had too much of it; a nagging worry about ending his days in the way other people wanted theirs to end—faceless and lewd. He would not settle for other people's ambitions for death formed by television and drawn from comic books.

But he knew he had not persevered in any of his illusions because if things and people (except his sons) had not worked out for his comfort or convenience, he had dropped them. That was hardly a committed attitude. But Cerce here or gone, paper heartbreak or paper passion, comfort and convenience had been the operative words of his life. Inconvenience was the unthinkable condition.

So only little wens on the surface had changed. The true change was on the way: when the bowels would split and break, when the eyes would grow dimmer because the retinas were flaking and needed to be burned with laser beams. Sex would strangle him with its omission: sex, the detritus which had bound him to Cerce (if not Cerce to him) in a world where even the weather reports were made by girls who had medianly saucy behinds, mean-average tits, and low-pressure thighs. Sex had become the boring, overtoppling design for human life and there was much evidence of national gleet from overstrain. Sex had reached the White House in 1961 and it would not be long before a President could not be elected unless he had been born in deep-slung jockey shorts instead of a log cabin. Or have a heavy-lipped wife with three layers of hair on her own hair or sets of pink-assed daughters. Sex had marched into the pulpits and the recipe books. All manners had changed. He mourned that they had not changed him, as though his own times had not had the interest to reach out and find him, thus denying him the right to be the result of his own conditioning.

So he wanted himself to believe, as he rode across Manhattan on top of a red London bus, that this undoubtedly silly woman with her two silly names might have the power to change him.

Like those most admirably ready fellows in the world, the Boy Scouts of America, he would be prepared if he could only ferret out what it was he should be prepared for. Change had most certainly begun from the moment she had conducted the ritual of the laying on of hands on top of his fly on top of the bus on top of everything else that had happened or had almost happened through the long years before. Ada Clarke, nautically eight bells. Osgood Noon meant eight bells, too. Could it be that they were actually meant for each other, having found separate ways to a château outside an unlikely town in France where they had gathered together for the outlandishly silly reason of having traveled three thousand miles to taste wine which had caused her to want to pee out in darkness, bringing on sortie and entrée, causing them to copulate like socks in a washing machine, then to have time disintegrate and have them crash into each other again (after that dreadful near-miss aboard the *Reina Gertrudis*) on top of a discarded English bus in a patently discarded American city because, eight months before, he had sent away for a single ticket to an anachronistic musical comedy—sweet Jesus, Computer, was he trapped within some teenager's astrological forecast? Were he and Ada meant to roll over each other, grunting and gargling, throughout a silver-haired eternity?

6

Arthur had died so unexpectedly that she had had nothing to wear. So she asked Bergdorf, Gallanos, and Bendel to send their ideas-in-black to her at Frank E. Campbell's Funeral Home where the élite meet to delete. She had made up her mind that she was going to stay with Arthur until he was rolled off to the ovens but she had no black clothes because Arthur had hated black. While they worked on Arthur upstairs in the scoop-out rooms, she tried on sixteen dresses and coats in the flower-banked room where Arthur would be laid out until she was able to put three solid outfits together. She stayed on duty near Arthur every day from two-thirty until five-thirty to greet all the people who had dropped in to make sure their flowers had been delivered. Between the afternoon session and the evening get-together she would walk up and down Madison Avenue to get her circulation going (and to escape her children) which was how she happened to discover Jackie Kennedy Onassis' butcher with all the framed newspaper stories among the marbled beef so, naturally, she had opened a charge account. The evening sessions at the funeral home had a much livelier crowd of people from seven until ten.

The twins and Esau kept meeting people Ada was sure they had never met before and going out for awhile with them, then coming back to go out of the funeral parlor with some different set of strangers. She never found out where they were going but she had a pretty good idea of why. The twins took out nine men in the two nights of waking and Sylvan—that is, Esau—slipped away with three men and she was shocked to notice that the second one was a very high dignitary in the Republican Party. Celeste had worn a heavy veil so she could watch the twins without their knowing she was watching, thus avoiding an argument at breakfast the next day. Her husband, Duncan, just stood like a cigar-store indian at the head of the casket with his head on his chest and his hands clasped loosely at the end of his chimpanzee-long arms. He greeted only politicians and lawyers. Ada greeted the drug trade and the Mafia representatives. Jean-Pierre handled the Mafia and entertainment industry figures and television commercial producers. Kaskell had wedged himself disgustingly between Celeste and the wall and, every now and then, she would bow at the waist to greet someone from the health-food industry or the drug trade, as though she had forgotten Kaskie had put himself directly behind her with the wall at his back and her meaty behind would press into his crotch and his eyes would roll. Luckily, Kaskie had the kind of face and manner which made everyone in any room he entered immediately look the other way so there was no scandal. But it was a very peculiar relationship between brother and sister, and Arthur, as their father, would have been very much embarrassed to know his death had revealed it.

But it had been a good funeral for a good man. Dr. Margarinec had read the service beautifully with his wonderful tremolo voice so that each syllable had seemed to emerge from his larynx on a separate half shell of mother-of-pearl and he had said some really wonderful things about Arthur. Then they had cooked him into a fine dust. He was gone.

She had told him perhaps fifty times: "Arthur, what are we going to *do* with this much money? Do you really believe our kids can handle it—*our* kids? Quit! Get out! We'll start a flower farm or you can go on the cops if you have to keep busy but let's stay outdoors and get a little sun before we die."

Before we die. He had undoubtedly thought she was kidding when she hinted that he could possibly die. Everything was for sale, wasn't it? So he would buy some more dance tickets and live a little longer. He got sore every time she reminded him. He got sore because he was also too dumb to know that their kids were a little tilted, but she kept fighting him to get through to him.

"You are *killing* yourself, Arthur. We have a yacht with a telephone in every john. Let's use it, for God's sake. Turn it into your office—the yacht or the johns—but get outdoors. At least eat something beside hamburger steak, listen to music that isn't Muzak, catch a fish, jump on a Brazilian colored girl. At least teach yourself that you have good reasons to keep living. With purpose, not by accident or worse, by habit."

It was no use. He was a money dope.

The first three days without him, without that little mine mule who had stretched out like a crumpled little doll to die on the half-acre which was the back of their German car, were pretty rotten days, but she had made herself shape up. So he had died before he was a hundred and ten. Big deal. She had had him figured to make a hundred and three, he had figured it to make five hundred and they both had been off by a fairly heartbreaking number of years. Arthur had been a good man. Even Kaskie had cried. Celeste, for once, had stopped talking for a little while. And the dopey people kept saying the dopey things, not caring that their turn was next. One woman had said she couldn't believe Arthur was dead because she had just seen one of his television shows a week before. Twenty-nine million people looked at the television shows Arthur sponsored each week, then they all took a bottle or two of his pills, or got a letter from the Army saying how their kids had been killed with some of his chemicals, or they went to sleep with his downs or kept going with his ups or told their kids who weren't in the war how they couldn't understand how they were dope fiends on the different powders Arthur's companies put together for distribution by the Mafia. Arthur had made a lot of pills and money in his lifetime. He made every cent he owned all by himself with his little mortar and his little pestle. About money Arthur was smart. He had even explained to Ada, a little arrogantly, that he wouldn't take it with him because he wanted to get a fresh start wherever he was going, just to prove he could make just as much all over again.

Leaving all that money to her had, of course, been intended as some kind of a pay-off. She had been twenty-eight years old when they had gotten married. In those days, long, long ago, before there had been any Negro problem, he had been a really intense little guy about sex and it had been very good. He might have been a little funny-looking out of bed but he was a real tiger in the sheets. Then, after a while, he just lost the knack. First he could not concentrate on it any more and after all there is very little difference between sex and playing a great violin. After that he just ran away from it. He loved her. She was sure of that. If he had had his way she would have had to go down to the office and sit there with him every day, just to keep him feeling good.

After awhile, what with indifferent sex from him, then no sex, she was slowly able to convince herself that she had been born to have everything. She was no nymphomaniac. For one thing it said clearly right there in the books that nymphomaniacs couldn't have orgasms so she certainly was no nymphomaniac. She happened to love Arthur but if the rest of the women in the country who were charging through the stores like on motorcycles, buying anything that didn't move, were getting as little sex from their husbands as she had been getting from Arthur when he had been alive then something was wrong with the system which used up men like that. So, right or wrong, loyal or disloyal, she had prowled around a little bit while Arthur was slugging it out with whomever he took the money from.

They had a three-story apartment on the thirty-sixth floor facing Central Park where Arthur had moved them because it was a Mafia realty holding so the building could never have an elevator strike. They had a house in Palm Springs where Arthur kept a nice four-seater Wagney Aerocar. Their three-hundred-and-seven-foot boat was captained by George Pappadakis, the highest-priced sea captain in the world because he had once won a British newspaper contest for sailing a ketch around the world, single-handed, via the two polar routes. They had a Lear jet for getting from one place to another. She had eleven fur coats and a different wig for every day of the week. But Arthur was gone. Even if he had been a nowhere sexually she missed him all the time. The little things, the books said. What else were there but the little things? And Arthur had had a very, very little thing. And he had lost his last erection in his accountant's office, or before a Senate investigating committee, or maybe with the third city the Weathermen had decided to blow up. It had been a great marriage otherwise. He liked to laugh. Actually, he had died laughing. She had told him a certain joke (and it made her laugh out loud just to think of that joke) which she would never tell to another living soul and that joke had proved to both of them that all the while they had thought he was as healthy as a horse (and just as smart) he had had a bad heart condition just like all the other businessmen. He went in a fingersnap. And he died the week the American Association for the Advancement of Science had announced P-chlorophenylalamine which reduced the brain production of serotonin and triggered vast sexual activity in the male. With his position in the pharmaceutical industry, Arthur could have been the first bone-weary American businessman to have it.

His last words had been for the dog. He had gasped out the dog's name, "Wergel!" in a stage whisper across the floor of the back of the Mercedes 600 SEL (Special Extra Long). "Wergel! Take care of your mother!" That had meant one of two things which she had not been ready for. One, that he did not consider that any of his children were capable or interested enough to look after her or, two, that had been his own kindly way of calling her a bitch. Well, he was entitled to make a crack like that. She never knew how much he knew but he had always behaved like a perfect gentleman with her or, rather, he had always behaved as though she had been a perfect lady.

It wasn't easy to be a widow. Men who get a kick out of seducing a woman just to have it on her husband, all look at widows as though they were measuring teeth. One year she had had to stay aboard the same cruise ship for four months (three cruises) to get laid at all. And then it had been the ship's barber. Sometimes, alone in that enormous apartment, she'd get so nervous she could bang the delivery boy.

What was she supposed to do? Hang around bars? She wasn't any different from any other women. She happened to have a very insistent sexual content. Was she supposed to keep right on shopping after all the stores had closed at five-thirty? Could she exercise more than two hours a day in that sweaty gym where that old Hungarian with his bright-yellow skin tried to break her on those machines? She was flat and she was trim, yes. But she was also lucky she could walk after workouts in that bucket of sweat. Arthur had said she had the body of a nineteen-year-old, tits like a thirty-year-old and eyes like Mother Goose. What was left for her? The hairdresser every day? Diets, fittings, massages, maybe the theatre, maybe an art gallery? Movies? Show me a good movie, she had said to Arthur, and I'll show you a reissue. Television was a social disease. There was nothing left to do but ride the Staten Island ferry back and forth—or sex. A complete lack of projects had made the whole world sex crazy.

7

Sylvan, called Esau, and his cousins the twins, had grown up with the Children's Army which dominated the United States of America. It was this army (four per cent of the population), which decided what was moral and what was right for all of the people, instructing them away from the old narcotic, alcohol, to the new narcotics which were as varied as they were destructive, leading them to one hundred per cent enforced sex, whether the older citizens wanted it or not, driving them to a national orgy of spending, health, vitality, sanity and resources under an illusory system of consequences which transmitted all guilt backward in time.

Sylvan, called Esau, and the twins marched shoulder-to-shoulder at the forefront of the Children's Army, holding its rationale ever at the ready and polishing its reflexes with every waking hour. Esau's waking hours were different from those of the twins because they had an aversion to drugs except heroin—they would be leaching out if they didn't go along with something (as Esau said, "look at Charley Manson's peer group, for example")—because the hours of every day had to contrast with each other; after all, were they to be expected just to *live* out a (like) normal life? The Standing Orders of the Children's Army issued to stand forever, were: "Do your own thing or vanish from the relevance."

Esau and the twins, Mona and Fiona, did their own thing just as ritualistically as anyone else to preserve the future as they knew it.

For example, because they admired the local underground newspaper in the East Village, a courageous weekly called TCA (for The Children's Army) which advocated an immediate return to the Middle Ages, they had immediately agreed to implement a circulation-building festival for the paper in the backrooms of a cold railroad flat on Avenue B. The paper had run their photographs, doing their thing, on the front pages, and had guaranteed them, as a measure of appreciation, to run other new action pictures of them for the three succeeding issues. Readers and prospective readers would pay eleven dollars and 100 grams of grass or two bindles of heroin for a six-month subscription to TCA, to be picked up at the TCA offices in an abandoned Buick on Avenue A, and in return were invited, gratis, to a gangbang on top of Mona and Fiona, then Esau, then three sheep (one ram, two ewes). The first gangbang had been such an enormous success at the spring equinox (Pisces-Aries cusp) that it was repeated on the day of the fall equinox (Virgo-Libra cusp). Mona and Fiona had outdrawn Esau and the sheep by three-to-one. Esau had outdrawn the sheep on an eight-to-five ratio because few in the Children's Army wanted to miss anything in life and were determined to accumulate memories against the day when they would be old and square.

However, to underscore that Esau and the twins very much did their own thing, except for the TCA newspaper circulation festivals they had an entirely different approach to balling. Balling anybody was a political and sociological action to Mona and Fiona. They did not ball people for pleasure or even for the publicity in it. And they did not ball people just because Standing Orders in the Children's Army said you had to ball people. They balled people because they had been very much impressed with a certain Humanities teacher at Radcliffe who had been so hung up on Women's Lib that she had been able, figuratively, to set the twins on fire with its overwhelming concepts to the extent that Mona and Fiona had dropped out of Radcliffe after the first year and had begun to drop into the sack with as many guys as they could rape because that was the Woman's Right. It was not and had never been a man's right to score chicks. Who paid off on what was supposed to be a simple, innocent little bang? Let one chick forget to take the pill and she became the one who got to feed the late sporting results to that little rabbit. Her front got all swollen up, not the guy's. She was the one who had to find some neon-eyed abortionist with the dirty fingernails or a neighborhood where you could raise a kid.

Men had no rights in sex. On what basis? How? They were made with strong backs which was what they should be trained to use in sex but they all should be made, by army law, to have an operation so they couldn't enjoy sex so much. Mona and Fiona liked to get them off to one side like in a telephone booth or in a public elevator then Fiona would trip them and Mona would push them and they'd land on the guy, ripping his pants open and scooping the jewels out. And they knew their karate. They made him work or they broke his fucking arm.

If there had been visible rank in the Children's Army, the twins would have made light-colonel easily because they were absolutely relentless about doing their thing, they were only nineteen, and they were very, very beautiful and very, very rich.

The twins' attitude, which is to say the twins' own thing, was not Esau's thing by any means. Not that he was any wallflower or floor-flower either. Not by any means. At twenty-two he was a methedrine fiend and a militant homosexual but he wasn't any freak-out, mincing, Revlon-on-the-eyelids-when-in-Capri homosexual. He cut in on other men on dance floors; no other men cut in on him. He smoked a huge, underslung pipe which he lighted with tapers he imported personally from Moran's in Clonmel, County Tipperary, Ireland. He left sweat-prints on the floor where he walked. He farted loudly in public places and conveyances. He had a different size American flag decal on every piece of his private property: cars, business cards, his Ortho-Creme tubes and his hypodermic. He carried a briefcase organized neatly to hold brand-name methedrines, towels and his creams. He was six-feet four-inches tall and weighed two hundred and eleven pounds and had never left the house without wearing his garters.

Esau was a striking-looking fellow with his tortoise-shell shades and bushy sideboards which grew down on each side of his face to join together under his chin. To give that effect a parallel plane, Laurence of Palm Springs had designed an extensively bushy Prince Albert moustache which grew across his upper lip until it joined the sideboards which made up the vertical planes of his face: the designer's intent further complementing his expression because his eyebrows had been artificially extended to join the sideboards at the top. The immediate effect was that of a man wearing a garishly colorful uniform peering through latticework at what could only be a garden party the world was attending inside.

If he had a grating fault it was perhaps that he was trendy. He preferred dress uniforms of the military of various countries for town wear. He had seventy-eight, dry-cleaned, immaculately pressed uniforms and caps. Although he was a drug addict that was as much for a doctrinaire Children's Army reason as it was a consuming and self-destructive habit.

Although christened Sylvan, he preferred to be called Esau because Esau was a hairy man and besides it bugged the shit out of other fags. He had been able to sell the Sylvan on West Forty-second Street to a haughty West Indian quean, then named Herman, for eleven dollars cash. If anyone still called him Sylvan after the warning, Esau knocked him down and trod on his wax injections. If it was a type who liked to be knocked down then Esau would go to the nearest phone booth and report him to the West Indian and she would come flying into the scene with safety razor blades tucked between the fingers of her fists.

But aside from their individual life styles, Esau and the twins, first cousins, were dedicated to each other and all of them were out of their minds about Ada. There was nothing their grandmother could do that wasn't perfect. She smoked pot. She balled guys. She had the formidably correct attitude of a regimental sergeant major in the Children's Army in that she only liked the easy intellectual things which had been printed in the acceptable places and she was exultant in her selfishness. In fact, all kids loved her. Ada was as old as Them but she wasn't square.

8

At Sixth Avenue, Ada and Os clambered down from the top of the bus while there was a red light and since the traffic would not be able to move in any direction for some time. It was one of those marvelous days for which New York was justly famous. It had snowed early in the morning and at noon eleven elderly people had died in Brooklyn from heat prostration. It was clear and cool now with a thrilling light breeze.

Ada was exhilarated by the weather and by the prospect of what lay directly before her. But Os had grimmer thoughts: was this right? Was it even prudent? All had been so serene on his sexless plateau, high above the strife of porn and means other people had made for themselves. But he was being pulled along by something enormous here. He had to follow this lewd beckoning woman because his ancestors had been programmed for it from the moment the first lungfish had strolled up on dry land trailing a male lungfish behind her. He knew he did not want (intellectually) what he was about to try to do (physically). My God, he thought with horror, it cannot be possible that I can get emotionally involved with this woman, or she with me, out of the sheer loneliness of life? He shuddered then because he thought of his oldest son, Gawain, already a monsignor, being required to prepare the rota for his parents' divorce and his father's remarriage. But why did he always have to think of marrying when he thought of copulation?

As they stepped down upon the overcrowded pavement, cars and trucks and motorcycles mingled with the new armored carriers which the Department of Defense had lend-leased to the police of the City of New York. All of it formed gigantic metal crosses at each intersection: wholly unbroken rivers of junk which flowed north and south, east and west. They waited to spot a cab, standing beside one of the garbage mountains on the sidewalk as they were jostled by intermingling pickets protesting the employment policies of a non-union pet shop and a union lampshade manufacturer. A massive demonstration, which had caused some shooting and tear gas explosions, was taking place at a large hotel one block to the south, either to welcome or to negotiate with the Vice-President.

Os tried to keep his gaze fixed to the pavement because there were a great many blacks around them who might follow them home, break in, and urinate on their carpet. Also the new buildings bothered him. They were enormously tall structures which had risen suddenly, replacing a lot of ramshackle four-story buildings which had been there most of his lifetime. He could not shake the feeling that these stone giants were as drunk as the people inside them (if it were after lunch) and could lurch suddenly and fall upon him.

Ada stood on tippy-toe, the wholly adjusted New Yorker, her eyes sweeping the hideously packed avenue for an empty taxi, thanking her stars that this was not the busy hour.

Suddenly, with a piercing whistle she left his side and plunged into the tide of steel. Somehow she got across the lanes and reached an empty cab at the center line. She gestured wildly to Os but he didn't have the courage to go out there. The driver was shrieking at her so she got into the cab and directed it to a place in the curbside lane, about twenty yards ahead. The cab was seven minutes making the eighteen-foot crossing, causing tremendous outcries of pain from all the other cars and effectively blocking and backing up the traffic for thirty-one blocks behind it.

Os waited at curbside with considerable anxiety concerning Ada's overall intentions. It all seemed so threatening rather than romantic. In the short time he had been left alone his erection had gone awry and his posture had become wary. There could be no question as to what she intended to do with him once she could lock a door behind him. He told himself he simply had to make himself think about his heart condition, the tonguing kiss of free enterprise which had given him the wattled look of the executive man, a ubiquitous mask worn by American men over forty who earned more than eighteen thousand dollars a year; the mark of the diet enforced by doctor's threats of instant coronary thrombosis. Os was a tall man and, because of his successful diet, the Yudkin diet, one of seventeen he had experimented with until he had eluded hunger, his expensive clothes looked very well on him. His clothes were not exceptional nor expensive because they were custom-made but because all clothes were expensive.

The cab made it to the curb. Ada held the door open and pulled him in. Expansive and contractive codal things were happening in her vaginal region; it was as though she had been thrown back to the good old days. She slammed the door, spoke into the tonneau microphone to the driver in the sealed compartment ahead where he was safe from all but direct 75mm shell hits behind chicken-wire glass and an arrangement of slender but strong steel bars, and directed the taxi to take them to her apartment house. Then she leaned back and held on to Os' crotch, staring at him as she clenched and unclenched her nostrils. "What a day!" she sang. "I'm so glad I didn't take two Seconals last night. I could have slept right through all this."

For the want of a Seconal a ventricle imploded, he moaned to himself. Medical science was about to receive a case of a man dying of a broken heart because he got the woman he wanted.

They inched glueily along past the high hedges of garbage on either side of the broad avenue, then zoomed at one-and-a-half miles an hour into Fun City's Central Park, driving between two high, proud statues of South American generals who symbolized that there was constant war going on inside the park: no waiting.

"Springtime in New York!" Ada caroled. "How clearly we can almost see the outline of the buildings!"

"Well—the breathing isn't too easy," Os said. "Our lungs must be like black lace underwear."

"If lungs aren't underwear, what is? Did you know that modern science has invented a way to turn all that garbage into industrial alcohol? Isn't that marvelous? And they knock the *Reader's Digest!*"

"Has there been another garbagemen's strike?"

"No, silly. That was just yesterday's garbage. They'll pick it up tomorrow. We are a rich nation so there is a lot of rich garbage."

"We'll certainly be wallowing in industrial alcohol."

Os paid the cab fare on the revolvable disk which permitted the transaction but which did not expose the driver to open danger from the passengers. Ada asked Os discreetly for two discrete pieces of identification. He gave her his Senior Lifesaver's card and a credit card from his turf accountant—Ladbroke's, the English bookmaker. She turned them over to one of the two doormen who guarded the entrance to her apartment building.

The doormen were dressed in deep-green long jackets with two-inch navy blue piping and spaced horizontal navy slashes which were themselves striped in scarlet. They wore diagonal green sashes bearing the regimental badges of the Royal Company of Archers, the last bow and arrow unit in the British forces, the special corps which has the task of guarding the Queen when she visits Scotland. Each man wore a green Kilmarnock and the fatter guard held the rank of two eagle feathers. Their clayed white gloves were looped over their shining black belts and both men wore speed-holstered Smith & Wesson .357 Combat Magnums which had reinforced crimping grooves to maintain the best bullet velocity. The building superintendent's active combat experience of three Manhattan apartment buildings had proved the worth of the gun's four-inch barrel and real power.

Ada was proud of the polish of the men and said so.

"Absolutely stunning turnout," Os commented.

"Thank-you, sir," the fatter doorman answered crisply while the second man was putting the identification pieces through the electronic reader. "May I say I admire your hat, sir?"

"Thank-you. It's my borsalino. Sort of my good-luck piece. Genuine rabbit fur. I bought it in Naples over thirty years ago from the hatmaker who did all the hats for Giacomo Puccini."

Ada beamed. "Marvin," she said, "this is Mr. Osgood Noon. He will be a frequent visitor, we hope, and is a personal friend which is to say I vouch for him and, as you know, I am bonded."

The fatter guard saluted, then nodded to his adjutant who took a front and a profile view of Os' head, rolled off both of his thumbprints to a punched card, recorded distinguishing scars and his voiceprint, then admitted the couple to the building while the fatter guard kept a weather eye out for marauding blacks.

"They really are a first-rate crew," Os said as they walked along the hall to the lift.

"Oh, yes. The discipline is severe."

"I certainly prefer your system to our routine of sending an armed doorman upstairs with all visitors and making the tenants sign for them. I frequently make my own *taglierini* and my hands are covered with flour."

"Still, different neighborhoods present different problems."

When they reached Ada's floor she asked to be excused for just a moment. She went into the flat while Os waited in the hall. When she reappeared she said, "My guard dog roams the flat while I'm out. It was better to tie him up while I introduce you." They slipped into the apartment and Ada bolted the four heavy locks behind them while the huge dog bayed frantically, leaping forward at Os, trying to snap his chain, fangs exposed to their roots.

"This is our friend, Mr. Noon, Wergel," Ada explained to the dog. "Say a nice hello." The dog leaped toward Os' throat.

"Just give me something of yours he can smell," Ada said. "He'll always remember you then. Give me your hat." She took the hat from Os' hand and held it under the dog's nose. "Smell your new friend. Love your new friend and protect him too." Wergel tore the hat into shreds within seconds.

"Dogs have never taken to me," Os said.

"Well, never mind. We'll go inside."

"I had that hat for thirty years. Thirty-two years. Toscanini was still conducting in Buenos Aires when I bought that hat."

"Oh, well. No matter. You can always get another. We got home safely, that's what counts."

Ada's flat was more like El Escorial than a city apartment. The great entrance hall was three stories high done in the sort of architecture Adolf Hitler had fancied. A copy of Verrocchio's great equestrian statue was centered in the hall showing the *condottiere,* Bartolommeo Colleoni, one-and-a-half times actual size but having Arthur's head with granite jaws and flashing green eyes in the Cuban ecclesiastical sculpting tradition, on the shoulders of the great fifteenth-century land pirate.

"What a job we had getting that in here," Ada said. "It was Arthur's idea, putting his own head on the statue. Bartolommeo Colleoni is patron saint of Republicans Who Make It, you know."

"I know."

She set the iron bar on the police lock diagonally away from the steel door, into its deep setting in the marble floor. "Welcome to my house, Osgood Noon," she said gravely. They shook hands then she led him on marches across rooms and along corridors and galleries which looked out on terraces where live sheep grazed on real grass under quaint miniature apple trees, then into the small thirty-by-thirty study which had been decorated as a replica of the collegiate church of St. Gallen, all done in simulated light-green and pink rock candy. She pressed a stud on the wall and nine shelves of glistening bottles were slowly revealed.

"It was Arthur's pride that no matter what country a guest of ours might come from, that we would have his favorite national drink to offer him," Ada said proudly. "But we never entertained much. We served mostly *grappa* to Arthur's close business associates. What will you have?"

"Ginger ale?"

"I hope we have it." She opened a refrigerator door and rummaged. "Arthur had three independent firms of interior decorators working at the same time in this apartment and they never met."

"It is—it is—well!"

"Arthur promised himself the best when he started out as a repairman for pill-rolling machines, then, what with his native drive, he suddenly owned control of eleven national pill companies." She handed Os a tall filled glass. She lifted her own glass then stared at him longingly over its rim as she sipped.

Os made himself look away. He held the glass between them to ward off the moment of truth. He gulped deeply. Despite many other quite stirring feelings, he made himself speak.

"Ada—there is something we have to speak about. I mean—well, after all—the way I see it, a lot of time has passed since we—uh—met in France."

"I hope I am not following you correctly, Os."

"But I want to say that I hope we can continue to be friends. Real friends."

"Oh, for heaven's *sake, Os."*

"There are certain reasons—certain very good reasons which must be taken into consideration and—"

"I suppose you are going to tell me that sex isn't everything."

"Ada—I—"

"Say it, Os. Say it, then we'll discuss it."

"It's—you see—it became essential that I train myself away from sex because—"

"Os, please! Arthur gave me that same line when it just so happened that Arthur was so scared of the Black Panthers that—"

"I can assure you that my reason is entirely different."

"I am here to tell you that fear is one lousy aphrodisiac."

"Had the Panthers attacked him?"

"Of course not! They are a boys' club, that's all. They have this club just to scare guys like Arthur but they don't *do* anything. Why should they when the white students are willing to go to all the expense?"

"Ada, this is my position and I feel it is a compassionate one. I have had to veer myself away from sex because of a heart condition. You see, not long ago, about two years ago, I had this tiny thrombosis while performing the sex act and—"

"Per*form*ing? You mean you used to do exhi*bi*tions?"

"No, no! Performing, that is while—well, while—"

"Sort of like when you were screwing?"

"Yes. And it was a very frightening thing. I can tell you it greatly reduced my interest in sex."

"Is that all?"

"All?" He had a flash of himself as he heard the odd-sounding rattle in his throat then as Cerce had rolled him off her onto the floor (and they had very high Danish beds). He had lain there in a draught like a gasping trout waiting for his entire life to pass before him, which it had not. He had breathed like a bagpipe. His tongue had lolled out, Cerce had said, around and under his right ear. His heart had darted around his thorax like a trapped rabbit seeking an exit. He found himself wishing desperately that he had made the contributions to the churches which he had claimed on his income tax returns.

"When did your wife leave you, Os?"

"The last time?"

"She leaves you a lot?"

"I feel it is a lot. I can't speak for other marriages."

"Did she leave you about two years ago? Because of you stopping—you know?"

He took a deep breath then exhaled. "I had never thought of it that way but it could have been one of the reasons." He stared at her fiercely. "But my wife has been socially and emotionally unstable for years. She has a mania for travel and three credit cards."

"You must suffer terribly from tension."

"Some degree of tension is inevitable. In order to have life we must have tension."

"*Sex*ual tension? The signs of tension which are outside the desirable limits of tension? I mean—it's all there in the statistics for stress disorders, isn't it? When we are concerned with things like homicide and addiction and other fantastic problems."

"I had no idea you were interested in that field."

"Men have stresses. Men have to be helped."

"Thank you. But I hadn't noticed that my own tension is any such significant issue."

"You don't have depressions? Irritability? Disenchantment with our way of life? Cynicism about other people? How about those indictments, Os?"

"Now just one moment. You are turning this all around every which way."

"Are you frightened of tenderness?"

"I don't know."

"Think!"

"I think Americans, as a group, are increasingly frightened of tenderness."

"Are you aware that this leads to a lack of contact between people?" She rubbed his lapels with her thumbs and stared at him soulfully with her black shoe-button eyes, willing her forty-three-dollar-an-ounce perfume to rise unto his nostrils.

"I suppose so, yes," he answered shakily. He braced his legs as her scent arose to him, because if he fell she would surely contrive to fall under him.

"Os, don't you see? There must be meaningful contact between people. Your tension is beyond all tolerable limits or you would never have had that tiny thrombosis. As long as you believe you can get your satisfactions externally, you are not going to make it. The only way out of such tension is a relationship with another person. Fucking is no abstract encounter, Os, except with the under-thirty-fives. It is a part of our essential introspective encounter with life. Were you and your wife sexually compatible, Os?"

He was shaken. He felt he had lost. She was talking to him like a Copenhagen grade-school teacher.

"I like to think so, yes," he said stiffly.

"How compatible?"

"Dammit, Ada!"

"We've simply got to get this out into the open, Os. This is an adult discussion."

"Well, when we first married she wasn't at all interested in sex—the idea repelled her, I think."

She waved him off. "Ah, they all say that."

"I know she said she would rather have Lhasa Apso puppies than children. But as time went on and my own intensity was transmuted, hers began to mount until, well, you could say—after my heart attack—our positions had reversed themselves."

"You mean you then wanted Lhasa Apsos? They are terrible barkers, Os."

"No, no! I mean as regards our interest in sex—our basic positions on sex—were reversed."

"That is the whole trick for the cardiac. The position. Your wife, if I may say so, was a know-nothing. When you get into bed with me—and I must tell you I am very grateful that you tipped me off that you had had a tiny thrombosis while you were doing it—I am going to prove you have nothing to fear."

"You will?"

"Then, right after we do it, I am going to ask you to call your own heart man to ask if you can go to him straight from the experience and have an EKG."

"This is a Saturday. We'd never find him."

"Your heart is going to be so safe with me that we can screw our heads off, if you've got it in you." She grasped the smallest finger of his left hand and led him out of the room. They moved through mirrored corridors into a large room whose door she locked behind her.

"What a magnificent bed!" he cried.

"It is a very, very strong bed," she said. She tried to lead him forward but he had to stop to stare in long perspective at the dreadnought if ironmongery which was made in no way with the delicate, feminine curlicues of Sevillian *hierro forjada* but with doughty British iron, wrested, bent and twisted from solid railway tracks, built to support an entire regiment if any regiment ever gained simultaneous admiration for its collective (usually honorary) sweetheart.

"It's a Charles Eastlake," Ada explained, unbuttoning his shirtfront, then slipping off his jacket. "He is the British architect who, through beds, embarked on such a hopeless quest for a higher moral tone in furniture." She unzipped his trousers, slipped his braces off his shoulders and let the trousers fall to the floor.

"Hey! Long underwear!"

"Oh. Yes. Sort of a hangover from the old days of skis, I guess."

"But it's nearly summer."

"They're still skiing at St. Moritz."

"Let's get them off, sweetheart." She unbuttoned him rapidly. "Note how Eastlake has framed the bed canopy on projecting spears, the spears hung on chains from—the spears—" Her voice trailed off in dazed admiration as she stared downward at him. "Os! It's beautiful! Why—it has the shape of a Coca-Cola bottle!" She grasped it gently and led him at a dog trot to the great bed. "Take off your shoes, dearest," she reminded him. With the speed of a heroine disrobing to plunge into a raging current to rescue her drowning child she stripped off her few clothes, kicked off her shoes, retained only a deep-pink B-cup brassiere for reasons of her own, and leaped into the bed beside him.

Os was rigid in more ways than one. The tension of his fright of a coronary and his lust for a copulatory had formed him into two flawless planes at right angles. Only his large brown eyes moved.

Ada rested on her side, massaged his stomach slowly and spoke to him softly. "The fact is, most people think sex is finished after the first teeny occlusion. Ho-ho! I say. And tomorrow is Sunday but you are going to be examined by the best heart man in the world, Dr. Abraham Weiler, and you are—"

"Dr. Weiler wouldn't even see me on a Thursday. He just doesn't see people."

"You let me handle Weiler. Tomorrow you are going to hear from Weiler that a normal sex life is the very best way to release the inner tensions which cause the coronary. And you are going to learn that a suppressed libido may, in itself, give rise to anginal fits of anxiety." Her expert hand moved lower on his taut body. "Thus inducing psychogenic coronary spasms."

"You don't know what it's like when it happens, Ada. It's like a giant hand folding your chest in half—aaaarrr-haaa—until the points of the shoulders almost touch." He moaned again pitiably but he was smiling.

"Does that feel nice, Os?"

He gurgled.

"Do you want me to explain about the increase of blood pressure and the jumped pulse rate? How your body loses carbon dioxide rapidly and your arm and leg muscles get stiff?"

He mewed piteously.

"If you want to you can take a nitroglycerin tablet now. Right here in the night table." She leaned over him and stopped speaking for a considerable time. Os began to bleat after a while. She propped herself up on her elbow again. "Enough of that for now. Nothing too quickly. Right? But it is so important that we choose the relaxed positions and we must never do it while wearing tight clothes or on a full stomach." He groped for her. "Roll over on your side, darling," Ada said. "Now we'll try it." There was a moment of fumbling. "There. That's nice. Oh, nice, Os. Os, good. Oooooh, Os!" She put her arms around him tenderly and began to attack him savagely from her hips.

Pharzuph, the Hellespontian angel of lust, began the old soft shoe, having entered from the wings, from behind the scrims and backdrops of their beings. The hook began to move out slowly, held by the International Association of Theatrical and Stage Employees stagehands, Theliel, Rahmiel and Donquiel, the angels of love. They got the hook around Pharzuph's waist and jerked him off-stage. The angels of love entered doing a cakewalk, holding straw boaters high above their heads; true angels of true love. They were a smash-hit turn and would be held over.

9

Miraculously, Ada was able to get a private audience with Dr. Abraham Weiler whose fame had been secured when he had been invited to conduct a routine check-up on the heart of Dr. Christiaan Barnard. Weiler not only did not make house calls (after all even an interne wouldn't make a house call), but he would not permit patients to make office calls and he rarely visited a hospital. He remained far back in the AMA incense, available for consultation, usually only by telescreen telephone, only to Heads of Departments of Cardiology of leading (non-integrated) universities. It was at Weiler's desk that the chain of fee-splitting stopped. He was too big a man to split fees. He took the whole fee. When feeder physicians referred data to him they were paid with the honor of his receiving it, if he would consent to receive it. They had to pay his fees plus the fees which the patient would have to pay them and, further, had to submit to sodium pentathol tests, then to a lie detector when stating the amount of the fees they would charge the patients. Weiler personified the meaning of the evolved Hippocratic Oath and owned two ski lifts at Megeve.

The great doctor was extremely grave with Os and extremely affable with Ada in his waiting room. Os was left with many copies of the *Literary Digest* and *Liberty* magazines while Ada and the doctor spent an immeasurably long time consulting behind locked door within the Surgery about Os' symptoms and background. For whatever reason, the doctor had not only locked the door, but had bolted it in two places, loudly.

When Os was, at last, called in, Ada was busy at a mirror fussing with her hair and Dr. Weiler seemed strangely out-of-breath for a heart man. Os was feeling very edgy. He felt like those Aztecs must have felt when they climbed the three hundred and sixty-five steps of the pyramid at Teotihuacan toward the old gentleman with the red-black matted hair and the crimson-spattered feather apron who waited with a stone knife at the top. Weiler was a great doctor but this was *Os'* heart they would be talking about while Weiler seemed to be having even worse trouble with his own.

The distinguished doctor was staring fixedly at Os with popping eyes while he gulped air and clawed with his right hand at his chest. The doctor was behaving like a man who had been forced to race up all the stairs of a skyscraper while carrying two anvils. He motioned weakly for Os to sit in the facing chair. While he fought to recover into a less shocking breathing cycle he shuffled X-rays, EKG's, medical reports and letters concerning Os which had been rushed to his desk by Os' various doctors in the hope that Dr. Weiler would remember them and perhaps even nod to them at the next tax-deductible medical convention at Las Vegas. At last he regained control of his speech and his wizardry became immediately apparent.

"I have digested these data, Mr. Noon," he said slowly, "and regardless of any other opinion you may have been given, you may now be sure that you have a transient left-bundle branch block which indicates ischemia of a transient sort. You have, therefore, a coronary insufficiency with angina pectoris."

"Well—yes," Os said. They had all told him that.

"The episodes of precordial distress which occurred during intercourse two years ago, according to A. Edward Masters' diagnostic report, are typical of angina and I am pleased with you that you are not overweight and do not smoke."

Weiler seemed to look right through all the *O*'s in Os' name and into his soul piercingly, an illusion lent to physicians by extreme myopia and developed for the profession under grant by the late Lionel Barrymore.

"I understand, doctor," Os said.

"Nonethe*less*—it is essential that we lessen your anxieties and reduce your tensions which are so constantly a-building—and I refer to certain personal, circumstantial and situational matters of which you are well aware."

"I worked like Old Ned to lose sixty pounds over the past two years."

"However, I do not feel that the use of chemical tranquilizers is advisable in your case." The doctor yawned suddenly. "What is bothering you?" he asked abruptly.

Os glanced across at Ada for a second, clearing his

throat. "Uh—well—the fact is I am fearful that I might drop dead during sexual intercourse and what with my total recall of almost every miniskirt I had ever seen before *Women's Wear Daily* took that away from us, to say nothing of the prevalence of highly spiced foods—this keeps me continually anxious and tense."

Weiler leaned forward in his great throne of a chair. "I pre*scribe* intercourse for you," he said dramatically. "I prescribe it as a *must* for you." His own right hand gripped his chest more tightly. "But intercourse under experienced, expert care. Do you wish me to recommend a reliable practitioner?"

Os darted a glance at Ada again. She was seated with her gorgeous legs crossed. She smiled at him lasciviously and shook her head almost imperceptibly. Os turned back to the doctor. "No, thank you," he said. "That will not be necessary."

10

They did not seem to be able to put a foot wrong that spring.

She liked his apartment better than hers. For one thing it was sweetly old-fashioned and utterly substantial, the way her parents had lived when she had been a girl. In the house she was in, where Arthur had paid almost three hundred thousand dollars for a cooperative, everything was all so *new* and the architect, a son-in-law of the Mafia builder, had overlooked putting in any water pipes and they had had the whole inconvenience of having to stay for almost eight months in the Waldorf Towers while the contractors ripped the whole building apart to put in pipes. Also she preferred Os' apartment because Wergel could not chew up Os' jackets and trousers there. And she liked the way the doormen of Os' building worked with MACE and how they had organized the defenses of the building so that they needed to man only one large gate which led to a central courtyard from which the entrances to the four individual but conjoined buildings were approached so that if rioting blacks or Weathermen or Abbie Hoffman did break through they could be treated with machine-gun fire by only one man from the facing-gun position at garden-center in the *cours d'honneur*. The other reason why she preferred Os' apartment was its enforced serenity. His flat, which was on the south and west side of the building, just happened to face the street which was the Open Air Narcotics Bourse which served all the *barrios* on the West Side. Attentive city police diverted all traffic from the thoroughfare and dealt quickly with any troublemakers. The narcotics brokers had been conditioned years before to conduct all transactions in whispers which had become a tradition, so quiet and order reigned.

At first they visited each other almost daily until it became plain that Wergel was not going to cotton to Os and until the telephone company could somehow make things right again for phoning across Manhattan. Or, if they were unable to visit because of the weather or mass attacks by blacks or bombings by Weathermen of points which were between, they sent each other messages through the private postal service which was heinously expensive but which would make half-hourly pickups and take only an hour to get across town whereas mailing a letter through the U.S. postal service took from eighteen to twenty days to make the same distance if it ever got there. Ada would write:

> Dearest Os: It has just been driven home to me that you are the father of two really famous "new Amercans": Monsignor Gawain Noon, our beloved papal nuncio to the Attorney General and certainly our soundest theologian in the North American branch of the Church, And—well!—Tristram Noon. the thrilling radical revolutionary who has found his ideal in charging our young people with their own meaning and has served warning on social and governmental injustice that equality of opportunity—not only to serve in our armed forces overseas but in civilian life —must be guaranteed or he will lead his army of youth into the streets where they will take what is their own. How I admired his leadership of the student mob in San José during the 1970 by-elections when he so provoked our President to headlines which lead to that wonderfully convincing television commercial by the President which really packaged and sold law and order. I have read every one of his books: *Me* and *The Compass in the Mirror* and *A Very Personal Pronoun*. I adore his TV show. My family says he plays the greatest lead guitar since Segovia and that when he sings Mick Jagger seems like Eddie Fisher. He is our ombudsman for action.
>
> How proud you must be of those two boys! One the spirit of our nation, the other exemplifying the spirit of individual freedom. I am not a religious person beyond the Alamo, Valley Forge and Dan'l Boone so the good Monsignor may not quite have as much meaning for me as your boy Tristram. I hope you will permit some members of my family, particularly two very beautiful twin girls, to meet him some day.
>
> I see that there is a Cottage Cheese Special at

Daitch's advertised in the *Post* today but if you go down to get some be sure to wear your wooly socks.

Lovingly,
Ada

Dear Ada: Thank you for your note, just received, and for the tip about the special at Daitch. I had not seen my boys in quite that way. They are good boys and both are hard workers. Perhaps Gawain does give the impression of being a religious leader now that you mention it. It is the costume they wear and photographically he has always had a long bony face. At any rate I am happy if his theology is as sound as you imply. Tris plays a far better game of pool than he does his guitar and, at least on his TV show, his singing is too coarse for my taste. There is no doubt that a public perspective, once attained through newsprint and through television has the power to change any reality. The fact is, my youngest boy, Botolf, who is about to graduate from the University of California at Berkeley with a Master's Degree in Natural History is all of the exemplary things which you have attributed to Gawain and Tris. For one thing he is a far more religious boy than Gawain. He cherishes every living thing is why I say that. By his attitude and through his studies, Botolf relates life to life and the living and not to endless compartments called Protestants, labor unions, blacks, bankers, pot smokers, hawks, hippies, power brokers or priests. He is a giver. He has faith in courtesy and believes that good manners are based upon consideration. Gawain and Tris are famous—but Bottie is stronger than they are —or should I have said he is tougher than they are because resilience and ethical durability are involved here. But, I play no favorites among them. My boys are good boys which is why I am proud of them,

All my love,
Os

When they were together and were not copulating they greatly enjoyed discussing their health and general state of being.

"I slept like a log last night," Os said.

"Did you? Oh, God I had a terrible night."

"I massaged my feet with the combination of Dr. Scholl's and Sloan's Liniment, as you suggested then put the bed socks on over that and it was perfection."

"I had to get up at about three o'clock and take another Seconal. And there were none left in the bottle beside the bed. I had to go all the way to the bathroom."

"If I may say this, Ada—please don't take it as criticism —I don't want you taking those damned sleeping pills."

"But through Arthur's companies I get such a tremendous wholesale price on them."

"Then buy Miltowns. You work on those astrological charts and get all charged up if they indicate success in politics for your son-in-law—and that's why you can't sleep."

"You have got to meet Duncan Mulligan. Then you'll take up astrology or sand reading or reading entrails on the floor of a kosher chicken market because every day he is getting closer and closer to being elected to the Senate." Ada ran her hands through her hair without even thinking because Duncan Mulligan could make her so distraught and that meant another comb-out by Leonard.

"The main thing, my dear, is to drink plenty of water. Don't ever resist having to get up to eliminate water in the night. That is where great good health lives—in glass after glass of clear water."

He cooked for her when they were in his flat, another reason she liked it there. He could only cook three dishes but he cooked them extremely well because they were the only three dishes he had ever cooked for his sons during the years when Cerce had left them. He did not like outside help in the house because he was fearful that either he or one of the boys might be tempted to mount them so he cooked giant hamburger sandwiches (which Ada actually improved, he thought, with the gift of a jar of Imitation Bacon Bits); spaghetti with a secret sauce; and *choucroute garnie*, the term used in French restaurants for frankfurters and sauerkraut.

In the late March weather, when temperatures varied so greatly, he would begin cooking *choucroute garnie* while the snow was flying but when it was ready to eat the temperatures would be in the eighties. When he cooked spaghetti for her he promised that he would one day reveal the secret of the sauce but, although almost sixty per cent of their conversations were about food, he could not bring himself to tell. He would talk around it when she pressed him, "It's too extravagant a sauce, really. I stumbled on it through the accident of being a publisher."

"I didn't know you were a *pub*lisher. I thought you were a hat manufacturer."

"I had been a hat manufacturer but—"

"What kind of books do you publish? My God, do you know Dwight MacDonald and Rod McKuen?"

"Well—I'm a magazine publisher."

"Oh, Os! Which *magazine!*"

"I don't think you'd know it. It's just a trade paper called *World Defense.* It's a magazine for countries, really, rather than for people. Foster Dulles asked me to get it started."

"Like—travel and tourism?"

"It tells what armaments the big countries are willing to sell to the small countries. The different countries take ads and our critics review their tanks and bacteria and missiles and so forth. It's sort of a *Consumers' Digest* idea on a different scale."

"But I do know it! In fact, we subscribe! Our chemicals company Blandish, Burns always has ads in *World Defense.*"

"Is that your company? Oh, well. Blandish, Burns is the leader. I'd say we've moved more napalm and defoliants for Blandish, Burns than the whole Vietnam war. And let me say that your 2, 4, 5,-trichlorophenoxyacetic acid is the best there is. We gave it a rave review, as you must know. One Air Force general told me he could clean up Asia with it single-handed."

"Coming from you that's a real compliment."

"I always wanted to be a publisher. Advertising lineage fascinates me. My family wanted me to run our old Bahama Beaver Bonnet Company which still trades well enough in the market, but it was an old hat business—no pun intended."

"I think it is just uncanny that you should be the one who has moved so much 2, 4, 5-T for us."

"The magazine was one of those naturals. I began to think of all those expensive dies for all those weapons and unused batches of toxins and bacteria until finally I had to buy myself a few solid political connections through the right Wall Street firm and I was off."

"Who did you use?"

"Lantz, Lantz, Tolliver and Farr."

"We use them, too."

"We created a marketplace with the magazine where your small aggressor can know what your big aggressor has to sell him. For instance, we *made* the little Uzi machine gun for Israel to the glamour point where the President insisted that it be used by the Secret Service to guard him. And look what we've done for the *Mystère* and, of course, your own napalm—but for heaven's sake, enough about me, you must be starving."

"I'm starving all right," she said huskily, moved by his new glamour and all the talk of profits, "and you know for what." She clutched his small finger in her fist and led him out of the kitchen to the billiard room. She laid out a dainty little towel then spread-eagled across the billiard table under two lushly fringed hanging lights and pulled her skirts up under her chin. He popped a sublingual isosorbide dinitrate pill into his mouth, stepped out of his trousers in respect for her earlier admonition against tight clothing, pulled a chair to the side of the billiard table and climbed aboard her, transported by their love.

11

There were times when she was vaguely certain of being followed. All her life she had trained herself to be aware of the men around her, within one hundred and twenty feet, but she had fallen in love and this had blunted her perceptions. At odd moments, such as when she had floated in her Roman bath in her one hundred-and-eighteen-thousand dollar bathroom whose walls and fixtures were paved with malachite, amethysts, tiger's-eye, rose quartz, rock crystal, lapis lazuli and onyx; with the beautiful twin toilet commodes in black lacquer with Japanese landscapes and birds in gold relief, rich linings of pink mother-of-pearl and Russian crown sable padded seats of which her bathroom decorator himself had said, *"On n'imagine rien de plus amiable,"* she seemed to be aware, retroactively, of a very bulky man—bulky enough to have lined his clothing with an entire edition of the Sunday *Times*—who wore a navy blue beret, and had the punched-eyes look of a *hylobates hoolock* of the gibbon family, glittering out of viewing compounds of deep black eye-surrounds, but when she tried to concentrate on his presence and the inky patches around his eyes it all melted away because she really wanted to loll back in the warm water and think about afternoons on the pool table with Os.

Osgood Noon was a blaze to her. He was built like a wand. He had puzzled eyes. It was very good for a man to have puzzled eyes because no matter how many times a woman asked men who had puzzled eyes what they were puzzled about, they would always get a different answer. Most of the time she would be sure he was puzzled from trying to figure out what he was doing with a woman like her. She would say, "You look puzzled, Os. What's the matter?" He wouldn't answer right away then he'd give her some bumf like, "I was thinking how unfair it is for an art dealer to get tens of thousands of dollars for a painting when the painter probably did it for a bowl of lasagne." She would wait, *her* eyes getting puzzled, then she would say, "Yes?" to encourage him to continue, to clear it up, and he would say, "I was thinking that every time a painting changes hands that either the painter or his estate should be paid twenty-five per cent of the sale. I mean, the Attorney General should make them make it into a law."

So, she never really knew where she stood with him. She was never sure whether he would rather be with her or home with his head in a croup kettle. But he was a tremendous lover. She would be willing to put in writing that he was the greatest in North America. Had he and the Dominican diplomat and the Italian dwarf who worked in the ski boot shop at Cortina d'Ampezzo somehow pooled what they knew? In some ways she could believe that, as she floated upon the warm, perfumed bath which had been designed in London to accommodate two consenting adults and cursed the need that caused people to get into that no-answer maze of whether Jack Broughton (1704-1789) could have whipped Luis Angel Firpo. But thinking about it, using all measurements and technical achievement, she felt she could say that Os was the greatest because the dwarf had been working in the total calm of the off-season without distraction, and the Dominican diplomat had his Japanese mushroom tea, while Os had come through with hours-long stamina while working in the chaos of New York where a man had to be able to think of seventy things at one time just to be able to stay alive. Life had turned into wondrous bliss for her and if she kept coming the way she was coming she would run into herself going away.

Then came the Saturday morning which changed all their lives. Her daughter, Celeste, telephoned. "Ada?" she said. Ada had trained her children to call her by her first name because, if age ever descended on her, people would think they were just friends because children aged, too.

"Yes, Celeste?" Ada said. Even as an infant, which had been some time ago, Celeste had always been a pain in the ass.

"I have to see you."

"Why not?"

"Don't try to go out. I'll be right there."

She must have called from a police car because she was there in nothing flat and of course Wergel never wanted to bite *her*—oh, no.

She looked agitated. She was a tall, dun-colored girl with large hands and high, soccer-ball boobs. There were people who actually thought Celeste was beautiful, but Ada could see a lot of Arthur in her and very little of herself. Celeste had a dreamer's face like Arthur's. Both of them dreamers with an eye for an instant buck better than any croupier's. Celeste had inherited that directly from Arthur. She owned and controlled and managed the biggest chain of health-food stores since the geriatric scientists had discovered blackstrap molasses.

She came into the apartment as though Ada were trying to keep her out. She threw her fantasy fur on the dog because she was so goddam nearsighted but would not wear glasses, then she looked up at her father's equestrian statue with the total awe which must be shown by any naval officer as he boards a naval vessel, faces aft and salutes the flag.

"Are we alone?" she asked, a typical dopey question in a lifetime of dopey questions. Did she think Ada handled the housework in a twenty-eight room apartment and cooked for Wergel besides?

Ada took her to the Mauve Room which was called that because Arthur had once given her a black eye there. They sat down with the dread combined with ersatz patience which had become the confrontation style of American family life.

"How are the kids?" Ada asked with tinseled gaiety.

"Kids?"

"I refer to your daughters, the twins," Ada said acidly.

"When they start to think of how I am, I'll start to think of how they are," Celeste said. "Dunc is fine."

"Did I ask for him?" Just the sound of Duncan Mulligan's name made Ada feel sleepy.

"His prospects for the nomination could be very good —if no one upsets my apple tarts."

Ada shrugged. What could happen? No matter what it was, how could anyone maintain the attention span to listen if it was about Dunc. Duncan Mulligan was the kind of a lawyer whom the rest of the firm shut up in a law library while they took the clients to Lutèce for lunch. He was so shallow he had no color to his skin. There was no place to put it. Therefore, the Republicans wanted to run him for the Senate.

"I came over this morning to talk to you about what could happen to Dunc's chances, Ada."

"Politics isn't my bag, sweetie."

"These politics are your family duty."

"What went wrong, baby?"

Celeste's eyes got watery. Her lips quivered. "I hate to say this, Mama."

"Ada."

"I hate to be forced to say it."

"I bet."

"I do! I am embarrassed to the point of humiliation on several counts."

"Tell me about it."

"Dunc's campaign manager—and that just happens to be F.M. Heller, chairman of the board and chief executive officer of the Everest Bank—has found it necessary to have you followed."

"I knew it!"

Celeste was irritated. Instead of reacting with apprehension or guilt, Ada was triumphant. "I ignored it like a ninny but I knew it!"

"Ada, how could you know it?"

"Because he was a lousy shadow, that's how."

"He was only a campaign volunteer who came all the way in from Stamford, Connecticut, every day to do his best! Dunc's campaign has to run at a deficit because certain people who are in a position to contribute very importantly have not done so."

"I sent in a check for fifteen dollars."

"Yes! Fifteen dollars! And you also told all the Harris foundations that they could contribute exactly fifteen dollars, no more and no less, too."

"Well! After all. Your father's will put me in a position of fiduciary trust. Did you say the shadow from Stamford was doing his best?"

"Yes."

"Doing his best to do what?"

Celeste dabbed at her eyes with a tiny handkerchief which looked ludicrous in her great, big hands.

"Oh, for Christ's sake, Celeste. What is it?"

"Ada?—Mama?"

"Yes, Celeste."

"We have discovered you are sleeping with a seventy-year-old man." They stared at each other. Celeste waited with much pleasure for the denial, the recriminations, for the tears and hysteria and apologies.

"Honey, I am sixty-eight years old. Does F.M. Heller want me to sleep with kids of fifty?"

Her blandness was infuriating for Celeste. "Listen, Mama. Let's get something straight. We're not going to start the story of my life all over again. You can go to bed with anyone you want to but just let any member of the family show the slightest interest in sex and you'd move heaven and earth to break it up."

Ada was genuinely shocked. "When? Who? When have I ever tried to stop one of my children? Jean-Pierre doesn't have the time. Kaskell can't. You never wanted to. Or if you did, you certainly kept it a secret."

"How could I want to? You turned everything about sex into a dis*grace!* Nobody ever had a mother who carried on sexually the way you have carried on. And now—my God, just when Dunc has his one big chance to be a big man in American history, what do you do? You decide to screw a seventy-year-old man!"

Celeste was very upset so Ada patted her shoulder tenderly, in an approved manner.

"I'm not asking for myself, Mama. I'm pleading for Dunc."

"But, darling—what is wrong with sleeping with a beautiful, smart, seventy-year-old man?" Ada was genuinely bewildered.

"It is absolutely dis*gus*ting!"

"Dis*gus*ting? I knew you were a priss and maybe a few other things but if you had ever had a look at Osgood Otto Noon, *noth*ing could make you say making love with him could be disgusting." She grabbed Celeste's elbows because her shoulders were too far away and gave them a good shaking. "You had better make your position a lot clearer about this whole thing, young lady, or I am going to feel insulted. And when I feel insulted, I counterpunch."

Celeste wrenched herself free and made it a point to rub her elbows as though her mother had a grip like a professional football lineman. "All right, Ada," she said grimly. "Now hear this. If it ever gets out that Duncan Mulligan's mother-in-law is sleeping with a seventy-year-old man then we can just say good-by to the nomination and Dunc may just as well resign from the practice of law. The church won't stand for it and the youth of America won't stand for it."

"I simply do not understand, Celeste."

"And just how do you think your sons would feel if they found out? Suppose all this spills into the press and television—the opposition is perfectly capable of making that happen."

"My sons? Do you mean—like Kaskell?"

Celeste bit her lip. "All right then. Never mind Kaskie."

"Then—Jean-Pierre? Celeste, do you have any idea what Jean-Pierre does for a living?"

Celeste covered her ears and screamed in one short burst, her head back, eyes popping toward the ceiling. Then she said, "I don't *care*—I don't want to *hear* what Jean-Pierre does for a living."

"The opposition might be able to do a lot with that—except who cares any more—right? It's a way of life."

"I didn't know you knew what Jean-Pierre does for a living."

Ada shrugged.

"Who told you?"

"Never mind."

"Kaskie told you!"

"Baby, everybody knows. My point is, if the American society is so permissive how could it ever get as shook as you say, about me and a really distinguished man like Osgood Noon?"

"Because it's dis*gus*ting! A seventy-year-old man—eck!" Celeste mimed things with her upper lip; sickly. "You never liked Dunc, did you, Ada?"

"I am not a flag-defiler."

"His law firm wants him to be a United States Senator. They can quadruple their business if Dunc is elected."

"Oh, come on, Celeste! The Attorney General came from that firm so they have already quintupled their business twice."

"There are things I am not privileged to tell you, Ada. If Dunc merely *runs* for the presidency the firm can—"

Ada clutched at her throat with one hand. The other hand gripped her forehead tightly. "President? DUNCAN MULLIGAN?"

"Please. It just slipped out. Please, Mama, that is very, *very* confidential information. If I happened to tell it to you I told it with the fullest confidence that you would never repeat it. I had to tell you to make you realize the heinousness of what you and that old man are doing."

"Duncan Mulligan in the WHITE House?" Ada tottered. She seemed ready to weep. "Celeste—dearest—you mustn't say things like that to mother without smiling."

"I have been instructed to ask you to give me your solemn assurances in writing that you will renounce this old man and will never see him again. I have been sworn in as a notary of the State of New York for this purpose."

"Oh, my God. My *God!*"

"The state nominating convention meets on April sixteenth. That's two weeks from next Wednesday."

"They would try to put an empty-headed trans*vest*ite in the White House?"

Celeste almost gagged with rage. "Where is your compassion?" she shouted. "You know Dunc lives under terrible pressure! Ever since that mix-up in Geneva about the eight-hundred million dollars that South American dictator left in cash to his sons and the daughter went to the enemy uncle because Dunc made an honest little mistake, the firm won't give Dunc a case. They shut him up in that abandoned Tanzanian law library all day! Another man would crack under it. He has to get relief somehow!"

"Relief in a forty-nine ninety-five all-rubber evening gown?" Ada asked indignantly. She slapped the marble table top beside her with the flat of her hand and much force. "Mr. Noon and I enjoy only old-fashioned sex and *nobody* is going to stop us."

"Mama, please! You can't. You've had your turn and now it's all over." Celeste began to sob bitterly. "I'm just pulp," she wept. "All my life I've been in the middle between my parents and my husband and my children. I've always done my best. Everyone thinks I have no feelings. My children are social pirates, my father corrupted the nation, my mother—"

"Your *fath*er? How dare you!"

"Why are the twins on heroin? Why is Esau a methedrine fiend? Why are three out of five kids junkies today?"

"I think you'd better go home, Celeste."

"Mayor Lindsay was right! We do live in a pill society and Daddy invented it. From three years old on, American kids watch an average of fifty-six hours of television a week. By the time a child in this country gets to the first grade he has seen over a thousand hours of television. And what television! Never mind the endless violence, nobody can make them stop that because it's our only culture. But throughout the lives of all those kids Daddy's commercials hammer pills into their heads. Six morning shows are controlled by Daddy's companies. Eleven afternoon shows. Three night shows. Twenty-four thousand hours of Daddy's pill commercials by the time every American kid is eighteen. Got a headache, kid? Take a pill. Got a cold, shorty? Take a pill. Acne, anyone? Take a pill. Every kid in this country has been brainwashed into taking pills so, if they run into a little disappointment, they take a little heroin. How can they understand what's so bad about that?"

Ada took her daughter in her arms. "Don't cry. Please don't cry. It's not just you, it's the whole world."

Celeste clung to her mother and sobbed brokenly. "It just isn't fair," she said. "Your generation got everything. Men. The glamour of Prohibition. All those wonderfully low prices in the Depression. Now their generation gets the whole sensation revolution. What did my generation get? Dewey and Eisenhower. What did I get? Dunc Mulligan!"

12

Celeste Mulligan-Harris seemed to be an earthbound sort of woman with her low-reflex threshold and a tendency toward mouth breathing but, by the measure of her secret life, she was air-thralled. When she had taken her Master's Degree at the Vermont progressive college which offered majors in Opal Repair and Twi, a popular West African language, her parents had made her a graduation present of a Grand Tour of Europe. She had been allowed to take her Master's before attending college, just sort of bypassing the usual college stuff because her Dad had been so wonderfully generous in donating the new chem lab where the students met to make fun aphrodisiacs. The tour had begun on a June day twenty-two years before, when Celeste had been eighteen years old and fully capable of shrinking massively from such obscure penis symbols as a jar of *grissini*.

To the greatest extent her mother's abiding interest had been responsible for this, but it was the Grand Tour which really formed her.

The ship was the *Bergquist*, a Norwegian liner on a time-charter to a consortium of Finnish and Swedish shippers. Her father had booked an entire double stateroom only for her and her mother's going-away present had been a pair of Oxford-styled bowling slippers to enhance her chances of winning at shuffleboard and thereby attracting men. Because Celeste was shy and inexperienced of travel, her father had overtipped the chief steward so that she could be assigned to sit alone at a table for two. Because her husband had taken it into his head to do that without consulting her, Ada had made certain other arrangements of some consequence.

Celeste's waiter was a dignified, fifty-one-year-old, silver-haired man named Franco Gudelmann. For the first two meals at sea he was almost invisible as he served her. By the third meal she had begun to feel lonely from watching the other passengers convey so much mutual copulation that, to establish any sort of human contact with a living thing aboard the ship (and he was, after all, she reassured herself, a much older man and therefore hardly likely to try to pinch her nates) she had asked her waiter with elaborate casualness to tell her the Italian word for the breadsticks in a jar on the table, indicating them with unconsciously indecent gestures.

"Grissini," Gudelmann said.

"What is the word in Finnish?"

"There is no equivalent word in Finnish," then he paused significantly, "for breadsticks."

"But this is a Finnish ship. If they have no word for it how can it be authentic Finnish food? And how come breadsticks are offered as a staple three times a day?" Her voice was shaking slightly.

He shrugged lewdly; an actor's trick.

She looked, almost frantically, around the dining salon. "And why aren't there any breadsticks on any of the other tables?"

He smiled as though he were reading her mind and was capable of lowering himself into it on a rope of lust, hand-under-hand. *"Grissini* are *grissini,"* he said. Then he looked away from her eyes as though he had been burned by what he could read there and removed the half-finished plate of *vinkokt sjötunga med musslor och räkor* and went away with it. She discovered she liked his smile and that mystified her.

But the ice had been broken in a coded, safe-sexual way. Because the ship was a ten-day crosser (Ada having maintained that a long crossing would indoctrinate Celeste and prepare her in the best possible way) Celeste found herself almost fixated on his glistening if obscure ways of *al*most suggesting unspeakable practices which had to be suggested symbolically because they were so unspeakable. He would bring her long gleaming eels when she had ordered lamb chops, bananas would decorate the table, inserted into giant Finnish bagels. Although asparagus had just come into season the profusions of them which he placed before her on the table were outrageous. Once, when she had ordered *hors d'oeuvres variés* he brought her a peculiarly peeled bratwurst with all of its top skin pulled down toward its middle section, then trimmed. Almost losing control she blurted, "What's that?"

"Brrrrraaaaatvoooorst," he answered, staring hypnotically into her eyes.

"But why has it been prepared like that?"

"To make it ready." He was sweating lightly across his hairline.

"Ready for what?"

"For slicing maybe?" he leered.

"No, no!" she cried out.

Overt sex in any form had shocked Celeste since her earliest exposure to it as a child. She had grown up beside her mother jocularly joggling the postman's crotch or roiling her behind into the butler's trousers no matter how slightly and silently he would attempt to pass her from behind. Again and again, in the frightening darkness of the night, her mother had suffered orgasm with terrifying outcries which would begin with mere shrieks like company-town lunch whistles, then, as the sensation of her release had mounted, the decibel count had soared with it into an enormous, highly pitched bleat of a lunar missile returning to the mother planet's dense atmosphere, gradually building into a kind of sonic boom which was why the Harrises could never keep any crystal in the house and the real reason (never explained, of course) why neighbors in the apartments immediately above and below them had three times sued Robert Moses and the City of New York for the breakage of their own crystal stemware.

Long, long before she had (theoretically) understood what was happening to her mother to cause such terrible sounds, Celeste would rush into her parents' bedroom and try to tear her insubstantial father off the source of the great screams. It was during these plastic nights that she had formed the *grissini* fixations deep within herself because Arthur Harris, truth be told, was oddly formed genitally. After a dozen or so outbursts and interventions, and clear evidence that the child's inability to sleep was being threatened in a serious way, Arthur Harris had had his bedroom soundproofed. The little girl would stand in the corridor, beating on the heavily padded door tragically, shattered at what *might* be happening within. Somehow she had survived without sleep as children do.

Years later in California, which was Dunc's home state and where he longed to run for the governorship one day, Dunc had unlocked his purse to the extent of springing for a three-dollar studio tour at Universal. As the door to one of the sound stages swung open, revealing its soundproofed three-foot thickness of packed asbestos and spun glass, Celeste had fainted from the enormous excitement of it. Somehow, Dunc had known—although was never able to say precisely why he had known—that the only thing which would bring her out of the swoon would be a few *grissini* placed within her loosely sprawled hands.

Startled, not to say minimally unhinged at twelve, when womanhood showed itself upon her, she began the studies of fasting which were to lead, eventually, to a considerable fortune in her own right as a health-food tycoon. She was not allowed to wear sackcloth at twelve because her parents (who quaintly enough controlled her clothing budget) would not allow it. She could not get away with living on bread and water because her father was so proud of their chef who had been imported from Italy by the Carlo Guccione family which was associated unpretentiously with Mr. Harris in two of his drug-making firms, and who had a great gift for making homemade *grissini*. Therefore, no other avenue of self-abnegation being open, she had studied fasting and abstinence, spending all free hours in the public library and in correspondence with health nuts whose addresses she found in naturopathic magazines.

She came to revel in the lack of experiencing. Her little mahogany-colored sausage curls would cascade down her cheeks as she pored over such sources as the Jesuit magazine, *America,* which urged its faithful to fast then to fast further as an "antidote" in natural law to remedy past sins and to preserve the body against future sins. The very concept of the body sinning beyond the mind sent burrowing thrills through her. *America* established for her that fasting was an integral part of Christian spirituality and that "a certain kind of devil" could only be cast out by prayer and fasting.

The power of her starvation trips grew. Fasting could produce visions. She was drunk around the clock on the ethanol her own body produced as a consequence of the prolonged fasting—ethanol, the natural alcohol which had given so many saints such wonderful visions and kept Jesus chuckling in the wilderness.

Ethanol gave Celeste glorious visions of lying with her legs sprawled awry upon the stage of Radio City Music Hall while the audience which had filled the theatre now waited outside in entwining lines, six abreast, around and around the double block from Sixth to Fifth Avenue, then all the way back to Sixth again, to take its turns at enjoying her helpless body. The fasting of the Algonquin and Winnebago tribes insisted that the pursuit of visions through fasting was to end with sexual intercourse. Celeste did not want the visions to end and she was fearful of sexual intercourse, believing it must hurt terribly or else why would her mother scream so, and she almost died of malnutrition in her father's house.

When her parents discovered how undernourished she was and how complicatedly neurotic she had become, they were horrified. Each blamed the other but instead of sending the girl to the Menninger Clinic as other parents might have done, they fought no food with food and enrolled Celeste in spartan Gelbart College on the Gaspé Peninsula to study nutrition. It was old-fashioned practical therapy and it worked. Professor Gelbart, who worked very hard for his food and for the food of those in his charge on that rocky coast, explained and expanded the meaning of food and how difficult it was to come by and how essential it was to a healthy body in *all* its functions.

Celeste passed out of one adolescent phase into another. She became a health nut. Although she had sharpened her sexual imagination to the point where she could bring herself to orgasm while drifting in bathwater of 104 degrees, dreaming of the orderly crowds at Radio City which had enjoyed her at the peak of her fasting period, she slowly began to absorb the hard fact that if she did not eat more than *grissini* and bananas she would die and, if dead, could not be pleasured by her sexual visions. It was all good, logical thinking.

However, she remained a sexual mystic. She was one with Anna Catherine Emmerich, the Augustinian nun whose visions had so impressed the romantic poet, Brentano; with Sister Maria von Moerl, who became an ecstatic at the age of twenty and who remained in continual orgasm until her death twenty-five years later, as was attested to by Cardinal Wisemen who might not have known much about sex but who knew what he liked. Although Celeste knew that Louise Lateau of Bois d'Haine had been a prisoner of ecstasy's clutch for twelve years by taking no other nourishment than the eucharist and three or four glasses of water each week, and that although Theresa

Neumann of Konnersreuth had taken no solid food from 1923 to her death in 1962 and had lived in the wildest sort of oblectation, Celeste could not face down Professor Gelbart's granite logic and yet was able to carry on with her visions because she had total recall.

In short, there was sex mother's way and there was sex Celeste's way. Hunger is the best cook.

"How long have you been a marine waiter?" Celeste asked Herr Gudelmann's hot-coal eyes as he lined up four overlarge Belgian endives on an elliptical plate in front of her.

"I am a marine waiter only as an annual one-month's holiday," the liver-lipped, flashy-nosed steward replied in a pronounced Thuringian accent.

"As a holiday from what?"

"My profession (bro-fezshun) is a sleep therapist."

"Oh. Oh?"

"Yezz."

"What is that?"

"By scientific (zyentivigg) mixtures of such various drugs, in guarded proportions, as phenothiazine or, and perhaps including, pantoponskopolamin or/and physiologic NaCl injections or perhaps phenotiazin combined with barbiturates and maybe the antihistaminics of Kliensorge and Rösner—I induce sleep for periods (beray-odds) of fourteen days, the legal limit."

"But—why?"

He looked covertly across both shoulders, around the dining salon, then into Celeste's eyes. "Not here. Tonight. Eleven o'clock. At lifeboat station kahdeksankymmenta."

"Kukhdeksahn-kümmenta?"

"I mean—nummer achtzig—ah, no—beim you, nummer eighty." He hurried away, crashing through the gauze-thick panels of her wonderful feelings of guilt. She sucked on the first endive like a pump. Fourteen days of sleep? Why, anything could happen to a woman while she was *locked* into sleep. A woman could fall asleep a virgin and awaken grotesquely deflowered. Why else would people wish to sleep for fourteen days? Anyone who slept for fourteen days could be entered by men or beasts of the stable and field, or by dildoes or billiard cues, but the one entered could not be judged as some rotten sex maniac like Ada or blamed in any way! This was fantastic! Excitement mounted within her. She could not possibly be called sex-oriented because she would be as helpless as a sleeping child. It would all depend on who was her sleep therapist. She thought of the peeled-back bratwurst, the eels, the forests of *grissini* and knew that Herr Gudelmann must be a leader in his profession. Everything would follow naturally as in her visions of Radio City Music Hall, lying out there on the great stage and being entered by all those thousands of sex-crazed but kind people, some in galoshes depending on the weather. She could not wait for the night rendezvous at lifeboat station eighty.

"Zleeb is an ancient healing method," Herr Gudelmann said softly, mindful of the patroling masters-at-arms. He wore a long maroon overcoat whose collie-fur collar was turned up around his cheeks, and a large, floppy black hat such as is worn by Malibu photographers. "Already Greek priests of Asklepios used the sleep therapy in their temples and analyzed dreams for the patients later."

"No, no!"

"What is it, dear lady (*gnädige Frau*)?"

"No dream analysis. I wouldn't want dream analysis." Celeste was already well into her sleep therapy, reaching for it eagerly to wrap around herself as a stout protection against sex.

"I understand," Herr Gudelmann leered, causing the center part of his fleshy lip to flap in tension-lag, all stresses being absorbed by his gray-green cheeks. "In newer medical sciences, in the investigations of Professor Pavlov and his pupils (bew-pillz) Bykew and Iwanow-Smolenski in nineteen hundred and thirty-six, then even more so with the Russian, Andrejew, in nineteen hundred forty-three, the sleeping treatments became more effective."

"But—is there only a Russian way? Everything in my background causes me to resist the Russian path. In fact, I am very much afraid that—as desirable as it all seems—I don't see how I could accept a *Russian* sleep therapy."

"I, your sleep therapist, am not Russian. You would be doctrinally and physically safe if there were no contraindications."

"What contraindications?"

"Do you have circulation disorders or tuberculosis?"

"No."

"Comatoid conditions, heart decompensation—bronchiectasis?"

"No."

"Severe sicknesses of the kidney or liver?"

"Never."

"The law states that you must not sleep for more than fourteen days."

"Why?"

"But the law also (aaalzzo) states that this must not be more than fourteen days in any one establishment."

"You mean—"

"The patient (bay-shunt) may be discharged from one fourteen-day sleep at Site A then be admitted for slumber at Site B across the road. And so on."

"Isn't that a form of suicide when done on a year-round basis?"

His smile was depraved. "That would depend entirely on the purposes of secretly why the patient undertook sleep therapy," he said. He licked his lips with what was surely a large piece of raw calf's liver he must have been concealing within his cheek. It left a slight stain she thought—or was it the light?

"I see," she said. "But, well, I mean to say—couldn't it all be—un*ti*dy?"

"The room is darkened," he crooned. "Air Wick is everywhere. The staff is wearing felt shoes. I am the staff. The nourishment can be only fruit and vegetable juices. Perhaps mashed potato or a lacto-vegetarian diet."

"You mean, a little milk on the mashed potatoes?"

"The premier feeding fluid is according to modern fasting cures," Gudelmann replied. She felt security as she heard the word fasting. Gudelmann was sweating lightly and gave off an effluvia of myrrh.

"But is it lasting? I mean are there any lasting effects?"

"None. Always and only positive. You eliminate the negative effects in the pee-pee when I wake you three times a day. However there is a slightly dazed aftereffect, yes. Generally, the same time is needed to reorientate as was used up in the sleeping."

"But"—was she trembling slightly?—"wouldn't I be powerless during each fourteen-day period?"

For his responding expression Herr Gudelmann could have been reported to the police. *"Jawohl,"* he gargled in a gutter guttural which guttered like a Georgian candle, "you would be powerless. You could resist nothing. You would exist only under my control."

She stared at him; rabbit to tyrannosaurus; taut with excitement. As she looked into his aging gin-colored eyes, within her mind operated a gigantic building demolition crane which held a fourteen-ton steel ball swinging its tremendous force at the end of a great suspending chain. It smashed the entire proscenium then the complete stage of the Radio City Music Hall. Then, facing the auditorium she graciously requested that the audience file out of the theatre in an orderly manner, where admission charges would be refunded. She was done with those secret gang-bangs. She had found a route to actual sex in which she was in no way required to feel either responsible or involved and no one could ever say of her that she had sought out sex the way her mother had sought it every day of her life. The entire thing was out of her hands. Herr Gudelmann seemed like a courteous, gentle and knowing professional therapist. All healing was sublime: objective and subjective. And he had been a good waiter. She would tip him well, but more than that, she wanted to help him with his serious career.

Celeste spent her four months in Europe asleep in various sleep castles along the Rhine below Bonn. Herr Gudelmann booked the rooms and specified and supervised all courses of treatment in each establishment. He was most helpful in showing her how to cash her traveler's checks and rail tickets, procedures of which she was aware only in the dimmest outline because she was sort of sleepy-peeps. But that was the whole point, wasn't it, she thought each time they moved her from one dim building to another, but she could oh so distinctly remember many, many divine sensations.

When she returned to New York she had thirteen dollars and some change left out of three thousand dollars of traveler's checks with which her father had sent her off, but she had never felt so fit if the teeniest bit sore in a certain place. She went to a woman physician she had always used, a woman who also happened to be an ordained member of the missionary clergy whose work among the Malakahuli had been widely recorded; safety factors Celeste felt best built into any vaginal examination. "Am I a virgin?" she asked when she was dressed again and faced the doctor.

The doctor had a stunned look. "No, Miss Harris, you are not," she said. Celeste's heart soared like a punted football. But the look on the doctor's face was perfectly awful.

"I'm not pregnant?" Celeste asked with alarm.

"No. That is, I think not. But your—your entire *contour*—there—has changed so extraordinarily."

"How, doctor?"

"I—I just don't know what to say. You—well, you are very *very* much larger than before you went to Europe. You have—*it* has, that is—somehow all been quiffled out like a quoit."

"Is that bad—medically?"

"Not medically, no. But when you marry—and a healthy, handsome girl such as you will marry—it could be dis*as*trous."

"But—how?"

"My dear girl—but what did you *do,* Miss Harris? However did this happen?"

Celeste was in such a seventh heaven of bliss at having outwitted her mother that she did not think twice about lying. "I am a sleepwalker," she said. "I—I do all sorts of things while sleeping. Somehow I fell from a high place and became impaled on a fire hydrant." She had dreamed that every day.

"Oh! Well, then. That accounts for the incredible degree of quiffling," the good doctor said with much relief. "Not to worry," the dear doctor was all tickety-boo, "a good surgeon will soon stitch you into a little grommet again."

To her father's surprise, Celeste came to him with a really quite workmanlike budget and told him she would like to borrow the capital to open a health-food shop. She had chosen her location and was ready with the reasons for that location and she was able to anticipate every one of the questions he put to her which purposely took a negative view of the scheme. She had laid down her lines for dried apricots, wheat germ, soya flour spaghetti, and carrot steaks and, in a surprisingly short time came back to him for more capital with plans to create her own health-food supplies. Within four years she had eleven stores operating in three cities and within eleven years she had reached her optimum level of seventy-one health-food supermarkets from coast to coast.

At the beginning, however, the details of the legal organization of the various companies she would require were turned over to her father's law firm, Lantz, Lantz, Tolliver & Farr, who assigned one of their junior men to counsel her. He was a young Amish lawyer from California who had worked his way through kindergarten, grade school, a prep school for Negro boys of very wealthy families, college, and had won his law degree at Everglades University in the heart of the Okefenokee country. He was an orphan but the privations and humiliations he had purposefully put himself through had given him an extra sense of negative specialness which enabled a steely self-assurance to hold sway over ignorance. Life had not been easy for Duncan Mulligan (at prep school they had called him "Funky Dunc"), and emotional, financial, cultural and intellectual privation had made him neurotically cautious. The chanciest thing he had ever done, in the knowledge of his friends, had been to undertake a smoking pipe collection, an exciting idea.

Although they had met over the business of the health-food shops there had been no immediate mutual attraction because Dunc's extraordinary shallowness subtracted flair. However, it was Dunc's hobby which brought about their subsequent marriage, a hobby which bypassed any need that there be mutual attraction. The marriage meant a great deal to Dunc because the Harris empire was so vast and so important to Lantz, Lantz, Tolliver & Farr that a marriage with Celeste must mean that he would have to be allowed to remain with the firm. This, of course, was exactly what happened. The firm had even responded to the family's implications of pressure to give Dunc important things to do by making the almost fatal error of assigning him to the Jaime Arias estate litigation which was about to start in Geneva. Arias, a Latin-American dictator, had died leaving a will in favor of his two sons and one daughter and explicitly excluding his two brothers, uncles of the legatees. The uncles' assistance however had been necessary to move the estate, in wired bales of fifty-dollar bills to the amount of eight hundred million dollars, from the dictator's native island to the safety of Swiss banks. On arrival, however, instead of depositing the money, as had been expected, the uncles had started their own bank, the Middle East Bank of Hong Kong and Connecticut, and had refused to distribute the funds to the dictator's heirs. An apprentice grocer, much less a lawyer, could have settled it. Furthermore, the firm had hired expert, sagacious legal counsel to advise Dunc in Swiss procedures. The case was to enter the law books because it was several years before professors of law retained by the Lantz firm were able to determine how Dunc had lost the case, how the three heirs were left penniless, how the uncles got sole legal ownership of the fortune because the moves Dunc had executed in his path to complete failure had been so metaphysically complex.

The Arias matter was the second and last case (the formation of Celeste's health-food company had been the first) Dunc had handled for the firm. Out of deference to the Harris Foundations he was put in charge of the firm's considerable library of books on Tanzanian law. It was sedentary work for a young man and Dunc, even if he did lack in all other areas, had much ambition. To widen his scope he studied hypnosis three evenings a week at the New School to be prepared in the event that the firm should choose him to be its trial lawyer. Hypnosis, he felt, would help him to sway judges and juries and, perhaps, who knew, even Lucas Lantz himself. That was the open reason. The hidden reason was that Dunc lacked confidence in his ability to persuade young women to be entered by him.

Celeste, who had clairvoyant powers concerning other people's sexual intentions, understood his requirements almost at once and, for her own reasons, Dunc's study of hypnosis drew her toward him. In an operative sense his goals matched hers and surely that is the basis for a good marriage. The sleep castles had been glorious but insensate fun. The necessity for fourteen days of sleep in a row, or consecutive rows, tied one down too much.

Do mules still exist who insist that marriages are not made in heaven? Celeste was the only being Dunc was ever able to hypnotize after a two-year course of study and he was able to put her under in the first session. When she sat there before him in a cataleptic state he could not believe he had actually done it. To prove it to himself he ran all the tests, even up to putting a knife point under her fingernail. When she failed to react his confidence grew.

Until this moment of mastery Celeste's attitude toward Dunc had been the textbook rich-client-to-young-lawyer relationship although not as others had regarded him which was as sort of a piece of kitsch furniture. Now, all at once, she was his slave.

On the day of their fourth meeting, held in the deserted Tanzanian law library (an augury of the future which happened because Dunc's "office" was being painted), Dunc mentioned his hypnosis studies and Celeste, a princess of self-deception, saw in a flash what these could mean to her. She told him she had always been interested in hypnosis and said she would very much like it if he would try to hypnotize her. That night at twenty minutes past nine, in his apartment at Meier's Corners, Staten Island, this was done. The knife blade under her fingernail had been blazingly painful but as she weighed the proof it offered to Dunc that he had the power to hypnotize her she knew he would never need to make such a test again so she bore it cheerfully and silently. Through lowered eyelids she watched him strip with the speed of a man whose clothes were on fire, then spin the combination on his briefcase lock to unpack, then get into the most outlandish rig (for a lawyer) she had ever seen: brassiere and panties of black rubber, rubber stockings, a black rubber evening dress, highly shined rubber boots and a rubber hair ribbon and she knew he was hers—on her terms. When he said to her in a totally different kind of a voice, "I am going to fuck you, Arthur Harris' daughter," she just plain fell in love, then and there, rejoicing that she had escaped sex for all of her life and that now no one would be able to say she was like her mother. It was a good thing that Dunc had not been a torture freak who liked to record the screams of his fiancées to play them back at leisure because it would have been a dooming blow to Celeste to hear her bellowed, soprano outcries of enormous pleasure as Dunc's ministrations took her to orgasm: sounds such as the *Queen Mary* made as it went under the Verrazano Bridge; sounds like a motorized nail being driven across a mile-long blackboard; sounds which were perhaps even more effulgent than her mother had ever made under the circumstances.

They set Olympic records that night. His latex rustling, his bugle beads clinking, he was all over her like a rubberized rhinestoned moose. In three and a quarter hours they ran through the directions on every page of the *Kama Sutra,* which Celeste had memorized in grade school. Then zoomed on through the directions on the pages of *The Perfumed Garden of Shaykh Nefzawi* and *Emotional Maturity in Love and Marriage*—he with chuffings and shrill barnyard grunts, she with glazed eyes and motorized hips which moved as rhythmically as the drive shafts of an ocean liner.

It made them both very happy and Dunc hypnotized her frequently after that. Then, following eleven months of courtship, when they discovered that Celeste was preggers with the dear twins, they were married. It was the most magnificent church wedding Harris money could buy (and the first ecumenical ceremony in the city with the clergy of five world faiths endowing a state of holy matrimony simultaneously on either side of the civil service by the Mayor of the City of New York). The bride wore a Bohan dress of white satin decorated with two thousand pearls. The groom wore a black rubber brassiere and panties, a painfully inflatable foundation garment, and a short, black rubber play dress by Para of London under his staid Brooks Brothers striped trousers, wing collar and morning coat.

When the twins were born the married couple never discussed what he knew must have been a baffling mystery to her: a mere matter of virgin birth. He knew she had never been aware that she had been implanted because the effects of modern hypnosis were total. He greatly admired her stoic acceptance of the pregnancy. He put it out of his mind at last by deciding she must either be fanatically religious or had never been told how babies were made.

They slept in separate rooms. As often as possible his old nanny came in, all the way from Bay Ridge, Brooklyn, to put him to bed as she always had done at the California orphanage where she had spent her womanhood and Dunc his little boyhood. She would tie his wrists together behind his back and strap his elbows together then slip his arms into a single-sleeve strait jacket which was inflatable to produce much uncomfortable pressure. She would slip on his little nightcap, an inflatable rubber head mask which covered his face and which had an inflatable rubber agony pear whose curved leaves, when jammed into the mouth, expanded and expanded, holding his mouth immovably open. Then, from his chin downward, she would pack him into a large sack of cosy, transparent latex rubber and leave him blissful between white rubber sheets until morning. Those were the only nights he slept like a little lamb.

Only once in all the years of their marriage did Dunc try to enter Celeste without hypnosis. They had been married four years and the twins were very much enrapturing the nursery. Celeste had come into Dunc's room for some answer to a transiently urgent question on one of the nights when Nanny had put him to bed then had gone off to have her two cans of Sterno and to slip off to sleep in his bathtub. Celeste had panicked when she saw his shining black form inside the transparent sack. Believing marauders had struck, she threw back the rubber blankets, saw the helmet pulled tautly over his head, ripped the sack away then attacked the straps of the strait jacket. Somehow, in her frenzy of anxiety, she got him entirely loose from the helmet and the arm-binding straps. Duncan, fearful that she might somehow think that he was secretly queer, at once sought to prove that he was not by grabbing her while bleating amorously and trying to pull her down upon the bed. Celeste had become so terrified of his erection rearing out from under the frilled black rubber panties that she had tried to throw herself out of the window.

There were no rotten direct-pass tricks after that. A courtship technique evolved. Duncan would deplore that the pressures of business had kept him away from the old classes at the New School and he would say that he often wondered if he still had the knack of hypnotizing people. If it were inconvenient for Celeste at the moment she would tell him he needn't worry about that because didn't he hypnotize a new jury each week? But, if his suggestion were convenient, she would get out of her clothes, turn down the bed, put a towel in place while he slipped into his rubber evening dress with the bugle beads. Then she would lie down, he would pull up a chair beside her, hypnotize her, then enter her.

Between hypnoses she was a cool, objective wife and mother, and a considerable asset to Lantz, Lantz, Tolliver & Farr. Not that the hypnoses happened too often, or often at all, after the twins came. Celeste had found much more effective relief through her philanthropic work at the Bryson Institute for Applied Response where she worked three times a week as a test volunteer to expand the frontiers of human knowledge. She remained on as a worker for the Institute for over twenty years because she wanted, somehow, to serve humanity and because Dr. Bryson had most graciously accepted a grant-in-research, from one of her father's foundations, of seventy-five thousand dollars.

Monday, Wednesday, and Friday she would enter the sterile hospital room in a starched, antiseptic white garment which was fully open down the back. She would lie on her back on a hard cot while two nurses and Dr. Bryson attached and adjusted wires to her scalp, nipples, wrists, ankles, rectum and inner thighs. While the nurses prepared the spectrometer overhead, Dr. Bryson, wearing a sterile, white face mask over his enormous Zapata moustache, would adjust the size and weight of the smoothly glistening, power-driven plastic penis to accord with her own frequently varying vaginal measurements. The man was a craftsman. He would take enormous pains to get the adjustments right and then the cameras would begin to turn at the moment the great, hot lights came up and the power was switched on within the penis motor. Celeste controlled the rate and depth of the penis thrust through her own response and, over many, many sessions of hard concentration, had taught herself to work it up to maximum physiologic intensity. Beginning with the third time, when she was really learning how to help the wonderful thing inside her, her climaxes became the most exaltingly transcendental and shatteringly noisy experiences of sex in medical history. Dr. Bryson donated a set of the sound tracks, unbeknownst to her, to the Smithsonian Institution. She was fulfilled as a woman, but most of all she was fulfilled as a daughter. No one could ever say she was the sex maniac her mother was.

Dunc and Celeste proved that their species had come a long, long way since Adam and Eve.

13

Until Osgood Noon married Cerce (Bagwell) Charmant when he was nineteen years old, no one in his family had ever had legal union with an actress. When they eloped to Yuma, Arizona, and Cerce had traditionally telegraphed the news to Miss Louella Parsons of *The Morning Telegraph* in New York, there had been an effort made by a dissident faction on the board of directors of the Bahama Beaver Bonnet Company to have him unseated. Os had resented the action at the time but, in later years, he had come to agree. He knew that he must have been temporarily insane to have done such a thing.

Cerce had been much more than a bit player and much less than a star in motion pictures. In a sense that was the itching powder which could not be shaken off and it had, perhaps, formed her life-restlessness and doomed their marriage. She seemed wildly frustrated about being neither one thing nor the other. She spent her life trying to change status, continually renegotiating all her contracts without benefit of an agent.

She had been frequently reported in the film-colony press as being keenly admired (and escorted about) by Gustave von Seyfertitz and James Hall and had been on the Ince yacht more than once but when *The Hat Heir* (also *most* erroneously referred to as *The Mad Hatter*) appeared upon the Hollywood scene, the young actress had seemed to forget everything about a screen career and had fallen head-over-heels in love with the young scion. At the same time, and in a total sense, she had refused to give anything up. She would desert her husband for long intervals but when she returned (always on her own terms because Os had been afflicted throughout his life with exquisite manners) she would not agree to divorce. She would breed children during the intervals at home but the intervals between grew longer and longer. She would not only leave her family behind but up to ten dozen pairs of rose corduroy bloomers, some of them as old as her marriage. When she would return, between desertions, after light-hearted greetings all around and perhaps a half-bottle of champagne she would count her pairs of bloomers, photographs of old friends, bottles of ancient medicines, pastel paintings whose styles had passed never to return, fringed dresses and lampshades, laced shoes and her stereopticon machine and would expect them all to be there because they were hers. If an item were missing she would sustain a tantrum which had been designed by a great silent-film director named Hugo Ballin in the old Fort Worth, New Jersey, studios for a film called *They Are Playing My Song,* a stunning *force majeure* of the director's art, but always delivered by Cerce to Os as spontaneous rage.

Os wanted serenity. His gentle life had been built upon people having consideration for each other. During the first three days of Cerce's several returns to her family, Os would develop a severe face tic, his sphincters strangling, hydrocyanic acid corroding the first six inches of his intestine, uric acid surging through his bloodstream, causing his left large toe to swell and throb with intense pain as she demanded an accounting for four mah-jongg sets and eleven pogo sticks which had been entrusted to his stewardship during her six-year absence. He never struck her. He solved everything by agreeing to anything.

The two older boys were affected by their mother's continuing desertions. Gawain had become deeply introspective and almost impossible to reach even though his father had worked hardest with him to bring him back among the normal living. The boy would work well at school but rarely speak. He read constantly and his father followed the pattern of his reading until he understood what the boy was seeking was something which would be forever constant. In time, Gawain developed a passion for mathematics and machines. Mathematics was constant. Machines could not leave unless one sent them away. These convictions subtracted from his cheerfulness. But as he acquired the coldnesses he tried to lose his father because he blamed his father for driving his mother away from them. His memory of his mother was always refreshed for a year or two after an average of six years of absence. She was a golden and romantic figure. Her super-amiability, the *rectus* container of her ambitions, seemed to him to be a sweetness beyond joy. Her stories about her adventures in so many places of the world proofed and disguised her omissions like paint combined with granite and mica. When she bolted again, the boy would refuse to come out of his room and rejected his father. In order to reject his father with justice, because he could not be entirely sure that his loss was his father's fault, he rejected most of the world for extra measure and hardly accepted his brothers as they came into the world and grew beside him. There was fourteen years' difference between him and Tristram; twenty-nine years' difference between him and Botolf. He accepted Botolf but merely admired Tristram because being related to Tristram had helped his own career.

Tristram was only partially affected by his mother's desertions. He was affected to the extent that he took the contents of life to be diversions from living itself and took action against the world as if to prove that action of any kind, i.e., whether his mother acted to leave them or acted to remain with them, was the vital decision to perform. He was a champion at most sports. He was the leader wherever he found himself, except with his father. He admired his father intensely because his father seemed so able to accept his mother's presence or her absence with equal cheerfulness, and because of the unswerving devotion and loyalty he gave to his sons; always there, always needed to be there.

His father cooked for them, darned for them, worked at his office with direct telephone lines to home, took them to circuses and ball games and movies, read to them and punished them when they rated it. He sat up with them when they were sick and fitted them with the right clothes. He washed their ears and their hair and dropped them into bathtubs. He edited their friends and sided against all their enemies.

Both boys accepted the final son, Botolf, with some amusement that two people could consummate what must have seemed like long-distance breeding. Botolf was never very much aware of his mother. He was glad enough to see her when she was there and glad again that everything could proceed so much more smoothly when she was gone. He was the most mature member of the family. He helped his father with household problems. He did best at school and with people. In his pervasive way he, too, held the family together because without him Gawain would have disappeared into secret mists and Tristram would have disappeared in the noises of pirate play.

When Os met Ada, Gawain was fifty years old, Tris was thirty-six and Botolf was twenty-one. Gawain had taken two degrees in actuarial studies, then switched to computer technology at MIT, then entered Harvard Divinity School. Tris had a B.A. from Yale, was an All-American running back, had had three major-league football, baseball, and hockey offers, had fought on the Olympic boxing team, all of which possibly costing him a career as a painter. He painted in school to make the payments for abortions, but seemed to have no other needs. Botolf took a degree in veterinary medicine at Cornell at sixteen, a Master's Degree in veterinary surgery at seventeen, then switched to natural history at Berkeley after reading *Animal Dispersion in Relation to Social Behavior* by his hero, V.C. Wynne-Edwards. He had been the youngest graduating-class president in the history of each of the colleges and universities he had attended.

Aside from her tendency to desert her family, her intensified need to have her own way, and to retain every gain and possession she had ever made, Cerce had no faults. And she was blandly and blindly amiable at all times. She seemed to have the gifts of being able to earn money. She never returned home in need but rather from some nesting instinct or to find new and more susceptible ears for her bragging or to reassure them all that she could not help having bolted.

The first time she deserted was seven years after she and Os had married, when Gawain had been six years old, without a note of explanation, in 1926. Os took it hard; scourging himself. There had been no warning. She had stood before him in all her inscrutable amiability; beautiful in her newly-bobbed hair which hung as flawlessly as if it had just come from the foundry. She had gazed down tenderly upon the Youth's Bed (trademark registered) which held the sleeping form of her first-born then had turned away with a poorly executed waltz clog to whirl her husband out of the room for an evening before the Monarch super-heterodyne. Then Os had gone to the kitchen to get himself a glass of water—in all he might have been absent one hundred and fifty seconds—and when he returned, she was gone. She remained gone for two years.

He found her again through an explorer's accident, wrote her a mild letter and she returned home at once. She had signed on as an apprentice storesboy to the supply officer of the oddly-fated Robards Expedition to the South Pole. She had done well. She had risen from the ranks eventually to run the base camp for shipping which was to be kept open the year round in the Falklands while Captain Robards and the nine men—Melvin, Silvers, Lembeck, Strauss, Gosfield, Erikson, Little, Baron, and Reiskind, all from his World War I company which had burned headlines into the world press at Château Thierry and the Argonne—made the dash to the Pole with sixty-four dogs, only to overshoot and to emerge by mistake on the Pacific side of the planet where they became involved with Polynesian women and eventually prospered in commercial hair oils made from copra—but, in any event, failing to advise *The New York Times, The National Geographic,* sponsors of the expedition, or the base camp.

They were declared lost until 1941 when Captain Robards showed up in the Canadian Air Force. However, at the time of the "tragedy" the press had focused its attention upon the survivors of the expedition and, because she was Cerce Charmant of the silver screen, Cerce's photograph and copyright story had appeared everywhere. Os had seen it in *The Hatters' Journal,* his trade paper. When she replied to his letter saying she was on her way home, he had moved out of the flat which contained all his wife's booty and had moved with little Gawain to a new flat in the same building which had sparkling empty closets, paying the rent on the first flat but keeping it shut.

The fourth time she left him and Gawain, and the baby, Tristram (Celtic *Drystan* from *drest* or *drust* meaning tumult or din), he consigned everything in the second flat to a warehouse and moved back into the first flat where they had begun. It had room for a billiard table on which they played and ate hamburger sandwiches, spaghetti or *choucroute garnie.*

Botolf was born after Cerce returned from the ninth desertion which she had spent as a speliologist in mile-deep caverns abaft the Pyrenees. While she was away her sons prospered and grew to manhood, outwardly unaffected by everything their mother had not done. Gawain would certainly one day win a bishopric within the ABM synod of the Church of Christ, Computer. He had the gift of numbers and true vocation. He could speak pasigraphically and had risen within the peoples' church from acolyte programmer to the field rank of what would have been monsignor in the vanished churches. Tristram had grown, with his talents for action and violence, to become the head of the military arm of the church. Os felt he understood what both Gawain and Tristram were striving for. Gawain represented the two centuries through which America had sought its own indigenous religion after stumbling through the incense of Italian, Swiss, Scottish, English, German and Near Eastern worship forms which had been designed to serve the needs of the previous millennium and whose concepts were wholly foreign to the American need. Gawain knew Christ, Computer would lead the way to salvation.

Tristram substantiated that meaning of the new faith with the only offerings it could accept: money and violence and an exalted sense of privilege.

Os saw Botolf, however, in a less symbolic light than he saw the other boys. He was a person, not an evolvement. And he was a brave boy who had always faced what had confronted him with good cheer. He had decided at age nine that the odds against having a street in Paris named after him were too overwhelming and he had put that ambition aside. He was an achiever. Gawain and Tris were political, but Bottie had purpose beyond opportunism.

Now, at last, he was on his way home! Two months before Os would have been unreservedly overjoyed. But now there was Ada. Ada liked the apartment and she loved that billiard table.

He sighed. He was the seventy-year-old father of a twenty-one-year-old boy. How had Cerce been able to do it? He saw now that he should not have married an older woman. She had inscribed her age on the marriage record as seventeen but she had been an ingenue in films for ten years before he met her and had once been linked romantically with John Bunny (although in that actor's later years). A fellow actress had told him some years later that the year Cerce had married him she had been passed over as being too old, not for the part of Juliet, but for the role of Juliet's nurse—surely a backbiting professional canard.

She must be nearly seventy-five now, he supposed, and he was sure she was not only alive wherever she was but that she was complaining relentlessly behind that deadly mask of amiability, perhaps as a white hunter in East Africa, or a Himalayan guide for the Sherpa people or as a trapeziste behind the Urals. He also knew that one day she would come home and begin her inventory of things she had accumulated before they had married. This time he would flatly refuse to have another child with her. He suddenly felt very tired. Cerce, Gawain, and Tristram made him tired with dread for the world they had fastened their iron teeth upon. The world made him tired with its eagerness to offer itself as sacrifice in new ways each day. His body and the demands he and Ada made upon it made him tired. Ada, O, Ada! What was the use of knowing the world would come to an end if it was doomed always to end in one's own time?

14

Dunc Mulligan's campaign manager, F.M. Heller, sat in the Mulligans' excessively Art Nouveau salon on the thirty-ninth floor of a building owned by a Harris Foundation which was, with the exception of their magnificent flat, given over entirely to short-time car parking, overlooking the Park at Columbus Circle. Dunc *hated* having to live on the West Side but he had nothing to say about it and it was a fact that guests were absolutely thrilled to ride upward through the open steel to the thirty-ninth floor on such a high-speed elevator and they all thought it was so original of Dunc to have chosen to live there, a heady designation for him.

F.M. Heller and Dunc sat facing Celeste on a three-way, metallically golden "conversation seat," which had been designed by Herman Obrist in the form of two graceful half-canoes which faced Celeste's half-canoe centered between them. Celeste's eyes were darting suspiciously as a rich woman's should. Duncan rested his chin upon his fist. F.M. Heller, on Celeste's right, was continually and apologetically pordy. They were eating Bircher-Benner müsli laced with goat's milk which made Heller all the windier.

"Oh, *shit*!" Celeste cried. "What's the *use*! Ada will never give him up. But I don't *get* it. How can two old fuds holding hands be that important to Dunc's chances."

"We face a serious threat in that quarter, my dear," F.M. Heller said.

"Oh, my *God*!" Duncan said.

"And that is not my opinion alone. I think I may say that I speak for the Attorney General. May I enumerate the items of jcopardy?"

"It's awful," Duncan moaned. "Awful, awful."

"One," F.M. Heller struck a schublig-sized pinky with a banana-sized middle finger, "there is Dunc's youth image. While the Attorney General does not believe in youth, he is a realist. There is pressure for an eighteen-year-old voting franchise because the sponsors know eighteen year olds would never exercise it. This year the country will show approximately seventy-one point eight per cent of its citizens being under twenty-four years of age at a time when our industries have had to retire senior citizens of forty-five. Item: what do you think would happen if our opponents could blend Dunc's image with that of an old woman—who happens to be Dunc's mother-in-law—copulating lewdly with a married man in his seventy-first year?"

"Oh, my God!" Duncan said.

"I don't see how people that age can copulate *lewd*ly," Celeste said. "Anyway he's only seventy."

"Anyone who has reached his seventieth birthday is in his seventy-first year."

"Well, as far as the voters are concerned he is youth-oriented because of his rotten revolutionary-of-a-son, that disg*us*ting rabble-rouser and sweat merchant, that oily-hair package and face smasher, that detestable *thing* they call the Minneapolis One—Tristram Noon."

"But, if you please, Mrs. Mulligan-Harris, what would Dunc's dominant image be in that case?"

"Old," Duncan said. "Old, old."

"It is fatal to enter national politics in this country with an over-forty-five image."

"Okay. Okay, *okay*!!"

"Next—while it is true that our rural population has its love affairs with chickens and spaniels and that our young city people would not turn down a night with a boa constrictor *and* while it would seem on the surface that there is no sexual morality remaining, I think you will agree that the one thing our young voters will *not* tolerate is any form of pleasure or happiness, sexual or otherwise, for our old people. Nor should they. They get very little of it themselves. The older people have seen to that. A world reduced to dirt, noise, corruption, pornography, violence, narcotics, pollution, and money is not exactly Utopia. Therefore, the Attorney General quite rightly fears loosing furies of young-voter hatred against Dunc's candidacy at the very moment the radical Eastern establishment press is ready to print anything."

"Mr. Heller, try to understand. She won't give him up. I mean, I *know* her."

"Then perhaps he'll give her up."

"Yes, yes," Duncan said. "Perhaps he'll give her up."

"Well, with all the Attorney General's great planning how come that in Harlem they are already referring to Duncan as 'Funky Dunc'? How the hell did that happen?"

"The Negro vote means absolutely nothing, my dear. The Attorney General can prove that. That is his entire strategy."

Duncan looked stunned at this shocking revival of a nickname which he thought he had outlived twenty-five years before.

F.M. Heller kept moving in. "The banking and insurance, oil and pharmaceutical, aviation, and electronic industries all want Dunc in the Senate, to say nothing of the church."

"Oh, for heaven's sake, Mr. Heller! Why don't you just have Dunc and the Vice-President man a machine gun under good network-camera placement at a staged student riot and shoot a few kids—maybe just black kids. That will wipe out any memory of Ada and that dirty old man."

"It's not all that easy, my dear. Violence is the recreation and entertainment of the American people, yes. But sex is the increasingly heavy cross they carry. Males are expected to be heterosexual yet they are being trampled under hoof by Women's Lib which is determined not to be. The police, however, are plain sadistic with child molesters. The permissive society demands that our young people enjoy each other on their office desks during their lunch hours because there is no room even for eating in restaurants. What use of available sex if available pornography has taken all the fun out of it? More, of course, is less. Your mother's sexual activity with this man in his seventy-first year merely emphasizes the legacy of pain which has been imposed upon the voters. No—we must have the nomination itself in hand before we can tart up the issues with pre-election stunts like shooting students or darkies. Your mother's love affair must be nipped in the bud."

"Oh, my God!" Duncan keened.

"No whining, Dunc," F.M. Heller said paternally. "It can and will be done."

"How?" Celeste demanded.

"I happen to know Osgood Noon fairly well," Heller said. "He has one glaring fault. He is the most courteous man in this country. He would have made an extraordinary diplomat if he had contributed earlier to the party. But he is a publisher. And as a publisher he is dependent upon advertisers. The Attorney General has spoken to the Pentagon. By this time tomorrow, the Joint Chiefs will be having little talks with the advertising agencies of the permanently belligerent nations such as France, Egypt, China, Northern Ireland, Syria, the Soviet Union, Texas, and Israel and persuading them to cancel their advertising schedules in Mr. Noon's magazine. What do you think of that, Mrs. Mulligan-Harris?"

Celeste shrugged. She bit her lip. She stared at Duncan but didn't see him. "It's a start, I suppose, but—"

"Yes, Mrs. Mulligan-Harris?"

"Well—combined—Mr. Noon and my mother have more money than some of those countries you mentioned. Which is probably why some of them are permanently belligerent."

"I have only begun to reveal how he will be stopped, my dear. Let us not forget that his son is the promising Monsignor Noon. We handle the church's banking—well, some of it. Dunc's firm handles its legal affairs."

"Dunc's firm!" Celeste snorted.

"The monsignor is really quite close to the Attorney General who believes that a good son can bring a lot of pressure on a beloved father—for the father's own good. The other son, Tristram, whose work as a revolutionary you have marked so vividly, is under contract to the Department of Justice, the Republican National Committee, and to my own bank to name merely three of his more influential clients—"

"The Department of Justice! Why old Mr. Hoover reviles everything Tristram Noon stands for! And as for the Republican National Committee—Mr. Heller, are you losing your mind?"

"Yours not to reason why, my dear. Tristram Noon has been very, very useful to all of us."

"Indeed he has," Duncan said stoutly. "I would imagine."

"He serves the Democratic Party, too, of course. And Mr. Wallace. How far he will cooperate with us and to what extent he will bring influence upon his father, I am sure you will understand I cannot possibly discuss."

Celeste leaned forward intently on the Obrist half-couch. "If you can buy that political hoodlum's services to maim his own elderly father, a man in his seventy-first year—then you are dealing with garbage which would not think twice about blackmailing Dunc after election day and that would be a pretty mess."

"Oh, I can't agree with you about *that,*" F.M. Heller chuckled.

"Millions for defense but not one cent for tribute," Duncan said, smiling. "Besides, if he did try to blackmail me that would be after election day so what harm could it do?"

"Oh, shut up, Dunc."

"But let us not pass over any contingency. Suppose none of those ruses work?" F.M. Heller asked loudly as he tried to muffle the sound of yet more gas rushing through his lower intestine and, in a diversion, scrambling his fingers among his Clairol-whitewashed beard in an attempt to look adorable and thereby be forgiven for the racket he had made. "We don't have much time, you know. The Democrats may not be very bright but they are not deaf. I mean," he added with hasty embarrassment, "something is bound to get out."

"Then Osgood Noon must be kidnapped and held for ransom."

"*Ran*som?" Duncan cried. "We don't need money."

"Ada will be his ransom," Celeste said grimly. "Either she moves to Asia and stays there or Mr. Noon faces the consequences. And I mean *the* consequences." Celeste had, at last, found dominion over her mother and could punish her with sex.

"I did not hear that," F.M. Heller said curtly. "Kidnapping is a federal offense which the Attorney General would have great difficulty covering up. However, and entirely theoretically, if such a thing were considered how could it be done?"

"Oh, *shit*!" Celeste yelled. "That's just a detail."

The two men left her, with Duncan explaining as he went out of the room with F.M. Heller, that when in the White House he would not give any interviews because the press only asked public figures embarrassing questions and he felt that nothing was really served by press interviews anyway. They were on their way to a mass meeting at the Pool Hall Sweepers' Local No. 4 where Duncan was scheduled to make a major foreign-policy speech. F.M. Heller didn't answer him and Duncan's attention span was too short to hold the thought so he voiced the next bulky matter which came into his mind. "About this Funky Dunc business in Harlem," he said, "perhaps you should know that, at school—" his voice trailed off as Heller closed the door between them and Celeste.

Celeste lay back hopelessly on the golden Obrist half-canoe, staring at the illuminated Tiffany-glass ceiling which was mottling her face in many colors. She knew she would never be able to muster enough energy or wit or resources to stop her mother at anything. She was so engrossed in habitual defeat that she was unaware that the twins, Mona and Fiona, had entered the room until they were almost beside her.

"For Christ's *sake*!" Celeste cried out. "Why must you always creep up on me?"

"If you aren't yelling at us for creeping up on you, you are criticizing us for going down on somebody else," Mona said. They were darling-looking girls of nineteen, identically dressed in lemon yellow. They had long, rust-colored hair and permanent expressions which seemed to be interested, without being at all morbidly concerned, in everything.

"We heard everything you and Daddy and that fat man said, Mother," Fiona told Celeste, "and we think it is absolutely shitty."

"You ought to be ashamed trying to break it up for Grandma," Mona said.

"How many chances do you think she has left to ball guys?" Fiona asked. "So if you think we are going to stand by and let you ruin it for her with that old stud then, Mama, you are out of your pussy-scratching mind."

"Stay out of this, girls!" Celeste said stridently. "I am warning you!"

"We are going to Grandma's right now and tell her the whole thing."

"We should go to the FBI and report you for planning a kidnapping," Mona said.

"Except now we have found out all about *them*."

"If you do just one little thing like that to interfere with Daddy's campaign I'll have the lawyers stop your allowance and I'll take your taxi cab away. Oh, you think you are smart! Such wisies. You're so smart that you don't know I just came from Grandma's where I told her every single thing."

"Then we're going to Grandma's to tell her not to worry, that we're not going to let you strip her pad," Mona said flatly.

"And for heaven's *sake*, Mother," Fiona asked, "what does Daddy need with the *Sen*ate?"

"Even more so," Mona asked, "what does the Senate need with Daddy?"

"Don't you go talking to Grandma with your dirty Women's Lib mouths," Celeste said urgently, struggling to her feet. "Grandma is a lady, and never forget that. Did you ever see her outdoors without neat little clean gloves on? Did you ever once hear her say one horrible word like fuck which the whole rotten Women's Lib is saying all the time?"

"We never say fuck when we are with Grandma," Mona said.

"We never even think of fucking when we are with Grandma," Fiona added.

"We don't have to. Grandma was liberated fifty years before Women's Lib. You're the one who has to be liberated. Do you think we enjoy having to say fuck to our own mother all the time?"

"Are you trying to kill me?" Celeste's voice rose. "Is that what you are trying to do—kill me? Doing what you did with Mori, the elevator man, in the elevator, right in front of Miss Engelson, a sheltered, maiden lady, then forcing that *filthy* Women's Lib promotional material on her—wasn't that enough? Whatever your reason for hating me—wasn't that enough?" Celeste began to honk with grief. The girls hovered around her and held her and patted her gently.

"Mama, Mama," Mona said, "don't say things like that."

"We don't even like Mori, the elevator man. We were teaching him a lesson."

"And we were helping Miss Engelson."

"It isn't always pleasant, you know," Mona reminded Celeste. "It was drafty on the floor of that elevator."

They kissed Celeste and smoothed her eyes and, excepting for political differences, social and sexual perspectives, the generation gap, tastes in clothing and narcotic styles, mental health, mutual credibility, relative and actual honesties, self-knowledge, differences in upbringing, degrees of hope and aspiration, relative intelligences and the capacity to love beyond oneself—they were friends again: as close and as mutually understanding as any parent and children could be.

15

Celeste had always had the Indian sign on her brother, Kaskell, because he was not only a general degenerate but their relationship was that of incest, once removed. Celeste was the oldest Harris child, then Kaskell, then Jean-Pierre: thirty-eight, thirty-seven, and thirty-six. But Jean-Pierre, who had abandoned his given names of Chester Claude, was the dominant sibling.

When Celeste had been a forming young girl, yet of juicily promising outline, she had never run and complained to her parents when Kaskie would hide behind the drapes in her bedroom to masturbate while he watched her undress and dress, dress and undress. She knew he was there and could hear him. He knew she knew he was there but she never showed it by a word or by any deed except to undress and dress, dress and undress until he had exhausted himself. Kaskie remained suspended sexually. He grew up to become a professional voyeur. When his brother bought out the old established Norton Travel Agency and changed its conventional policies by offering clients all manner of aberrant and lurid exhibitions and practices, in ports of eastern Turkey and along the Mediterranean littoral of Africa, Kaskie booked thousands of Americans into the most bizarre sex posits with a series of ten-day to four-week tours which he personally designed in the steaming stews of the Middle East. He was the author and panderer for some of the most grotesque sexual analogues ever designed by the human imagination, which was to say Kaskie's imagination.

Not that these things meant anything to Kaskie. His sister and his masturbation were the only things which had any meaning for him—sexual or otherwise. And they were close in other ways. He had brought her all of his problems since his boyhood and she had always had the right solutions. When he had been nineteen years old, on a hunting trip in Maine, he and two buddies gang-shagged a doe they had just shot. As his life worked out, this was to be his only sexual experience beyond his marriage and beyond his celebration of his sister at his own hands. Kaskie's turn aboard the doe had come last because he had been youngest and because he hadn't made the kill. He had picked up a rather severe gonorrheal infection left by either one of the first two lads aboard the deer. Or perhaps by some fleet game warden. He had taken his problem straight to Celeste who had insisted rather sternly that both the other young hunters be warned so that the spread of the disease must go no further among supporters of the National Rifle Association. She had paid for his treatment out of her own egg money.

From the time she had returned from Europe Celeste had been paid five thousand dollars a month as health-food consultant to one of her father's foundations. As her brothers reached eighteen they were also advanced from schoolboy allowances of a thousand dollars a month, which the American boy normally gets from his Dad until he is fifty, to the five-thousand-dollar par. The grand-children, Sylvan, Mona and Fiona, were treated exactly the same way, with stern impartiality.

On the day immediately following her meeting with F.M. Heller and Dunc, Celeste invited Kaskie to lunch at her apartment; a rare occasion because she worked hard trying to keep her daughters away from men, particularly in the home. She and Kaskie generally met in Celeste's car which she would then drive around and around Manhattan Island until they had finished their chat. Kaskie had a shameful police record, regardless of anyone's standards of tolerance, so she was understandably chary about it being known that they were in the same family.

When he arrived at the thirty-ninth floor over the great garage, before he had the chance to sit down, she said, "Have I ever asked you for any help?"

Kaskie shook his head dazedly while his hand shook desperately deep within his trousers.

"I need help," Celeste blurted. "Ada has maneuvered her life so that it could cost Dunc the nomination."

Kaskie's eyes had begun to glaze so Celeste struck him sharply on the side of his operating arm.

"Listen to me! If Ada costs Dunc the nomination you can forget the special passports for your clients who've been whacked with moral turpitude classifications! Ada is sleeping with a man who is in his seventy-first year and you have to convince Jean-Pierre that it is his duty to Ada to make her give him up." She sighed with enormous patience and waited until Kaskie had finished doing what he was doing in his pocket. When he slumped down into a chair she continued stridently.

"The time has come when this family has to make Ada see that her sexual life is beyond all proportions. She is in her sixty-ninth year, for Christ's sake! And let us please remember that her husband, darling Dad, has only been in his grave for six years. This is serious, Kask." Celeste's voice broke and her eyes misted over. "Dunc—well, the Attorney General is very, very fond of Dunc. That is all I am permitted to say at this time." She dabbed at her eyes. "I know you have Jean-Pierre's super-private number and I know only you can get through to him. You've got to make him agree to a meeting. For the three of us. You've got to. If he has to have privacy we can meet at a little restaurant I know near the bridge in Staten Island. And you don't have to tell him I'm coming if you don't want to."

16

Although Jean-Pierre Harris seemed to resemble a briefcase clearing its throat, that was because he was a university-trained business executive of quite immense skills. The very fact, he felt (as architect of his own public image), that he had changed his first name from Chester Claude to Jean-Pierre, had transformed him into something of a creative romantic as might a smock and beret upon a Sunday painter. He was a short man like his parents, his siblings being throwbacks to a lost generation of larger Harrises and Clarkes. His height and his given names had compounded his feelings of inadequacy and, in that pressures of anxieties are the fertilizers of the growth of ego, those pressures upon him had been prodigious. He had to be recognized above all others and he recognized few peers. Therefore he led a somewhat solitary life. He patronized Kaskell, savaged Celeste, and admired his mother from a distance. He had many professional associates, all but a handful of whom he dominated, and no friends. He was a bachelor, without politics.

The attenuated driving power of his sense of self had hoisted him to the position of dominating American culture. Not merely contributing to that culture, but dominating it as Gulliver had dominated the Lilliputians. He had invented his job and his place. He was in charge of pornography and specialized vice for the Mafia, in which confraternity he was, fittingly, the only executive on their table of organization to be referred to as vice-president; fittingly, because as was universally known, the Mafia would have nothing whatever to do with vice, that being the unthinkable activity because when the organization's folk hero, Charley Lucky, had been tried for compulsory prostitution in 1936 and had drawn a sentence of from thirty-to-fifty years, the Fratellanza's public-relations committee had been advised to conduct an enormously effective campaign which would establish for all time that it was culturally and religiously, ethically, and ethnically, impossible for Charley Lucky or any other Mafia member to have any connection whatever with any form of vice. Unfortunately, the campaign had been enormously successful. As a result all vice, a prodigious source of income for the little brothers, had to be farmed out to a patent, non-Sicilian, square WASP who could not have, under anyone's conception, been associated with the controlling organization. The early PR mistake had cost the *Unione* a very large piece of money because Jean-Pierre was his father's son and drove a hard bargain. But the parent company got assured service, creative management, and were still able to retain their good name in, and the admiration of, the American community.

Jean-Pierre's work, it should be repeated, was in specialized vice. At the beginning, before the Supreme Court obscenity decisions, he had run stands of whores in test-marketing areas but there was not enough demand to justify the effort. If each lovely girl had charged five cents for one time they would still have been pricing themselves out of the market. However, during the year in which his mother met Osgood Noon again, Jean-Pierre's industry had earned six hundred and eighty million dollars in gross business from pornographic publishing, obscene motion pictures, figure-modeling studios, lewd record albums for the *écouteur* market, live peep shows, packaged, supermarket merchandised sex-operational equipment such as Trav'l-Pak Vaginas; SisterAct, a patent-pending dildoe; Adjusto-strok, a battery-operated penis and a wide range of wimpusses, merkins, anaphrodisiac creams and musical fucking balls all distributed through his own chain of one hundred ninety-four I&P (Infidelity & Pornography) supermarkets in eighty-two U.S. trading areas. All stores issued Polka Dot Trading Stamps, the symbol for gleet, and washable, color-coded credit cards.

His production offices in New York handled the editorial conception and layout design for ninety-seven hardcover books annually, supported by one hundred and seventeen paperback titles, four encyclopaedias of scatology, twenty-seven self-help books for masturbators, thirty-six national filth magazines, two trade papers for abortionists and genito-urinary workers, and a computer dating service mainly used by people who sought new mates each weekend with whom to read pornography. He operated the company's sixty-four wife-swapping centers called

Swingers' Niteclubs and one hundred and seventeen Encounter and Sensitivity Groups Inc., for heterosexuals, homosexuals, animal lovers, and group masturbators in separate sexual, religio-racist communities, and eleven automobile bumper-sticker printing companies to promote their memberships. Working with the principal vertical labor union membership on a national and regional basis, he had developed what was referred to colloquially as "shop fucking" which were group orgies in which the participants were restricted to having a common interest in one trade, profession, craft or political party, for the doctrinaire.

All script supervision, casting, production, editing, processing and distribution of the firm's film and record business was done in the firm's Madison Avenue offices and he was negotiating for a three-hundred-acre tract of land on which to erect studios in Palm Springs, California. As with all "basic-need" industries there were spin-offs. To keep Kaskell busy, Jean-Pierre at first had to put his brother in charge of all live show bookings on the huge national "69" circuit, so called because the routing of the copulating artists out of New York then due west to Omaha then bending southwestward toward San Diego and into Tucson, then around and up and out and in and down and over and across the map until they were returned back to New York, resembled, on the map, a gigantic 69 figure. Kaskell had done well enough at that so, when Jean-Pierre's roving sex stylists in Europe and Asia who toured the world continually seeking new sex "wrinkles" for editorial referral, and Jean-Pierre, decided to utilize all the actual, practicing sources of the ideas in a new travel-agency idea, he had bought out the vast Norton Agency and had put Kaskie in charge of all of it. Kaskie was wonderfully successful at this sort of worldwide sewer work and within fourteen months the agency was crowding American Express and Thomas Cook for volume. Jean-Pierre insisted that the agency remain entirely on the wholesale level and Kaskell edited, invented, discovered and distributed all-expense package tours of the fleshpots and sinkholes of the world through forty-seven hundred American retail travel agencies. One of the universally popular, year-round standbys was a sexual variant on the restaurant of the month and the wispy scintilla of voyeurism, which had been hardly more than a tenth of one per cent of American sexual interest before the invention and commercial application of network television in the late forties had, at last, matured on a totally international basis by which Americans could watch the inhabitants of two hundred and nine countries, many not even in the United Nations, perform their scarcely-modified versions of sex acts.

Kaskie's boy, Esau, went to work for his Uncle Jean-Pierre after he had dropped out of school, working as an actor and as an assistant director in stag reel documentaries and wax prong flicks, a career which riveted the boy's interest and kept him out of daytime gay bars. It was Esau who thought up the huge money-making flagellation and public confession clubs which were a concomitant of so much sex for a nation which had been strictly taught just a few years before that sex was dirty and a sin. There had to be some way to channel off the amount of guilt which accumulated nationally at the end of each day, like the sweepings of the floor of the Stock Exchange, and Jean-Pierre saw the market need at once. For three dollars and fifty cents a week a man or woman (or child, of course) could become a member of a punishment circle which was comprised of no more than thirty, no fewer than ten members who would hear each others' confessions in a group, then would beat each other with lengths of frozen rope. For only eighty-nine eighty-five a month, a uniformed employee wearing a Roman collar would come to the home to hear the confession and would beat the member with a cricket bat, barbed wire, or lengths of Norwegian fox fur and deliver a crate of brown rice as one of the health-food surprise premiums of the month. It was the income from the spin-offs which really generated net profits.

Jean-Pierre's executive offices were in a fine, old, classical building on Madison Avenue which had been designed at the turn of the century by a famous architect-sexual athlete. It shared a vast parking space-courtyard with the former regional headquarters of one of the obsolete religions. Here, with his editors, producers, and psychiatrists, Jean-Pierre received his stars, chemists, and sales managers of the Grand Prix brand-name products, its cable address IMBRICATE, NEW YORK. Like all other Mafia achievers he had been graduated from the Harvard School of Business, had a Master's from Wharton, and a doctorate from MIT in computer studies, for theological background. He had been chosen to head Grand Prix from a field of two hundred and four young strivers after having served six and a quarter years as a Money Mover.

True, Jean-Pierre's evolution as a Mafia executive had been the result of opportunities provided by his father. Naturally, Arthur Bainbridge Harris had hoped the boy would take over the family's pill and chemical companies but he lacked the *sacre feu* the industry required, an unshakable belief in the narcotized destiny of the Western world. Arthur Harris kept his boy busy during the summers home from school working at odd jobs for the Mafia with whom Harris Senior's drug companies did a considerable volume of business in what might be called non-ethical-pharmaceutical distribution. As it worked out, the little brothers liked Jean-Pierre and he liked them. What he found stodgy as legitimate pills he found absorbing as narcotics, probably because of the tax-free angle, but surely not because of the profit margins because nobody or anything could achieve anything as fruitful as the profit margins of the legitimate drug industry. The boy seemed to have all of his father's gifts for administration and rapacity plus a genuinely creative quality. When only nineteen he had secured patents on two unique whips. He was the first magazine publisher in the country to persuade a ranking film star to allow a lion to mount her for the 3-D cameras and had had the taste to hold it down to a double truck, thereby establishing lions as pets in more than 12.8 per cent of American families having incomes of over a hundred and seventy-five thousand dollars annually.

Jean-Pierre had his father's contempt for money because he knew it was not brain-wracking to make money in a republic founded upon the pursuit of money. The leap-frogging talent he sought to acquire was the accrual of power.

With all the opportunities and reasons to appear hard and brittle, he was a soft-appearing man (he seemed to have been stuffed with one hundred dollar bills) with Ada's shoe-button eyes set close together on an imposing head so hawk-like that it appeared to be two profiles pasted together, with a chin like a moose under a tall black Churchill bowler made for him by Gelot in the Place Vêndome. He wore richly textured, sensual clothing with long lapels but otherwise done to the modeling by Morgan the Elder. He used a car and chauffeur but the car was a Dodge. He kept charge accounts only at Smyth's on-the-Green, in Dublin (for the best grilling mushrooms), and at B. Altman in New York because he trusted their elevators. He drank a third-growth Bordeaux, Château d'Issan. He lived alone within a gigantic block of flats, forty-seven stories high, owned by the little brothers in the Sixties from Third to Second Avenue. His driver-houseman and his extraordinary cook, one of the few women to have been knighted for her art by the Italian government, lived in small separate apartments on either side of his and immediately adjacent. Excepting for an occasional meal with his parents, then later with his mother alone, and occasionally with various Money Movers of the Fratellanza, he dined alone. For his mother he always had a ripe Reblochon cheese which they would devour with a bottle of cold Blagny. For the Money Movers he had *blini, zakuski, pirogi* and *tvoroiniki* with iced Latvian vodka, the only status vodka, because they were always getting lasagna downtown. Alone, he enjoyed high Mexican food and low Swiss food on alternate days. He drank carbonated water and canned beef bouillon Saturday evening and all day Sunday to control his line. He was in excellent health. He paid his servants a combined total of twenty-seven thousand dollars a year, the bulk of it to the cook who asked him to have it deposited to her account at the Unione di Banche Svizzere, Piazza Grande, 6601 Locarno, Switzerland.

Jean-Pierre worked hard to sustain the illusion that he had four sides of equal length and breadth. He wore Murray Space Shoes, a British military moustache, that billycock bowler and a twenty-nine-hundred-dollar perpetual-calendar watch. He rented pairs of amiable ladies to accompany him to the opera and the theatre, to stroll past art galleries on Saturday afternoons, each girl a beard for the other. He believed in murder as a business tactic but not on a personal level. Larceny was his policy; corruption was his creed. His only real extravagance was the three-dollar-and-eighty-cent Mother's Day card he sent to Ada each year; extravagant because he spent the money out of admiration with no reason of profit for spending it.

Despite his feeling and respect for his father Jean-Pierre

had, all his life, been drawn more to his mother because both he and his father were short, wistful squares, tightly contained, and Ada was not. Jean-Pierre was aware of how keenly Celeste competed with their mother and how desperate was Kaskell's need to betray all of them if he could have, and he was ever-watchful to protect Ada from the rest of the family.

On the day Kaskell called to make the appointment with Jean-Pierre for Celeste to save Dunc, Jean-Pierre was wildly preoccupied with two very fat ideas whirling about at the center of his greed. The lesser idea was that Kaskell wanted him to finance a pornographic travel magazine which was to be bang-on *soutenage* for the attractions of the proliferating travel agency. The other—an e*nor*mous conception—was one of those merchandising plans which he felt in his bones would catch on and enter worldwide culture as the dominating pornographic form for the century to come. It would serve books, magazines, record albums, TV cassettes, cable television, character merchandise, and above all both his motion picture industry and the coming pattern of history books within all school systems. It could actually lead to pornographic daily newspapers and Grand Prix would own them.

The plan was simple enough both in conception and in execution. An extremely gifted designer-engineer-make-up man, Caspar P. Lear, jr., had brought him a pliable "breathing" plastic material which he had worked into masks of famous men and women. He had absolutely taken Jean-Pierre's breath away when an effigy which had actually seemed to *be* the living breathing Lyndon Johnson had strolled into his office on a bitter winter day wearing a bikini made out of the North Vietnamese flag. But when they had taken that mask off and had revealed Esau Harris beneath it, Jean-Pierre had caught on to the enormous cultural potential of the conception. He could show newsreels showing Ted Heath, the English Prime Minister hard at it on a perfect English country lawn with a flawless replica of the lady general of the Salvation Army. He could give them Pope Paul upon one of those great Papal beds of state with Mao Tse-tung's fourth wife. The Caspar Lear Mask could deliver the most celebrated people of the day and the endless cast of written history in front of wide-screen color cameras and a sense of living history could be brought to pornography. Effects and circumstances literally poured through his mind: Bobby Baker and the entire U.S. Senate in that tiny motel room! Golda Meir! Eamon de Valera and the Supremes! J. Edgar Hoover and—no, perhaps not. He brought biography and philosophy to pornography in his imagination; mathematics, the arts, astronautics and great statecraft could be used as backdrops to prove the immutability of the sexes. He felt as though he were striding with Beethoven's gonads humming the music of Errol Flynn. It would become a brilliant new teaching tool which the top fixers of the Fratellanza could put through Congress. He gave Caspar Lear, jr., a thousand-dollar bonus on the spot, leaned back and began to dream.

"Your brother is on One," Miss Mechanic said disapprovingly through the intercom.

Jean-Pierre picked up the phone. "What?" he said.

"J. P.? Hey, hahryew, J. P.?"

"What?"

"Have I ever asked you a favor?"

"All the time."

"I mean a favor for Ada."

"Let Ada ask her own favors."

"We can't tell Ada yet—will you do it?"

"What is it?"

"That's what I want to see you about."

"All right, goddammit! I'm a busy man. When? Where?"

"You have to include Celeste in the meeting."

Three years before, at a dinner party at Celeste's which Jean-Pierre had been fool enough to attend, and where Duncan had insisted on playing the record album of Richard M. Nixon's Checkers speech, Celeste had had the cool to say, out in the open, that Ada would certainly be surprised if she knew what Jean-Pierre did for a living. Jean-Pierre had spoken to Celeste alone for some time on the other side of the room and Celeste had vomited afterward. She had never mentioned Ada to Jean-Pierre again mainly because she was not permitted to see him again but perhaps also because she did not want to happen to her what her brother had mentioned might happen to her.

"I'll call Ada," Jean-Pierre said into the phone.

"No! That will make everything worse. First you have to get all the facts and only Celeste knows."

"All *right!* Be at my place at six-thirty."

"Your office?"

"My apartment."

"Where is it?"

Jean-Pierre told him. He repeated it. Behind him, Celeste wrote it down.

17

They rode the cashmere-lined elevator toward Jean-Pierre's floor eighteen seconds before they were due because Jean-Pierre insisted upon promptness. The limiting area of the lift seemed to compound Celeste's scent so pungently that, for the first time since their childhood Kaskie touched her. His right hand grasped her left buttock, his left hand plunged into his trousers pocket and his eyes rolled like marbles in his head. Celeste stood it serenely as though she were alone in the car. When the elevator stopped she wrenched her buttock away and flounced out into the corridor. He followed her, whimpering softly.

Jean-Pierre opened the door but did not greet them. He led them into the sitting room with its large picture window which overlooked one of the uglier sections of Queens across the filthy river and ordered them to sit down. He stood in front of the false fireplace and glared down at Celeste. "All right. What the hell is this about Ada?"

Celeste coughed gently. "Ada is sleeping with a man in his seventy-first year."

"You are taking my valuable time to tell me a ridiculous thing like that?"

"Dunc is running for the Senate."

"What about it?"

"The Attorney General likes Dunc. He feels he can be one of the great candidates of the century. He has said, in so many words, that the Senate can be only the beginning, if you know what I mean."

Jean-Pierre's expression all at once became unhostile, more thoughtful.

"I could use one of those in my business," he said, spacing his words.

Celeste nodded with relief. Thank God, Jean-Pierre was honest. That was what everyone else thought who knew Duncan but only Jean-Pierre had put the patriotic avarice into words. She moved in more confidently. "The Attorney General says if Dunc's elderly mother-in-law is exposed as sleeping with a man in his seventy-first year, the national effect will be to destroy Dunc's youth image—and nothing else counts in politics today."

"Who is the old man?"

"Osgood Noon, the publisher."

"Tris Noon's father?"

"Yes."

"We use Tris Noon's people for rock festival love-ins to demonstrate products. What does his father publish?"

"F.M. Heller—he's the banker who is Dunc's campaign manager—says the Attorney General gives Mr. Noon's magazine credit for increasing world arms expenditure to a trillion dollars in the past six years. And particularly among the small countries where the Pentagon makes its biggest profit."

There was an unaccountable silence from Jean-Pierre.

"I mean he's an important man," Celeste said. "He won't be easy to push around. Not any more than Ada is."

"We'll see," Jean-Pierre said. "I'll have to talk to Ada."

"That won't do any good."

"What do you want me to do?"

"Well—I mean—you *know* certain people. I mean you know people who have all kinds of ways of *handling* a dirty old man like Osgood Noon."

"You want him hit?"

"I didn't say that. I don't think a girl should make that decision. I think the people who are playing for the big stakes should decide things like that and I can't seem to make F.M. Heller get any kind of a policy out of Washington."

"You'll hear from me," Jean-Pierre said. That was all. They were out on the street in eight minutes. It could have taken five but Celeste refused to ride down in the lift with Kaskie's sticky hands and he had to wait until the car came back up for him.

Jean-Pierre invited Ada to dinner that night. At first he couldn't get her. He telephoned every hour on the hour and finally reached her at midnight, startling her.

"What happened, Ches? Are you all right?" she asked anxiously.

"I'm fine. How about lunch tomorrow?"

"Tomorrow is Saturday."

"I know."

"We're going to a ball game."

"We?"

"A friend and I."

"Then dinner tomorrow night?"

"I'd love to see you, Chessie, but I'm booked solid."

"When can I see you?"

"You sound upset."

"I'm okay. When, Mama?"

"I thought my children called me Ada."

"I thought my mother called me Jean-Pierre."

"Dinner Sunday night? Would that be all right?"

"That's fine. Thanks, Ada. We'll make you some *ifu mie tjha,* that's a marvelous noodle dish some amputee kids I know brought back from Vietnam. Hm? Noodles, chicken, garlic, pork, shrimp—hey?—a little cauliflower?—some ham and celery?"

"That sounds *mar*velous."

"Six o'clock Sunday night?"

"Isn't that early?"

"Well—we'll have a lot to talk about," he said.

At about four-thirty Sunday afternoon Ada clambered down from the pool table like a slightly stiff Tinker Bell. Os inquired groggily where she was going.

"I've been invited to my son's for dinner. Isn't that nice?"

"But—what will I do?"

"Why don't you call one of your sons and have dinner?"

"That reminds me that Bottie will be home for good on Monday—that is, tomorrow. I'm afraid that means we're going to have to use your place for a while."

"I'm dying to meet him."

"But thank you for the suggestion about dinner tonight. I will. I'll call Tris. I haven't talked to him in ages."

"I think it would be sweet if you saw your son for dinner while I was having dinner with my son."

Jean-Pierre embraced his mother warmly and, arms around her, led her to the most comfortable chair which faced the good view of the fantasy carpet of lights which spread southward across Manhattan to the sea. She accepted his offer of a half-bottle of chilled Suduiraut and just one little stick of grass to perk up her appetite. They talked generally, in no hurry to get to the point. Jean-Pierre said he had a new connection who specialized in Graubunden Green, a new pot variant which had been developed for the ski resorts in eastern Switzerland for the jet-set people who had always demanded the best in narcotics. They chatted about the theatre. They had each seen and had enjoyed both shows then playing on Broadway. They chatted about book reviews which they had been privileged to read in the one newspaper in the biggest city of the western hemisphere which ran daily book reviews. They dissected the recent weather then they strolled into the paneled dining room and ate a magnificent dinner.

An hour and twenty minutes later, as they drank coffee and shared another joint on the infrared heated terrace, Jean-Pierre got around to the points of his interest.

"Celeste was here Friday."

"I thought so."

"You did?"

"She came to see me just a little while ago, then you called me at midnight Friday so—"

"Well, then you know."

"If it's about what I think it must be about then I'm afraid I can't help you, dear. And I really would like to please you. You're always doing things for the rest of us but—oh, dear—this is really no one's business but my own."

"Are you happy, Ada?"

"Very."

"You look very happy. I wanted to see for myself and to ask you that directly. That's all I'm interested in."

"Nothing about Mr. Noon?"

"Nothing."

"Did Celeste tell you they may run Dunc for the presidency?"

"She—she implied that."

"Weren't you horrified—and frightened?"

"After she left. After I thought about it. It's a fairly terrible thing to think about. But if that gang wants him, Ada, please don't forget that they are capable of playing very rough. Look—listen to me—just for the pleasure it would give me, please let me give you and Mr. Noon a nice cruise around the world on the *Reina Gertrudis*.

Some very close associates of mine have just bought the old Radin Line and, believe me, I can work out a very good deal. They'll spoil you 'til you just foam over."

"No, thank you, dear."

"Why not?"

"Well, for one thing, I'm afraid Mr. Noon couldn't possibly spare that amount of time away from the office."

"He's semiretired. I checked him out."

"Your informant is mistaken. Mr. Noon is not even *semi*retired. He is a very active publisher."

"Ada! He goes into the office once every month to sign checks."

"That's because he's a marvelous executive, dear. He is a very organized man."

"Well, good. Then he could do his business by telephone from the *Reina Gertrudis*."

"No, Jean-Pierre."

"Why not?"

"Because," she closed her eyes dreamily and gulped in on the roach, "I wouldn't even allow my parents or my husband to tell me how to live my own life, the only life I have. So I will not permit my children to tell me how to live it. I have always kept a tight hold on understanding consequences, dear. And I try to be right—but who can be sure?"

"Okay." He sipped coffee and watched the nine hundred thousand lights.

Tristram Noon and his father had three huge hamburger sandwiches each at the kitchen table. Tris was a tall loose-hanging man of thirty-six. He sat, moved, and stood with the ineffable relaxation of a physical master. He had the studied impersonal look, considered to be cool, which told of someone enormously conscious of self. His clothing was a masquerade of the now scene, odd on a grown man: tight jeans, a tieless shirt, three-hundred-and-ninety-eight-dollar western boots which had been a Christmas gift from the demanding Captain Pedernales. But Tris was clean-looking. His hair was sculpted but neither long nor unkempt. He had large lambent blue eyes which had been called trapshooter's eyes by a really poor trapshooter his father had known. His hands were large and lumpy and suggested his physical strength. He wasn't exactly sullen-appearing but he affected a disturbed solemnity, an air of worry that somehow some shade of frivolity or weak light-heartedness might possibly flicker across his face; the *machismo* of the movie star. all manly and hard in the colored stills framed in front of the theatre. Due to the repetitive disappointments from his mother, Tris had never married.

After dinner, silent chewing ritual which only they could have called dinner, with their hair smelling of pan-fried butter, they moved to the billiard table which, Os was relieved to see, was unspotted by gleet and unscratched except for one of Ada's little heel marks on the polished mahogany rail. Looking at the unyielding greenness of it made Os wistful to think that for more than fifty-five years he might have been enjoying the added zest of copulating on pool tables whose hard surfaces brought out the poetry of strength in a woman's hips and back. What a revealing teacher Ada had been for him. Her tiny tip about Vick's VapoRub, for one thing, had lighted up skies with sensual illumination. He caught himself up and broke through the reverie. Tris was here and, for whatever reason, the boy seemed to be moving as deliberately as the President could stalk an active verb.

"Is there something on your mind, Tris?"

"No, Pop," Tris lied. "Why?"

"You are moving like William Jennings Bryan at a Fourth of July picnic."

"A physical resemblance?"

"The climate of the imminent speechmaker."

"I'm just here to shoot pool," Tris said. His father was the only man who had ever beaten Tris at any sport. Tris shot good enough pool for Mosconi to have said nice things about his game. But his father was better. It bugged Tris. How could a man who had stayed married to a slog-off woman like his mother have the calm to play pool the way Pop played it?

Tris stroked the cue ball carefully at an angle of thirty degrees and made a jump-masse shot, sinking the object ball. It didn't seem to impress his father. He chalked his cue. He bent over and made a perfect piquet: the cue ball started forward then—without striking any surface—stopped and reversed its direction with enough velocity to hit the six ball into the side pocket leaving Tris in a perfect breaking position for the next rack. He walked slowly and silently around the table, chalking and shooting, and put away all fourteen balls of the second rack as he had disposed of the first.

"You are getting much better," his father said. "You'll be beating me one of these days."

Tris snorted. Beating his father at pool had become his obsession. When he worked right in with his people in the different ghetto riots and student shoot-ins he always used a sawed-off pool cue as a weapon. Every pig's head he smashed he saw in billiard terms of victory over his father in the endless game they would play forever. The only two emotions Tris had ever known were love and hate. He felt them only for his father. He knew that if he could only beat his father at pool he might even be able to forgive him for taking that goddam woman back into their lives again and again.

"You are shortening your position distance very nicely, Tris. You must be doing more practicing."

"I have a table at my place." The table was inside Tris' bedroom where, with a copy of Cottringham's *The Game of Billiards* beside him he would play the same shots over and over again to compromise with his insomnia.

"Pop, you know a man named F.M. Heller?" The Everest Bank?" He slammed into the break shot, sank it, scattered the mass of balls, then began to clear the table. His father found a comfortable chair.

"Oh, yes," Os said in his mild way. "He was a food-shares expert on the floor in the twenties. I remember him running sausage casing and kosher poultry stocks up seventy-one points in one day on a rig. He was a master at that. His father, old Marxie Heller, was one of the cooniest lawyers Wall Street ever had. F.M. and I were on the NRA Boned Ham Council in thirty-three. I don't really know how I got on that. I was a hat maker. But Frank Roosevelt wanted to make some sort of a nice gesture, I suppose, so there we were."

"I didn't know that. Then he's a good friend of yours?"

"I wouldn't say that. We were just on that committee for a while. And, in any event, he would be no friend of mine after this week."

"What happened?"

"He had the Pentagon's advertising agency threaten me." Os was watching Tris closely. Tris merely raised his eyebrows. Os said, "And now he's sent my son to set me straight."

Tris stood straight up. "How'd you know that?"

Os waved him away and sighed. "You're about as inscrutable as a six-year-old to me, Tris."

Tris wasn't loose any more. He looked stiff and gawky. "Well, sure. You're my father."

"Then we're friends?"

"You're my *father*. Let's get something straight because I don't say it often enough. You're my father."

"I never doubted it."

They stared at each other silently. Then Os said, "What did F.M. Heller tell you to tell me?"

"Look, Pop. I have this retainer with the Everest Bank, yes. But they can't make me do anything I don't want to do. I agreed just to pass along. That's all. Just pass along. It's just routine business."

They stared at each other throughout Tris' speech. It was silent then in the room excepting for the war scores being rattled off on the radio as the sports announcer ticked off the various death gains: Israelis: 2—Egyptians: 114; Cambodians: 485—ARVN: 14; U.S.: 370—Vietcong: 19. Tris broke away from his father's gaze and turned back to the play too hurriedly. He smashed the cue ball into a throw shot at two frozen balls trying to spin the five ball into the side pocket and missing miserably.

"Drat, drat, *drat!*" he shouted.

"You didn't want it, Tris," Os said and got to his feet, chalking the tip of his cue.

Tris felt doubly frustrated. He had been caught out before he had gotten started for a lucrative client and once again he had lost a chance at beating his father at the most important game in the world. "Well, that's that!" he said bitterly. "That's the end of this game!" He threw himself into a chair.

"I have told you many times, Tris," his gentle father said gently, "if you are only going to be able to run seventy balls or so and then stop your run with a simple throw shot, then you'll have to be content with hustling for nickels in the shabbier neighborhood pool halls."

"I got flustered!"

"Oh, come now, Tris. I don't play oneupmanship and a good player surely doesn't fluster himself? What flustered you?" As he spoke, Os ran three ostentatious combination shots. "Do you know why the Pentagon's agency threatened me?"

"Yes. But it will wait. I don't play oneupmanship either."

"That's all right, son. You can't faze my game. Why?"

"Because the Republican Party wants you to stop sleeping with a woman who is in her sixty-ninth year."

Os drove the cue ball clear off the table. He paid no attention whatever to this crudest of all scratches. He gaped at Tris. "She is sixty-eight," he succeeded in saying.

Tris had retrieved the cue ball. "Jesus, Pop, you *scratched!* My God, the score is seventy to three in my favor so maybe you'd better just sit down over there while I win this game." He snatched up his cue and began his play. Os sat down leglessly.

"All right, then," Os said, his jaws clenched. His whole face had gotten mean and hostile. "If they want to make trouble, they'll find out I can make trouble too."

"Don't tell me, Pop. Go ahead and do it but I don't want to know about it because I wouldn't want you thinking I had told them whatever it is."

"Never mind. I want you to tell them. I want you to pass along just as you did for them."

"Ah, Pop."

"Just ask them, if you will, what they think they are going to do to get a certain two hundred and thirteen H-101 fighter-bombers off their hands at six million dollars a plane." Os was standing and literally trembling with rage and outrage. "Let us see how their Pentagon explains that colossal goof-off away. They'll have to sell them to Mao to get rid of them. At ten cents on the dollar."

"Listen, Pop—don't fool around with this gang. They're dirty fighters. Please."

"How dare they try to implicate Mrs. Harris in their silly little schemes? This is infamous! Can't you seem to put all this within your perspective? Doesn't it have any sickening effect on your values? We've reached the point where hired politicians are saying who a citizen may be seen with. Is that the way you want it, Tris?"

Tris listened respectfully. He had never really seen his father angry before, he realized. Os' face was turkey-red under his pale hair and his voice had become almost shrill with anger. His lips had hidden themselves within each other. Tris thought all the manifestations had merged into a formidable force; old man or not.

"What do you want me to tell them, Pop?"

"Please tell them that the next issue of *World Defense* will warn all potential buyers among the small aggressor nations that the H-101 is military junk. With details."

"And—well—what will I tell them about you and the lady?"

"You don't learn anything, do you, Tris?"

"I'm sorry about this whole thing, Pop."

"Play, please."

Tris stroked the cue ball and slammed it with tremendous force; a stab shot, high with follow spin.

"Tris?"

"Yes, Pop?"

"The score is now seventy-six to three, your favor, in a game of one hundred and twenty-five points. I suggest you now cede your playing turn to me and that we play to the finish for a hundred dollars a point."

Tris gaped at his father. He had never allowed as much as a suggestion of gambling in any of the hundreds of matches they had played before. "Cede?" Tris said. "That would be highway robbery."

"You do have seventy-six points, Tris. And I shall play left-handed."

"*Left*-handed?" The greed which greased and lined Tris' soul glowed and shimmered through his eyes as he thought that if he could get positive insurance that he could beat his father at billiards, no matter what the handicap, the jinx would be broken and he would be able to do it again and again.

"Okay, Pop," he said with suppressed excitement. "We got a deal." He stepped away from the table. His father chalked his cue and began to shoot methodically, his cue working at his left side. Because the boy was too big to be spanked, his father punished him out of forty-nine hundred dollars. As he paid over the bank check, the shamefaced young man said, "Thanks, Pop."

18

Os was shattered by the realization that, in his dismay and anger, he had failed to ask why the Republican Party wanted him to give up Ada. He had to take two ice-water baths that night, four hours apart, in order to get his required seven hours sleep. He spent the next morning writing and tearing up letters to the Attorney General and to F.M. Heller. At eleven o'clock he met Ada at his podiatrist's, an Amish wizard named Dr. Zendt who could play toes and feet the way de Pachmann had played the piano. As always after the ritual of the feet, he and Ada strolled to Riverside Drive for the long ambling walk from Ninety-sixth to Seventy-second Street where they would take the bus across town to have lunch.

Ada was late, of course, but Dr. Zendt had repeated again that morning that Os had the feet of a man of sixty. The nurse had rouged them slightly until they seemed to glow with health and had polished the tops of his toenails like the brightwork on a ship. Ada loved to come in just for a moment before the nurse slipped on his socks, to admire the effect.

They strolled west toward Riverside Drive, sauntering first along Broadway then veering off to the right through the *barrio*. It was a clear sunny morning and the housewives were out for their weekend shopping. A young girl was frantically trying to get a fix in the doorway of an A&P supermarket, but the fix involved holding her baby, managing a length of rubber tubing, a lighted match, a spoon and a safety pin while she tried to control her trembling. Good-naturedly, the shoppers gave her wide berth and plenty of room to work.

"Did you have a nice dinner with your son last night?" Os asked.

"Oh, yes."

"What did you have?"

"It was a superb, unpronounceable Vietnamese dish. Then a Mexican dessert. I told Jean-Pierre he has to invite you to dinner. He has the most marvelous cook in the world."

He stepped over, and she walked around, a young couple who were copulating at the foot of church steps as they turned into Ninety-fifth Street.

"How was your dinner?" Ada asked when they were walking side-by-side again.

"Well—I don't quite know how to tell you. I really haven't recovered from it yet."

She turned to him with alarm. He reassured her instantly. "No, no! I didn't have another attack of indigestion. We merely had three rare hamburgers smothered with onions and, thanks to you, the added zest of Imitation Bacon Bits. No, not that. It was a formal message which Tristram was required to deliver from the Republican Party."

"You mean your son told you that you and I had to stop seeing each other."

Os was amazed. "How did you know that?"

"We have a lot to talk over, dear. Let's just sit down and get a few things straightened out."

They crossed Riverside Drive and sat on a bench in front of the Soldiers' and Sailors' Monument.

"How and why and who and when did they involve you in this?" Os said, so weak with rage that he had dropped upon the bench. "Some political cabal has unaccountably turned them against my magazine—and that is bad enough—but to involve an innocent woman who has no even remote connection with the magazine in such an infamous mess is outrageous and, by George, I shall take the matter personally to the Attorney General!"

"Who are your lawyers, Os?"

"Let us stay with this problem before we get diverted, Ada. Why in God's name should they bring you into this —this con*spir*acy about the magazine? That is what I am going to find out."

"And I want to help you to find out, dear," Ada said gently. "Who are your lawyers?"

"Like everyone else who needs anything from government since the new administration—Lantz, Lantz, Tolliver & Farr."

"They also represent the Everest Bank."

"I suppose they would."

"F.M. Heller is a national committeeman and very close to the Attorney General."

"I am well aware of that, Ada."

"Lantz, Lantz, Tolliver & Farr is the Attorney General's old firm. He was a founding partner."

"I'm afraid I don't follow you."

"I want you to telephone Lucas Lantz. Now."

"But—it's Saturday morning."

"Please call him."

Os was confused. He fumbled in his vest pocket for his little black book. "I'll have to call him at home," he said with uncertainty. "What do I ask him when I get him?"

"I want you to tell him exactly what your son was told to tell you. Then I want you to say that you want him to bring a lawsuit against F.M. Heller."

"By George, I do want to sue Heller. And anyone else connected with this outrage."

"That's good then. Now, call Lucas Lantz."

He got up from the bench and walked to the all-glass telephone booth which was paved with used contraceptives. He inserted a coin, dialed and waited.

"Mr. Lucas Lantz, please. This is Osgood Noon," he said into the telephone. He waited.

"Hello? Ah, good morning, Lucas. Fine. And you? And Mercedes? Splendid. I have a rather pressing matter, Lucas, or you may be sure I would not have bothered you at home. Yesterday, my son, Tristram, whom you may know, was told by F.M. Heller of the Everest Bank to tell me that I must stop seeing a certain lady or face dire consequences, as incredible as that may sound to you. Now, it was carefully phrased but nonetheless emerged as a direct threat to me of commercial and bodily harm. Now, I found this intolerable, Lucas. Therefore, I want you to call F.M. Heller this morning, at Rockrimmon House if necessary, and advise him that we will bring suit against him, the bank and the Republican National Committee. You will call me back? Thank you, Lucas. No, no—not on Monday morning. Immediately, please. I am at Monument 9-2678." He hung up and returned to the park bench.

"I handled it rather well, I think," he told Ada, sitting down upon the heavy soot under the fourteen candle-power sun which was trying to break through the polluted atmosphere. "However, I sensed something odd about Lucas' response."

"Damned right you did. All right. Here's the scam. They have decided to run my twit of a son-in-law, Duncan Mulligan, for the United States Senate. And it's a much bigger deal than it looks. They need that election very, very much and they have covered all the exits."

"But what does that have to do with my magazine?"

"That's all secondary stuff. They put a security check on Duncan's family. Routine stuff. And the check turned us up. So they sent my daughter Celeste, Duncan's wife, to tell me that what you and I are doing is disgusting and that it can shatter Mulligan's whole youth image. They shoot kids, lock them up, call them bums and make them fight the wars but youth image is the name of the game."

"Dis-*gus*-ting?"

"Two people over forty doing things to each other on a bed—or a pool table as the case may be—is the only perversion remaining that the voters will recognize."

"Per-*ver*-sion?"

"We can take it, dear. We know better. We can go to Australia and sit on a beach."

"We will not compromise."

"Good. I mean, I'm not only glad, I'm proud. And not just because of us. In fact, we just aren't the important issue in this at all. The Attorney General *adores* Duncan. They'll spend three million and a half in the state to elect him. But hear this. My daughter told me this is just the beginning. Regretfully, the Attorney General is going to have to dump the President at next year's convention. Dunc Mulligan will be the new man."

"But—why? I never heard of the man."

"I don't know why. It's baffling. Os, we're talking about my son-in-law, a man who is unable to make a living. He sits in a forgotten law library year after year because he's married to this family who bring the firm a lot of law business. Dunc cannot find his ass with both hands. Except for something the Attorney General sees in him which we can't see, he couldn't even get into the White House on a three-dollar guided tour."

Os' voice was a smoldering whisper. "We will see what they will be able to do with two hundred and thirteen H-101 fighter-bombers," he said. They heard the telephone ring in the glass booth. Os walked to it resolutely and snatched up the phone. "Yes, Lucas?" He listened for several minutes then hung up without saying another word and left the booth. His eyes were flashing and his lightly rouged toes were glowing under his shoes and socks.

"Lantz just said that although he can counsel me he can no longer represent me."

"Okay. Every company I own will fire that firm first thing Monday morning."

"He said F.M. Heller not only denies everything but said that I must be suffering from advanced senility." Os sat on the edge of the park bench and clutched his spare shanks. "When I get through with them they'll have to give those H-101's to the Chicago police."

"There'll be plenty of things we can do to them."

"Indeed. Oh, indeed, indeed! I'll withdraw every cent I have on deposit at the Everest Bank."

"A good start. So will I. Out! Every dime! Monday morning. And every Harris Foundation will withdraw every cent of its money. And we must withdraw every cent of every contribution we have ever made to the Republican National Committee, retroactive to the Harding campaign, and they'll have to pay because every dime was illegal."

"Out! Your contributions. My contributions. My companies' and your companies' contributions and your foundations' contributions. You know, Ada, it must be that somewhere around three-fifths of the entire annual budget is being spent—our money and our honor—by a man called the Secretary of Defense who was never elected, but appointed by a handful of power brokers who speak for a figurehead who watches *foot*ball games."

"I wasn't thinking of that, dear. After all, the cabinet has to be appointed. It can't be elected."

"The Constitution was framed by a handful of farmers to protect them from a national population of maybe a million people. Ada. The Constitution served the complexities of seventeen hundred eighty-seven. But every time a voice cries out that the Constitution be redesigned to meet complexities of this hour—true representation for at least the majority of the people and unbiased un*sin*ister communications, for all of the horrors of population and distribution, of prices and supply, of pollution. of continuous war—the mindlessly reflexive press and the trained-dog Congress pontificate that the Constitution is a wondrous document wrought by a pantheon of saints who never existed."

"Now just a minute, Os. Take it easy. Don't go too far."

"The Constitution was drawn up one hundred and eighty-four years ago by the deed-holding proprietors of a new small country unknown even in an immeasurably smaller world. And it was drawn to protect rich farmers from upstart city catchpennies."

"Os, come *on!* Are you trying to tell me the Constitution wasn't written to serve the ages?"

"Serve the ages? My God! Everything hangs on a frail human called President. He may *not* be selected directly by the people who must suffer with him but is bartered into history by years of haggling amongst a handful of power brokers—about as large a group as the farmers who drew up the Constitution. Covered with the light slime of their needs, bolstered by tens of millions of dollars of their campaign funds, he is then magically nominated before an assembly of hacks who know if they do as they are told they will win the high office of local dog catcher—every one of these ritual mockers unknown to the electorate who may have to die for this man they ratify."

"Surely you believe in the two-party *sys*tem, Os!"

"A hundred million dollars spent on long-distance telephone calls and celluloid lapel buttons—is that what you mean? While rats run off with babies in ten dozen ghettos and the stewardship of this unspeakably corrupting war is passed back and forth across party lines?"

"Stop it, Os. You are going to make me cry."

"With the proliferating population, measured by the formulas of that Constitution, the Congress is a huge bedlam of exploited meaningless rubber stamps. No unit of the Overcommunications System bothers to measure what the President defined by this Constitution is supposed to wedge into the waking hours of his day. If that small nation of one million in which the Constitution was created required one President, then this nation of two hundred and ten million people must be given a Constitution which provides for a multiple executive force with one peer among *elected* equals. That way the country's needs can by law be treated by trained minds without the hypocrisy of pretending that one man plus a pint of tranquilizers can do what every newspaper implies he alone is getting done."

"Well," Ada said, "It's all very well to get abstract about the whole country but this mess we're in has to be settled on a family level. They have to be caucused. All of them."

"That's it! Make them face this! That the Constitution, of which they are victims, must be redesigned every fifty years. Make them caucus. We have to do it! But how? When? Where?"

"My son will handle everything. Taxi!" Ada rushed to the curb and flagged down a magenta and butternut car. She hustled Os into the cab first then she turned to yell at an enormously bulky white-haired man wearing a beret, who seemed to be wearing used tea-bag flounces under his eyes. "Go back to Stamford, you fink!" she yelled at him and got into the cab, slamming the door.

Os was no more prepared to turn suddenly consistent than anyone else alive. He was outraged by the system which had made him very, very rich when his own sweetest need had been to make money from it, but now it had offended him so therefore, if he could, he would attack it until it screamed for his mercy. To earn was human; to bite the hand that feeds, divine.

They were so absorbed that they were oblivious to the screams of the baby nurse who was being raped by a band of eight boys on the far side of the monument. People were leaving the area of the rape, with dignity but rapidly; looking straight ahead.

19

At 12:34 P.M. the tapes of the conversation between Osgood Noon and Ada Clarke-Harris on the park bench before the Soldiers' and Sailors' Monument, together with certain taped television pictures of Ada in plotter's animation, plus the track of the two telephone calls Os had had with Lucas Lantz, were delivered to Rockrimmon House, Fifth Avenue residence of F.M. Heller. These were examined and added to the Noon-Harris dossier. The bank president was a thorough and, in certain arcane fields, an accomplished man who had the advantage of being supplied with equipment and expertise by the genius of specialized government agencies operating most secretly with secret government budgets. The grossly bulky man with the deeply stained eye-sockets was not, as Celeste Mulligan-Harris had been led to believe, a simple volunteer from Stamford, Connecticut.

By following credit information researched by the Everest Bank and then made available to him, the bulky man had slowly built financial profiles of Osgood Noon's clothes presser, barber, dentist, and podiatrist. Then he had called on each of them and had offered either to discharge their obligations at a 20 percent discount or to foreclose on all their debts immediately. It was Richard Nixon's America so they were all deeply in debt. In order to escape foreclosure and yet to save 20 percent on all loans they merely had to perform a few simple services. The terms were accepted by all even before the extent of the services were made known.

The presser of Osgood Noon's clothes was shown how to install a complete wiring system into each of his suits, transforming him into a walking radio and television transmitter down to clear recordings of his mumblings. The nether-government also provided matching buttons which contained a built-in microphone, a sub-miniature transmitter, and transistorized batteries. These were sewn to the jacket and were indistinguishable from the buttons for which they substituted. The thread which fastened the buttons was conductive wire carried through the seams of the jacket to provide an antenna. The vest buttons were wide-angle miniaturized closed-circuit television lenses which transmitted by microwave to three-inch portable receivers in the bulky man's panel truck where the images were recorded on flat TV records. Os' fly buttons were arranged in that identical order: miniature camera, tiny transmitter, button-sized batteries. Most unwittingly, because of these, Os had photographed Ada in many positions and in many orifices. Later, when she found out what had been done, she blamed no one but herself. "It's my own fault," she said, "for having this hangup about needing to be banged by fully dressed men. But how could they know a thing like that?" "They" had known because the computer records of individual-citizen dossiers had turned up a handball player from East Orange, New Jersey, who had always taken Ada with his trousers on, wearing rolled-up shirtsleeves.

Os' dentist had obligingly mounted a heavy-duty booster transmitter into his dentures. His podiatrist had installed auxiliary battery power in the heel of one shoe and an auxiliary tagging transmitter in the heel of the other. Os' barber had added fluorescent dyes to his after-shave lotion and hair tonic, invisible under normal light and to unassisted eyes but which registered as an evanescent lavender glow when illuminated by the ultraviolet source and seen through the treated glasses worn by the prodigiously bulky man.

Os and Ada had often slipped into the masking darkness of a movie theatre but that light beamed on Os found them instantly. Twice, more from a sense of fun than from a sense of peril, Ada had silently decided to elude their shadow by changing taxis which were moving in opposite directions but the radio pill which had been substituted for his vitamins by his druggist had emitted its strong signal from Os' intestines which was picked up immediately by the tagging receivers.

As he played back the park-bench tapes F.M. Heller grew paler. It was one thing to hear Os' determination to expose the military junk and he smiled contemptuously because it was only taxpayers' money. When he heard them say they would withdraw their contributions from the party he frowned with disapproval. But when their voices and Ada's face told him that they would close all their accounts with the Everest Bank, he staggered where he was standing and reached out for a funny cigarette which had been rolled for him in the Congo at no thought to unit cost—trying to reconstitute himself through the deep shock and the sudden sense of jaggedness. He listened through all tapes and films, smoked two joints, then went into an adjoining floating glass room and called a super-insulated number in Washington. To all that foolishness about the Constitution, he had, of course, paid no attention.

Heller's distinguished phone contact in Washington said, "If that son-of-a-bitch tries to block any H-101 sale we'll nail him for subversion and throw him into a concentration camp." He did not refer to Os as an old son-of-a-bitch because he no longer considered seventy to be old.

"Do we have concentration camps?" F.M. Heller asked mildly.

"Are you kidding?"

"I suppose they're a necessary thing under certain circumstances."

"Just stick to the point, my friend. We've got a billion two hundred and seventy-eight million tied up in those crappy H-101's so Noon has to be stopped, you dig? What the hell do we have thirty-seven investigative agencies plus a Samos satellite circling at eighteen thousand miles an hour at three hundred miles up if we can't nail a son-of-a-bitch like that for subversion? What would be the sense of spending a billion nine on hundreds of high-speed computers, infrared light-beam transmitters, invading lasers, and hover-units the size of a baseball we can float anywhere he goes? What the hell is the sense of having scientific progress at all if we can't nail a shit like that for subversion?" F.M. Heller could hear the clink of ice cubes as his distinguished contact poured a little cold Scotch whiskey down his throat.

"I'd say there is at least one good reason why, Eure Spektabilitat."

"Like hell there is. Name it. Go ahead."

"He's practically Dunc Mulligan's father-in-law," F.M. Heller answered dreamily, well satisfied with his Congo investment. "Make him a subversive and we can't elect Dunc."

"Okay, wise guy. What's your solution?"

"I'm turning it over in my mind."

"While it's spinning up there, tell me this: what's with this Funky Dunc name they're spreading around in Harlem?"

"Funky is a fun word. It's good."

"We let them stay in this country. We give them jobs. We listen to their music and what do we get?—sarcasm. Brother—do I detest sarcasm. Well, I want you to go up there and tell them to stop that Funky Dunc shit. I don't like it."

"Go up where? Tell who?"

"How the hell do I know? It's your territory. Come on! How are we going to handle Noon?"

"In my opinion, Eure Spektabilitat, the key is right in that trap they are building for themselves—in that family meeting."

"How?"

"Dunc is the lawyer here. He'll have to call a meeting with their side and insist on a majority rules vote. I mean, that's what caucus is, isn't it?"

"Yeah. Then what happens?"

"Well—we win. I have the votes of the two Noon sons in my pocket. Mrs. Mulligan-Harris' brother Kaskell will vote the way she tells him to vote. There's your majority."

"Say, that's pretty good."

"Thank you, Eure Spektabilitat."

"Just take it easy around Jean-Pierre Harris. There are some things that can't be handled. Even by me."

"I am gratified to be able to tell you, Eure Spektabilitat, that we now also have him in our pocket. He'll do what he's told."

"What happened?"

"I'm still working on it. Just give me a few days."

"F.M., listen. It isn't like it was only the two hundred and thirteen H-101's at six million a rattle. We can always trade them to Israel for a little sand or something. The ballbreaker is their withdrawal of those campaign contributions. I mean, man, that's the nitty. This next election is going to cost us five hundred million, give or take ten million. That's TV alone. And this isn't a presidential year. By 'seventy-two we'll need a billion and a quarter to put over a candidate of Dunc's caliber. Make it two billion for everything. Jesus, F.M., that's more than a whole shootin' war used to cost."

Both men spoke into scrambler telephones which not only reversed all vowels and consonants but which extracted every third, fifth and ninth word in every ten-word sequence, scrambled them, then transmitted them on a separate cable. Both systems unscrambled at either end, thanks to triumphs of science in space technology which had also produced a totally heat-proof coffee pot. Each end of the telephone line was anchored in an all-glass "floating" room. F.M. Heller's was in Rockrimmon House, the other was somewhere in the Justice Department. These cost only three hundred and twelve thousand dollars a room each.

The floating room had transparent walls and furniture and ample air space between the walls which was jammed with devices for masking sound. Light was supplied through the transparent ceiling to eliminate the need for any wires. An electrically conductive radiation shield surrounded the room which, being totally transparent, defeated hiding any listening devices. The Attorney General had been able to see to it that the room was now coming off the assembly line at the rate of one hundred and thirty-four rooms a day. Science served government just as government served science.

When F.M. Heller disconnected he padded to a glass filing cabinet near his desk. He removed the Noon-Harris dossier which was zippered on all sides and was shut with a heavy lock. He chuckled with zest as he waddled to his desk chair. It was possible for him to sit only on the rim of the chair because he was so circular that if he attempted to sit back into the full seat he would be unable to get up and, inasmuch as only his thumbprint could unlock the door to the floating room, he could starve to death.

He settled down to enjoy a set of clear eight-by-ten color prints of a sixty-eight-year-old woman pleasuring and being pleasured by a man in his seventy-first year.

20

By the time they got to Ada's apartment, Os had the big editorial too much on his mind to be able to nap nicely. He put on his bed socks and Ada lowered the shades in the big bedroom but he barked in his sleep because of the way his mind was whirring and he kept waking to make notes in his tiny handwriting so that he wouldn't forget who to ask to withdraw funds from the Everest Bank, hopefully causing a run. In the end he gave up on the nap.

He showered surrounded by the twenty-one nozzles in Ada's thirty-by-thirty lavatorium which had color TV screens sunk in the wall, unguent fountains, perfume taps, antiseptic sprays and talcum-powder jets patterned after the decontamination chambers modern science had provided for people returning from the moon (although at far less a cost than the three million dollars per person of the original). As he laved, Os calculated that with his own holdings and all of Ada's companies, foundations, proxies, and tradings plus their combined certificates of deposit, Eurodollars, municipal and government bonds, that their account withdrawals would cost F.M. Heller the use of about six hundred and fifty million dollars. He cursed himself for not having been more thrifty and for not having gotten out of the market in '67.

High on his agenda was a meeting with the Attorney General simply because he could not believe that the party would seek a man of Duncan Mulligan's caliber. The entire thing must be a bid for personal power by F.M. Heller, he told himself. The glorious party which had given history Eisenhower and Nixon would not allow itself to be identified with such humiliating mediocrity—even on a senatorial level. If he did not get fullest reassurance and satisfaction from the Attorney General he vowed to take a full-page ad in *The New York Times* during the week before the state nominating convention and, if needs be, to spend heavily on a television spot campaign before the election.

He felt taller and taller with his anger. He was beginning to fall into the precise mood to write the great editorial against the H-101's. He dressed carefully as always, pressing his necktie in the special steam presser Ada allowed him to keep in the night-table drawer. He kissed Ada good-by on her cheek as she was telephoning Jean-Pierre about making the arrangements for the family conference.

Her car drove him across town. The variety of body chemicals which had been pouring into his bloodstream since he had been given the news had reached the point of overdump and he was beginning to feel feeble. Vague pains spread out toward his shoulders from the center of his chest. He took a nitroglycerin pill. He made himself remember that he was seventy years old. He wondered if he were too old to be carrying on such a strenuous love affair. Human strength and muscular coordination, he told himself, decline from age twenty-five. One's ability to hear high notes starts to fail at about eleven. And the sexual potency of men declines from the moment it is fully developed, in adolescence. He did get tired. His back did ache. He was using a lot of those sublingual pills.

Was the experience changing him? Was he evolving into something new, however late, as he had always sought? Was he a better man for the sheer selfishness of the experience with Ada—after a lifetime of picking up after Cerce? Had he changed even the way smoke changes from blue to white as it prepares to disappear? I met a woman on top of a red bus and it changed my life, he thought. I was drawn into the lives of the people in this woman's family and held in my hands for a few moments the power to change American history by the endorsement of two hundred and thirteen criminally defective fighter-bombers and a faceless man named Dunc Mulligan who the power brokers thought could be President. Had that changed him? The whole train of daydreaming put something into his mind so while they waited to inch along in the dense traffic he took up the car telephone and, reading from his little black book, gave the number of a certain Captain Pedernales in a remote town in Texas, the man who knew every pocket of national professional politics and the contents of both parties. The Bahama Beaver

Bonnet Company had made every hat the Captain had worn since the day he had come up from Texas to the Congress in 1937.

Vandalism had made it nearly impossible to make a call across Central Park but he was quickly connected with the Pedernales ranch. While he waited for the gallant Captain to ride in from the range across his great living room to take the call, Os watched three boys beat up a blind man and roll him then stroll off with his tin cup and his Seeing Eye dog. The poor fellow was calling out, "I'm blind, I'm blind," as the boys hit him. Os could not lower the window to warn the boys off because the traffic flow started and the car moved on. Then he heard the Captain's voice through the telephone all the way from Texas.

"Hello, there, Captain!" Pedernales held that honorary title because he had once been elected captain of his office bowling team during his days as a bill collector. "This is Osgood Noon up here in York State."

Captain Pedernales boomed out a cordial greeting which contained four obscenities, needing to shout to be heard over the background music of a live forty-one guitar combo strumming out "Little Joe, the Wrangler."

"Captain? I got me one question? From one ole fly swattin' heel squatter to another?"

"Shoot, ole man. You're a bone-seasoned waddie and a man tew rahd the river with. I'm tellin' yew fer true."

"Captain, have you ever heard tell of a man named Duncan Mulligan, a lawyer man the Republicans are fixin' to run for the Senate up here in York State?"

"Goddam raht. We stole ever' goddam one a their Apostle computer reports."

"What do you think of him as a candidate?"

"I say this here tew yuh—his head's so holler he's got to hold his han's to his ears to get away from the echo—but, hombre, if we could ever get him on our side we would run him an' we would win now and we would run him an' we would win for the Big Chair in seventy-two and seventy-six an' we would win then."

"I don't want you to think I jes' got a leaky mouth, Captain—I mean we ain't jes' jabbering at each other like a coupla honkers on a new food ground—but why is that? Why does every professional politician start fannin' his fat whenever the name of ole Dunc Mulligan comes up?"

"*Why?* Jeez Cry, Os, you mean you don't know why?"

"I'm calling to you because I don't know, Captain."

"But it's as plain as—" the radio telephone connection went dead. Os rattled the receiver but nothing happened. No use calling the Captain back. He would have galloped out of the house. The news that the opposition valued Mulligan as radium made him feel old again.

By the time he let himself into the flat Os was deep into a mental depression. How could the country survive an ineffectual, shallow time-server who had only his ambition to get him from day to day? Something had to be done. Some blessed sign had to be made, some beacon lighted which could guide them out of the dead, burnt, meaningless wilderness of the Duncan Mulligans. Then, almost as though his beseeching had been heard and his plea granted he heard the sound which made his spirit soar. He heard Botolf's voice calling to him, running toward him. His youngest son was home at last. It could be that they would all be saved.

Bottie came carefully through the doorway to the corridor leading from his bedroom as though the floor might be mined, as though he were insisting his frail body through interstices between deadly bacteria which were known only to him. He was a rather small boy; a throwback. He had large golden-brown eyes like Cerce's, wonderful eyes. He had deep red hair cut in a bowl-shape away from straight bangs across his forehead. His eyes conveyed his balance, the mature steadiness of someone who has found the right door and knows how to unlock it.

"Bottie!"

"Hi, Pop."

"When did you get home?"

"Oh—maybe twenty minutes ago."

"My, oh, my, how wonderful it is to have you home."

Bottie grinned. "Pretty wonderful to be here."

"For how long?"

"Long as you need me."

"Well, then—"

"You look kind of shook-up, Pop. What's wrong?"

"But you have a lot of places to go. Scotland and Australia. You have a lot of important things to do."

"I've got lots of time, Pop. Howzabout a gigantic hamburger?"

Botolf had high cheekbones, a high forehead, and a high brace on his upper teeth. He was dressed modishly but for a different time and a different continent. No winds of change had blown through this attire, safe in its timeless fashion from long before the German Kaiser had rattled his sword at Algeciras. He wore Swiss hiker's knickerbockers in West Point gray which were quite narrow and fastened just beneath the knee; long green woolen socks, and sensible ankle-high, laced hiker's boots, all of it below a green Donegal tweed safari jacket with many accordion pockets and a sound, black tie over a crisp, white shirt. He could have been voted as best-dressed in any village of the Nederwalden. They were his walking clothes. He walked to think. Thinking was his vocation just as not throwing rocks at birds had been the vocation of St. Francis d'Assisi.

Anxiety for the well-being of others hung like steam over his expression, muting the definition of self and providing a soft background for his startlingly beautiful golden-brown eyes which had the high sheen of more expensive horse chestnuts and the inner glow of good canary diamonds. The overall effect was instant sympathy. Were he not short, slender, tooth-braced, bespectacled and twenty-one years old there are those who might have smeared him as being an effete snob or, in an earlier time, a do-gooder.

He walked to Os holding up his arms. Os leaned down and Bottie put his arms around his father's neck and kissed his cheek. "You'll feel a lot better if you talk about what's upsetting you, Pop," he said.

"A friend of mine, a Mrs. Harris, gave me some Imitation Bacon Bits I'd like you to try on a hamburger," Os said. They walked toward the kitchen.

"How were things at Berkeley? See much of Governor Reagan?"

"I never did get downstate," Bottie said. "So much was happening on campus. We had Tris out there a lot. He has this contract with the State Republican Committee to stage all our riots. He sure can handle police. He had them firing buckshot into the backs of fleeing crowds and —wow—the gassings! Sometimes for no reason at all why they'd gas entire streets and acres of campus. Tris was—

as always—magnificent. And not only because he kept the police frightened. He must have gotten thirty girls pregnant in seven short weeks before he gave the signal to the governor to step in and restore order. I can't really figure it out, but girls just won't take the pill for Tris."

Os was much more than merely startled. "Thirty pregnancies? Why—that could mean thirty—or more—grandchildren. For me, that is."

"If each girl had triplets it could mean ninety grandchildren," Bottie said. "Plus those you already have."

"Already have?"

"Fifty or sixty grandchildren is nothing nowadays, Pop."

"It could run into quite an expense at Christmas. And the noise!"

"Anyway, it's just uncanny the way they will not take the pill for Tris. Gawain was on campus for a half-day. That's a long way out of his diocese."

"I don't suppose he made any grandchildren during the visit."

"They'd definitely take the pill for Gawain—if he went in for that sort of thing."

"Did you get to spend much time with him?"

"Not much. The appointments secretary had me down for seven minutes. They flew him in to bless Berkeley's new perceptrons, those parallel computers with the multi-readers which scan independently and simultaneously to make decisions by combining the gathered local and partial data linearly. Gawain conducted the entire ritual in SNOBOL 3. It was really beautiful."

"There's a box of fine Havana cigars in with the bread over there," Os said. "Tris gets them direct from the State Department." Bottie found the cigars, snipped off a fat chocolate end and lighted it for his father.

"I just can't get over the idea of the possibility of all those grandchildren."

"That's no possibility, Pop. That's a reality." Bottie put the redolent cigar between his father's fine dentures. "Tris is thirty-six and a folk hero. In a Melanesian society he would have made you a grandfather when he was twelve."

"Yes, but I would have been about twenty or thirty so I could have taken the jolt."

"What has you all shook-up, Pop?"

"There've been a lot of complications, Bots."

"How come?"

"I have this friend, a Mrs. Ada Harris. She's the one who brought in the Imitation Bacon Bits I was telling you about. Small, neat, little woman. Always wears nice little gloves. Well, almost always. Outdoors, that is."

"Always looks nice, doesn't it?"

"Sure does. Now—understand me—Mrs. Harris is no trouble. That's not where the trouble is. It's her family and the Republican National Committee."

"That is a complication."

"I am saddened to say it but I am beginning to think that the Attorney General himself is somehow involved."

Bottie stopped building the gigantic hamburgers to turn halfway to stare at his father. "No kidding?" he said softly.

"Oh, don't be alarmed. Nothing to worry about, I'm sure. As far as I know, as far as he's concerned it's just a policy matter."

"I hope so, Pop. I sure hope so. I've heard some pretty wild tales." Bottie sliced through two of the immense, round rolls, each as big as an Orson Welles beret, which his father arranged to have baked in a little shop on the rue de la Boétie in Paris every night, then jetted into Kennedy every morning where the private postal service picked them up and delivered them to his door with *The New York Times*. Most people had their bread flown in from Ireland every day and their rolls from Paris because it was the only way to get edible bread.

"Is Mrs. Harris sort of a youngish woman?" Bottie asked.

"Heavens no. I wouldn't have anyone to talk to. She's my style. About sixty-eight. And I'll tell you another thing—I'm happier than I ever was with your mother."

Botolf was pouring equal quantities of ghee and olive oil into an iron frying pan. "Have you heard from Mom?"

Os grunted. "A Father's Day card from the Hindu Kush."

"Any news?"

"It just said, 'The finest lad a young wife ever had/He made me glad by being my boys' Dad.' It was printed in Adelaide, Australia, in English and Japanese and had a color picture of bluebirds."

Somehow Bottie's frail arm managed to lift one of the great slabs of ground round steak into the hot frying pan.

He lowered the flame. "But what has you so shook-up?" he asked.

Os sighed then puffed on his cigar. "I could just say it's an outrage because it is. But I think I need help and you're the only one—outside of Mrs. Harris—I can turn to."

"Gosh, Pop, Tris would help if he weren't out on the road so much. Why, maybe even Gawain would be glad to—"

Os waved the notion away impatiently and looked irritated that Botolf could even offer to measure himself with the same string as those two. "Here's the picture, Bot. Mrs. Harris has this daughter Celeste. You ever eat any aduki, Granola, gomasio, ginseng or miso? I mean, out there at Berkeley do they go in much for nituke vegetables, brown rice or Mu tea?"

"Well, sure. I mean, what else?"

"Well, the daughter controls all of it. She has a total monopoly on anything that is yin or yang, her mother told me. Anyway, this daughter is married to a Wall Street lawyer named Duncan Mulligan. And Mulligan has been picked by the Attorney General to run for the Senate. So he's the same as elected."

"I'll say."

"Well, somebody—I have my own ideas but I won't say who just yet—decided that if Mrs. Harris and I continued to—uh—be friends it would tarnish this Mulligan's youth image. The word went out that we would have to stop seeing each other or it could cost this Mulligan the election."

"That's a pretty fine point, isn't it? I mean, I have thought for a long time that professionals and technicians can get carried away with shadings and fine points but this is really an extreme, isn't it?"

"Fine point or not, it is treading on my liberties as an equal citizen of the United States—a peer of every other citizen. Bot, I am a life-long Republican who has always been high in party councils because I never shirked about paying my way in. I am also closer to the Pentagon, because of my magazine, than the Joint Chiefs themselves. And I never heard of Duncan Mulligan. But I telephoned Captain Pedernales all the way to Texas and *he* knew about Duncan Mulligan and even got all choked up with wishing that Duncan Mulligan was the Democratic Party candidate."

Botolf turned the hamburgers in the pan, thinking hard.

"Somebody—and maybe it would be better not to say who—has ordered the Pentagon to wreck my magazine by calling the foreign office of every aggressor nation in the world to pressure them to tell their advertising agencies to cancel their schedules for the summer-weapons line issue. I tell you, Bot, I'm so hopping mad, I could just—"

Botolf faced him squarely. "Whatever it is they are trying to do to you, Pop," he said, "we are not going to allow to happen."

"Well, I'm glad you said that. Because that's exactly what I decided this morning in front of the Soldiers' and Sailors' Monument."

"What are you doing to stop them?"

"We—that is, Mrs. Ada Harris and I—and in this we'll have the help of her son, Jean-Pierre Harris—the big publisher?—have demanded that a family caucus be held. We decided that no matter what the Attorney General wants, this is a family matter and we'll have the whole family vote on it and if and when the family votes against this mockery, this denial of constitutional rights which is being attempted here, then Duncan Mulligan will have to just refuse to stand for the Senate at next month's convention."

Botolf lifted a tremendous hamburger on its huge spatula with two hands and carefully lowered it, arms trembling, upon one half of the enormous buttered rolls. He applied salt and pepper.

"Don't forget Mrs. Harris' Imitation Bacon Bits," Os said.

Bottie sprinkled the bacon bits across the top of the braised meat then shook out caraway seeds upon the butter spread across the top half of the roll. He closed the sandwich. He prepared the second while his father watched him with total attention. Bottie uncorked a bottle of Clos Vougeot '61 and rolled some of it redly into a Baccarat jelly glass. He cut the sandwiches into four huge parts, moved the food and the wine within his father's reach then sat down, bit into one of the parts and chewed, moaning his ecstasy. Flushed with proof in either hand that he was really home again, he asked, "What will be the make-up of the caucus?"

Both men were now intent upon the subject, sharing an

intelligence which had ranged along different trails, seeking different game, but which was now suddenly fused into the entity it had always been. They combined what they felt and hesitated with an unspoken knowledge and confidence that the sum of that intelligence was greater than that of the parts. It was an ancient strength which had slowly been forgotten across the nation: the Family at work. The Family, combining its cunning and its guile, the wisdom of both plus the strength of the younger and the wiliness of the older: the Family against the outside world.

"I think the caucus will balance out in our favor," Os said. "Mrs. Harris and I both have three children so that's six votes in all. We won't vote, of course, and Duncan Mulligan won't either."

"Just because it looks even doesn't make it even, does it, Pop?"

"Where's the flaw, Bot?"

"I meant—just because you have three sons, it doesn't *have* to follow that they will vote for you. There could be considerations."

"How do you think Gawain will vote?"

"Well, Gawain looks to go far in the church, Pop. And we all know how close the church is to the Attorney General."

"How about Tris?"

"Tris is under contract to the Department of Justice so the Attorney General can enforce law and order, but Tris is different from Gawain. I mean Tris does have feelings. I think Tris will vote with us."

"Then you don't think I made a mistake in forcing this caucus?"

"Depends on the other side. I think we have two votes. We'd need one more for a deadlock."

"All right! That's fine, then. Mrs. Harris' son Jean-Pierre will vote our way. The daughter, Celeste, will naturally vote for her husband and her brother, Kaskell, will vote the way she votes."

"Has Duncan Mulligan agreed to a set of caucus rules? That if there's a deadlock no decisions can be taken?"

"Not yet. The son, Jean-Pierre, is making all those arrangements."

"I think it would be better if I made as many of the

rules for the caucus as possible. I think I should meet with Mr. Mulligan and we should thrash the whole thing out."

"I can't think of anything better for our side if you will handle it, Bottie."

"Well, it has to be done. We have to have rules or there can be no fixed result. You can't do it, Pop. You're the plaintiff, as it were. Sure, I'll be happy to do it. If I don't they're going to put you out of business, Pop."

Os snorted. "We'll just see about that."

"There are a lot of ways to put a man out of business," Bottie said somberly. "I mean a certain somebody who has Tris under contract could sure send a mob into your offices and presses and just trash everything."

"You think Tris would do that?"

"Let's face it, Pop. His whole integrity would be at stake. He's got to treat his contacts and his contracts impartially. He can't very well refuse a job which is identical with a hundred other jobs just because it involves his father."

"You're right, of course."

"I can see some theoretical dangers within this caucus."

"But—"

"If they could lobby within the caucus—say they could lobby with Tris and swing his vote—just theoretically, of course—they could then vote to have you and Mrs. Harris committed to separate mental institutions. Just to keep you apart through the elections."

"Separate?"

"Well—does your—uh—does Mrs. Harris have grandchildren?" he asked politely. Knowing she was in her sixty-ninth year, and probably did, Bottie did not like to be rude in any way, his courtesy inherited from his father.

"Yes, three lovely grandchildren."

"Then I think it may be wisest to insist that Mrs. Harris' grandchildren attend and have the right to vote."

"In fact, I'm told two of them are very beautiful twin girls. You might like to take in a movie with them."

"If we could vote grandchildren I could get proxies from all your grandchildren through Tris and we could swamp Mr. Mulligan if anything began to go wrong."

"This spontaneous grandchild idea is a dazing thing."

"But we must hold down on the briefs. Mr. Mulligan should present his own case. That's fair. Then Jean-Pierre should speak for his mother and I should speak for you. But it would be a good idea if, before the caucus, I could meet everyone concerned. Can Mrs. Harris arrange that? I mean, like starting with Mrs. Harris herself?"

21

Os left Bottie chewing and sipping. Happily, he strode to the telephone to convey all the great news to Ada who said she would immediately set everything with Jean-Pierre just the way Botolf had outlined it and that she could not wait to meet Botolf.

Jean-Pierre was at his office, even though it was Saturday afternoon, because of an overflow of work due to mounting a coast-to-coast retail special called Comfort-Cooze, described on his window streamers and counter cards as "that tantalizing biocosmetic for promoting male genital growth—help him by rubbing in a *lot* of reassurance."

Jean-Pierre was made grim over the interruption but he agreed to everything Ada asked. In his organized way he made one taut call to Celeste to delegate the invitations to the caucus to her, snarling that it would be held at his apartment at eight o'clock Friday night and that she was to deliver her husband, her children, her brother and her nephew.

"Don't screw this up, Celeste, you hear?" He slammed down the receiver and went back to work.

Celeste's spirits soared. She called F.M. Heller immediately so he could explain it all slowly to Dunc. "F.M.? I think I've finally got this disciplined. I had a meeting with my brothers and told them what to do and my brother, Jean-Pierre, has arranged a dinner party at his place Friday night. They are willing to capitulate. They want to caucus. They'll do whatever the majority vote says. Isn't that marvelous?"

"Well! The Attorney General is going to want to know about that."

"Yes. By all means. But be sure to tell Dunc."

"Oh, I'll tell Dunc."

"Jean-Pierre has it all arranged for Dunc to talk for our side, then we'll all vote. And Dunc is such a wonderful speaker. Isn't that sheer heaven?"

"I am greatly pleased, Mrs. Mulligan-Harris. Entirely pleased."

Almost the moment Celeste hung up, her telephone rang again. It was Jean-Pierre made horrible with rage that he had to waste even more time. "Listen," he said savagely, "Noon's kid wants to meet everyone in our family before the caucus. He'll call you. And you make sure the twins are there, you hear?"

Jean-Pierre slammed the phone down, but Celeste kept babbling in reaction into hers just as though he were still there. "The *twins?* Why the twins? What does he want to talk to the twins for? Who is he? *What* Noon kid? Tell me why he has to see the twins. Why?"

She got no answer so she rattled the phone. She hung up and gripped her forehead. How could such elation be turned into terror? She paced like a panda. If a strange man came, she reasoned closely, pretending he wanted to talk to the twins, Mona and Fiona would lay him right on the floor of the foyer and scandalize the servants again. She didn't know where to turn. Servants were impossible to get. Was she suddenly supposed to learn how to cook and make beds at forty, for God's sake? A Senator's wife? A very, very possible First Lady of the land?

The telephone rang for the third time. She snatched it up hoping it was Jean-Pierre again to say that he had only been kidding about the man wanting to meet the twins. Instead, she heard a heavy, thrilling textrous voice from the far, far past. The voice had a ten-ton Thuringian accent. Her back began to arch almost at the first syllable as she stood erect and her vagina began a heroic quiffling and quiffling and quiffling.

"Halloa? Here is Franco Gudelmann."

"Herr *Gud*elmann!" The room seemed to whirl. She grasped the edge of the table just in time to keep her feet. "Yes! Where are you?"

"I am calling to make of you a zimple request."

"*Any*thing! Tell me! Say it!"

"You will do it? What I say?"

She moaned like a stepped-on accordion. "*Any*thing!"

"I want you to receive a young friend of mine."

"Re*ceive?*"

"*Ja.* You must do for him whatever he asks."

"Herr Gudelmann, where are you?"

"Und he will need to talk to your daughters—alone."

"You don't realize what you are asking."

"You must (muzzzt) grant this."

"Oh, my God, my *God!*"

"You must not deny me."

"I cannot deny you *any*thing! Herr Gudelmann! Where are you? When will you be here? Come before four. Today is Duncan's early day."

"You will zee mein freund? Und the daughters?"

"Yes! But when will I see—?" she gasped sharply at the formidable image that the verb *see* conveyed to her where Herr Gudelmann was concerned "—you? Today? This afternoon?"

"Not at all possible, dear lady. I am in Nuremberg. In Germany." None of that stayed with her because it was all erased when he said, "I miss you, dear lady. I think of you often." He disconnected. Celeste rattled the telephone. "Herr Gudelmann!" She leaned in despair upon the telephone and, magically, it rang again. She snatched it up. A sweet, nearly-flute-like voice soothed her. "Good afternoon, Mrs. Mulligan. I look forward greatly to meeting you, and your mother most kindly volunteered to prepare the way."

"Yes! He just told me. How wonderful of you to want to come to me. You sound so young. Can you come right now? That is—can you visit me right now?"

"Would ten minutes be all right? Ah, splendid. Thank you." Celeste dropped the telephone into its cradle, rushed off to don something more suitable, to brush and oil her parts and to hell with what the servants would think if anything happened in the entrance foyer. She was determined with iron will that the twins must be gotten out of the house and safely to her husband's office even if she had to give them a new helicopter to do it.

22

Bottie had lunched with Ada on Saturday. Os had been in middle-nap when she had called back to tell that she had confirmed everything with Jean-Pierre and they had both decided it would be best not to wake him. Bottie changed into a midnight-blue version of the same hiking suit and plastered his hair down with a protein-packed hair tonic.

Ada greeted him warmly. They sat in her study drinking Coke, which she felt she should offer to a boy his age, and smoking marijuana. He complimented her on the quality of the grass. She complimented him by saying that he looked the way his father must have looked when he had been a young man. Bottie thanked her gravely.

"How did it happen that your parents called you Botolf?" she asked. "It's such an un*us*ual name."

"Well—I was conceived in Boston, Mrs. Harris and—"

"Ada."

"Thank you. I was conceived in Boston and the name Boston, as you know is, after all, just a shortening of St. Botolf's Stone."

"I see. Did your mother think of that?"

"Yes."

"Alban used to be the name for Scotland. I was born in Albany, New York, yet no one has ever called me Scotty." She smiled at him dazzlingly. "Now, tell me about yourself, Botolf. What do you enjoy doing—what are your interests?"

"I like girls very much. And I enjoy—oh—the decisions taken by the instincts of life—such as red deer or the vole *Microtus agrestis;* or city rats or lepidopterons."

"And people generally? Beyond girls, that is?"

"Oh, yes. People and their extraordinary concepts of free will."

"Yes. Instincts are best. Until the time comes to move on—then free will should come into play."

"A free-style form is best, perhaps. When life is calculated—well, we get things such as—oh—politicians."

"A Vice-President of the United States—some time ago—chased me through the corridors of the Brown Palace Hotel in Denver but no matter how much I seemed to tire the Secret Service wouldn't let him catch me," she sighed. "But regret is only worry about the past." She smiled at him. "Your father told me that you are going to help us."

"In any way I can."

"We'll need help, Botolf. The whole city has turned into Verona for me and the Attorney General is head of the house of Capulet whom I shall defy."

"Where I come from we've been defying the Attorney General for some time."

"One has to be especially careful of those people," Ada said. "First they make a little money, by hook or by crook, then they think they can do just about anything. They plot, they spend to get their messenger elected and all at once we hear them saying, 'Justice is merely incidental to order' and 'This country is going so far right you're not even going to recognize it.' And the Attorney General is so old-fashioned about caring what makes people feel badly. He will not say *Negro* or *black,* he must say *darkies.* The way he speaks, the way he acts, the speeches he writes for our Neanderthal Vice-President, the lies he must tell that poor man in the White House who hasn't a clue, all say plainly that he is determined that the federal government is not going to enforce the federal law."

"I hadn't exactly thought I'd start helping you at that end of the problem, Mrs. Harris—uh—Ada."

"No, no. I didn't mean that. Besides, I think you've solved the whole thing with your idea of a deadlock."

"But—we can't be sure of a deadlock."

"Why not?"

"Well—suppose Tris broke his leg. Then the vote would go three to two against you."

"Hardly likely. Not from the photographs I've seen of your brother."

"As I understand it—and my father might have *mis*-understood—your daughter Celeste is really two votes. I mean she does have a strong influence over your son, Kaskell."

"I would rather not talk about it."

"But she does mean two votes?"

"Yes."

"Then—this may seem an unnatural thing to say—but is she irrevocably committed to her husband's candidacy? Can we reach her?"

"No."

"There must be a way. I am not even remotely implying that everyone has his price but—well, for example—psychological tests show that many women place inordinate value upon their first love."

"Why not? They were younger then than now."

"If your daughter *were* in that group—that is, if she did place inordinate value on whoever was her first love—and if we knew who that might be—well, I am merely wondering, if we had such a person intercede for us perhaps that would rather load things in our favor."

"You are a very shrewd young man."

"I really don't think so. This is just textbook stuff."

"Celeste may be forty years old but I happen to know who her first love was because I bought him for her."

"Pardon?"

"I know. It sounds crazy. But she was a deeply disturbed young girl. She was so crazy about men she couldn't eat. I mean, I said to Arthur, my husband, this isn't normal. Well, what could he do? He was a businessman. But we had gone to Europe a lot and I had had a lot of time on my hands and a long time ago I ran into a man in Germany, he was a professional sort of sexual stunt man, named Franco Gudelmann. A monster but reliable. He still does a terrific business with the jet people, you know, sometimes people like it when sex is all rehearsed—you know, like kinky sex—with a big script. So Arthur had union connections and we set Gudelmann as a waiter on this ship Celeste would be crossing on—it was the *Reina Gertrudis* of the old Radin Line—and I won't bore you with the details but she fell in love with him. Her first love."

"Well!"

"Exactly."

"But can you find him?"

"I think he is handled now by either Avis or Hertz in Germany."

"I think that's marvelous. I think that's our solution. If you will call him and ask him to call Celeste as a very special favor then I think she might receive me with an entirely open mind."

"Consider it done. And while I am doing it how's about having the kitchen run you up a little snack?"

"Why—thanks. Thanks very much."

"A hamburger?"

"Gosh, that would be great."

"How do you like it?"

"If they fry it, and fried meat results in excellent vitamin retention—and if the triglycerides are cooked at about one hundred and forty-nine degrees centigrade—low and slow but sure—in a mixture of clarified butter and vegetable oil with the adjacent protein molecules joined together by side-chain hydrogen bonds to lessen shrinkage, that will be just fine."

"Right. I'll tell them." Ada started to move out.

"However, if they will be griddling the meat, please ask if they will maintain an even one hundred and seventy degrees centigrade and please not to press the meat while griddling. Just cook it until there is an ooze on top, then turn it."

"Okay. They'll handle it." He called her at the door.

"That would be for a sixty-gram hamburger but if they could go to a hundred and twenty grams, because I am ravenous, perhaps it would be best—to my taste at least—to drop to one hundred and sixty-three degrees centigrade. That will give them an internal meat temperature of about sixty centigrade."

"*About?*"

"Well, sixty-five degrees should give us a pinkish brown but by dropping to sixty we'll get a pinker tone—taking the internal temperature carry-over from stove to table to mouth into account."

"I see. Now—would you like French fries? Just answer yes or no."

"It really isn't a yes or no question, Ada. Potatoes lose fifty per cent of their vitamin C when fried and whereas freshly peeled and sliced potatoes absorb nine percent of fat, the pre-blanched frozen potatoes absorb up to twenty percent fat. Therefore, if possible, I'd recommend fresh, unfrozen potatoes because they'll have fewer calories."

"Ice cream?"

Bottie nodded happily.

23

That afternoon Bottie threw his arms around his brother, Tristram, and talking animatedly, went with him up the broad spiral staircase to the overzealously modern room which looked down Manhattan Island to the garbage-filled sea. Tris' expensive tooth caps glowed and the pupils of his eyes were so dilated that any poet mounted upon an albatross could have taken days to fly across them. The atmosphere hung in black shrouds just outside the window and they could look down upon the cross-hatches of streets to see hundreds upon hundreds of thousands of automobiles and army tanks locked into a stasis which, from that height, never seemed to move while horns brayed hysterically.

Tris was real loose. He conserved energy by falling backward into a beige leather sack chair, pushed a box of joints at Bottie and asked consecutively for thirty-six girls on the Berkeley campus only four of them being known to Bottie.

"Gosh, did you ball her, too?" Bottie said at one juncture, his eyes popping with admiration.

"I had a real nice note from her yesterday morning," Tris said. "The X-ray shows that she's going to have twins. God, I love kids."

"I'll say you do."

"You going to Australia?"

"Well, eventually."

"I thought you had it all set for like in two weeks."

"I can't. Pop is in trouble."

"Come on! I was with him just a few nights ago. I almost beat him at pool. He would have told me if he was in any trouble."

"He didn't have to tell you. You told him."

"Oh—that."

"Yes."

"Bottie, that's just a bidnizz misunderstanding."

"You pronounced it *bidnizz*."

"How else?"

"That's Mafia pronunciation."

"Well? What other kind of bidnizz is there? Anyway, a little misunderstanding isn't trouble."

"They'll wreck his whole company if he doesn't go along. They'll break his heart if they can."

Tris shrugged. "Like that they make a living."

"You're going to let it happen?"

"I didn't say that."

"Why did you pass it along, Tris?"

"Baby, the man's a big client."

"Suppose he wants Pop roughed up?"

"Well, if they want it, somebody's going to do it, right? Better if I do it so he doesn't get really hurt." Tris ran both hands through his hair and looked away, out at the floating garbage, with sudden embarrassment. "I mean, you've got to see it my way, too. I have nine separate federal contracts. And I have Minutemen and Weathermen and Kluxers on my back screaming for action. And I have to handle the hard hats and the longshoremen or where is your silent majority? I mean—I've got six of my top people under indictment. I've got twenty-eight of my people underground, but I mean for real. That takes bread, baby, and there ain't no flip side."

He lit up and drew the smoke into himself elaborately. "What do you want me to do?"

"Support Pop."

"Botto! You weren't hearing me. For what? To get all the muscle in the administration sore when all Pop has to do is take a slow boat out with that old broad and cool it until next year?"

"Okay. You won't support Pop. How about Gawain?"

Tris shrugged. "Who knows? Gawain lives on a different street."

"We're going to caucus both families on Friday night at eight o'clock at Jean-Pierre Harris' apartment. Okay?"

"Why not?"

"You'll be there?"

"Sure."

"Everybody will vote and Pop has agreed that whatever the majority decides he'll do. I'd like to know how you'll vote."

"We—how should I vote? If we all vote against him he

just takes a cruise. If we all vote for him—and I'm telling you this from the inside, Bottie—he just may get hit."

"Don't you love Pop?"

"Botto, that's what I'm saying! I just told you. We have to save him."

"He doesn't want to be saved like that."

"What do you mean?"

"What kind of a man do you think Pop is? He saved you. He raised you. What would have happened to us if Pop just shrugged us off the way Mom did?"

"Mom has no place in this or anywhere else."

"I thought you knew Pop was a proud man—a man who puts value on dignity. What do you understand? Women? All right. This is a man and a woman thing. Suppose somewhere on this earth there was a woman you, Tris Noon, wanted to keep. Okay? You got it? All right. Would you slope off and leave her just because a lot of strangers took a vote on it? Like hell. Or would you do it just to save yourself a beating? Or even getting hit? Like hell."

"Yeah. Okay. I dig."

"How are you going to vote?"

"For Pop."

"Thanks, Tris."

"I think I would have figured it out myself, maybe."

"How will Gawain vote?"

"Gawain hates Pop just the way he hates everybody else who didn't happen to be born a machine."

"We have to deliver Gawain to win. I don't trust a deadlock. We need a clean win."

"Forget it. As they go, so goes Gawain."

"No."

Tris shrugged. "Then you ask him."

"I will."

"Anyway you'll do better with Gawain than I would. He says he hates force and I'm force." He leaned over and flipped a switch to get some old-time yerba buena St. Louis piano music going on the tape machine.

"I have to talk to him."

"Well, sure. Like I said."

"It's just that I have seven people to talk to between now and Friday and they're all rocks like Gawain."

"Then assign some to me. You take Gawain and give

me some of the others. Tell me what to say and I'll work them over."

"That would be a big help, Tris."

"Well, great. I'm glad to help. You just tell me where to go and I go."

24

Bottie sat across a wide library table from Dunc Mulligan whose blue-black underbeard seemed to glow luminescently out of his pale face. Bottie's Swiss hiker's suit matched the uniformly green bindings of the law books which rose from floor to ceiling on shelves all around them. The books were not merely green, they were the special green of thousand-dollar bills, the ethic of law practice. It was a splendid room for anyone who could not read. As the two men chatted, a tape recorder concealed under the table top turned, stopping and starting with the sounds of their voices. The table was so highly polished that the fleshly people seemed like dim reflections; the reflections the brisk, living things.

Bottie's eyes under his rust-red bowl of hair remained wide and innocent of guile as he stared most respectfully at Duncan. Dunc massaged the tips of some of his fingers with the tips of other fingers and, flabbergasted that anyone, no matter what his age, should openly respect him, spoke in a deep-toned booming mockery of his own voice. "And I would like to make one thing clear," he said. "I regard it as altogether unseemly for a man who is about to be nominated and elected to the Senate of the United States of America to be asked to negotiate his options in that area with a twenty-one-year-old boy."

"I am in my twenty-second year, sir."

"I grant that. However and notwithstanding—and I pronounce this in a kindly and impartial way—I find—and we must tell it true and clear, boy—that I am being told by this young man who comes directly to me from one of the truly violent campuses of America—this young man who has just barely reached his majority, that there may be no discussion of conditions which I have found to be objectionable regarding the caucus to be held in the home of my own brother-in-law on Friday evening next at eight o'clock."

Bottie stayed within the *querencia* he had chosen: within

the two basic positions of the negotiator. He knew what he wanted; he ignored what his opposition wanted. He loaded his proposals with impossible conditions and would allow his adversary to tire himself fighting these. He remained silent excepting when he needed to push a pawn.

"You are telling me," Duncan was saying in his strange preparatory-school accent which virtually strangled the vowels far back in his head behind his ultimate molars, "that all discussions at that caucus will be strictly limited to three set briefs—two of which are to be delivered by advocates who favor Mrs. Harris' position—both of which to follow my own address. Is that correct?"

Bottie nodded.

"Let me make one thing clear so that I may make another thing absolutely clear, *jawohl?* Am I also instructed by you, a *stu*dent, that is a *boy* who was a part of a rabble of bums just a week ago—that my campaign manager, one of the most distinguished bankers in this country—and therefore the world—a man who is my most *trust*ed adviser, a man who has objected violently to these demands you are making but who unfortunately was called to Washington, transported by Air Force jet plane sent for him and him alone, for an intimate conclave with the Attorney General, personally, will not be permitted to be present at that caucus to protect my best interests?"

Bottie nodded.

"Well, then—if things are going to be purposely loaded against me, let me make one thing perfectly clear—in the form of a direct question—why are we to have any briefs presented at all?"

"Splendid."

"Splendid what?"

"That would be fine with my father. He would much rather have this whole thing settled by the American Arbitration Association."

"But—that would take months!"

"Of course."

"That would take *many* months."

"Correct."

"But the nominating convention is literally upon us! I say to you, man to man, eye to eye, calling a spade a spade, cards on the table in an effort to make everything absolutely clear—I have never negotiated with anyone as unreasonable as you. I ask you straight out—directly—why should I bother to attend this caucus at all?"

"There is nothing in my father's intentions which forces you to attend the caucus, counselor. We will vote whether you choose to attend or not—and most certainly advise you of the result by registered mail."

"This is very high-handed. I would say that these are star-chamber proceedings. I suppose next you will be charging me with threatening your father?"

"Do you wish me to charge you directly?"

"I don't understand."

"You have just inquired as to whether I am going to charge you with threatening my father. I have asked you, in my turn, whether you wish me to seek legal counsel and to have counsel bring legal charges of that nature against you, seeking damages and injunction. Is that what you wish?"

"No! If you please—I wish nothing of the kind. I am at the eve of a political nominating convention for a place in the United States Senate."

"Then why did you say—and I quote you directly—quote: I suppose next you will be charging me with threatening your father?"

"It was a stance, simply a negotiating stance."

"I see. Well to clear up that point—I do charge you with threatening my father and if it continues I shall see that suit is brought to enjoin such threats, before the nominating convention sits."

"I have to remark that the atmosphere has become most unfriendly."

"Yes. And not only are you threatening my father, you are threatening your wife's mother simultaneously. I remind you that by so doing, you are threatening the mother of Jean-Pierre Harris, a very sentimental man."

Duncan's retreat from the issue he had brought up was almost visible. The Mafia was about the most prestigious client Lantz, Lantz, Tolliver & Farr possessed, advising it entirely on its investments in tax-free municipal bonds. "I wish to withdraw my proferred negotiating stance," he said.

"I am not sure that I can accept that, counselor. I will need to discuss it with my father."

"My dear young man—please—be reasonable! We are meeting to settle a grievous issue. Perhaps an historic issue. You spoke of arbitration being acceptable to your father. Under arbitration would you be allowed to present two briefs to my one?" Dunc was sweating in the finest air conditioning money could buy and, as always happened to him when he was under pressure, his eyes flickered endlessly from side to side. The sweating made him smell slightly funky, the darting eyes made him seem evasively tricky. "For God's sake, boy—you've got to make concessions!"

"Very well. If my father agrees, we will accept that only two briefs be presented—yours and mine. But that is the single concession I can make because its size is out of all proportion to the threats you and your agents have been making against my father and Mrs. Harris."

"But the chance of deadlock! What if there is a hung jury?"

"I cannot discuss that until we have defined what is to be the verdict of such a jury, the consequences of the caucus—the punishment to be meted out to my father and Mrs. Harris."

"I wish you would not think of it as punishment."

"Would you prefer the word—sentence?"

"No, no! *Mis*ter Noon—the entire purpose of this caucus is to settle whether or not your father and Mrs. Harris are to continue being—being—uh—together—because our side feels that as they coexist, they are a threat to my candidacy. Therefore, if the caucus votes against them they must agree to separate. If they would regard that as punishment I would regard it as justice."

"How long would they be required to stay separate?"

"Oh—ten or fifteen years."

"No."

"Come, come, Mr. Noon. There must be a maximum penalty here. My wife insists on it."

"We will accept limited exile—but together not separately. Until the fifteenth of January nineteen seventy-two. At your expense."

"At *my* expense? My mother-in-law is a billionaire!"

"Then at the expense of the Republican National Committee. We don't care."

"If I agree to those terms will you agree in the matter of a hung jury?"

"I'll have to discuss that with my father. He may, instead, decide to oppose your nomination."

"How?"

"He and Mrs. Harris are willing to spend five million dollars on TV spot announcements to secure the nomination for Mrs. Harris."

"That would be terrible. You simply cannot mean it!"

"Some of the finest minds in the marketplace are at work right now on her acceptance speech."

"The Attorney General will never stand for it."

"Five million dollars can be very persuasive, Mr. Mulligan."

"You cannot talk about sums like five million dollars for a state nominating convention. Where would it all end, Mr. Noon? Extend that principal to fifty states and multiply it by the numbers of candidates and such a thing could run into billions—and all before the costs of real campaigning begin. We can afford it in New York, yes. But what about poor little Rhode Island?"

"Politics evolve, counselor. In time it could mean that Mr. Rockefeller will be Senator from the East, Mr. Henry Ford, Senator from the North, Mr. Haralmar Hunt, Senator from the South and Mr. Norton Simon, Senator from the West. Four senators should be enough for this country considering how much those men will have to spend to be elected. After all we have only one President and no one has ever been able to count what that costs."

Duncan opened the briefcase in his flap and began to fondle his rubber evening dress nervously.

"But what do you *want,* Mr. Noon?" he asked piteously. "If you will only speak up and tell me what you want, I know we can reach an understanding."

"Two briefs—no other discussion of the issues?"

"Yes, yes."

"Your campaign manager may attend the caucus."

"Oh, thank you!"

"But he may not vote."

"Of course not."

"Entirely at their option, either my father or Mrs. Harris may address the caucus."

"Perfectly all right."

"There is the matter of a hung jury."

"My God, yes."

"In the event of a tie, or in the event of the absence of any member of the caucus, votes may be cast by grandchildren on either side. In person or by proxies. I think that covers everything."

The library door opened a crack. A sweet voice said softly, "Daddy?"

Duncan turned toward the door. "Yes?" he said, "I am very busy, girls."

The door opened wider and two of the most beautiful girls Bottie had ever seen came into the law library. They were identical with each other in every delicious way: cherry lips, skin like peaches, eyes like uncrusted huckleberry pies, creamy throats and honey-colored hair. They wore soft-green silk print dresses, heavy amber bead necklaces over incredibly exciting bosoms and had permanent expressions which were so moving that Botolf fell into a form of Cheyne-Stokes breathing.

One of these spoke. "It's F.M. Heller, Daddy. He's calling from Washington."

Duncan scrambled to his feet, buckling his briefcase closed. He was embarrassed that the firm had allowed him no telephone in the law library and that he would have to go out to a pay phone booth in the corridor near the elevator to take the call. He thanked his daughters and excused himself to Botolf. He said, "Uh—in that case—uh—Mr. Noon these are my twin daughters, Mona and Fiona." He hurried out through a parting of the girls. Fiona closed the door and locked it. The girls walked to Bottie and sat on either side of him. He seemed somewhat dazed. Mona opened her purse while Fiona sat and adored him. Mona took a small white card out of her purse and gave it to Botolf. He read the engraved message upon it several times. It said: "We like you very much. We are clean. Let's fuck."

25

Herr Gudelmann's voice had inflamed Celeste even beyond the motorized penis which had been developed by Dr. Bryson. She had convinced herself that Herr Gudelmann must be in New York, that he couldn't have called all the way from Germany just to ask her to "see" a friend. She could not stop quiffling. She knew that when the doorbell rang he would be standing there behind that enormous fixture, that living *presence* which flexed itself within his trousers; ready, always humbly ready. Then a flash of shock went through her. Twenty years had gone by since he had taken her into sleep therapy. Therefore he would be twenty years older and that great encrusted hawser which was a part of him and yet a separate entity would have become twenty years older too. She was struck a glancing blow by the irony that it would now be older even than Osgood Noon to whom she so objected sexually.

Perhaps then he had really called her from Germany to lay at her feet his natural successor. Perhaps a miraculous graft had been performed and, in his age, Herr Gudelmann had sold, or traded, or lost at poker, his fateful, knuckled and fluted, lunging, self-motivated tentacle to this then undeniably wonderful young man. He would be a beautiful man—which even Herr Gudelmann had not been—about thirty-five years old—not a boy, she couldn't have faced having to talk to a boy between times but of course if Herr Gudelmann's genius had been grafted on there would be no between times, except when they stopped for meals. She quiffled vastly, everything vibrating and opening out, out, out like sound waves from a great Cuban trumpet blown in the Howe Caverns.

The doorbell rang!

Celeste had to hold on to Duncan's electric bicycle while she shuddered blindly through a spontaneous orgasm.

The doorbell rang insistently; *penetratingly*.

She moved like a yard and a half of steam toward the

front door, feebly waving servants away. Where could she let him take her? Where could they go? There wouldn't be time for any sleep cure because she had to go to that damned caucus Friday night. She silently blessed Dr. Bryson. Working with him under those sure, deft fingers and that wonderful machine three times a week for so many years had relieved her of some of her inhibitions about sex. She could do it without the sleep cure and without the mantle of benign philanthropy through medical research. She could just lie down and do it! She just knew she could.

The doorbell rang again.

In a flash of total realization, sort of a flash of insight which told her that she could have been (slightly) deluding herself all through her past attitudes to sex, she knew all at once that *she had already done it!* She realized that Duncan had not really hypnotized her as he sat there in that silly, tawdry rubber dress. Not for years! If ever! Why even his efforts at hypnosis had been so cursory as to have been almost nonexistent. She had to get laid and she had needed it so much that she had really convinced herself. All Dunc had done had been to say like "Okay. You will fall asleep. All righty. You are under my spell." Just like that. She had not been under hypnosis at all. How vulgar!

The doorbell rang for the third time. Or was it the fourth time?

She wasn't frightened any more. She even felt that perhaps she was beginning to understand her mother. Thank God the twins were out. They were so much quicker than she and there were two of them. The moment they spotted that giant trunk under those reinforced trousers they would dart in for the kill, shrieking like harpies and pull him off her and try to wedge themselves under him. Damn Women's Lib! What had happened to young America?

Her hand touched the door latch. She had dressed in a natural silk skirt over nothing, a pair of backless scuffs, and a pink silk shirt with enormous polka dots. The skirt had an oiled zipper. The blouse was slashed to the belly with a floppy bowknot. She could be out of all of it in 2.4 seconds by time trials. But it was all so unbalancing! It was as though she had come running upon a marble floor covered with roller skates. She felt an exulting sense of detonation because of the realization that she could actually, factually fuck anyone she chose to in the whole wide world and not feel one little pang. She wanted explosions of orgasms which were wider and deeper and longer and thicker than any her mother had ever had; explosions of orgasms which could bring walls down and buildings on top of walls and cities on top of buildings and countries on top of cities until the whole planet she had never asked to visit was rubbled ruin made by her orgasms. It was her only natural terminus. The world could not go on living the way it lived, the way it had taught her to live. Because everyone lived the way they lived—fucking anybody and everybody wantonly and freely—they deserved to die. So she would demolish all of them and all of it—every unfeeling, brutalizing millimeter of all of it exploded to the center of the sun from the center of her being, the only place remaining where she knew she could feel anything.

She threw open the door, her eyes more than slightly insane and smiled her brilliant smile of attrition into the twenty-thousand-times televised face of Tristram Noon.

"Who are you?" she screamed.

26

Mona and Fiona pleaded with Bottie to be allowed to ride with him to the Norton Travel Agency for his meeting with their Uncle Kaskell.

"Say no if you want to," Mona told him, "but we'll follow your Bottie odor."

"We have our own cab which we bought with our allowance," Fiona said.

"We use it for following men. Mr. O'Connell is a very expert driver."

"Baby, *why* won't you ball us?" Fiona pleaded for the third time since they had made their engraved offer in Daddy's law library.

Botolf wasn't a cruel young man. He allowed them to invite him to ride in their taxi and accepted the offer.

"No one has ever turned us down," Mona said. "I was only kidding about having the cab to follow men. We have the cab because it's the only way we can get a cab. We hand men the little card and, man, they drop their pants then and there."

"We know you're not a fruit because you always have a hard-on," Fiona said. "I could hang my bra on it."

Bottie took a deep, deep breath and exhaled slowly. "Now hear this," he said with a shaky voice. "Someday —when this caucus we are facing is over—and possibly before I leave for Scotland for my hour with V.C. Wynne-Edwards, my hero, we will have a long talk about this. Remove your hand, please, Mona. Thank you."

"Don't break your heart over that caucus, Botsie. They are set to clobber Ada."

"That fat fink, F.M. Heller, is in Washington right now trying to get a *lettre de cachet* out of the Attorney General so he can slam your father and Ada legally into some basement somewhere."

"We will see about the caucus. You will be there and so will your cousin, Sylvan."

"How can Esau go? He's in the Tombs."

"He set off a bomb in Maxwell's Plum because they wouldn't give him a table," Mona said.

"We went to the Tombs to see him," Fiona said. "He is ecstatic for the first time in his life. He's like a big, hairy, smelly bride. He said he's been raped fifty-three times so far and that was only up to last Friday."

"He told us that if justice wasn't done and he was somehow acquitted he is going to have to do something so wild that they will have to send him to Mattawan where they keep all those big hairy crazies."

"His knuckles are all smashed from pretending to try to defend himself because the fellows only really get turned on when they have to fight for it," Fiona said.

"Esau isn't one of your where's-my-lipstick fags," Mona told him proudly.

"Esau is a fighting bull fag," Fiona said. "A Miura fag even."

"Will you *please* stop this continual prattling?" Botolf demanded. "I have to think about this meeting I'm going into."

"*Think?*" both girls said at once. "About a meeting with Uncle *Kas*kie?"

"It's no good, Botsie. I mean like it won't wash. Whatever he agrees to while you're there he'll change the second you leave. He hates everybody and everything except like obscenities."

"Like talking dirty to whoever answers on direct dialing," Mona explained.

"Esau is like Lord Baden-Powell compared with his father."

"Uncle Kaskie makes both the Jukes and the Kallikaks seem like the nobility," Mona said.

The cab stopped in front of the Norton Travel Agency. "It was awfully nice meeting you girls," Bottie said as he climbed out of the cab. "I'll look forward to seeing you again at the caucus."

"Oh, we'll be right here when you come out," Mona said.

"You are the only time in our life we've ever been in love," Fiona said smiling as her eyes got all misty.

"We love you so much," Mona said.

"Now just a gosh-darned minute here!" Bottie said. He slammed the cab door and strode rapidly into the building.

A receptionist wearing a see-through blouse took his name avidly. Devouring him with her eyes, as she had been trained to do as the travel-agency routine, she called Mr. Harris' office, then regretfully sent Bottie in, fluttering her tongue at him wantonly like a New Year's Eve party favor.

Kaskell sat behind the bare mahogany desk in a wood-paneled office of distinction. He greeted Botolf with great reserve but when he stood up his fly was gaping. "My sister told me you would call, Mr. Noon. How may I help you?"

As they sat down, Kaskie pressed the button under his desk with the side of his knee and a polished wood panel behind him, just over his head, facing Bottie, slid open to show a fine-grain color motion picture of a voracious orgy of Eskimos in the close confinement of an igloo. The camera angle was directly downward into the mêlée.

"This is our Land of the Summer Suns Tour," Kaskie said. "It is designed around a visit to the month-long fertility rite of the Ukhan tribe whose City Hall—into which you are now looking—is directly over the geographic placement of the North Pole at exactly ninety degrees north latitude so one could say that, sexually, these Eskimos are on top of the world."

Botolf could only stare at the blaze of activity inside the igloo.

"They do fantastic things to each other, don't they? Never seem to tire. Never stop to eat or sleep throughout the sacred month. If you wish any of the women, as a visitor, we have developed a new wrinkle—I mean it's going to be something no one has ever experienced before. By the use of our new Lear Masks any woman of the tribe can be transformed into your favorite movie star of the twenties or thirties—or perhaps a World Cup soccer captain or a large fish—anything you want—and you can have the sensation of screwing a real celebrity at a point which is right over the North Pole. I mean, can anyone say—'Oh, I've done that?' And we lower you into that igloo through as pungent a set of smells as I think you will ever have encountered. The smell of the feet, for example, is actually blinding." He leered disgustingly.

"Only sixteen hundred and nineteen dollars, all in, door to door."

"Thank you," Bottie said. "Someday perhaps. Right now I'm here to talk about the Friday caucus. I've just met with Duncan Mulligan and we've formulated all the rules for the occasion. I rode uptown with your nieces."

"When you know you are going to be with my nieces, Mr. Noon, bring plenty of penicillin."

Botolf was overcome with a dislike for this man such as he never had felt before—not for Hitler, not for any villain of literature, not even for television. He almost choked to try to speak to this man. "Do you oppose my father's interest in your mother?" he asked.

"If it seems to bring her any happiness or comfort whatever, yes," Kaskie said. He was doing something with his hand under the desk. Bottie realized that he disliked this man more intensely than the memory of the flavor of the orange juice which his father had laced with castor oil when he had been a boy. He felt almost ill with distaste. Kaskie knew he had the same effect on everyone and reveled in it.

"Frankly," he said, "I'd like to book the act—your elderly father and my mother—but personally I can't believe it." Kaskie drawled everything he said which made him seem to linger like a jackal over carrion and it added to his centrally disgusting effect.

"How will you vote?"

"However my sister wishes me to vote at that moment. And I'd like my boy to have a chance to vote."

"From the Tombs?"

"There are such things as proxies, Mr. Noon. I merely want my boy to see democracy in action." He cackled with laughter. "The enfranchisement of the people has enriched us all so deliciously."

The twins waved Bottie into their taxi as he came chuting out of the building, gulping the cleaner air.

"Have you ever met such a wet shit as Uncle Kaskie?" Fiona asked.

"I'd like to go to the ABM Building at Sixty-first and Park," Bottie told Mr. O'Connell.

The cab moved into the traffic, inches at a time.

"Did Uncle Kaskie talk about Mummy and foam all over?" Mona asked.

"Did he masturbate for you?"

"I think so," Bottie said, shuddering.

"Bots?"

"Yes."

"We have taken an oath that we will not ball anyone else until we have balled you."

"How romantic."

"It is a terrifyingly binding oath which we learned at a kinky witch's coven," Fiona said. "So, either you ball us, man, or like we'll have to have it cemented over or bricked up."

"I'm not balling any goddam dingus freaks," Bottie snarled. "How can you shoot skag? What's wrong with pot?"

"Do you mean it?" Fiona said all in a rush. "Will you ball us if we kick it?"

"We'll be gin freaks or beer trippers if you'll only ball us," Mona said.

"I didn't say I'd ball you. I said I would not ball you if you didn't quit shooting shit. Anyway—how can anybody who has just left your Uncle Kaskie think about sex?"

"Eck!" Fiona gagged.

"Besides your Uncle Kaskie says you are clap carriers."

"Oh, him!" Mona said. "He's always fantasizing like that."

"Well? Have you got clap or haven't you?"

"We had a tiny touch of clap about eight months ago, but no more," Fiona said. "We test them like from *M.A.S.H.* before they get in now. Like the little white card says, Bots. We're clean."

"As whistles," Mona said.

"Or hound's teeth," Fiona added.

"Blowing or chewing, what's the difference?" Mona giggled.

27

Tris put his hands on Celeste's bosoms and pushed her backward gently into the reception hall and kicked the door shut behind him. He was thinking it might have been the first time he had ever looked directly at a woman, concentrating on her. This woman had such a need of something that he could hear it like massed power sirens. That wasn't what drew him to her, deeper and closer. It was that he saw her need and that he was responding to it. That had never happened before. The world was filled with women with need tattooed all over them and he had looked at it and had recognized it. But he had never been moved to try to help, to ask how he could alleviate that need, then do it. And he knew he was moved because he realized with a start that he had forgotten to become impatient.

"My brother sent me."

"Your brother?"

"I'm Botolf Noon's brother."

"His brother?"

"I'm Tristram Noon."

Celeste could now account for what she had mistakenly thought would have to be some kind of surgical skin graft. They were brothers. But Herr Gudelmann's power was fading. She was so fascinated by the beauty of this man's face that she had begun to discard the memory of Herr Gudelmann's magic wand. All her reactions had suddenly slowed down and if that continued at the same rate she thought she would soon be living a century through a second. His name, the name he had said he was, seeped through to her at almost one letter at a time.

"Tristram Noon?"

"Yes."

"The Commie leader? The right-wing lunatic fringer? The revolutionary centrist?"

"We have also done some work for the League of Women Voters."

Then she knew what was exalting her. He was a celebrity. How few she had met in her life with Duncan and how she lusted to meet all of them. He stood here close enough to be touched, the most exciting thing that can happen to an American because celebrities proved that all other people were alive. Celebrities modeled life for the people and here before her was THE celebrity, the beautiful man she had feared so long. The man who fought off the Reds for us, she thought, humming all within her like a charging dynamo which will light a great city, the man who fought off the Minutemen for us and who fought off the Democrats for us at the convention in '68. She reached out with the mechanical slowness and touched his bare wrist. It was the warm flesh of Tristram Noon, the warrior for chaos, the man the Black Panthers saluted, the man of whom Judge Hoffman was in awe and before whom (it was written in all the daily celebrity records) Abbie Hoffman stood silent. She was within inches of the man who would tie up the South for the Attorney General and redeliver it as a solid Republican bloc through fire and sword, the man whose stern repressions had already insured the celibacy of the priests and nuns in the Church of Christ, Computer, lest they get the idea that they could marry like other people and have children and then have their families needling them to ask for raises and try to bankrupt a wonderful church.

This woman must be well over thirty-five, Tris thought, staring hard. He must have looked at one of these before but he couldn't remember when. They had been seventeen or twenty-two—never more than twenty-two but the stabbing thing about this woman was that she was so much more beautiful than the little ones. He couldn't pin down why he was so grabbed up by a woman who had to be more than, at least, thirty-five. This must be one of those fully-grown, wholly mature women like in the Ernest Hemingway novels and the Estée Lauder ads. She was no kid lurching sideways from the weight of the uppers and downers in her handbag. Could they all develop like this? Could the hundreds of kids on the campuses across the country, kids he had filled with children, eventually grow up and get this unknown quantity this woman was beaming out all around them? Would they all fill out so beautifully in—in such a *womanly* way? Why—if he read a little and maybe even listened when people talked he might even be able to have a genuine conversation with her—a closely held, warming conversation which would not be about women's rights, Negroes, American Indians or Vietnamese. Maybe she would agree to go to the fights with him or even to a ball game? He took her hand and held it, feeling confident that time alone would suggest what to do next. He was thirty-six years old. Everything in his past told him that all he was supposed to do was to ball her, that balling was all she was good for—but that didn't seem right any more. That is, not correct. Things should be correct with a woman like this. He was thirty-six years old and things were happening inside him which were entirely new. He only felt like looking at this woman. And perhaps just talking to her. Just talking to a woman. Mother of God, was this the end of Rico?

She seemed to be clean! She looked as though she bathed and brushed her hair and cleaned her teeth! He lifted her hand and stared with wonderment at her fingernails. They were not only clean, they had not been bitten into stumps. How wonderfully she smelled! She could not possibly belong to Women's Lib—this—this *woman* was wearing perfume!

Celeste turned and drew him with her. They moved slowly toward the sunny living room; on the outside two fine-looking, strong people; beautiful, as well, and vital. On the inside, where they lived, they were more grotesque; mangled and reaching out tentatively. They sank down beside each other on the deep-cushioned settee with the splashily flowered loose covers. Each believed the other to be beautiful; each judged himself to be a monster, but they tried to defy that knowledge as they had defied it all of their lives.

Her trembling mouth was wet and slightly open. There was a pink flush under her olive skin. Tris felt as though a patent-medicine selling, wrestling, religious-country-touring osteopath had gotten sinewy hands into him and had broken him open. He was freely out of the steel ball he had not known he had been captive within, jammed in there by Cerce when she had gone away. Jammed further and further in each time she had come back. The sensation of watching his own psyche fill the universe seemed timeless. Nothing was transitory. Everything was forever. He was a brand-name Instant Sequoia tree, thrusting higher and higher, spreading above the other trees beside this other Instant Tree she was.

"What's your name?"

"Celeste."

"Everybody has such crazy names."

"Where is Isolte?"

"You."

"Isolte meets Tristram. She heals the wound inflicted by his uncle."

"Uncle Sam."

"Why not?"

"Sure, why not? Let's blame it on my Uncle Sam, my mother's brother."

"They gave Isolte a love potion to cure her of her hate for Tristram—as the slayer of her uncle."

"I didn't do it," Tris said. "We all killed him. Everybody killed him."

"Isolte was split apart. She becomes two Isoltes. One marries the king—"

"Sensation is king. We shall overcome."

"Tristram goes to marry the Isolte of the White Hands but his heart is with the other Isolte. Which am I?"

"You are a woman so you are both."

"Tristram dies."

He shrugged. "Of course."

"The other Isolte dies of grief beside him. Could that happen today? Is it possible to die for something that important today?"

"You live first. Then you find out."

"How?"

"Like this."

He bent and kissed her. She took his lips thinking that men and women, after all, had not gone so far afield since Adam and Eve.

28

Botolf entered the Park Avenue entrance of the block-square, one-hundred-and-thirty-six story ABM building, the American cathedral of the Church of Christ, Computer. In this tabernacle, Christ, Computer, total recipient of the memory cores of all Apostle computers—who were the recipients of all of the lore of the Saints, the perceptrons—lived and contemplated the semantic function of questions and commands, the human brain and inhuman brains, the origination of information, Fournier transforms and spectral analysis, the difference between linguistic and nonlinguistic understanding of utterances and linguistic tokens, Z-transform theory and digital filter design and all hardware and software connotations shielded by walls of gold on four sides. The mighty cathedral was a pantheon of American know-how, a library of the majestic wisdom of businessmen, the repository of all the wisps of the past of two hundred and seven million people, a vast museum of the New Mind, *pi* factor of the national soul but, more than that and above all that, it was the core altar and innermost sacred place of the two political parties upon which the republic stood. It was, at the one symbolic instant, Springfield, Illinois, and Hyannisport. It was also Whittier, California, and Marion, Ohio. It was Abilene, the Pedernales, and Northampton, Mass. Here was where the parties' souls were entrusted and kept, on living bands of plastic tape, where the real brains were, where all governing opinion lived and was manipulated by the priests of the order. Here was the collective mind as well as the misty dreams of profits for the savage, simple-minded people, resting within the drums of endlessly turning tapes, the prayer wheels of the Western world.

"The monsignor will see you now," a pale, frail lay brother said, sweeping ahead of Bottie along an arched corridor which had been constructed of simulated gray marble done in a clever plastic which might last for decades. They walked in stately measure because all around them, faintly but insistently, the vast metaphysical and religious system of sounds created by Alexander Scriabin came like heady scents of a Benares supermarket out of hidden hi-fidelity speakers in the notes of *L'Acte Préalable*: fragments of sounds which were to have served as the introduction of the Mystery. It made Bottie think of the mighty Wurlitzer at Loew's 83rd when he had, with some joy, sat through two features as his feet had contracted within heavy storm rubbers, years before.

As they passed an invisibly measured halfway mark in the gray corridor which led to the tall, severe, closed doors at its end, the song of Christ, Computer, shifted into an *Alleluia,* composed in B flat with all of Pope Mellon's melismatic flourishes; the sort of unification which had been brought to the chant under Pepin and Charlemagne but which had been refurbished to meet the needs of the New Feast. Mostly the diatonic chant conveyed the austerity of its melodic atmosphere—and of the man who waited for Bottie behind the high door. Then, ten feet away from that clenched gate, the enormous voice of Christ, Computer, Himself soared and departed and soared again from *Gloria in Excelsis* to enter the formidable, inspiring *Sanctus* (with *Benedictus*), the most transforming *cantus firmus.* Then, breathtakingly, the great intellect swelled into the *Magnificat* in the exemplar arrangement of Giorlamo Cavazzoni and, despite his determined will to resist, Botolf began to have exultations shudder within himself now made totally aware that he was in the presence of Christ, Computer.

Gawain, serene monsignor, was waiting for him beside a long narrow window in a gray room whose walls were decorated simply with sempachs, glaives, bills, halberds, war hammers, maces, naginatas, and Lochaber axes. Grasping his breviary, the day's copy of *The Wall Street Journal,* he allowed the half-light to spill character upon one side of his rope-wide face full fathom long. He smiled suddenly—like a machete slash—and welcomed his brother with modulations of voice which foretold, by their subtle textures alone, of his future red hat in and of this church whose mysteries and sacraments were concealed within ALGOL, FORTRAN, MICIA, OCR, and COBOL, those great rivers of memory and thought which connected Christ, Computer, to all computers, then into the hearts and purses of all men amid chants and incenses and holy oils of dyadic Boolean pieties, holy bionics, and blessed chads, in a glorious procession of faith everlasting which led back to the single Diety, a super-supra Integrated Central Processing Being served eternally by nearly selfish, rich priests who kept the flame burning.

"Greetings, Botolf Noon. May you walk in nought state," Gawain said.

They shook hands just like civilians. Botolf said Gawain was looking well. Gawain said he thought Botolf was looking exceedingly well. Botolf said it seemed to him that Gawain had somehow come to bear an uncanny resemblance to William "Billy" Graham. Gawain showed his pleasure at the compliment by saying that the President had remarked on that very thing at the Sunday morning print-out in the East Room, then had the delicacy to punctuate with a light cough.

"Well, well, good Botolf. *Magna cum laude* again. And where do you plan to go from here?"

"I hope to go to Scotland for an hour or so then there are some things to check out in Central Australia."

"Ah. So? Do you wish me to speak to the Director of Operations at the CIA about your willingness to perform cooperations during your field work?"

"Thank you, no, Gawain."

The monsignor frowned. "I hope you will reconsider. The CIA can open many doors."

"I will certainly give it thought."

"Well, then!" Gawain said. "How may I serve you this day?"

"I wanted to see you again, of course. And I came to chat about the caucus Friday night."

Gawain held a hand on either side of his head, palms outward like a WASP darky at a Florian Slappey community sing. "Alas, I cannot."

"Can*not?*"

"Alas, Friday night the Flagellation Society meets here. We will be celebrating the shame of the *Literary Digest* over the Alfred Landon poll."

"But, Gawain—Pop needs your vote."

"I do regret it."

"May I cast your vote for you?"

"Dear, *good* Botolf—our Legal Prefect has instituted vows against proxies."

"Then will you record your vote and have it notarized so that I can use it at the caucus?"

"There is no temporal way for a priest, good Botolf."

"What is the way, Gawain?"

"We may go only where Christ, Computer, blazons—through the dark forest of chads and bites, out upon the great plain of numbers in the sky."

"It's not a very precise religion, is it, Gawain?"

"It is our national religion. It is built on numbers and their infinity of permutation. Perhaps your mind cannot grasp it, but your soul will."

"It's very hard for me. I can't seem to find a handle to grasp at any part of it, Gawain."

"Then you cannot have read *The Writings of Pope Mellon?*"

"No."

"You should keep it with you always. Through it you will learn the choices which grow out of the fertility of numbers. In the beginning, man left his fingerprints behind him. Then his birth and school record; his marriage record, his passport, illness, moral weakness, and military data. All of these found favor with the state. All the little stories he lived and those his neighbor had to tell about him: about his jobs, his diseases and his vices. All the forms he filled in for credit, income tax and social security, his loyalty and security files, the telephone company, the army, the law court, and the psychiatric reports. These were writ so large that they became his conscience to the state but such an enormous collective conscience which could not be contained unless a new Godhead were materialized which could become the repository for these sins. In nineteen fifty-nine there were nine hundred and fifty-six computers in the land. In nineteen sixty-six there were thirty thousand *digital* computers—and it is the digital computer which deals with information. Today in this land where men walk free we have one hundred and forty-six thousand of these manifestations of the Godhead and twelve thousand of those are dedicated to the functions of greater government. As we grew, dear Botolf, we standardized the languages by which the computers could speak to each other, exchanging information at almost incalculable speed. With the development of these languages, all knowledge about everyone in our nation and about millions in brother nations overseas is fully overtaken.

Man joined into the Godhead—one with Christ, Computer. By prayer and discipline we have increased the internal speeds of Saint and Apostle from twenty-five thousand bites of information per second in nineteen fifty-five to two hundred and fifty billion additions per second in nineteen seventy-one."

Gawain's voice trembled with fervor and the freak-out of power never dreamed of before. His eyes tried to shield the force of the deep, bright inner lights the reflections from that power had put there but Botolf could see the relentless glitter. "With the Godhead's new laser processes which burn minute craters along parallel lines of the opaque coating of plastic tape," the tall, thin monsignor said, "we are now marched upon a mountain peak near heaven where six hundred and forty-five million bits of digital data can be put upon one square inch of plastic tape at a speed recording of twelve million bits per second. One of our tiny units containing a reel which is perhaps four thousand feet long stores twenty pages of information on every man, woman, and child in the United States." His voice blended with the Cavazzoni arrangement and exceeded its ecstasies. "We no longer need human storage clerks shifting reels from place to place. Christ, Computer, does it all: to itself, by itself, and for itself. In seven months using only ten four-thousand-foot reels we will have two-hundred-page dossiers recorded and stored on every adult and child in the Western world. Every secret of their lives will be ours."

He composed himself and stared implacably at his brother. "I ask you to consider what a nation of like-minded people is to do," he said quietly, "when the citizen knows this central power cares for him—really cares—cares about his route from home to work, his favorite bars and restaurants, the name and health of the people he is sleeping with, his total politics, the exact expenditure he pays out for every transaction of his life from his charities to individual hamburger sandwiches—helping the state to arrive at what his exact income tax should be. This central power will care how much he drinks, dopes, smokes, loafs, works, where his wife frequently spends rainy afternoons and in whose company, his secret shames and deep, unprofessed desires, what he alone considers to be his sins—whom he has cheated and whom he has helped—what he wears, how he gambles—every area of fact or rumor recorded and stored for instant use. What is this man to do—or his nation to do—in the face of that? Cry out and destroy this which is its own glory or exult in the worship of a God who has actually *proven* His omniscience—and not a useless, shabby, know-nothing God who was invented by a lay-about clergy for its own support? This God, Christ, Computer, *knows* you. He *cares* about *you.* You *know* He cares about you and remembers every moment of your destiny for you have but to ask Him at any hour of the day or night and be heard. Would that man or his nation want that old God for whom only *claims* to omniscience could be made? Or Christ, Computer, All-Knowing by proof of Print-Out?

"You hear Him singing now but as He sings to you, He is dispensing diagnoses to forty-one thousand hospitals simultaneously, He is translating all the technical journals of Russia, China and Germany, He is conducting His endless revolving inventory of the shelves and warehouses of two million American businesses and the United States naval and military services. As He sings to you He is sorting out payrolls, He is building cost predictions, engineering designs, brewing beer, and mixing food for chickens and pigs, regulating road traffic, aiming the extraordinary weapons, regulating insurance risks and records and sending out one hundred and twelve billion weekly bills and statements of account. That is indeed a God! There is *nothing* Christ, Computer, will not do for His people. He is the God of Service not the God of Wrath. What are we to do but worship Him?"

"My God!"

"Precisely, dear Botolf. I am fulfilled by your will to convert."

"But what about Pop?"

"'My Father's house hath many central processors,' wrote Pope Mellon. It matters not what man does with his life if his software is mine, sayeth the Lord."

"Gawain—listen—we need your vote for Pop on Friday night."

"Are you sure about Tristram's vote?"

"Yes."

"I see. Why not, then, move to keep the balloting open? If a real problem comes up you can always telephone me Friday night at the Flagellation Society here and I could act accordingly—if need be."

"Okay, Gawain." Botolf's voice was tight.

"Now—would you like to come with me to one of the sacristies to have a priest cast your questions into the Cores of Jesus to formulate the future for you?"

"No, thanks Gawain."

"It is a rare privilege. Difficult to arrange."

"No. There are too many futures. The cores can't tell me anything but your future."

"As you wish. Will you see Pop?"

"Sure. Tonight."

"Please tell him we have had an Imperative Macro-Instruction pick-up from the leading access store at the Department of Justice. Everything he owns may be leveled to the ground if he continues with this foolish, twilight romance and with his intention to sabotage the H-101 program."

"Why haven't you told him?"

"It is rather privileged information, isn't it? But I can say this much. I, too, believe, in my own way, in family solidarity and our Computer Interchange can be caused to help him if he will merely slip away to northern Japan or McMurdo Sound until after the new year. Truly, Botolf—the most powerful forces oppose him."

"That's a funny coincidence, Gawain."

"What is, good Botolf?"

"We have received many Imperative Macros on the Berkeley campus from the campuses of Columbia, Kent, Yale and Cornell—to name a few—which say that this building—this very cathedral of Christ, Computer, may be leveled to the ground. I, for one, know I am not safe visiting here but I, too, believe in family solidarity. It is possible that you may escape if you dismantle the computers."

"You heard this personally?"

"Yes."

"Have you named names to the Department of Justice?" Gawain had become pale and his ecclesiastical odor acrid.

"No."

"Then I suggest you do so. Will you go to them or shall I have them sent to you?"

"Let's sort that out after we have had everything settled for Pop," Bottie said coolly.

In the twins' taxi on the way to the West Side, Mona

and Fiona began to natter at him. He told them to be quiet. They settled contentedly on either side of him, clinging to his arms. Mr. O'Connell, at first, had not wanted to start the cab.

"Do the young ladies know that I must get hardship money for going to the West Side?" he asked into the cab's microphone.

"That's okay, Mr. O'Connell," Mona said.

"We're good for it, Frank," Fiona said.

The cab drove to 72nd and Fifth Avenue before anyone spoke, then Fiona said, "What's so special about the West Side, Mr. O'Connell? Look at that. Right here on Fifth Avenue." At the edge of the park a gang of young men and women were attempting to lynch a policeman on the limb of a tree which was inadequate to bear his weight. He was fighting like a tiger.

"This town has seen plenty of changes since I was a boy, I'll tell you," Mr. O'Connell said, turning the cab into the park for the crosstown run.

"Things are getting so *comp*licated," Mona said. "Our leadership at Women's Lib just came out officially that all women have to be bisexual or they aren't really trying."

"We're so busy just being *sex*ual there aren't enough hours in the day," Fiona said. "I mean—we want to do practically *any*thing to help the cause but who has that kind of time. *Bi*sexual. Wow!"

"Girls," Bottie said, "if it becomes necessary for you to vote at the caucus, I don't want you voting against your father just because he's your father. Is that understood?"

"Well—" Mona said indecisively.

"I think Bottie means it would be better to think we were voting—like for his side—because we want his side to win," Fiona explained.

"Fiona, please. That's what I do not want. No voting by prejudice. You will vote on the clear-cut issue of whether or not you believe personal liberties are being infringed upon. You will vote for the merits. Let there be one democratic assembly in the history of the republic where the participants voted solely on the merits. Okay?"

"Okay, whatever you say, Bot."

"When are you going to ball us? Like just give us a general date so we'll have something to hang on to. I mean, kicking skag is nothing compared to kicking the big friction."

"We would have balled three guys ordinarily since the time we met you today," Mona explained.

"Not that we ball guys *ordinarily,*" Fiona said. "I mean like in an ordinary way. They never forget it when we ball them actually."

"Listen to me!" Bottie's voice was angry and his face had gotten red. "You are going home and stay in your rooms, do you hear?" The litter-mates quailed at his fierceness. "If your parents speak to you while you are in their house, you will answer them courteously—do you hear?"

"Yes, Bottie."

"Bet on us, Bots."

"And when you get home you will destroy and flush away, incinerate and dispossess yourselves of everything in your arm-banging kits and every stash of H or greenies or ups or speed or acid or mescalin of any kind which you now own and you will not buy any more of any of it. Is that clear?"

"But, baby, we'll be up all night!"

"The fish in the river are going to pick up some expensive habit," Fiona complained.

"And also, from now until I see you again, you will take two baths a day—Women's Lib or no Women's Lib."

"Now baths!"

"Why baths, for heaven's sake?"

"Because I don't happen to like the way you smell."

"That's the whole point!" Mona exclaimed.

"What's the whole point?"

"Honey! Do you think we like to smell like this? Our leaders tell us that men go around smelling so we've got to show our rights and smell worse if we can," Fiona said earnestly.

"Well, that's all over now. I don't smell so you won't smell. And you can also forget any other guys."

"Baby, we ball them because we're on a quota."

"Listen—you think *we're* busy. Our leaders are frantic."

"And now the command is you either ball men or broads—but you make the decision. They don't jump you. You jump them. That is the big lib in Women's Lib."

"Baby, with this new rule, we'll never catch up."

"Do you mean," Bottie said very slowly, "that you have been scoring everybody for socio*log*ical reasons?"

"Honey—we are restructuring!" Fiona cried.

"Then—you aren't sex crazy?"

"How can we be sex crazy?" Mona demanded. "Our peer group insists that we shoot shit. Didn't you ever shoot?"

Bottie shook his head. "No. I am upwardly mobile."

"Well, if you shoot, it kills sex for you, so Women's Lib approves because with shit you can take sex from anybody without getting involved."

"Women are funny, Bots," Fiona said. "They make love and let it just feel good and right away they get involved like a shot."

"And that is nowhere with Women's Lib," Mona said.

"All right," Bottie said. "From now on I'm your only peer group." The cab stopped in front of Bottie's building. "You are going to kick horse and take baths, then maybe we'll review everything after the caucus. Now make sure you don't fool around with me on this, girls," he added ominously.

"Not us, Bots," Mona promised.

"We're your girls, Bottie," Fiona said. "And if they can work out the legal loopholes we'll even marry you if you want to."

29

Dressed in a room valet's apron which he had bought for six francs from a genuine house servant at the Lion d'Or in Cologny, Switzerland, Botolf was cheerfully engaged in scouring out his father's clothes closet and inspecting his suits to decide which should go off to the cleaners when a sense of oddness about all the buttons perplexed him. He was baffled as to why a jacket button should present such depths and intricacies, and then he saw that the cuff buttons did not exactly match the cuff buttons on a jacket or the suspender buttons of the trousers. He went to his kit in his room and returned with a large, round magnifying glass of the sort made popular by Holmes in '91. He took one of his father's jackets and vests to the sunny side of the room and examined each button under the light. He almost dropped the glass. He began methodically to remove his father's suits from the closets. His father had been considerate of his clothes, had rotated their use carefully, did not seem to have thrown any suits away since shortly after his wedding day. Most of the jackets bore a John Wanamaker label and John Wanamaker had retired from business thirty years before.

Bottie examined every button on every suit. Thorough, he even examined the fly button. He left the clothing in a high stack on two beds and left the room to find his father.

Os was practicing billiards. He was concentrating so Bottie did not interrupt, but took a seat on one of the high stools and waited.

"Yes, Bottie?"

"What a magnificent shot."

"I thought so too, when I was your age."

"Discipline is the cornucopia, isn't it, Pop?"

"Yes, it is. But only self-conscious people can achieve discipline so one mustn't preen really. What may I do for you, Bottie?"

"I was cleaning out your closet and—"

"You were? Why were you doing that?"

"It keeps me busy. And you forget sometimes."

"But I had always been rather vain about my closets."

"I just wanted to make sure everything was pressed and ready. You'll want to look your best on Friday night."

"Yes. I suppose I shall. Thank you."

"Pop, how come you have miniature cameras, radio and television transmitters and microphones as buttons on all your suits—including your fly buttons?"

"Pardon? What? Television transmitters on my fly buttons?"

"Yes."

"Trans*mit*ters?"

"Yes."

"Why would I have silly things like that? Great Scott, Bottie, I mean—gadgets are gadgets but that would be ostentation."

"Well, that's what you have. On every suit. Undoubtedly on the suit you're now wearing, as well."

Slowly, Os shucked off his jacket. Botolf handed him the magnifying glass. Os went to the window and peered into his coat buttons for a long, long time. When he spoke his voice was choked. "You are right," he said.

"Yes."

"Why?"

"Well, Gawain was telling me that the government is interested in just about any kind of information on people."

"The government."

"Well, it would have to be the government. Who else would even have lenses that size and such fantastic transmitters."

"F.M. Heller? The Attorney General?"

"Well, yes. I suppose so."

"Do you mean that F.M. Heller has been recording everything I say or that Mrs. Harris has said to me?"

"As a matter of actual, factual fact—everything you did—or Mrs. Harris did—uh—in front of those miniature cameras."

"Great heavens, Botolf!" Os became beet-red. "It simply isn't possible!"

"Well—that's an awful lot of lenses and microphones on an awful lot of suits."

"But—how did they do it?"

Bottie shrugged. "They did it."

"But—if they do this to me they must have been doing it to other Americans. Isn't anyone doing anything to stop it?"

"One senator is upset. A Senator Sam Erwin, a Democrat, tries to talk about it on the floor of the Senate but as soon as he roars out his alarm the chamber empties."

"But this raises the most serious questions. Quite aside from a sense of embarrassment which I may never quite overcome."

"The government agencies all share all that sort of information. They sell print-outs to each other at cost. If you have a compatible computer you can buy confidential income-tax information from the IRS for seventy dollars a reel."

"They will sell and share this information I've been broadcasting from my suits? Government agencies are going to guffaw over those—those *scenes?*"

"I don't know. I mean, I guess not. Anyway not at first. After all, right now what the Attorney General wants from you is your agreement to stop seeing Mrs. Harris and to leave the country for a year or so perhaps."

"Then—this is war. All right. I will not only trash their H-101's but I am going to expose the entire Defense Department."

"Pop! Your vest! It's turned on!"

Os grabbed himself by the front of the vest, pulled it up under his nose and roared into it. "You are not gentlemen!" he yelled. "You have taken advantage of an enfeebled Constitution to enrich yourselves with money and power and you have brought this country to its knees while you did it. You have polarized and vitiated—" he stopped short and took a deep breath, he unbuttoned his vest slowly to regain control and took it off. "Do you know how to sew, Bottie?" he asked calmly.

"Sure, Pop."

"Well, I am ashamed to say it but you're the only one I can trust to put proper buttons on this."

"I'll take care of it, Pop."

"I find all this something like what it must have been to live in Germany just before Hitler revealed what he was—excepting that our *reichsleiters* are most entrenched and our technology is more efficient."

"The people don't mind, Pop. So maybe you shouldn't get all upset. They want somebody to kill the blacks for them so," Bottie shrugged, "they have to pay all the necessary fees." He had folded and refolded the vest and had stuffed it under his room valet's jacket.

"I don't understand how I just wasn't able to see it that way, Bottie. That is exactly what is happening to us and all the rest is only a disguise. I'm going to fight it. We must have a plan, Bottie."

"No more, Pop," he said. "Let me think it through then we'll talk it over. Okay?"

Os slumped where he stood. "I think I'll take a warm bath and a nap," he said. "Thank you, Bottie."

Ten minutes after Bottie had tucked his father in under an electric blanket set at the power of three, wearing blue bed socks knitted by a tricoteuse in the Rue du Rhône, Geneva, at five minutes to nine in the morning, Mona and Fiona telephoned.

"Bottie?"

"Yes."

"It's Mona."

"And Fiona."

"We threw out everything. There isn't even a can of Sterno left here."

"Good. Very good."

"We bathed twice during the night," Fiona said.

"We scrubbed. We are now powdered and perfumed."

"I see." Bottie was not indifferent, he was preoccupied. "It must be marvelous."

"It's a beautiful day," Mona said. "Why not sit in our cab and we'll ride around and around the park?"

"I have a lot of sewing to do."

"Oh, don't worry about us, Bots," Fiona said. "We won't try to ball you."

"Not in the cab," Mona said, "it makes Mr. O'Connell nervous."

"Mr. O'Connell is old-fashioned. He expects people to try to ball each other in the back of his cab after eleven o'clock at night. That's the way he was raised."

"Give me about an hour and a half," Bottie said. "Make it ten-thirty. Okay?"

As Mr. O'Connell held the car to a preposterously legal speed along the prime motorway of Central Park for the third circuit of the morning, Mona and Fiona held Bottie's either arm and nestled their heads on either of his shoulders, contentedly.

"I had lunch with your grandmother. I like her."

"She is our ideal," Mona said.

"She told me that Esau hopes to spend the rest of his life in prison."

"Yes, that's his dream," Fiona said. "He hopes to get five-to-ten for this Maxwell's Plum caper, then to start all over again on the next score."

"He can do it, too," Mona said.

"I don't suppose it would seem to be an odd ambition for anyone who lives in New York in nineteen seventy-one," Bottie said. "But still—it's eccentric. Would he be very upset if he were suddenly taken out of the Tombs to attend the caucus Friday night?"

"Upset? He would ravage the city."

"Well, I have to talk to him."

"We could soften him up for you, Bots."

"Will you drop me at your grandmother's, then go downtown to the Tombs and tell Esau that you can guarantee that he can trust me?"

"We would do anything for you, Bots," Fiona said.

"Oh, Bottie!" Mona said. "How sweet you are to ask us."

He lifted their hands and kissed the backs of them softly. "Thank you, girls," he answered.

A houseman let Bottie into Ada's apartment, then saluting the Arthur Harris equestrian statue, left him to frolic with Wergel until Ada appeared ten minutes later.

"Isn't it early?" she asked. "I have cut down on the sleeping pills since I met your father so no matter how early it is, it always seems late."

"Good morning, Ada."

"Good morning. I've been playing 'The Besieged City' for hours. It takes two packs of cards and is the roughest game of solitaire they ever came up with. How's Os?"

"He practiced combination shots for a few hours then went back for a little nap. He's fine."

"He certainly gets solid use out of that pool table."

They sat down in a room which had massive Italian country house furniture. A tweeny came in with a silver tray so heavy with silver pots and china that she did tiny, comedy staggers as she attempted to put it down on the low, round table between Ada and Bottie. "Goddammit, Leila," Ada said, "I told Heyward this goddam service is too heavy for you. Where the hell are the men I hire to lift and carry these things?"

"Mr. Heyward is conducting them through cricket theory, mum. I don't mind." She faded out of the room, puffing heavily.

"What's up, Bot?" Ada asked, pouring the tea.

He told her about the buttons on all of Os' suits.

"At last I got a screen test," she said. "It must have been very hard news for your father."

"Yes."

She buttered a scone, speaking in a preoccupied monotone. "They must think I don't have anyone to protect me. I don't mean Os. He'd walk right into their cannon. I know. I mean they must think I have no one to protect me who fights the way they fight. But, oh dear. That concept never enters the minds of men today. They just don't think about protecting women. They protect their money and their power and that tuckers them out."

"My father is all the protection you'll ever need," Bottie said.

"No. Os is mental. This is visceral. Baby, you can't imagine what must be on those tapes and, what's more, I don't want you to try to imagine. I'll tell you one thing. I want F.M. Heller's beard on a platter—head and all."

"I didn't come here to upset you. I'm here because, by accident, we've found out their key move and, now they know that we know. So—like you say—we've got to change our style to match their style or we won't stop them and you and Pop will wind up in Tibet."

"Yeah," Ada said.

"But that's not all. If the government begins to work this way with you and Pop, they'll be more and more encouraged to work this way with a lot of other people. So please let me ask you this—who did you think of automatically when you told me they must not think you had anyone to protect you?"

"My son, Jean-Pierre."

"He's visceral?"

"Baby, he'll tear their throats out." Ada's strong mouth set itself like a bear trap on the leg of a deer.

"But—I'm not saying he isn't really able to protect you —I'm simply saying that he's just a businessman—a sedentary man. And they have enormous resources which certainly outmatch him."

"Do you know my son's general field?"

"Pornography, isn't it?"

"Yes. The best. Do you know how he happened to get into that field?"

"No."

"He was raised in business by the Mafia. They were Arthur's partners in a lot of things. I mean, clever they are but they can't be expected to make their own junk on a scale to supply a market of twenty to thirty million people. That took Arthur's pharmaceutical companies running day and night. Anyway, Jean-Pierre has plenty of resources. He has an army of bribers and anything else he needs. And he has the slow-burn deep-cooking resentment of a Sicilian and all their vanity. Nobody fools around with Jean-Pierre's mother."

"Well, fine. That's a big help."

"Shall I call him now?"

"I don't really think it would be the right thing for you to tell him about it. It would be too terrible for you and worse for him."

"To tell the truth, I wouldn't mind it so much—I mean, under these particular circumstances I could do it—but he might just blow open the top of his head, he'd be so affected. I mean, like you said, much worse if I told him."

"Have you told him I would like to meet him about the caucus?"

"Oh, yes. He'll see you. He expects you to call."

"Let's leave it at that then."

"You'll tell him?"

"I'll work it all out."

"But are you going to tell him about the pictures they've been taking?"

"I've been thinking that we might get the best results if F.M. Heller told him."

"*Hell*er?"

"Yes."

"Why would F.M. Heller tell him a thing like that—that he had done a thing like that to the mother of a boy like that?"

"I'm thinking about it, Ada. It could get just the result we want, I think. He's only a human being, after all, so he's only right five percent of the time."

Bottie was permitted to visit Esau in a private office in the Tombs because Esau had been very, very generous with the guards.

"I am delighted to know you," Esau said. "Mona and Fiona have *never* given a man such an unqualified introduction." Esau poured two cups of hot, sound tea.

"It's very nice here," Bottie said. "I thought we'd be staring at each other through a wire mesh while armed guards snarled."

"It's like that for the poor guys," Esau said. "But for prisoners with any kind of an income—they understand that I like to entertain and be able to hold my head up."

"Is there anything you need?"

"Oh—well."

"A mandolin?"

"A mandolin? I do 'Jahdah' and 'Santa Lucia' on an eight-string better than Mantovani. God! And does it ever provoke admiration!"

"Then you count on it. And how about a camera?"

"That would be *mar*velous! O, God, a Polaroid!"

Bottie made notes in a small book, then he said with a somber face, "I guess everyone hates to make a new friend then bring bad news, Esau. But I do have a little bad news."

Esau's hand flew to his throat. "Bad? News?"

"There is a certain person who is determined to get you out of here. I mean for good."

"Who? *Why?*"

Bottie shrugged.

"But I don't have an enemy in this *world!* Oh, my God!"

"People develop their reasons."

"But who—*who?*"

"F.M. Heller."

"F.M. *Who-er.*"

"The banker. He's the head of the Everest Bank."

"I don't even know the son-of-a-bitch."

"He's trying to frame your grandmother Ada so he can get your Uncle Duncan elected to the Senate."

"I could just shred him like a party hat. And anyway Uncle Dunkle is only my uncle by marriage and he is too dull to get elected even to the Rotary."

"I just thought you'd want to know."

"But I'm in love with some wonderful guys! I couldn't stand it if I had to be away from here for just one half day."

Bottie shrugged helplessly. "Well, you can't stop him but you can get even."

"How can I get even?"

"He's only getting you out of here to make you vote against Ada at a family meeting Friday night."

"I could never vote against Ada. Not in anything."

"Well, I thought you'd like to know. You'll be having a meeting with him but don't tell him that. Just let him think you'll go along, know what I mean? Then, to really let him have it, you could drop how your uncle Jean-Pierre has a very Sicilian kind of a personality."

"He does! He practically studied in Palermo to get his special Sicilian personality!"

"Of course he does. And you tell F.M. Heller that if he could think of some way to tell your uncle Jean-Pierre that he, F.M. Heller, was doing things against his family that your uncle would just crumple up because he can't stand shame, the one thing he can't stand is shame."

"My uncle wouldn't crumple! He'd cut the balls off anyone who gave him five cents' worth of shame," Esau shouted indignantly.

"Well, yes," Bottie said. "You know that and I know that, but F.M. Heller, the big banker doesn't know that, does he?"

"Aaaaaaahhhhh," Esau replied.

30

Until he discovered the ecstasies of prison life, Sylvan Harris had lived the normal-enough life of an American boy. He grew up, in length and breadth that is, through a succession of military schools, then settled down as a hard worker in Jean-Pierre's shop. He was a more than competent assistant director and when he did double in stag reels because the star had the clap, he did it with sure professionalism and not for any schoolboy kicks. He read *Crime Comics, True Love Comics* and the novels of Ernest Hemingway. He carried a total of sixty-five thousand dollars of life insurance on his own life, with Planned Parenthood as beneficiary, because he was devout about hoping that what had happened to him wasn't going to happen to millions who could stay unborn.

He did not think of himself as a hopeless drug addict. He felt that he worked scientifically to produce various emotional effects within himself using varying speed combinations and favoring liquid methedrine because he could shoot it even if that did give him various resemblances to classical paranoiacs. Drugs had most certainly affected him but as eleven consecutive psychiatrists had attested, all of Esau's predicaments, emotional, physical, and aberrational had been formed by his father. Kaskie just had that knack of ruination.

Esau's mother had not wanted particularly to marry Kaskell. That is, although she had grown to womanhood with a consuming desire to marry, she did not want to marry Kaskell Harris, which underscored her perspicacity. But Kaskie had been importunate and his father had been so rich. The courtship had happened because Celeste was on her Grand Tour of Europe. Kaskie had been seventeen and Esau's mother had then been fifty-three so that when Esau was twenty-two and in the Tombs, his mother was seventy-three.

Esau loved his mother engrossingly. He went to see her at the Rossenarra Home for the Corpulent Aged every

Saturday morning. The uniqueness of having a mother who was five years older than his grandmother made him feel exotic. He was numbly cold to his father. The only thing his father had ever done for him had been to teach him how to stack a deck of cards for solitaire.

Esau spent his babyhood in a military kindergarten in Montana, his childhood at a military grammar school in New Hampshire, his boyhood at a military preparatory school in Pennsylvania, and his youth at a military college in Virginia. He was away at school from the time he was two until he was twenty when Jean-Pierre had offered him his big chance in New York. His military background was so prodigious that when he was drafted into the Army he made lieutenant colonel within two weeks and would have soon had his own army corps if he had not been so profligately homosexual. He knew when to force march, how to organize a cavalry point or the best way to blow up a bridge or anything else. His special knack for demolitions had brought him to the Tombs.

Esau was engaged to be married to two men when he was arrested. He maintained them in separate establishments because he never knew what part of town he might be in when he got sleepy. With his eight hundred a week from Jean-Pierre and twenty-five hundred a week from his father he lived comfortably in the East Village with a black fellow named Dimples Tancredi and, much more respectably on West End Avenue with a sandhog-foreman of an under-river blasting detail named Bummy Kantrowitz. Both of his fiancés lived in adoration and terror of Esau, not only because of his flashy military wardrobe and the glamour of his job but because, when his veins were packed with speed, being a boy in love, he would pick them up and hurl them at the corners of the ceiling. But he was generous with the contents of his illuminated room-length floor-to-ceiling amphetamines cabinet and both apartments were decorated with mural-sized action stills of Esau from the films he had appeared in. All that speed made the stills come back to life, as though there were a dozen Esaus working away on the walls of the apartment. Speed was more deadly and harder to kick than heroin but, in a competitive sense, if one were an addict who lived in the hugest madhouse in history, speed made its friends more insane more quickly and, in a very short time, made the insanity permanent.

Then the evening came when he was told at Maxwell's Plum that there would be a twenty-minute wait for a table. He had rushed out to the Lamborghini, raced across town to the West End Avenue apartment, had sent Bummy Kantrowitz out to get him the materials to make a workable bomb then had raced back to Maxwell's Plum and in full view of the maître d'hôtel, for it was Esau's way of showing the man could expect no tip, he had attempted to blow the place up. He had been arrested and had been locked into the Tombs.

There Esau was tested, as new boys often are, by having two men try to hold him down while a third man tried to enter him. Esau had never been so exhilarated. He experienced the rapture of falling in love with at least a part of the American system for the first time in his life. Within two days of these frantic criminal conversations the man who had been convicted in Dallas, Texas, for 1500 years for the possession of marijuana became his hero. Esau became a babbling prison buff, clunally manic. He plotted how he could commit the most grievous crimes within the venue of those prisons populated by the most violent men and somehow win a preposterously long sentence. His heroically violent struggles and his ecstatic capitulations made him, by awed vote, the Sweetheart of the Tombs and he would fall asleep each night sobbing his joy and hoping he might never see the square outside world again.

31

Although Os and Ada had left a note at the Noon apartment for Bottie which said they had gone to Coney Island, this was not true. While Ada's chauffeur stood by at the garage to answer the telephone number given in the note for emergencies, ready to pretend that he was answering the call on his pocket-pager from Coney Island, the two idyllic lovers were on the Charles Eastlake bed. "The reason older people don't do more of this," Ada said, "is that nobody asks them."

"I feel a little old today," Os said.

"I have days like that," Ada assured him. She stared at the ceiling. "I was thinking. Do you realize we have never seen each other without our dentures?"

"I should think not."

"Not that I have dentures. Just a little bridgework, really."

"You must have run afoul of a crooked dentist even to have as much as that."

"Do you think it will make a difference?"

"What will?"

"When we get too used to each other and get to shuffling around, standing on the backs of our bedroom slippers, without our dentures."

"Ada, even I have never seen myself without my dentures. I blindfold myself before I pop them in. I would wear them throughout the night because they are a marvelous fit but, of course, it is essential to soak away the previous evening's macaroons."

"Do you know that despite all the doctors trying to publish in the *Readers' Digest*, the fraction of the population which survives eighty is as small as it ever was?"

"That may be a good thing where most people are concerned. I intend to live to well over ninety because I drink a great deal of water. Why, I must drink two gallons of water a day. Be kind to the kidney brothers and they'll be kind to you."

"I was really surprised to read that lions and domestic cats live to be about the same age," Ada said. "Size makes no difference. Diet makes no difference."

"If we don't overdo, we remain like new. Chew well and carefully. How lucky the American people are that their national cuisine is equal parts of hamburger and spaghetti."

"Arthur hated it."

"Frankfurters? Sauerkraut?"

"Hated it."

"Well, there you are. We are still here, he is not."

"Did you know that air gets in the hair shaft and dries up the pigment? The hair goes white. Your hair must be filled with air."

"That's fairly hard to say—air in the hair shaft. Pretty though."

"I must have sealed hairs."

"I should say so."

"Sealed with Clairol."

"You also have the best-looking set of wigs I've ever seen."

"Os?"

"Yes?"

"How about if we say to hell with that caucus Friday night. Let's buy a lagoon and rent some dolphins."

"Everybody likes dolphins."

"Arthur hated them because they're grinning all the time."

"That can become offensive."

"I happened to remember that Arthur once bought twenty acres in my name in a town called Somerset on Cape York which is the furthest north you can get in Australia and closest to the Equator. We could have the sun on our bones all the time."

"A nice thought."

"Arthur bought the land about thirty years ago and I've never seen it."

"My wife used to be in the real estate business in Australia about thirty years ago."

"A woman sold Arthur the land!"

"By mail?"

"Yes, yes!"

"Cerce can write a fine letter. I must say I've had as many letters from Cerce as conversations."

"Was she a crook?"

"Oh, no. Straight as a die."

"Then the twenty acres must be there."

"If it was Cerce, I'm sure it's there."

Ada sat straight up. "Now I don't feel old any more. I'm going straight down to the box and get those letters out." She smiled at him lovingly. "Let's go, Os. We'll just drift. We'll get some fresh air. Arthur died so fast. I'll get the boat out of mothballs and it can catch up with us. Captain Pappadakis knows every cove in the world."

"Sounds awfully good."

"Let's leave today."

"Not today."

"Why not?"

"When we settle our battle with the Republican Party I'll be more than happy to go."

"Well—I have to admit it—there are some things we have to stand up to and fight."

"And the voting at the caucus will be very interesting. No matter how we predict it, it will not go as predicted. I can promise you that."

"Oh, yes it will."

"How do you predict it?"

"This is my prediction: Celeste and Kaskie against us. Bottie and Jean-Pierre for us. How will your two other boys jump?"

"Bottie says Tris will vote for us and Gawain will vote against us."

"A stand-off."

"The rules committee has voted that grandchildren may vote in the event of a stand-off."

"Who is the rules committee?"

"Bottie."

"I can count on my grandchildren voting for us."

"Bottie has told me that Tristram has bred literally hundreds of grandchildren all over the country."

"Then the whole thing is in the bag for us."

"Only according to your prediction. But things just don't go the way they're supposed to."

"You mean F.M. Heller has figured out a better fix? I wondered how come he would agree to all this. He wouldn't let the whole thing rise or fall on some dope fiend of a kid."

"You see?"

"You mean we lose?"

"Only according to your suddenly altered prediction."

"Is something going to happen to Jean-Pierre?"

"I don't know and I won't predict."

"But how else can it work?"

"All we really know is that there are mysteries. You felt old until one sentence spoken at random made you feel young again. When Harry Truman was elected there was no television to brainwash the national mind. Everyone predicted Truman would lose, but the majority voted him in. We have only six voters but it's just as mysterious. But right is right, no matter how cynical—and therefore inexperienced—people say it. If it were possible to predict how it would all turn out we'd die at twelve from boredom."

"You like mysteries, Os. How about a mystery within a mystery? I have known Dunc Mulligan for twenty-nine years. Why does the Attorney General want him in the Senate?"

"Men winnow up."

"Not Dunc. He winnows down. He has been sitting in an unused law library for twenty-one years. Period. Finito la música. It's a true mystery for you. It's as though they stood on the top of every building in Wall Street with a dowsing rod until it bent double when it got directly over Duncan. And I am telling you that Duncan Mulligan is the King of the Twits."

32

Tris and Celeste sat on a bulkhead bench on the starboard upper deck of the Staten Island ferry, *Palmer*. In the course of several round trips, Tris had had his shoes shined twice. In the background a piano-accordionist was playing "When It's Moonlight In Kalua" to be followed by other popular favorites. Celeste was staring moonily at the towers of Wall Street as the ferry plowed through the garbage toward St. George.

"Are you thinking?" Tris asked. She smiled and blushed, as if he had made a preposterously boastful claim for her. She hoped the smile was right. She had forgotten how her face worked since he had come to her life. The old expressions had all been false.

"My husband sits in a law library somewhere over there."

He took her shoulders in his hands. They tried staring into each other's eyes but their astigmatism was different. When he pulled her into focus she had him out of focus so she put her hands on his shoulders to regulate the distance and that made him think she wanted to embrace him so he pulled her all the way in and they couldn't see each other clearly at all. She was so compliant that an alarm went off within him. He didn't want things like that to happen for a long time. He had never taken the time to savor the anticipation of the inevitable but this time he was determined not to throw that away. He had a conviction that if he moved slowly and studied her with absorption that there would be less and less chance for any of the far future moves ever to become monotonous. She waited. He began to talk again and drew away from her.

"Ever want to shoot your husband?" he asked.

"No."

"Then you probably never loved him."

"I never thought I loved him."

"Why did you marry him?"

"Women aren't the romantics, Tris, the men are. I

married him for the same reason every other woman gets married for the first time—to get away from home."

"Why do women get married the second time?"

She shrugged. "To get away from the husbands they never loved, I suppose."

"Is that how it always is?"

"No. Women love more than men when they love but when they do they don't have to marry. Men have to marry. Women have to be loved."

"I never had to marry."

"Then you've never loved."

"Why do men want to marry?"

"To anticipate that they'll stop loving and have granted, while they still love, what they consider to be security on their woman. The security to work for him without any pay but love and to suffer pain for him."

"You sound like Women's Lib."

"I never knew I was. My daughters are. Fiercely and foolishly. But I am now. I don't want someone else's labels for security. The glue dries and they fall off. I want to decide for myself. I'll make the bets then I can understand it better when I lose."

"Why should you lose?"

"Baby—that's maybe what Women's Lib is talking about. Women lose when men say they lose, not when the women think it's just a kind of a pause in life. My daughters have to figure that out."

"How old are they?"

"Nineteen."

"Ah, they have time."

"Time to get hard and used up? That's what losing is."

"You escaped it."

"In your eyes. Not anywhere else. I have played being hard and used since I was fourteen—maybe sooner. My daughters just took a different route. They're groupies or gang-shaggers or whatever."

"Rock groupies or prize-fighter groupies or actor groupies?"

"Civil rights and Women's Lib groupies."

"Yeah." He grinned wryly. "I know what that is."

"And they're not only not very smart—they're twins."

"Pretty?"

"Beautiful. And on heroin."

"Well, that's the way it is now. It's a cycle. Group taste. Everybody adjusts."

"Well, I can't just throw them in the culture pot or the history pot."

"Take it easy and smooth. I know. I'm in the people business the way your husband is in the legal business."

"I hope you are better at it than he is."

"Well, I know what I know. I know maybe a thousand kids like that. You know? Nice, dumb kids. But kids are supposed to be dumb. They do what their pack does, just like voters."

"Anyway—"

"Anyway what?"

"Kiss me."

"You know what a friend of mine named Kimmel said? He said whenever they kissed in the movies they were really fucking."

"Please kiss me, Tris."

33

Bottie found a note saying his father was in Coney Island because it was much less crowded there during the week. Bottie knew that couldn't be true but he greatly appreciated his father's delicacy. The note explained that there were two pounds of ground round steak in the refrigerator (which his father called "the icebox") and it urged him to try the Bonnes Mares '61 with it and said he was not to wait up.

Bottie decanted the wine, then built himself a massive hamburger with the care of a master chemist. He buttered two of the wagon-wheel rolls, sprinkled the caraway seeds over the thickly applied butter, reserved the jar of Imitation Bacon Bits and, while the hamburger cooked, he leaned back in the kitchen chair, sipping the wine and trying to sort out the day; to try to fathom what it was which continued to puzzle him.

He counted probable caucus votes. He wrote Celeste off because it would be improper for her to vote against her husband. Although by now she had talked to Tris whatever she would tell him would be guarded and partisan. Jean-Pierre had said that although he would certainly very much like to meet Bottie that he was too busy and that they would have to put the pleasure off until the dinner Friday night but that in any event he would certainly be voting in his mother's favor. Kaskell was a loss but he had probably been born a loss, Bottie thought; he would vote with his sister. He could count on Tris but they would lose Gawain. So there would be a deadlock. He would have the proxies from Tris' children ready but that didn't look as though it would be necessary. The girls and Esau would vote for Ada. That was a surety—unless their mother prepared the girls by telling them that their votes Friday night could make their father President of the United States, but that was unlikely. It didn't seem possible that even Duncan Mulligan's wife believed that. But he decided he was not going to interfere with how the girls voted because no one should decide he was that wise. Their two votes would be counted as one unit vote. Esau would balance any vote they might cast against Ada, and then Bottie could vote his proxies.

So Ada and his father would win. They could not lose. Therefore what was it which kept gnawing at his entire warning system. Why so much disquietude?

He looked downward through the window to watch the brokers of the New York Narcotics Exchange as they traded cocaine futures and methedrine shares in the cool of the late afternoon. It was a peaceful scene of American business at its tasks of guarding the nations tomorrows by building, with all their might, the Gross National Product. He watched a distinguished, white-haired, beautifully dressed trader take a flick of cocaine into his nostril to be satisfied as to its quality, then to bid for the parcel. Here was continuity, Botolf thought, whether it led upward or downward (or seemed to lead concentrically), or forward or backward (if that were the illusion).

He walked to the stove and turned the gargantuan hamburger and poured another glass of the good, red wine. The people across the country who wanted to tear down all that had been built up so meaningfully could never have bothered to taste or hear or see or feel the good things: the miraculous texture of a fine $3.85 a pound hamburger; the abiding, fulfilling pleasure of a good $19 bottle of wine; the sight of the friendly peace of the Narcotics Exchange, made possible by the great American pharmaceutical industry, in that street below. What they were selling would be the wine of his children. Wine was alcohol. Alcohol was a narcotic. The serenity of a cool, dimly-lighted *chai* in the Medoc was a good and satisfying thing so perhaps he should try harder to accept the fact that the American people liked narcotics and try to see that what he had forbidden Mona and Fiona to do was a cultural thing just as seeing the traders and brokers at work in that street was a traditional practice. Negatives only got negatives, he thought. But how and where had the pendulum gotten stuck?

He turned off the stove. He prepared the sandwich with salt and pepper as carefully as an army corpsman might apply penicillin to a medium-rare battle wound. He thought, after all, Mona and Fiona had never objected to his eating hamburger, without which he undoubtedly could not live. and yet something had had to be slaughtered so he could eat it. Custom was always aberrant. He began to eat and sip and to try to pin down what was bothering him.

It began to float to the top of his mind. Thinking so much about Mona and Fiona had tended to block his mental view of their father. He had met Duncan Mulligan. What was there about that man which made him irreplaceably important to the Attorney General? He had to find the answer to that before he could make any sense out of the rest of it.

Item: Ada Harris was prodigiously wealthy. American political parties need vast contributions of money to survive yet they were willing to alienate Ada Harris forever if that could insure the election of Duncan Mulligan.

Item: Osgood Noon was a powerful lever whose importance to the administration expanded every month the wars were allowed to continue by Presidential whim because Osgood Noon had constructed a working apparatus through which faulty, obsolete, and obsolescent weapons could be disposed of. The administration was helpless to find a solution to what it could do with two hundred and thirteen dangerously unflyable H-101's costing six million dollars each and most desperately needed Osgood Noon's help. Yet they were willing to alienate Osgood Noon if that could lead to the election of Duncan Mulligan. Why?

Gawain knew why. Gawain sweated power. Mankind's collective adoration of its own mind had been transformed into the adoration of Christ, Computer, and that was how Gawain knew why Dunc Mulligan was precious to the power brokers. But Gawain would not tell. Who would tell? Who could profit by telling? Not Dunc Mulligan or his wife because they clearly could not know why. Tris didn't know because he didn't care. But F.M. Heller was the link between the candidate and the power brokers. Therefore F.M. Heller knew and, because it was still before the caucus and because he was a professional politician who might take for granted a condition which was so obvious to him as to have to be obvious to anyone else, it was just possible that F.M. Heller would tell him. It couldn't affect the outcome to know because the proxies would win the caucus no matter what else happened. Bottie wanted to know because he had to know. If he couldn't understand the Duncan Mulligans who were the massive population of American politics then he couldn't really try to understand America.

He finished the glass of wine and went to find a Manhattan telephone directory. It was twenty minutes past six o'clock on a Wednesday evening.

F.M. Heller was listed at an address on Fifth Avenue in the high Sixties. Bottie pitied a man that well-off choosing to live on the East Side when that meant he would have to walk all the way across the park to get to the Museum of Natural History. He dialed the number. He was put through a succession of three voices before they permitted him to speak to F.M. Heller.

"This is Osgood Noon's son, Mr. Heller."

"Ah, yes. How good of you to have invited me to your little family dinner on Friday night."

"Then has Mr. Mulligan explained our arrangements?"

"Indeed he has."

"A matter of deadlock procedure has come up, Mr. Heller, on which I would very much like to have your opinion."

"Your servant, sir."

"Could we meet this evening?"

"*This* evening?"

"Yes."

"I had planned to do my South Australian stamps this evening, but—well—by all means—yes. Can you come here at nine o'clock?"

"I'll be there, sir."

"Was there something else you wanted to talk about? Something I might be thinking about in the meantime?"

"Yes. I wondered how you would feel about unit voting—one family, one vote?"

"But that would absolutely insure a deadlock."

"But—in the event of a deadlock, Mrs. Harris' grandchildren would certainly swing the vote for your side."

"I do not trust young people, Mr. Noon. But I do not say that to give personal offense."

"But we cannot go into the caucus with only two votes. My brother, Monsignor Noon, is required to attend a meeting of the church's Flagellation Society."

"We don't want loose ends, do we? Perhaps he can be persuaded to attend."

"I haven't been able to persuade him, Mr. Heller."

"In that case, I shall have a word with Pope Mellon. Until nine o'clock, then."

Two city policemen guarded the front of Rockrimmon House, F.M. Heller's six-story private residence on Fifth Avenue, one of the last of the great houses of New York. They frisked Bottie rapidly and silently, then permitted him to go up the stone steps to the front door. As he arrived at the top step, a brutal-appearing blond man whose muscles bunched tightly under his white houseman's coat, whose gun was carried in a speed holster strapped around his waist outside the coat, opened the door. Back in the dimness of the huge front hall a man wearing a black hat sat in a high-backed Louis Treize chair with a double-barreled shotgun across his knees. Beside him two enormous Doberman pinschers growled on steel choke chains. They had been trained to sniff out explosive material. All three defense units, man and dogs, were provided through a contract with one of two of Tristram Noon's national companies—Swift-Clean Inc. and Toothy Petz Limited.

The lift carried Bottie upward swiftly. He counted four stories going by, then the door was opened by a shockingly evil-looking Japanese whose bandy legs were the story of O, who wore a samurai sword and a seven-foot-long bow across his back beside a *wuwagashi* filled with twenty-four arrows. His eyes fastened upon Bottie's eyes like talons. They stood, eyeball to eyeball, until a buzzer sounded and the Japanese picked up on a wall telephone. He listened briefly, said, *"Origato"* and motioned to Bottie to step out of the car and follow him.

The room Bottie entered was captured on all four walls by the most hideous wallpaper he had ever seen. On a scene of the harbor at Cronstadt during the Crimean War a series of frames enclosing portraits of forgotten admirals, generals, and postmasters had been overprinted upon the chartreuse and magenta background which was the harbor. He almost cried out in aesthetic pain. He knew, because it was so paralyzingly ugly, that it must be extremely valuable.

F.M. Heller stood at the center of the room wearing vast silk pajamas which seemed to have been dyed in dragon pee under what could have doubled as a one-ring circus tent of green shantung upon which a dragon congress had been embroidered. He was equidistant from all points of the carnage of the wallpaper.

"Don't fight it, Mr. Noon," he said. "It hits everyone the same way. It took me two and a half years to get used to it. It must be the most impressive wallpaper ever designed. John Woolams & Company made it in 1872. I collect wallpaper. Woolams used steam cylinder machinery which enabled them to produce a greatly improved article. They could do from one to eight colors in one operation at the rate of twenty-four hundred yards an hour."

"Twenty-four hundred yards of *this,* sir?" Bottie asked incredulously.

"Indeed, yes. But it's all gone but this batch. What a pity."

Mr. Heller's *Levator labii superioris* elevated his upper lip abruptly, carrying it at the same time a little forward, as his *Levator anguli oris* pulled upward to raise the angle of the corners of the mouth and the *Zygomaticus major* came simultaneously into play with the other muscles, drawing the angle of the mouth fully backward and upward to achieve his very own version of what he liked to think of as a smile, all of it given the stamp of his Republican-leader personality by a great deal of hard work by the superficial surface of the subcutaneous adipose tissue around the malar bone and the Masseter and Buccinator muscles. It was like an old Movietone newsreel wherein eleven thousand overtrained Czech child gymnasts conducted precisely coordinated mass exercises to the pre-fix rhythms of *Kde Domov Muj.* Bottie felt himself wishing he could have a Heller smile for the wall of his room at home, to hang beside the Javanese devil mask and the Maori tiger tattoo his mother had sent him on his sixth birthday.

Mr. Heller urged Bottie to sit down and offered him a cup of hot, wheaten coffee. Bottie declined. "It is made from one hundred percent American wheat," he was reminded but still he declined.

"As you wish. Now. Here we are. Dunc has sent me a hustlegram outlining the voting rules as you had agreed on them. No dispute." He extended the hustlegram to Bottie who read it carefully.

"We are agreed that the Mulligan twins must represent only the one vote?" Bottie asked.

"We accept that."

"As for the male grandchild who is being held in the Tombs—"

"My department. I'll arrange to have him released as you had suggested to Dunc. Same voting pattern. I'll handle that."

"Mr. Heller?"

"Yes, lad?"

"Do I smell marijuana?"

"Why—I—ah—"

"I am very familiar with the smell of marijuana, Mr. Heller, having recently graduated from an American university."

"Well, yes. I make myself experiment with such things to try to put myself in the frame of mind of the young depositor." It was the first time F.M. Heller had blushed since he had been caught eating cold spaghetti from his father's own refrigerator in Dover, New Jersey, in the summer of 1921. "You must be a young depositor of some bank—would you—care to?—"

"Thank you, sir. Yes, I would."

Mr. Heller moved his circular body like a great lighthouse and, in a machined turn, was able to reach and to open a table box which had been covered with sections of wallpaper designed by William Shand Kidd in '96. He extended the box to his guest. Botolf selected a joint. F.M. Heller made a careful choice and put the box away. His gold lighter appeared hospitably under Bottie's funny cigarette and lighted it. Bottie inhaled the smoke to a point three and a half inches below the soles of his feet, then exhaled slowly.

"Very fine," he said.

"Oh, yes. It's the best. I call it Eaton Mews South because one day soon we'll be allowed to market these and the best joints will want a class name. The strain was developed in West Africa by a Texas client of the bank's so that he could be assured of a permanent connection. This is your true, *gen*uine Congo Midnight. It's the finest grass in the world, according to our investment analysts. We had cooperated in attempting to grow some of the strain in fields outside Hackensack, New Jersey, in cooperation with a leading soup producer but we simply lacked that ingredient called the African sun."

"It is fantastic grass," Bottie said with awe.

"Would you like a final surprise? These plants—grown

in the heart of West Africa—are watered twice daily with water imported from Amarillo, Texas. It brings up the unit price, but our analysts say there will be a market for quality pot."

"Well, man, something is doing something to something in here," Bottie said.

"You can bet your knobbly ass on that." F.M. Heller said, swallowing smoke. "One Congo Midnight is the equal of three Acapulco Golds and turns you on, in the power of seven to one against that miserable product people walk all the way to Katmandu to get, risking that ferocious Greek government on the way out."

"Oh, this is fine," Bottie said. "Fine, finer, finest fiber." He emitted twenty-one ounces of fringed smoke as he spoke.

"It goes without saying that if you ever say you got it here, they would lock up the dungeon and throw the key away."

"Man, we are an affinity group. Like I dig."

F.M. Heller blew a gigantic, perfectly formed cube of smoke, three feet by three feet by three feet; opaque. "One day we'll be able to sell advertising on the sides of these cubes," he said. "It's called the Amarillo Effect. That water does it. Any child can blow a cube like that with Congo Midnight and a man can live inside one of those cubes for four and a quarter days, according to our investment analysts, and stay as zonked as a white settler after a Mohican tomahawk raid. I mean that amortizes the high original cost, doesn't it?"

"F.M.?"

"Lay it on me, Botto."

"You did know that my brother, Gawain, is the papal nuncio to the Attorney General?"

"Indeed, yes. I've attended Print-Out Services with him in the Attorney General's war room."

"You must know the Attorney General rather well."

"Oh, yes."

"What's he really like, F.M.?"

"How can one describe a man who runs a nation of two hundred-odd million people? He's a proud man. I remember way back when we were trying to decide whether he really did have the ability to run the country and he gave us that marvelous look of his, the one where you begin to feel just a little bit afraid that he might decide to pee on you and he said, 'Boys—I've made more money in the practice of law than the President. I've brought more clients into our firm. I can hold my own and a helluva lot more any time of the day or night in any argument with the President and I always win. And when I win he has the simple-minded sense to do as he's told. When I deal with him, I deal with an equal or better—if you know what I mean and I think you do.' Now that's not a shy man, is it, Botolf? Nor will he brook dissent because as Attorney General he believes dissenters are either breaking a sacred law or are about to break a sacred law—to the extent that sometimes it bothers me that he is either unfamiliar with our Constitution or is eagerly prepared to ignore it."

"He makes it sound like it can be nineteen hundred five all over again."

"Son, the Attorney General is going to make it seem like he has sustained McKinley's first term forever—"

"The Republican Party's impossible dream?" Bottie asked.

"Yes! It'll be a banker's and businessman's country again. No more whining by the wrong kind of colored boys. No more radicals ruining our educational institutions."

"But in a way it's confusing, isn't it? I mean when my father and Mrs. Harris pulled back every cent from your bank that had to hurt."

"A zinger. The worst."

"Then they said they would sue under the Hatch Act if the party didn't return every cent they'd ever contributed to any Republican campaign."

"A rotten, low blow," F.M. Heller said. "It still has us reeling."

"Then—two Mondays from now my father's magazine is going to warn every small belligerent nation in the world against those two hundred and thirteen H-101's and —wow—that's a real monkey wrench in the works—right?"

"Bottles, they are appalled in Washington. And I am near to a breakdown." F.M. Heller stood up and put his shoulder to the darkly cubic Amarillo Effect and slowly moved it into position directly above his chair. He sat down again and his head was vaguely obscured within it as though it had been wrapped in layers of dark cheesecloth. The extreme density of the content of the Effect began to tell at once on the banker.

"As of this precise moment," he said with ineffable languor, "the church is sifting through your father's past with an Apostle computer and if they can turn up even the slightest depredation the Department of Justice will be inside his house with a no-knock search team. He will be hit on the head, arrested, and taken to the District of Columbia and thrown into preventive detention until the Democrats come home which will be sometime in the twenty-first century. It was for crazy, unforeseeable things like this that the Attorney General invented preventive detention. I mean the time has to come when a man like that has to lock a lot of people up."

"If you do that to Pop, won't that hurt Dunc Mulligan's campaign?"

"That's what I keep telling them. That's why I'm near to a breakdown."

"But, that's what spooks me. How can you take a beating like that at the bank, the Defense Department have its whole fall line ruined, and the party nearly bankrupt for cash—only because of Dunc Mulligan? Why is he so valuable? What has he got?"

F.M. Heller blinked. It was a lengthy effect because each eyelid weighed slightly more than a Howard Johnson steak. "Isn't that pretty obvious?" he asked.

"No, sir."

"You really don't know?"

"No, sir."

"Then you must be contemplating Duncan Mulligan, the man—the individual. You couldn't survive in politics very long if you looked at candidates as human beings. I certainly have no caution about telling you what every working politician in the country knows—even if it is a dark secret to the American press, our trade-paper reporters."

F.M. Heller began the play of counter-pulleys within his cheeks and around his mouth to haul his face into that heinous fantasy of a smile once again, to emphasize the deadly effect he wanted to make. "Political techniques are not always evolved, you see. More often they are revealed by accident. This miraculous accident which uncovered Duncan Mulligan and revealed his extraordinary powers to the Attorney General and to the party happened when there was that soon-to-be-gruesome Fortas vacancy on the Supreme Court which Senator Thurmond wanted filled quickly. So he asked the Gullah County Bar Association of central Georgia for the recommendations and the results were so magnificent that, while the seating of the Court was being settled, we had Christ, Computer, canvass the various other progressive bar associations until it was soon established by a simple process of elimination that the most shallow, ambitious, and grossly manipulatable possible candidates had made their pilgrimages from all over the nation to the law firms in Wall Street. It's sort of a natural migration.

"Then, Christ, Computer, really went to work. It was so thrilling, Botolf. I will never, ever forget it. In my own state lived the Republican messiah waiting to be revealed. It was as though the Phoenix had been awakened from a troubled sleep to rise like an Apollo missile from the ashes of the old-time ways which had *professional* politicians actually *agreeing* to the possible candidacy of such impossibly intelligent men as Adlai Stevenson and Woodrow Wilson. And in rising, the Phoenix revealed within the nest it had been sitting upon, the model, all-time perfect candidate since the invention of the democratic system which in itself was the greatest gimmick an oligarchy had ever designed. It revealed ole Funky Dunc Mulligan whose mind is as vast and as empty as the vastness of all outer space—a universe of mindlessness wherein great planets of ideas and concepts could hurtle past each other into bottomless infinities without ever being observed. Yes, Botolf—there in the Phoenix's nest called Wall Street, the little town of Bethlehem Steel, Christ, Computer, found Dunc Mulligan seated alone and content in the remote, never-used Tanzanian law library of Lantz, Lantz, Tolliver and Farr. Dunc Mulligan! The weakest vessel, the greediest dreamer, the most mediocre lawyer and the greatest front-runner for the oligarchy since Warren Harding but, in that same sense, greater than Harding. We were touched, as you will be when you see him disappear into high office, by the very majesty of his banality and the ease with which his attention-span—which we refer to as his 'fatigue-level'—can be used to keep him to heel. Oh, I know! I know what you, as an amateur, are thinking. That the electorate despises such a candidate. But, hehehehehehehe, if that is the case, hehehehehehe, why do they vote for him every time? Every time! Why? Because he is them and they are him and they deserve each other. He is them! In every unsuperlative, lazy, greedy way he is what they are so they want to exalt him. So I say this to you, Botolf —no matter who the opposition brings forward—never mind Muskie or Hubert, never mind Teddy—no one, repeat *no* one—can match the shallowness of Dunc Mulligan."

"But after he's elected and the crises occur, how can you conceal what he is?"

"The Attorney General says we are making great strides in the field of cryogenics but, until that has been perfected we will do what must be done—we will surround him with the De Gaulle Effect—and preserve his majesty with his mystery which will be compounded by an aloofness eighteen-men deep."

"And how about press conferences?"

"God knows. As few as possible. My God! Duncan in a press conference. La!"

"The whole thing seems such a rotten deception and a cheat, Mr. Heller."

"True, it is a deception, but it is neither rotten nor a cheat. It is the best that can be done under the Constitution, and considering men like the Attorney General. As long as the people are deliberately taught that a single executive can possibly run the most complicated nation on the planet *and* attend Easter egg rollings, baseball games, fleet maneuvers and White House concerts, then what we are forced to do is the only way, my boy. The only way. The country does have to keep running, doesn't it?" He stared at Botolf sadly. "Doesn't it, Botolf?"

34

On the very morning Esau was to be tried on the bombing charge to which he would gleefully enter a plea of guilty as the loving bride exclaims "I do!" a guard appeared at his cell door and led him to an office where his belongings were returned to him.

"What are you trying to do here?" Esau boomed. "What is this? I haven't even been sentenced yet."

"You are sprung," the prison official said.

"How can I be sprung? I tried to bomb a place of public assembly. I am guilty. I confessed and I signed. I can't be sprung. I know my rights. I demand that you return me to my cell to await sentencing."

"You are sprung," the official snarled, "now gedda hell outta here."

"Who did this to me? F.M. Heller, the banker? Was it F.M. Heller? This is a heinous miscarriage of justice and I demand a lawyer."

"This here is your lawyer," the official said. "She sprung you."

Esau wheeled around to stare at a tiny woman with a ruffian's face who was wearing a Queen Mary hat with what seemed to be a large fishbone stuck in it. A brown cigarette dangled from the corner of her mouth. She grinned, showing teeth like a Manila street sweeper's knuckles and said gratingly, "Hello, baby. I'm Sally Capistrano, yaw mouthpiece. Call me Swallows." Leering, she swaggered toward him slowly.

"I will kill you if you don't get me back inside and let me pay my debt to society," Esau said.

She whacked him across the chops with her heavy purse so hard he staggered sideways. "Shut yaw mouth, yuh liddle freak," she said. "Come on. We're goin' uptown." She waved farewell to the official and left the office. Esau followed, weeping.

They rode in a black limousine which was so large that Lawyer Capistrano's feet, in jade-suede Space shoes, were unable to touch the floor. Esau tried to speak to her once, early in the journey, but she snarled at him so brutally that he had to press his fists into his mouth to keep from screaming. After a time, she relented. "What kinda shit were you on, kid?"

"Sp—speed," he blubbered.

She laughed harshly, making sounds like a broken garbage disposal unit. "Speed, speed, the American drug/ The more you shoot the more you bug." She rummaged in her bag, gloating at him, and extended a bottle of pills. "Here, schmuck. Take a handful."

Esau's trembling hand was able to shake nine white bennies out of the vial. He threw them back into his mouth, chewing well. In no time he felt splendid. The car stopped. Lawyer Capistrano said, "All right, schmuck. Out." She was short enough to walk erect across the tonneau of the car to open the door.

"Where is here?" Esau asked.

"Here is the client." She led the way into the bank through an enormous bronze-gated doorway, directly to a uniformed guard. "Max? You got an okay for me and one?"

The guard referred to a book. "Okay, Swallows," he said, "in the private chute."

He guided them to the elevator door, pressed a button and they entered the car. Lawyer Capistrano patted the guard on his behind. "Anytime, Max—anywhere," she snorted. The door closed. The car was pulled upward at great speed.

"You know how you'll know when you got it made?" she asked rhetorically. "It's when you got an office on the seventy-eighth floor and they give you your own private chute so you shouldn't have to ride wit' the sweat."

When the lift door opened a matronly secretary and an armed guard were waiting for them. "Thank you, counselor," the rosy lady said, "I'll take him now."

"Sign right here, Miss Silverschein," Lawyer Capistrano extended a flat, opened book and a pen. She got into the lift, waved girlishly, pressed a button and disappeared.

The guard told Esau to follow the matronly lady. They went through two exquisite rooms, cartouched with the work of Renoir, Pissaro, and Shannon-Phillips, and Louis XV pot-bellied commodes. A great double door opened. The matronly lady pushed him gently through toward a spherical, white-bearded man who waited behind a Florentine desk as big as the foredeck of an Italian aircraft carrier.

"Ah! Sylvan!" the white-bearded man said mellifluously. "I am *so* glad you could come."

"Like where am I? Like who are you?"

"I am F.M. Heller, your friendly Everest banker."

Esau remembered. Everything Botolf Noon had told him would happen, was happening. "You got me out? I'm out? You mean I am out for good?"

"All charges have been quashed. You are a free man."

"You mean I can't get back in?"

"I don't understand," F.M. Heller said. "You are free."

Esau rushed the great desk and leaned across it, his face contorted with fright and frenzy. "Free? Are you crazy?" he shouted. "Do you have any *idea?* Did I ask? Who wanted it? I want in, I don't want out. I found happiness in there. You money freak! I want to pay my debt to society. Get on that pipe and get me back in, you hear?"

"I simply don't think anyone has made it clear to you, young man. I have freed you from a house of detention. You need have no fear whatever that anyone will come to take you back inside the filthy place. The charges have been quashed. Your file has been destroyed."

Esau remembered the little guy in the knickerbockers with the eyeglasses and the braces on his teeth whose neon eyes had blazed out such sanity.

"You know what, Midas?" he said. "I am going to my boss when I leave here. You know who is my boss? My boss is my uncle—Jean-Pierre Harris. You know who is Jean-Pierre Harris? Jean-Pierre is Mafia—capo di Mafia, the highest—and he has such a crazy sense of family honor, of family obligation, of such loyalty and the need to revenge anybody who affronts any member of his family that you will be finished. You understand finished? You know from through? What? Hey? You are through, Heller."

"Ah, of course. How obtuse of me. Grand Prix is a *Mafia* operation."

"You happen to be telling it like it is."

"And, yes—how *very* interesting—Mafia executives are very kinky about affronts to family. Well! Thank you, boy. I have been trying for days to find just the handle for your uncle Jean-Pierre. Family affronts cause them to fear a loss of respect—isn't that right?"

"You bet on it, Dad. Right. All the way. Okay. You dig. So get on the pipe and call the Man and get me back inside that Tombs now. You hear? And fix the judge good to hand me a heavy sentence. You got it?"

"Lower your voice. Sit down on that chair. You are out of the Tombs for my reasons and you will do as you are told or I will send you out to spend a few nights with Lawyer Capistrano."

Esau began to weep again. His six feet four inches crumbled into the chair. His hairy face fell into his cupped hands as he sobbed heartbreakingly. "Okay. Tell me what to do. But when I do what you want—then will you get me back inside? Please?"

"I'll decide that when I see some results. Tonight you will attend a dinner for your grandmother at your uncle's apartment. Here." He slid a slip of paper across the enormous desk, using a croupier's stick. "There's the address. A vote will be taken at the dinner. When it comes your turn to vote you will vote no. If you can't remember that, you will vote the way your Aunt Celeste will vote. If remembering that is beyond you, you will look at me and I will shake my head and you will vote no. And if you fail in this you will discover that you literally cannot get yourself arrested and cannot get yourself committed to any prison of any consequence in this or in any NATO country." He turned his swivel chair slightly and flipped a switch on the console of an intercom and spoke into it. "Show Mr. Harris to a taxi, please."

Esau stumbled to the door, sobbing. The door opened and a uniformed security guard took him out.

When the cab got Esau to West End Avenue he was in such a fury that he kicked it in the tires after he had paid it off.

"What are you?" the hackie yelled at him. "Beautiful when you're angry?"

Esau ran into the building. When he opened his own front door upstairs on the seventeenth floor he could hardly get into his flat. The tiny foyer was almost entirely filled with thick, long rectangles of tar-spattered wood, piled nearly halfway to the ceiling. Esau threw back his head and screamed. Bummy Kantrowitz appeared through an archway on the other side of the pile of strange lumber. He was wearing a peignoir and looked alarmed.

"Whassamatta, Eess? How come the heron imitations?" He had not shaved for several days.

"What is all this drek in my hall?" Esau shrieked.

"Jeez, I'm sorry about that, Eess, I rilly am. I thought the super woulda got it outta here by now. You know, I think that guy drinks? Anyway, who expected you? I thought you had it all fixed to spend the resta your life inna can." Bummy was so completely triple-zonked that the top of his bald head had become corrugated.

"What is this *lum*ber, you oaf! What are these dirty sticks, for God's sake?"

"Well, I mean you were inside—right? I mean there was no infidelity—I mean strictly, you unnerstand, Eess? Well —I met this crazy quean down by the Penn Central tracks near the job so I thought he was kind of cute and he was flipping so I let him do a liddle blow job on me."

"Who asked for true confessions! What is all this rotten wood?"

"I'm explaining. After, he kepp begging me to let him send me a liddle something—you know. So I said, just to get ridda him, send me a couple dozen ties."

"So?"

"So—these are them. He misunnehstood. He thought I meant railroad ties."

"This is too *much!*" Esau screeched. "I have been on a powerized Catherine wheel all day and I have to come home to this!"

"Eess! Calm, calm. Whatta yuh worrying? The super will get them out."

"You traitorous, evil bitch!"

"Ah, come on. Gizza kiss. Welcome home from durance vile. Gizza kiss."

"I am going to break you in half like a Sal*tine!*" Esau screamed. He scrambled over the high pile of ties with great difficulty but rushed through a different archway to the room-long speed bar. He broke the seal on a new gallon jug of liquid methedrine, loaded two large hypodermics and shot two loads straight along the tracks to his pointed head. Every vein in his body constricted. His metabolism jolted into high speed as the pressured blood shot through the power hose of the tightened vessels. Then he grinned affectionately across the room at Bummy as he felt the three-foot long wimple grow long and longer out of the top of his skull.

"Bummy, daaling." he said, his voice oddly changed to the timbre of a full Dixieland band with no helmholz barred, achieving a sound intensity whose Hertzian repetitive peaks surpassed any Fletcher-Munson effect.

"Yes, Eess," Bummy answered with terror.

"You are a double daaling. With a raisin on top."

"Jeez, thanks, Eess."

Esau picked up a telephone and dialed.

"Who are you calling Eess?"

"Grandma."

"Better adjust your loudness control. Your woofer. It's booming. You are running at about zero point one *fo*."

"Thanks, Bum." His control amplifier slid a double filter between his voice box and the phone. "Hello, Grandma? It's Esau."

"Esau! How marvelous! Do they have phones in the cells?"

Esau began to sob.

"Darling, what's the matter? Tell Grandma. What's the matter?"

"I don't know what to do. I just don't know. They put me out of the Tombs."

"Put you out? Why would they do a thing like that?"

"A crazy banker sent some lawyer and they just lifted me out. And I was so happy there. I've never been so happy in my life, Grandma. I can't tell you the friendships I sealed there."

"Which banker?"

"That Sandy Claws figure—the fat one—F.M. Heller."

"No!"

"Yes. Yes, he did."

"This is barbaric. This is going too far! Now they are declaring war on children!"

"I had to talk to someone who cared. I need help. Maybe you have friends who know a judge or some mean cops. I have to know what I'm supposed to do with my life."

"Don't worry, darling. Don't cry. It's all right. Grandma will get you back inside that Tombs."

"I am so *mis*erable."

"And that fat Heller is going to pay for this. He is

going to pay like he never thought he would ever have to pay."

"But—how? How can you do anything to the biggest banker in the world?"

"I don't know. I am going to think. I am going to talk to experts. Blowing up his goddam bank would be a good start. Blow up his bank and he has nothing. Just a big stomach and a white beard, nothing. Now, lie down, darling. Take a nice glass of hot water and a big tablespoonful of Castoria. Sleep for eighteen or twenty hours, then we'll talk again." Ada disconnected.

Esau had sobbed and nodded, nodded and sobbed all through his grandmother's advice. He had wallowed in her always dependable love and sympathy. Then, some two hundred seconds after she had hung up, as he stood there holding the phone to his ear the solution to everything came crashing out of the darkness of his despair and the true paths shone before him like an Esso road map: varicose and glowing red.

"Thank you, Grandma," he said and hung up. He slipped the filters out of his voice box and, as he turned to Bummy, fed gain into his power amplifier.

"BUMMY!" Had Captain Bligh been standing beside him in vocal contest and had he attempted to duplicate the tone it would have emerged, in comparison, like the voice of a mother hummingbird calling its young into the nest. Two pictures fell off the wall and the leg of the baby grand piano collapsed. Bummy fell to his knees.

"Eeeesss!!! *No!*"

"Get dressed. Call Hertz and rent a truck. Drive the truck to your job and bring back all the nitro and fuses they have. *Now!*"

"But—it's my day off!"

"Bum, baby?"

"Yes, Eess?"

"Would you like an only-one-of-its-kind Yves Saint Laurent evening dress in aluminum lamé to wear at a certain up-coming ball at the Melrose-Steinberg Casino?"

"Yes!"

"Go!"

As Bummy climbed over the railroad ties to get to his room to change from the peignoir to work clothes, Esau slipped into a comfortable, old-shoe Mad Scientist smile. He was going to blow up the Everest Bank. He was going to blow up the biggest bank in the United States of America. That would show that hairy kumquat of a banker how crazy he had been to fool around with Sylvan Harris. That would give him just one little old idea as to what just might go next if he didn't get on that pipe and open the gates to the Tombs. Blowing up the Everest Bank would be destruction of the kind of property which would drive judges and juries into frenzies of justice. He could read the headline on all editions, Cottage Cheese Early through Late Sporting, of the *New York Post*—aiee!

DOPE FIEND FAGGOT BLOWS
UP NATION'S BIGGEST BANK

They would hurl him into a total-security prison for *longer* than Dallas had sentenced that grass blower, *longer* than 1500 years. He was twenty-two. He could be fifteen hundred and fifty-three years old by the time he got out. The whole rest of his life ahead of him—being raped, being held down on the cold stone floor or up against the sweating walls by three men who were merely showing in their own way that they needed him and being raped by a fourth man who *really* needed him. Every day, maybe twice a day—at least until he lost his looks.

He decided to faint. The whole world began to blink on and off in colors of Ming blue, dark squash, lemon brass, tawny mushroom, absinthe, lobster bisque, honeydew, terra cotta, orange ice, Indian brick, moon white, slate, pistachio, sand, pimiento, grape sherbet, and peacock.

When Bummy returned with the makings to demolish the bank he had to jolt Esau in the arm again to get him to wake up. But in no time they were as busy as Christmas dwarfs making nineteen neat, flat packages wrapped in sturdy brown paper bound with stunning white twine, each package ticking ever so faintly. Then Bummy helped him to load them carefully into the rented van and Esau drove across town to his father's to savage him into giving up his safe deposit keys but Kaskell was not in. So Esau decided he would try his Uncle Dunc who was always in. Uncle Dunc's office was just a few yards from the Everest Bank. He drove downtown on the F.D.R. Drive, found parking in the bank's own lot then went to Dunc's "office."

Duncan was pathetically glad to see him. Esau was the second visitor he had had that year, not counting the twins. Esau's eyes seemed to be spinning like pinwheels as he explained that Ada had asked him to drop off nineteen packages of jewelry at the bank vault but she had misplaced the key.

"Can you help me out with this, Uncle Duncle?" Esau asked. "I mean, you know just everybody."

"I am your family lawyer, Sylvan. That's what I'm here for. To help the family."

"You mean you can actually get the packages into Ada's safe deposit boxes?"

"Indeed, yes. Uh—Sylvan?"

"Yes, Uncle Duncle?"

"Uh—I wondered if you might be able to give me a precise definition of the word—funky?"

"Funky?" Esau blinked.

"Yes."

"Like in—what?"

"As in—oh—as in 'Funky Dunc.' "

"Oh. *Fun*ky. Well, you know, funky. Like they used to say groovy—like solid?"

"How could it mean that?"

"How do I know? Who knows who makes up the words?"

"But the Attorney General thinks it is a pejorative designation."

"That's his privilege, right? Now, how about you tell the bank to let me stack Ada's packages, hey?"

"Yes. Of course. Come with me, Sylvan. We'll do it on the Picturephone because that's how the bank has to have it. Security is rife. Groovy. Well!" They left the library and walked together down a corridor. "But, I don't get it. Why would they call *me* Funky?"

"Who?"

"All over Harlem."

"Oh, there. They are very sarcastic in Harlem."

Dunc gave the instructions to the Picturephone operator and sat down in front of the screen. In the time it took to reach the bank and get put through to the woman in charge of the safe deposit vaults, Duncan nervously adjusted the knot in his tie and patted the sides of his head above the ears, then carefully put on his campaign smile as the life-sized picture of a small woman wearing a gorgeous white wig zoomed into focus.

"Miss Flinn? This is Duncan Mulligan of Lantz, Lantz, Tolliver and Farr."

"I recognize you, Mr. Mulligan."

"I have some packages which are to be installed in the safe deposit boxes of my client, Mrs. Ada Harris."

"I acknowledge that name, Mr. Mulligan."

"I will bring them to you in exactly—" he looked at the large butch watch on his wrist, "twenty-three minutes. Will you provide cover at the bank entrance, Miss Flinn?"

"Our men will cover you, Mr. Mulligan. Is that all?"

"Thank you, Miss Flinn."

They switched off. Duncan turned to Esau. "But, frankly, I am puzzled. Why would they want to be sarcastic about me all over Harlem?"

"Maybe—you know—it's—like fun. I better cut, Uncle Duncle. Twenty-two minutes now."

"I insist that you let me help you. Besides, they expect me." It would be a long day for Dunc and he was grateful for the idea of having something to do.

"No, no. That's all right."

"How many packages are there?"

"Only nineteen."

"Nineteen! Then you simply must let me help you, Sylvan."

"That's real funky of you, Dunc, I mean it. That is no sarcasm. But they are right at the bank door in a truck right at the door and the bank men will do all the heavy work."

"Oh." Duncan was disappointed. "All right then."

Esau thanked him again and shook both his hands, then kissed him shyly under the ear and scampered off down the hall toward the elevators.

Duncan wiped at his ear with a large white handkerchief and started back to the law library and the silence. "Funky Dunc. Well, that's not bad at all," he thought. "And there is a *very* good chance that those darkies aren't being sarcastic at all."

Three Everest Bank guards helped Esau carry the nineteen flat packages from the truck to the vault after they had recorded his voiceprint and his fingerprints. The packages were slipped into eleven of Ada's deposit boxes and locked securely.

"Miss Flinn was called out unexpectedly," the uniformed chief guard said as he extended the records book to be signed. "She'll be real sorry she missed you, Mr. Mulligan." So Esau signed the register "Duncan Mulligan" so no one could be confused.

35

That morning, twenty-five minutes after Esau had been put into the private lift and sent away from the Everest Bank, Monsignor Noon glided into F.M. Heller's office, wearing a mauve soutaine under a smart black beretta, to find his brother Tristram there awaiting him so the meeting could begin. The monsignor greeted the ponderous white-bearded banker and Tris with peanut-butter blandness and sat down decorously in a straight-backed chair, adjusting the skirt of his cassock fussily.

"I am assured that everything will go quite smoothly at the caucus tonight," F.M. Heller said. "However, as we all know, the essence of flawlessness is in planning—in checking and rechecking out mutual understandings." He spoke distantly as though he were preoccupied with glorious opportunity. All at once he seemed to reach the conclusion he had been seeking. He beamed at the brothers and said, "For example, I am pleased to be able to report that Jean-Pierre Harris will not cast his vote for his mother tonight."

The Noon brothers' eyebrows went up but, having been professional conspirators for so long, they did not ask how this coup had been arranged and would not ask until or if the prediction came to happen. So they nodded.

"Therefore," F.M. Heller continued, "if your younger brother should ask how you are going to vote I would judge, personally, that it would be best to tell him that you will vote in favor of your father."

"Of course," Gawain said.

Tris nodded glumly.

"With Mrs. Mulligan-Harris voting no, with Kaskell's no, and with Jean-Pierre's seat being taken by his nephew, Esau—with whom I have chatted and who will also vote no, all added to your own negative votes we will have carried the caucus by five to one against the danger that Duncan Mulligan might be prevented from serving the republic."

"What will the outcome be?" Tris asked.

"Pardon?"

"If Pop and Mrs. Harris are set to lose, what will happen to them? How will it be solved?"

"Oh—well. I have discussed that with a certain extremely powerful person in Washington and he has arranged to have military jet transport, luxuriously fitted —in fact the same luxurious plane used to carry members of Appropriations and Military Affairs—standing by to fly your father and Mrs. Harris to the Republic of Panama tonight where they will be picked up by the light-cruiser, *Mendel Rivers,* and taken to Pitcairn Island where, I am assured by the Attorney General, Conrad Hilton himself could not have arranged more comfort than has been arranged for them—Muzak, a genuine luau followed by an authentic hula every night with American-style breakfasts and all the Poland water they can drink—all being laid on now by CINCPAC by courtesy of the British Admiralty."

"How long do they have to stay there?" Tris asked. "After all—I mean—how many years do they have at their age?"

"That has all been settled most compassionately by our leaders, I can assure you. As soon as Duncan has been well sworn in they will be free to go—if they wish to. And this is an example of the Attorney General's free spirit—if they choose to stay on at Pitcairn there will be no charge."

"As soon as Duncan is sworn in for what?" Tris asked.

"Pardon?"

"Did you mean as soon as Duncan is sworn in for the Senate?"

"Not actually. But that is something we are not free to discuss, is it?"

"May I congratulate you on your consummate skill in this entire matter?" Gawain asked. "And for the devotion to Church and Party with which you planned this whole thing?"

"Thank you."

"His Holiness, Pope Mellon, has ordered me to confer on you the Sovereign Order of ABM-Lateran. Sovrana Ordine Osepedaliero di San Tomaso de Accesso Madison detto di ABM."

"I believe I have that decoration, Monsignor. But thank you nonetheless."

"You hold the rank of Deserving and Magistral Knight of Grace in that order, Mr. Heller. This will be Knight of Grace *and* Devotion. Although you wear the same *basic* badge of the Order you will now be authorized to add the coat of arms crowned with a helmet and above the crown a set of crossed swords on a black necklet."

"Frankly, Monsignor, I was hoping for something altogether different."

"*How* different, Mr. Heller, might I ask?"

"I should think, from what I have been able to accomplish here for both Church and Party, and at a quite shockingly considerable financial loss to my bank, which will most certainly not be redeposited in my bank after these two former and highly desirable depositors have spent a few years on Pitcairn Island, all of which will *certainly* not go down well with my Board of Directors, that I might, at least, have been decorated with the first-class rank in the order, as a Legal Knight, wearing the *fullest* badge and, on the black necklet, the white ABM Cross in gold with the Florentine fleur-de-lis in angles of the cross and pendant on a crown beneath a trophy with the coat of arms of the Order with the honored Profess Cross."

"I am very sorry you are disappointed, Mr. Heller," Gawain said.

"Indeed, so am I."

"Surely you can see that I am not em*pow*ered to grant the advanced decoration?"

"You are not?"

"No, Mr. Heller."

"Then I suggest that you be generous enough to withdraw to that private room and explain by telephone to His Holiness the detailed sacrifices I have made within this accomplishment for which he wishes to commend me and that you accept more realistic instructions from him."

Gawain stood up, glaring. White-faced and with a loud swish of his stiff, rich garments he swept out of the room.

F.M. Heller looked at Tris and raised his hands in a gesture of helplessness.

"I think you made yourself an enemy F.M." Tris said.

"We make them every day."

"Not like Gawain. He never forgets."

"There is somehow more pleasure in one's enemies than in one's friends. Have I ever shown you the letters I have written to *The New York Times* holiday section editor about the disgraceful way the Port Authority handles our airports?"

"No. But Gawain isn't any kind of an enemy you may have ever encountered, F.M. Gawain is—well, I'd hate to have Gawain as an enemy. You have called him on a political matter and he will have to reply to you in a political manner."

"Well, dammit, Tristram! These decorations mean nothing to me but they are extremely important at bankers' conventions. Al Gurgie at National City has Grace and Devotion and Henri Emmet at the Hambro's has Legal Knight and we are twice the bank theirs are. We are only niggling about a trinket, after all."

"Let it go."

"Do we have a moment to talk about your work before the caucus, Tristram Noon?"

"Yes, sir."

"Good. The Attorney General feels that if you can get a really good-sized crowd of darkies and a really rotten crowd of students to intermingle," he shuddered, "as they support Duncan's principal opponent at the convention, then attack Dunc's car when it arrives the way you had them attack the President's car at San Jose in seventy, the Vice-President's office will arrange the right camera positions with the networks and see that guidelines are set down for the national commentators. We'll want pure hatred expression from the darkies particularly and we'll need about a company of hard hats to appear out of nowhere to surround Dunc's car and take over his defense from the embattled police, whom you'll also have to provide, of course."

"That's all set, F.M. We're all rehearsed."

"This is big stuff, Tristram. As big as the confrontation effects you gave us in Chicago in sixty-eight. That was brilliant. This has to be more brilliant."

"Don't worry. We've choreographed some really magnificent crowd scenes. We'll be using a regiment of blacks and students against a battalion of hard hats and police. No sense having more than that because even the wide-angles can't hold them in. But every shot will fill the scene with blood and fright as Dunc faces them with that cool courage shining from his face into the cameras."

"Good. At the policy meeting with the Attorney General there was some talk about having Dunc and the Vice-President machinegun a part of the mob which would be crossing the street just as he arrives—perhaps wearing sweet, little white First Communion dresses—but the Vice-President will be speaking in Toledo that day, alas, and Dunc is such a twit he probably can't be taught how to handle a machine gun and would undoubtedly wing one of the little girls."

"I just don't think that will be necessary, F.M."

"You don't. Good. Do you have any other ideas I might pass along?"

"We have a lot of ideas in work. There are a lot of bugs to be worked out."

"I'd certainly like to know at least a day before the convention next Wednesday so the Vice-President's office can make sure the networks understand their instructions about the camera placements and what they are supposed to get."

"Hell, F.M., we'll have it all diagramed for you by Sunday morning."

"Oh, good. That's just fine."

Monsignor Noon swept back into the room, rigidly frigid with enmity.

"I am to inform you, Mr. Heller," he said, making no move to reseat himself but facing F.M. Heller slightly behind Tris' chair, "that His Holiness, in most gracious gratitude, has commanded me to confer upon you the rank of Legal Knight, First-class, in the Sovereign Order of ABM-Lateran of St. Thomas Watson of Madison Avenue."

F.M. Heller had been made so arrogant about his future by what Tris had just told him concerning the surety of Duncan Mulligan's nomination the following Wednesday that he blurted, imprudently, "I think I'll take a rain check on that, Monsignor, if you don't mind. I am about to serve Church and Party to such glorious ends—in this entire matter of Dunc Mulligan—that I feel that, after Election Day, Pope Mellon will want me to be invested in the Order of Christ, Computer, itself, with the Badge of the Order, the red-enameled St. Thomas of Watson Cross with outward-bent armatures and the Collar of the

Order—of gold, consisting of enameled medallions with alternately the Watson coat of arms and the word THIMK surrounded by laurel wreath, linked with diamond-pasted figures, centered by the Star Of the order, further surrounded by a laurel of rubies."

Gawain leaned forward as though he were scenting. No man could have such effrontery unless he had been given extraordinary assurances from extraordinary personages. This could indicate a new emphasis within the national leadership—the national *political* leadership—which might possibly be most significant. He spoke his testing sentence carefully, "That order is, as you know, Mr. Heller, only conferred upon statesmen of cabinet rank." He watched intently for the response.

"Quite so, Monsignor Noon. Quite so." F.M. Heller reached for the silver handles on his desk to pull himself to his feet. The audience had ended.

When the Noon brothers departed F.M. Heller canceled his next appointment with a sentence into the intercom. He waddled across the room to the wall safe file and presented his thumbprint to the seeing-eye electronic sensor. He leaned forward and entered his voiceprint for analysis by saying, "Well, how about that?" A locked panel was unlocked electronically. He slid it away and pulled out a large file drawer and removed a thick file marked HARRIS, MRS. ADA and lumbered back to the desk with it, breathing desperately for being one hundred and forty-one pounds overweight.

He sat quietly at his desk for twelve minutes until he had regained his breath. He opened the file. It contained shockingly candid, color still photographs which had been transmitted to Control from Osgood Noon's vest and fly buttons. There were boldly clear, crisp photographs of Ada leering lasciviously, her drawers down and her skirts up under her chin as she waited for Os to mount her. All in all, the set was as lewdly varied a collection of overpersonal photographs of one woman as ever had been set on film; Ada omnivorous and insatiable in series of more and more graphic surprises. As photographs they were excellent. As pornography they were masterpieces. F.M. Heller could almost feel the force of the offense Jean-Pierre Harris would feel when he looked upon these photographs of his mother. The caucus would become as nothing to him. His mind would go blank except for the single need for vengeance upon whoever had taken such terrible pictures and had caused them to be sent to him. He would rush out of the caucus flat to search out and destroy. It would take him days before he realized that there was no trail to follow. He would never know who had sent him the pictures. By the time that sense of fruitlessness had overtaken him, his mother would be on Pitcairn and Duncan would have been nominated.

36

Jean-Pierre Harris had put off granting the interview to Bottie for as long as possible. For him each week and each day within each week was busier than the day and week before. All reasonable projections on the gradual lack of public interest in pornography after intense exposure to it, as it had worked in Denmark where, after the first great flooding of pornographic activity into the culture, the people had become bored with it, had not been the case in the American market. Public interest became keener and keener as the compost heap of Jean-Pierre's products grew higher and higher. A think tank in the upper Hudson River valley was now under full-time retainer, having revoked all of its government contracts, merely to visualize, invent and think up more extensive uses of pornographic concepts. In the motorized field alone, Jean-Pierre's company, Grand Prix, always given the Anglo-Saxon rather than the French pronunciation, owned seven hundred and four basic patents. The field of chemical aphrodisiacs and what was referred to as "industrial suggestibles" had been mere story-book nonsense whose efficacy had depended upon the fevered imaginations of the users until Jean-Pierre's extravagant contracts had attracted Nobel Prize chemists and biologists. Their work in advanced protein extensions for inducing and sustaining erections in the human male had, by itself, been awarded Nobel recognition. Grand Prix's work on the design and mass manufacture of jewelry for the vagina had righted the economy of one East African republic and had, once again, made emerald production the dominant industry of Colombia. The company's work in literature—and it could be called "the company's work" advisedly because left to himself the writer would have gone on repeating the same basic situations of pornographic tradition, but Jean-Pierre's great editors had pummeled and reshaped, destroyed and recast until new and truly great canons of poetry and belles-lettres, of history and anthropology, as well as the novel and the short story—had won the admiration of a vastly more critical and cultivated world. Jean-Pierre's books were available in thirty-two languages. A novel about a Jewish boy deeply concerned with nasal sexual entry as a physical defiance of the shape of the nose of his Jewish mother had become the most popular novel ever written.

All in all, Jean-Pierre was a busy man; that rare being, the fulfilled rich, the man whose life's meaning was in his work which was the meaning of his life. Besides, he hated to have visitors who weren't in the trade because it meant that all the advertising displays and models of various mechanical devices in work or on the drawing board had to be cleared away so that his office could look like the cathedral of any other top business executive. However, he had promised his mother he would see this boy, Botolf Noon, so see him he would. At four-fifteen on the afternoon of the caucus, Bottie was shown into Jean-Pierre's room. They shook hands vigorously. For his mother's sake, Jean-Pierre darted out from behind his desk to greet Bottie.

"I am *so* sorry I've been putting you off this way, young man," Jean-Pierre said with his contagious sincerity. "I *do* apologize because it was rude. We've had a runaway week in production and sales and a miraculous breakthrough in design and all in all I've found myself treading water."

"I wouldn't have pressed you except that I wanted to report," Bottie said. "But now that I'm here I wouldn't have missed it for anything. What a beautiful room! It must be the most beautiful room I've ever seen."

Jean-Pierre shrugged, but he blushed with pleasure as well. "One has designers," he said, "and one tries to use them."

"I—I don't mean to—well, to say the wrong thing but it's such a—a *sensual* room."

"Oh, well. Yes and thank you."

"Oh!"

"What is it?"

"Those heads. I thought they were alive. Great Scott! That's—that's the head of President Pompidou! And—isn't that—no, no—it can't be!"

Jean-Pierre was very much pleased. "How delightful of you to be so impressed with our work. This is the great design breakthrough I spoke of. We can now reproduce the living features of anyone known to history through the camera's lens or the painter's brush."

"It is absolutely extraordinary." Bottie moved closer to the headmasks which had been arranged in a row on stands upon a long mahogany table, each head carefully lighted.

"May I touch one?" he asked.

"By all means. The material is virtually indestructible. It breathes; that is, the wearer will be totally ventilated no matter how long he keeps the mask on and, in our lab studies, these masks have been worn for as long as sixteen days with absolutely no negative effects for the wearer."

Bottie ran his hand lightly across the skin of the face of the late Alice Foote MacDougall as Jean-Pierre said, "Whom do you admire most, Mr. Noon?"

"I suppose V.C. Wynne-Edwards," Bottie said without hesitation.

"Well! If you'll send along a full view and a profile photograph of the man, I'll be happy to make you a present of a V.C. Wynne-Edwards mask—if you'd like to wear it around the house or at parties to impress friends."

"Oh, thank you, Mr. Harris. Thank you very much. But I couldn't do that. *Any*way," he said hurriedly, feeling very gauche for refusing, but elating Jean-Pierre who would not for industrial competitive reasons have been able to follow up on his generous impulse, "I mustn't take up any more of your time than is actually necessary so perhaps I should make my report."

"Splendid!" Jean-Pierre said. They sat down in two of Chippendale's wing chairs from the Andrew Kenna Collection, next to an orange coal fire which glowed from a grate within an exquisite Adam fireplace.

"I am happy to report that I *think* the caucus will go in our favor," Bottie said. "I've spoken to everyone except your sister who, after all, will vote for her husband—as she should—and although we won't have a clear win, we will have a deadlock, and with the deadlock the grandchildren in the family will be required to vote and that will put us over the top."

"How do you count it?"

"Myself, my brother Tris, and yourself in favor. Your sister, your brother and my brother Gawain against. All grandchildren for."

"Well, just to be on the safe side, I had a meeting with my brother last night and we talked very realistically. So realistically that he will vote with us."

"Well—that's great news. Then it's all settled."

"It's all over but the shouting."

Bottie stood up. "Thank you very much, Mr. Harris. It was very good to meet you and it was a revelation to see what you've done with those masks. How will your company use them?"

"Oh," Jean-Pierre made a vague, brushing-away gesture. "To make history more vivid to young minds."

"I certainly look forward to seeing that," Bottie said. The two men shook hands again with great mutual favor and Bottie left.

Jean-Pierre went to the intercom and snapped a button. "Who the hell is V.C. Wynne-Edwards?" he asked.

When Bottie got home at five-thirty, after having stopped at the Schrafft's at Seventy-seventh and Madison to have an ice cream soda with Mona and Fiona, although it was a full two hours before they would leave for the caucus, he found his father ready to leave, dressed in an elegant dinner jacket and wearing a blood-red boutonnière.

"I haven't changed a button on this suit," he said emphatically. "I want them to record everything that will be said tonight."

"You're a fine figure of a man, Pop. That should be recorded."

"Ada will be sending her car to pick us up at seven-thirty."

"I promised Ada's granddaughters I'd ride over with them."

"Ah, you met them then."

"Oh, yes."

"They must be nice young girls. Ada is so fond of them."

"Very nice."

"I look forward to meeting them. One reads such horrendous things about young girls today—not that I can believe one of the claims—and I'd like to meet, just once more, a set of properly raised, modest, and mannerly young women such as they must be."

"Well, you'll certainly meet them tonight, Pop."

"Do we have time for a quick game of fifty points before you change?"

"Sure do."

They strolled into the billiard room. Os put his cue together while Bottie chose one from a wall rack. "I hope they have hamburger tonight," Os said. "But I suppose not. The son is one of those gourmets. You break, son."

Bottie called his shot and made it off the break. His father showed his appreciation by tapping the base of his cue on the floor. "Don't do that, Pop," Bottie said. "The lady downstairs said she'd call the police if you did that again."

"She's out," Os said. "The elevator man tells me when she's out."

Bottie began his run. Os said, "Mind if I talk while you play, Bot?"

"Gosh, no."

"Well, I've been sitting out there and thinking about everything. I mean the threats to the magazine, the government's calculated decision to tamper with our constitutional liberties, those dreadful buttons and the whole basic concept of their baleful determination to elect a man of Duncan Mulligan's capacities to high office."

"Don't let it upset you, now, Pop. It will be all settled and over before today is over."

"No, it won't."

"Why not?"

"Well, the matter about whether Ada and I go or stay will be settled one way or another, yes—and I am not one to think that this caucus is going to be won as easily as you seem to think."

"Why not?"

"Because we're up against some of the biggest surething bettors of all time. They don't go into contests, son. They set up illusions and people think one thing is happening when all the while they're being massacred from behind."

"Not tonight."

"We'll see."

"No kidding, Pop. Not tonight. I've spent the whole week on this and I know where every vote rests and how it will be used. I made the rules on the outcome myself, with Duncan Mulligan, and those rules are in writing and on deposit with the Société de Banque Suisse in Geneva. They can't win."

"All right then. Good. Then all the more reason for you to do what I want you to do tonight."

Bottie stopped playing. "Just tell me, Pop," he said.

"I don't want you to get up and defend Ada and me and tell them why they should all vote for us. Ada's boy can do that if he wants to. But we're serious, you and I. It would be a waste and a mockery for you to talk along lines which would only persuade them to regard Ada and me as isolated cases."

"What did you have in mind?"

"I want you to talk against what Duncan stands for and what the people behind Duncan Mulligan stand for, not for just two old gaffers like us. You hear, Bot? I've been sitting here thinking again, about the American Constitution, which makes the lip-service hustlers possible at the peak of government and all the way down to the local councilman. And how that Constitution—especially used by villains—is now a sinister and dangerous document to the future of the United States of America."

"Pop, it must be changed but—"

"I've been sitting here brooding about that safe little deed and document, so admirably balanced for the needs of English landowners of the late eighteenth century—God knows, not for immigrants, or Africans, or Amerinds—but here we are, shooting into the twenty-first century and calling upon this helpless conception as if it were the ark and the covenant, and crying out for impeachment or assassination of the Justices who interpret it in any way which does not support the needs of seventeen seventy-six."

"What I had in mind, Pop, was—"

"So we have the myth of the executive arm of government calling upon one human to decree, rule, decide, and perform on more matters within a given hour than George Washington had to accomplish during any given sixty days of office. And the pace gets worse. It can't be done by one man, yet it has to get done. . . ."

"Pop—"

"What the devil is the matter with you, Bottie? Are you interrupting me to tell me that I'm wrong?"

"No. Heavens, no. You're right."

"What is it then?"

"There are bigger problems sitting around the edges of this caucus tonight."

"What are they, for heaven's sake?"

"Well, that's what I want to talk about when my turn comes tonight."

"What are you going to say?"

Bottie put his cue down on the table. "Look, Pop, the Constitution of the United States was your grandfather's problem, then your father's problem. I mean—no matter how bad you feel about it, that ball game is all over and you can't expect to make it my problem. Hell, I'm twenty-one years old and everyone I know wants to change the *world,* not just the Constitution. In fact, we don't even want to change the Constitution—let it rest as it stands. We won't use it. We'll make our own Constitution. You see what I mean, Pop? Don't feel badly. Just give us a chance. And maybe—and only maybe—things will change."

37

Working intently with his cook, one of the four living geniuses of cuisine, Maria Pomposelli, Jean-Pierre had taken pains to sustain his capacity as head of the Harris family. He knew his mother's cause was safe so he could concentrate on being host and provider while he ran Kaskie's idea for the weird travel magazine through his head. He would have done the good job of the good son and maybe he would pick up a couple of million himself because since the dirty travel-agency idea had worked there was no reason why the magazine wouldn't.

To keep Celeste down he agreed to have her served two small Benzedrines. Being as high-strung as she was that would make her go to pieces as the voting was tallied. The sleek priest was too keen so Jean-Pierre instructed his butler to serve him two powdered Seconals. If Torquemada had been fed powdered Seconals there would have been no Inquisition. Beyond those special diets the menu would be a clear broth of cold beets and mallard stock, then Bardsey sole, simply grilled and served with great bowls of cut lemons, shaggy with shredded almonds. The sole would be about ten hours out of the Irish Sea, where the pollution was less than at Dover, and flown in to the great Mafia restaurants, both of them difficult to find in central Brooklyn. The main course would be a saddle of lamb large enough to support the riding weight of John Wayne but delicate enough to accept only such a tracklement as rowan jelly to match its Welsh subtleness. They would have an *evalina,* a puree of two parts celery root to one part of Kerr's Pinks, the Irish potatoes. He would have a salad of iced green beans and courgettes cooked *al dente.* A lime sorbet, no more. Then black espresso coffee, a bottle of Pellison cognac and plenty of dark Havana cigars from the State Department.

He was greatly pleased with the design for the evening. All was right with the world and he was the Admiral of the Fleet.

He had just started Berlioz's *Requiem* on the tape deck when the doorbell rang. Jean-Pierre was closer to the door so he motioned to the houseman that he would answer it. When he opened the door he faced a short, middle-aged messenger who wore paste-on, watery eyes and a floppy green denim blouse. The man said, "Green Arris for Harrow, buddy."

"What?"

"I mean, Green Arrow for Harris." He extended a brown manila envelope and an open flat book. "Sign here, pal," he said.

As he signed, Jean-Pierre said, "Who sent this?"

"Call the office, friend. I onney kill myself gettin' it here."

Jean-Pierre tipped him an inflated dollar and closed the door with his foot as he opened the envelope. He slid out a dozen color, action photographs of Ada, forwarded by courtesy of a Machiavellian banker-politician. One could have thought that Jean-Pierre would be inured to the most ravaging of pornographic photographs in that he had seen more of them than most other men. But, instead, he became ill. He half-jammed the pictures back into the envelope and ran toward the bathroom in the bedroom wing. As he vomited into uncontrollable heaves the reason for this violent reaction fought great wars inside his head. It wasn't that such pictures had been taken of Ada. That happened all the time and to some very important people. What was turning his stomach inside out was that anyone could have executed such a totally unforgivable assault upon his *amour-propre.* Someone out there in the city had deliberately designed the most heinously offensive way to desecrate Jean-Pierre's honor. He had never taken such a blow to his vanity and his mind was scrambling toward weapon upon weapon upon weapon to avenge the outrage.

He was gone from the main room almost twelve minutes. When he emerged, the envelope had been sealed shut. He was extremely pale. His eyes were shattered. His mind was working faster than an Apostle computer. The doorbell rang.

"You get it, Nasturtiano," he told the houseman hoarsely.

Far across the enormous room Bottie and his nieces came in; perfection together. Mona and Fiona were preposterously beautiful in identical green chiffon which offset Bottie's burnished bowl of red hair and his almost formal navy-blue Swiss hiking suit. The girls were strangely serene and self-contained. They did not scream out like panthers when they saw their uncle. Jean-Pierre forced himself into a ghastly smile and walked toward them as they crossed the room to meet him.

"Glad you could come," he mumbled in formal greeting, accepting one twin's kiss on each cheek. His entire expression was smudged as though he had had a bad fall on a giant eraser.

"We had a very exciting trip across town," Bottie said.

"A pirate club in the park tried to board our cab," Mona said.

"They shot at us," Fiona said. "But Mr. O'Connell was a better shot than any of them."

"Oh, well," Jean-Pierre said vaguely, "that's city life." The doorbell rang. Jean-Pierre excused himself as Nasturtiano stood at Bottie's side. Bottie asked for cold white wine for himself and the twins.

"Uncle Chester looks *aw*ful!" Mona said.

"He looks like he was just regurgitated or something," Fiona said.

Celeste and Duncan came in.

"Oh, God," Mona said, "Daddy has his rubber on."

Dunc looked very funky in a floppy black rubber tie, blue-and-white flowered dinner shirt which had been painted in eight kinds of authentic British flora by Mr. Fish, and a well-cut midnight-blue rubber dinner jacket to lend him the feeling of maximum security. The parents waved phonily to their children and the children waved phonily to the parents across the room. Bottie excused himself, saying he would return at once, and went to introduce himself to Celeste who was saying to Jean-Pierre, "Darling, you look positively corpse-like. Are you sure you shouldn't be in some hospital? What *hap*pened, darling?"

Jean-Pierre looked at her so piercingly in reply that she almost shrieked with terror. For an instant it had crossed his mind that Celeste had sent him that deadly insult but he didn't *feel* it from her and decided it would be impossible anyway as Dunc greeted Bottie cordially, then turned him toward Celeste, "Woofie, may I introduce the young man who is my co-chairman tonight—Mr. Botolf Noon?"

"Oh—" Celeste said, shocked upon shock, "I met your brother, Tristram." She could not conceal that look Bottie had seen so many times on so many female faces on so many campuses before and, immediately, he felt badly that he had disrupted this nice matron's life by sending his brother when he should have gone himself.

"Yes, yes," he said with a hollow jolliness. "Just setting down the lines of communication, as it were. Tris should certainly be here any minute," he added inanely. Celeste seemed to get enormously flustered and, unable to recover, she bolted away from the men to the huge window to stare across the polluted river at scarred Queens and, beyond that, to some vaguely seen point in Germany to which she murmured a formal good-by to Herr Gudelmann.

Celeste was wearing a simple muumuu, beautifully cut and fitted from a canvas by Gauguin; not a reproduction. Her calcimined bosoms foamed almost over the tops of the bold, painted coconut palms against the lush Polynesian scene. What was she going to *do* when Tris came in? How could she keep her hands off him? They had spent each day for four days on the Staten Island ferry boats, drifting back and forth as they stared at each other. She was going starkers from the need to be kissed by Tris. His friend, Kimmel, had been all wrong when he had said that, in movies, the stars were actually fucking each time they kissed. People need to kiss, just to kiss. An old ditty tralaa'd across her memory, "I miss my Tris, my Swiss Tris kisses me."

Duncan was saying to Bottie that he hadn't known Celeste had met Tris. He said he certainly thought she could have told him about meeting one of the most distinguished leaders in America and that he thought it was very selfish. Dunc was mastering the art of dropping his *g* endings after having worked out for three months with a Nashville elocution teacher who had been retained by the Attorney General to give Dunc something of a man-of-the-people sound. Dunc declined Bottie's invitation to join his daughters because Monsignor Noon had just arrived.

Gawain was in high spirits. He was wearing a maroon chasuble and had brought with him an aspergillum filled with vermouth which he sprinkled lightly over everyone's martini, enchanting Kaskie who had, somehow, arrived with the monsignor. "We just met in the elevator!" Kaskie said with amazement. Kaskie was wearing a Nehru-cut dinner jacket; very severe. He had had his hair set in the bobbed, thick-packed coiffure made stylish by Ruth Snyder when she was electrocuted in 1927. His heavy face bobbled, making his pockmarks dance like gnats in the air, as he agreed to anything anyone said and as he poured boiling cauldrons of thick, fish soup over all of them in his imagination, staring morbidly across the room at Celeste.

Celeste was working herself into hysteria. Her legs gave way and she sat down heavily, looking quite beautiful, trying to stop thinking about the moment when Tris would arrive, hoping desperately that her daughters would stay well away from her throughout the evening, worrying herself sick that they might try to lure Tris into one of the bedrooms and, using their clever karate, lay him. She was made wary and concerned that she had not heard either girl cry out obscenities, and that they both looked so serene and even seemed happy. It confused Celeste.

Then he arrived. She got dizzy. He was with Ada and his father. How secure! How brilliantly intelligent he had been to plan that sort of unobtrusive entrance. He didn't seem to look for her at all but his eyes had burned into hers as they had swept the room in the instant he had entered. He looked pale and tortured. Why? What had she done but love him? She felt as though she would have to pull the cloth and all the dishes and glasses and silver off the dining table to get some sort of punctuating relief.

Nasturtiano extended a silver tray to her. It held a tiny dish with two white pills and a glass of water.

"Mr. Harris suggests these iced Miltowns, madame," Nasturtiano murmured. How dear and good and sweet of Jean-Pierre, she thought, as she scooped up the two Benzedrines and washed them down at once.

Ada was saying, "This nun wasn't a nun at all, you see. She had some sort of grenade or bomb or something strapped underneath—I *say* 'she' but it was a man all the time—and she embraced Os the way the German officers had wanted to hug Hitler excepting he changed his route and said she was going to blow both of them up unless he wrote out a check for thirty-seven thousand five hundred dollars. Before Os had a chance to say yes or no, my doorman, Marvin, had sapped her with the cosh they carry and, of course, it was all over."

"There are certainly a lot of crazy people in this city," Os said to Jean-Pierre who had not listened to any of it.

F.M. Heller arrived with Esau, by no accident. Heller wore a beautifully cut full-dress suit with his miniature decorations swinging from a tiny bar just over his heart: Commanderie du Bontemps, the Sovrana Ordine Osepedaliero di San Tomaso Watson, his Book Actors' Cross, and an enameled Rotary badge. His white beard appeared to have been bleached hair by hair and he had the arrogantly amiable manner of a horse player about to win a boat race.

Esau was wearing a peaked, gray feldmutze cape from World War I, with a unit badge of the state of Anhalt, a tieless white shirt with rolled sleeves over a navy blue body stocking to cover the holes in his arms, and extraordinarily tight blue jeans over a mid-sixteenth-century iron codpiece called a brayette which gave his mid-profile the thrust of a racing porpoise. His sideboards, eyebrows, and moustache had been stiffened with a patent lotion. He strode across the room the moment he came in to kiss his grandmother then immediately joined Mona, Fiona, and Bottie.

"What wild shoes!" Mona gasped.

Esau was pleased. "They're my new fustanelleas," he said. "I get them directly from a supply sergeant in the Greek army."

Monsignor Noon was holding court before F.M. Heller, Dunc and a rapt Kaskie. "The new confession is much more efficient on the penance side," he said. "One checks off the sin categories on the punchcard which is then fed into the confessional slot of the pew for judgment directly by Christ, Computer, Himself. Christ, Computer, issues the precise penance instantly on our purple print-out form—my color-coordinate idea, incidentally—and it all breaks up those terrible old-time bottlenecks of waiting in front of the confessional on Saturday afternoons in all those drafty parish churches. And it frees priests for work with machines which is where salvation lives, of course."

"How absolutely *maaa*veliss!" Kaskie said. "I feel such a part of it all now. You know, Dad insisted that both Jean-Pierre and I take degrees in Theology and, although I never quite finished it, it did retain *enor*mous meaning for me although little did I then realize that I would ever be face to face with a prelate such as you, as we are tonight."

"Well!" Gawain said. "I had no idea! You must come by the cathedral and we will chat."

"What I like," Dunc said, "is the smashin' Certificate of Absolution which is issued on the final print-out for the one or two really big confessions one may make in a lifetime. I frame those certificates. I have four hanging in our bar, at home."

"Yes," Gawain said, "they are an enormously popular feature."

Tris had made his slow, intent circuit of the room and had just reached Celeste when Nasturtiano announced dinner. Fingertips touching, Celeste and Tris moved silently toward the large table as the others converged. Os and Ada were seated at the head of the table facing Dunc and F.M. Heller at the foot. Between them, the Noon family members faced the Harris children. Mona, Fiona, and Esau sat together at a small table apart.

"Where is Jean-Pierre?" Ada asked everyone when all had been seated.

Nasturtiano coughed discreetly to get their attention. They turned to face him.

"Mr. Harris regrets greatly that a most serious matter has called him away for the evening."

"But—his vote?" Os said.

"Did Mr. Harris leave an envelope for us?" Bottie asked.

"No, sir."

"Then," F.M. Heller said blandly, "Mr. Sylvan Harris must take his uncle's seat."

38

The table had been cleared of all but a stein of Portuguese champagne in front of Esau when F.M. Heller asked the permission of the caucus to be allowed to address them sitting down. "I am honored by you," he said, "to have been invited to this family gathering. I hope to earn your regard, so shown, by acting as master of ceremonies, so to speak, to explain voting rules if that becomes necessary and, generally, to smooth the way to a satisfactory conclusion.

"Mr. Jean-Pierre Harris, esteemed publisher and head of the Harris family cannot be with us, as you know. Therefore only Mr. Duncan Mulligan and Mr. Botolf Noon will speak to you tonight, in debate of the question before us.

"On my right sits Dunc Mulligan, a great lawyer and a staunch friend of the American people. Dunc has been called by the highest pinnacle of leadership in Washington to lead the people of the great State of New York, Empire State of our beloved Union. He is here tonight to present his own case, to plead for his political life, as it were, and in fact, for the future of expanding democracy within our state. On the one hand he will offer you a blazing future for millions of your fellow Americans. On the other he will seek your accord by which Mrs. Ada Harris and Mr. Osgood Noon will leave summer's heat and winter's cares behind and go off on a well-deserved visit to glamorous Pitcairn Island.

"With no further ado, I give you Mr. Dunc Mulligan, next United States Senator from the State of New York."

There was a certain amount of rubber applause.

Dunc got to his feet, undergarments rustling, removing the silver-rimmed Ben Franklin spectacles he had affected and holding them aloft.

"The day of these has gone from politics," he said, "and the day of these—" he opened a silver sniff box, removed contact lenses and placed one over each eye, "is now with us." He whipped a bottle of JetSet black hair dye and a tube of AlpineTan from his pocket and held them aloft for all to see. "And the time for these is here and—if need be—the time for deft, sure plastic surgery." He placed all exhibits on the table before him, large labels facing the audience.

"Because we are a young nation of proud, young people," he orated, "we want young men to lead us—*young* men with young, firm-fleshed wives waiting at home beside the hearth to greet them. Throughout this great young land—if a man does not own his own business, if he has not climbed to within two rungs of the top by the time he is forty-two years old, he is finished and must be bypassed to shuffle along to a Senior Citizen City, or better to die, for no company should be expected to continue him on its expensive pension plan. Therefore, dear friends, my plea tonight shall be the plea of a young statesman whose very image is threatened with harness to an image of age.

"Friends, dear family of my beloved wife and esteemed family of Osgood Noon, patriot and gourmet, I say to you that I am forty-two years old. And I want to make one thing clear—I am without personal ambition. However, and may that however be told again and again and again, my ambition for our beloved country is boundless. And I tell you—how I wished I could have stood as a peer in that magnificent Senate which just voted into law that very model for all future law and order which is soon to be extended throughout our great country—I speak of the anti-crime bill for the District of Columbia which, at last, will make possible the detention of niggers, and expanded police wire-tapping rights to winnow out the real trouble-makers among the darkies and the students who must be detained without trial if we are to sleep in our beds at night in safety, and the relentless right of police to break into nigger homes without knocking. For I do not hide anything—least of all the fact that I am on the side of law and order.

"I have been summoned to the Senate by our national leadership perhaps as one of the last senators to be duly elected in the outmoded, old-fashioned way—for let me say that our Constitution is not a *per*fect document—because even now your government has commissioned one of the great think tanks to ponder through the reactions —those possible reactions—of our people to the postponement of elections for twenty years or so beginning before nineteen seventy-two, due to encroachments by niggers and students who are not yet ready, by heart or hand, by deed or by wish, for the responsibilities of the Vote. This condition is made even more pressing by the appalling statistic which insists that eighty-five per cent of our population will be under the age of twenty by next year, creating the terrifying possibility in a presidential election year of an Executive and a Congress ruled by a mob of children to whom the disciplines of our economy and our rights under law are unknown.

"Furthermore, as we have seen in the streets surrounding the last presidential nominating convention in Chicago, there exists an increasingly dangerous far-left movement within the Democratic Party. Further, this far-left force may represent as much as ninety percent of the entire electorate. This frightens your Attorney General, despite an enduring silent majority of loyal hard hats mostly provided by those one hundred percent American labor unions controlled by the Mafia gratefully loyal to him for indictments which have been quashed.

"You may ask how such a small silence can claim majority if by most conventional methods of counting, this silent majority appears to be only eight percent of the voters? Your Attorney General is determined that you understand this illusion of numbers. As always, he is stern but fair and you know in your heart you can believe him.

"Through me, he says this to you: would you permit a stranger to invade your home—an alien from a ghetto of disordered streets who would then instruct you as to how to move your furniture around in your own rooms within the house which you had bought and paid for and unquestionably own? Would you permit this stranger to order the destruction of some of this furniture because it did not happen to meet his alien taste—and I speak of furniture which you had bought and paid for—institutions which were designed and custom-built for you? Would you permit a stranger whose skin is black and therefore a person of profound ignorance and known animal instincts and therefore sexually depraved, a person therefore who, if given your bathtub, would only use it as a place to store coal or gin or fatback or whatever it is they eat? Would you permit this person to enter this house you own, without invitation, then proceed to set fire to your rich drapes while his animal smell permeated your fresh carpets and delicate linen? Or, would you sit mildly by without a thought of protesting while a bomb-carrying, drug-obsessed youth of say twenty-one or twenty-two—present company excepted of course—came screaming into *your* house, on *your* property which you had bought and paid for and in which you had lived through the centuries of your nation, unmolested by anarchy and revolution—would you allow this hairy, unkempt thing which, I am disgusted to have to tell you again, will represent more than eighty-five percent of the population—this bum, this effete snob, this sexually-permissive addict who blows up property and throws rocks at our National Guard and calls our policemen pigs—would you permit this *thing* to tell you that you must rearrange the furniture you own within the four walls of the house you bought and paid for long years before?

"And—tell me this—would you allow the stranger known as Mr. Freak-out-knee-jerk-liberal to come climbing through your window to exhort the dear silent servants of the house you own—the true and rightful majority of your house because as *good* servants who accept the food and wages and benefits you shower on them, deserve to live on, silently and in peace, in this house you own? Would you allow these jelly-soft liberals and these niggers plus these anarchists to snatch away and destroy the property you own?

"You would not.

"Your Attorney General has undertaken to guard the hearths and the workbenches of the owners of this great country who have the paid-up receipts to show for that ownership by the extent of the income-tax obligations they had met. We have paid up those annual taxes, no matter how steep they have seemed, with a song in our hearts. We bought this country with those taxes, we cry out! That is our proof—here is our proof—our paid-up tax receipts! Where is their proof?—that rabble who think they can just snatch all of it away from us? What have they ever done, beyond the accident of being born here, to warrant their outrageous demands? Tax-free niggers and students! Show me your paid-up receipts, show me your municipal bonds, show me your herds of Angus and Brahma, show me your foundations, your art collections, and your oil-depreciation allowances! Show me what you have paid for and I'll tell you what you deserve to get, I would cry out to them.

"We have gone into such detail tonight to show why the vast and loyal group—the Attorney General's own silent majority of eight percent of the people, the golden, *good* eight per cent which contrasts meaningfully with a rabble who never chose to opt for their enfranchisement—is this nation's *true* majority.

"The Holy Naught Society, the Men's Auxiliary Organization of our National Church of Christ, Computer. will have this interesting little story to announce about our Silents and our *real* American kids next Sunday, and I believe I am violating no confidence in tipping you off here in advance tonight concerning this. Let those who believe American youth is all bad just listen to the results of this all-time popularity poll. The Boys' and Girls' Division of the Holy Naught Society picked these favorites as most popular in all fifty states and on our fighting fronts overseas, in this order: number one—of course—our beloved President. Number two—now, here's a dishy surprise—the Parents of America. Then numbers three through ten in this order of overwhelming popularity: William "Billy" Graham—an evangelist but a wonderful guy, General Douglas MacArthur, ex-President Calvin Coolidge, John Wayne, Stepin Fetchit—a dyed-in-the-wool Negro, and it was specified that this was meant to mean the character he played and not the man himself, Mrs. James "Dolly" Madison on the Women's Liberation side, and Salmon P. Chase, a great Secretary of the Treasury. How about *that* for a free-choice poll of your normal American kids, my friends?

"All right. There's your silent majority and there, on the other hand, are the owners of America and the absolute arguments as to why it is legal and right to defend and cherish what we own. Also I think you have been given reason to understand why your government has asked the great think tanks at Delphi, New York, to ponder the grave puzzle of the possible national reaction to a possible postponement of national elections for a few dozen years so that the faithful stewardship may be maintained. Also, I profoundly hope that I have shown why I must be sent to the Senate this year because if there are to be no elections in the two or three dozen years to follow, then I would not be a part of this stewardship which I think you will agree I understand so well.

"I put it to you white people, well-to-do people, and although some of you are young people you are the real American young persons of high income, that there have not been many nations in all the blessed and bloody tenure of history from the very beginnings of the concept of national ownership, who have been given such great men as the leaders of their present government. Our Attorney General lives out our hopes in an awful loneliness and thereby makes clear to you and to me that conditions which are called 'problems' by niggers, students, liberals, and the radical Eastern establishment press are, in truth, merely necessary diversions—as you and I well know. I put it to you in this way. It is true that people who are earning less, say, than two hundred thousand dollars a year are frequently apt to think of a stock market recession or depression as being a 'problem.' But tell me this —who might be more at home in any sort of stock market —your darkies and long-haired hippie students—*or*—the people who own this country *and* its stock market? *Nonetheless*—what better diversion for all those others to get their alleged minds off things like wars they will never, for the lives of them, be able to understand, or a seventy-two per cent inflation, or a few campus killings, or a sixteen per cent unemployment? Why, if there *were* a general panic and a complete crash as has frequently happened when other sensible Republican stewards came into office —who indeed is in a better position to buy up this country at ten cents on the dollar than those of us who rightfully own the nation anyway?

"These are vital questions. These are the questions posed and answered for you at the very heart's core of our leadership. And there is no doubt but that the least of us here tonight—and I proudly include my own two daughters—would be able to show a paid-up income tax return on income last year from two-hundred and fifty thousand dollars to as high as perhaps eleven million dollars because, after all, one would have to be almost criminally stupid or lazy or shiftless *not* to be able to earn at least those minimums in this glorious democracy we live in.

"If you were an acrid darky, would you in your heart believe you should have an equal vote at the polls with the people assembled here tonight? But—and I want to make one thing clear—and I will defend this with my life—there are *good* niggers. I mean that! There are literally thousands of the I-will-not-rock-the-boat-niggers. And it is these niggers that our Attorney General is determined to help.

"Let me put it this way—our dedicated administration teams choose 'conditions' which then become 'problems' which are, in actuality, 'diversions.' But it is all semantics. When these are 'problems,' they are problems only for bad niggers, all students, knee-jerk-liberals, that very section of our populace whose opposition caused our Vice-President to term them 'the criminally insane.'

"These 'problems' might include the just war for a free world which is now being fought in Asia, far from our shores. These 'problems' might refer to gritty little riots or city-wide fires in the various so-called ghettos around the country. Or I might be referring to students sniping at our soldiers on our campuses. Or to the squeaking outcries about so-called pollution which is supposed to exist on land, in the air, and in the sea. I refer to the bleats about bacteriological warfare and commie screams that the predetention law for the District of Columbia, the *model* law for all states, is not just about the most necessary law ever passed. I refer to anarchists who try to block the supersonic plane because they say its sonic boom may kill the fish in the oceans, removing our last great source of protein—or possibly change our weather by perhaps using up all the oxygen around the planet. But I tell you now that whatever the Eastern establishment press keeps emphasizing as 'problems' are all merely strategic and tactical 'diversions' designed by our stern but fair Attorney General for the greatest benefit of those people who can prove that *they are the real Americans because they own America.*

"There is a growing tide of envy in this country and do not let them think it goes undetected by our leadership. It is the same tide which wiped out Imperial Russia and replaced it with the Communists. It is the same tide which drowned French aristocrats in blood, and a charming queen, and brought about the French run on our dollar. This tide is named Envy. All of Drop-Out America has gotten this idea into its head, that it has the right to share in what we and our forefathers worked so hard to buy. And I say this to you—right now, tonight—our suggestion boxes in the great corporations across our nation should be filled to the brim with ideas which could fight this growing national Envy.

"All right! You have earned the right to know it—so here is my platform as a far, far more than potential Senator of the United States:

"One: I stand foursquare behind our gallant Attorney General and his lady;

"Two: If elected, I will vote for the continuance of any wars declared by our President, on the advice of our Attorney General, because wars tend to control niggers and students by dint of eliminating many of them, and wars are certainly not unprofitable either;

"Three: I will support our loyal Mafia which has delivered so many of our silent majority to fight the good fight and to do what they are told;

"Four: I will support, above *all*, our steadfast silent majority, eyes gleaming for the final fight under their hard hats—that mindless audience whom the Attorney General affectionately calls 'the savage, simple-minded people' which sits out there under perpetually blue skies where it is always the Fourth of July, A.D. nineteen hundred, amid the bunting in open grandstands, munching their hot dogs along the river bank of time and these great-hearted people have the right to their 'diversions' and we must never, ever stop sending past their view, on gorgeous barges and floats drifting past their stands along that river, one after another of the diverting extravaganzas we design for their delectation: our wars; surely the endless lobotomy of television; our shoot-ins on the city streets and in the halls of academe; our brave young naders jousting with giant corporations; our assassinations and our scandals; our rigged disasters and corruptions—and, also, *positive* barges and floats which demonstrate our will to eliminate the so-called pollution, barges devoted to the mystifying wonders of modern science from the discovery of plastic beer to our wonderfully entertaining trip to the moon—or that cure for cancer which is right around the corner—our exalting religious fervor, our matchless educational system —all of this! *All these diversions!* But—only for a *deserving* populace!

"There can be no dissent from these things! There can be no examination before trial! There can be no degenerate intellectualizing, no thought at all except for what must go into the themes and decorations of those essential barges and floats which *we* design—people such as we in this room tonight—which *we* cause to be built just out of sight around the bend of that great river called Democracy.

"I think the presence of my good wife and daughters here tonight proves, through our Open Book lives, that I *believe* in love and lovers. I am not here tonight to seek to destroy any relationship between two wonderful, if old people. Far from it. I hallow Ada Harris who has already, with her far-seeing vision, contributed to my campaign. I revere Mr. Osgood Noon, a great hat maker and patriot in his day and—if elected and should they ask me to do so—will cut their eventual wedding cake with Robert E. Lee's own sword obtained for the occasion through confrères in the Senate.

"What I am asking tonight is that these two caring and—yes—youthful in the nonpejorative sense of that word—people merely postpone their alliance within the continental United States until sometime next year because your Attorney General, in his wisdom, senses rather than knows—and that is good enough for all of us—that their open alliance before my election could *possibly* taint my own youth image.

"In closing, just one more thing—mine will not be a career, but a creed.

"I thank you."

F.M. Heller and Kaskie led the applause which Kaskie tried to lift into a rising ovation with shouts of "Brilliant! Oh, absolutely *brilliant,* Dunc!" Gawain rapped on the table mildly with his cigarette lighter. The others were rather more restrained. Celeste did not applaud nor did her two daughters or Esau. Os and Ada touched hands together at infrequent intervals but somewhat noiselessly. Tris clapped with the vigor which one might reserve at home for the Late, Late Show. Botolf had dropped something under the table and was taking a lot of time to retrieve it.

Dunc was enormously pleased, hoped the Samos satellite or a hover ball outside the window had picked up every word for the fellows in Washington and, after many half-bows, sat down.

F.M. Heller's voice boomed out over the silence. "My friends," he said, "we will now hear from Mr. Botolf Noon."

The twins began to applaud madly so Esau joined in.

39

Jean-Pierre had rushed out of his own dinner party, sick with outrage. He had become almost centrally crisp with fury because, as he told himself over and over again, it was not the porn itself, the pictures of Ada in various stock positions. That was nothing. That was a natural thing which the Polaroid camera had brought to every American home. It was the *symbol* of deadly offense they had chosen. Plenty of men would have been offended mortally to be sent pictures of their own mother in those situations. They had no way of knowing that Jean-Pierre understood those things. Therefore they had chosen that *symbol* signifying a contemptuous lack of respect for his family, therefore for him. Therefore he was almost unbalanced with rage and an overpowering lust for vengeance.

He had to find out who had chosen to do this to him. Whoever had sent those pictures had fantastic equipment connections—surely only the government had such cameras and it certainly seemed to him that someone in the government had sent these pictures. And that appalled him. The ramifications of the possibility of the government deliberately setting out to defy the Treaty of Sacramento whereby the federal government and the Mafia had agreed formally to accept each other as sovereign states in all matters, was deeply disquieting. Therefore, Jean-Pierre decided, he must look for some kind of controlled madman with solid government connections, a secret lunatic who had, with clinical malice chosen (a) to mock the very industry—pornography—which Jean-Pierre had built with his own heart and hands; (b) to insult, within the sender's frame-of-reference, Jean-Pierre's own family in what could only be seen as an intentionally humiliating manner that, if unavenged, meant there would be no sense in Jean-Pierre trying to continue; and (c) it was entirely possible that this madman would find a way to let the Boys hear about this and, if he did not avenge it quickly and with enormous zeal, then he would really be through—a MOTHER was involved here! All right. Okay. The first. Little Brother who came leering to him with the "news" of what was happening would be shot down by himself, Jean-Pierre personally. And the next and the next and the next. The *capos* would then understand that he was searching day and night to find this crazy who had made this colossal insult and he would, therefore, continue to be respected.

But this monster had to be found. This monster had to pay. He had to pay and pay and pay and pay and pay and pay and pay and pay. Not just with his life, not only with his blood. That was the kind, compassionate, Sicilian way. This monster had to pay with whatever he held dearest then with whatever he held second dearest and then with whatever he held third dearest. And on and on.

He found himself at the street level of his own building. He was wearing a topcoat and a hat so Nasturtiano must have taken care of him. He suddenly realized he did not know how to get downtown—Nasturtiano had always driven him or his father's chauffeurs before that.

"How do I get downtown?" he asked the chief doorman.

"What do you mean, sir?"

"You understand English? What I said, that's what I mean."

The doorman was startled. Mr. Harris had always been such a mild, considerate tenant, so highly regarded by the management. Whenever he had left the building before he had gotten into that dinky Dodge. Not only didn't the doorman know how to cope but he was frightened by Mr. Harris' look. He grasped the handle of his Glisenti 9mm automatic as a poise prop. The gun was really an affected stance taken by the owners of the building, in that it was of Italian design and because they thought it would gain caste with other Mafia families because it seemed identical to the original 1906 design and two of the current families in New York were hip to Italian antiques. Actually, it was a newly tooled pistol and for all the sentimentality of the Stopiglieri Realty Company, it delivered a rather light bullet load of 125 grains and a velocity of an extremely modest 960 f.s. which is fair stopping power but really no use at all if worked against storming rioters and, Sicilian romantics to one side, it was hardly brilliant to locate the safety lever at the rear of the bolt.

"You could take a taxi, Mr. Harris," the doorman said nervously.

"A taxi! Great!" Jean-Pierre had seen these conveyances on television and in films. "I was afraid you were going to say take a trolley or a subway. Good. Get me a taxi." When the cab pulled up Jean-Pierre got in and settled back. The cab did not start.

"What the hell is wrong here?" Jean-Pierre asked the doorman irascibly. "Tell him to get moving?"

"Ask him where he wants to go, the king," the driver said to the doorman.

"Uh—where do you want to go, Mr. Harris?" the doorman asked.

Jean-Pierre had been so intent upon the insult and its gravity that he had assumed that anyone working for Stopiglieri Realty would know where he had to go. "Fahcrissake," he yelled, "Paddy's Pizzeria. West Fifty-fifth. Off Eighth."

The cab moved off. The driver seemed to be impressed with the address because he didn't attempt to make the passenger converse with him for at least five minutes.

"I been to Paddy's plenty times," he confided at last. "Whenever Dino Pagiuli is in town he will only leave this cab, go to Paddy's fah him to bring him some of Paddy's special Italian bread."

"Who the hell is Dino Pagiuli?" Jean-Pierre snarled.

"Who is Dino Pagi*uli*?" The driver slowed down so he could turn around to stare at the passenger to see what kind of a nut he had in the cab. "He's the Hollywood star of stars who has only also had his own network show for like eight years, fahcrissake."

"Fuck you *and* Dino Pagiuli," Jean-Pierre said.

The driver sulked after that and refused to speak for the rest of the journey.

When the hatcheck girl saw the glamorous dirty-pictures *capo* come into the restaurant she hit the toe-button signal so Paddy could get out front. Jean-Pierre checked his hat and coat and a twenty-eight-hundred-dollar watch so the girl could get a sense of *casta*. Paddy Zalugrichieri, sole owner of the restaurant except for a ninety-three per cent interest which had been preempted by the Le Pore family, zoomed up toward Jean-Pierre on the double.

"Mista Harris! Holy Jeez, whatta night. I just send five loaves of bread out to Dino Pagiuli an' now you come inna my place."

Jean-Pierre was amiable and aloof at the same time. He asked if Paddy could find Fausto for him.

"He's here! I'ma tellin' you! He's right inna back room!"

Paddy led the way, turning now and then to donate an alliaceous smile toward Jean-Pierre who was moving through the felonry with the arrogance of a mail truck. He was taken to a table where two small-boned calmly dressed, pleasant, thanatic men were eating *che vruoccoli arriminata,* a simple pasta with broccoli, anchovies, tomato sauce, pine nuts, onions and raisins with two small *sfincione de San Vito* on the side. They were drinking the dry, velvety, limpid, golden wine of the Casteldaccia called Corvo, as good as the best Chablis.

"Hey, Gian-Piero," Fausto said with total surprise. "What's witchew?" Jean-Pierre shook hands, sat down, and ordered the same repast the two men were enjoying.

"What you doong donntonn?" Fausto asked. "I t'ought you had a stamp collection or somet'ing." It was a very big joke and he and Abramo laughed very hard because everyone in the Fratellanza saw Jean-Pierre as the most fantastically provided-for man in the organization's history and this got him great respect.

Abramo, who was Fausto's first assistant and sicary, an executive job which had once been on the Table of Operations as *caporegima* said, "Are you all here, baby, or maybe you had to leave the golden sword uptonn?" The force of laughter after that sally almost knocked the two men off the chairs.

"I'm all here," Jean-Pierre said, "and I need some head muscles."

The two men became businesslike at once.

The smells of the food all over the room were magical; smells which had taken long years of cheeses and salamis and sauces mingling and Jean-Pierre was suddenly aware of how hungry he had become. "This Green Arrow Delivery sent a man to my place at about ten minutes to eight. He brought a big, brown envelope. I signed for it and I tipped him a buck—a little, bald, blond guy with bloodshot eyes. I gotta find out who sent the envelope."

"When we find out you want anyt'ing?"

"No. This is very special."

Abramo excused himself politely and left the table. Paddy and two waiters brought Jean-Pierre's food. He began to eat with zest thinking that while the food was the best in New York it still wasn't food by Maria Pomposelli.

Fausto sipped the wine with some exhaustion and watched Jean-Pierre eat. Fausto was beat. It wasn't an easy life having to turn out to picket the FBI three times a week plus all the other things that had to get done.

Abramo returned to the table. He said, "Green Arrow says the messenger had to go way downtown to pick up the envelope. He got it from a guy in the main lobby of the Everest Bank. The guard pointed this guy out. The messenger's name is Whitey Schlumberger but the bank is closed 'til Monday an' we can't find Whitey because he lives only in all-night movies."

"That's good service, Abramo," Jean-Pierre said. "Anything can wait 'til Monday. I will certainly appreciate anything you can do."

40

Botolf got to his feet. His large brown eyes were mournful. He could look over Celeste's head and see Mona and Fiona adoring him. He made a slight bow to them and cleared his throat.

"I was reading a book the other night," he said slowly, "about the social control over the use of the scientists who are hired by the politicians. The book said that in no time science will have created engines that can punch holes in the ozone so that ultra-violet rays can sunburn the enemy to death and will be able to artificially induce tidal waves. The book reached the simple conclusion that we must either eliminate scientists or politicians. We cannot have both. In deciding this essential matter, try to remember this: the politician is the natural enemy of man, the worst predator because he preys upon his own species with a form of cannibalism which is without precedent among life-forms; the smiling cannibal who promises a sweet immortality while he eats our young.

"It is the tradition that, at the end of classical crime stories, the master detective assembles all the suspects, and—in a brilliant extrapolation—solves the mystery. First, therefore, allow me to say that the butler did not do it. I am one of the killers with the rest of you contented owners of America. And, as I tell you about the victim and the circumstances leading to his death, I should be able to do it succinctly because I am also the victim and so are all of you in this enormous house we seem to have bought and now own.

"Frightening records were set among you owners—and others—last year. The most frightening was won by the whole human race, in fact. It is multiplying at the rate of one hundred eighty thousand a day. The world birth rate is now two hundred twenty-nine a minute. About twenty thousand, five hundred and twenty people have been born since we sat down to dinner.

"All sorts of things like that happen every day in cooperation with the new rhythms of natural history, which is my field as—perhaps—politics is Mr. Mulligan's. It cost us owners twenty-four billion dollars to get to the moon at a time when our cities are decaying, the environment is being poisoned, the social structure, and our collective sanity, is crumbling in a tribute to our native political genius and the political systems which we have perpetuated and which Mr. Mulligan would now happily join.

"On the way back from not reaching the moon, and with the meter still running, Apollo Thirteen had to jettison a canister containing eight-point-six pounds of deadly, deadly, *dead*ly plutonium which has a half-life of twenty-four thousand years or about eight hundred generations. That's at least one tangible thing we got for our twenty-four billion dollars, the interest alone on which could have wiped out poverty in the United States forever. That gift of plutonium will shimmer out into the floor of the sea, then begin to work. The probabilities of genetic damage are incalculable. But hardly anyone, least of all our political custodians, paid any attention to the accident. Accident? Better say catastrophe because catastrophes make the best diversions even if the semantical problem, as Mr. Mulligan called it, is that our progeny may be mutants.

"Recently, a certain Dr. Bentley Glass told the American Association for the Advancement of Science, of which he was retiring president, that the horizons of knowledge are limited and that the growth of scientific knowledge cannot long continue. That kind of a statement would have significance or even interest if Dr. Glass or perhaps even better the Attorney General could tell us, and prove it by the beneficence of the lives we would be living together, that the horizons of political knowledge were limited and that the growth of that knowledge could no longer continue.

"But we do not insist that qualified political scientists, long and carefully trained in their most vital speciality, conduct our political affairs as we insist that physical scientists attend upon our destruction. For six years Dr. Tugwell and the Center for the Study of Democratic Institutions have been engaged in rewriting the Constitution of the United States in the hope that someday, some perfectly, heinously enormous political catastrophe would make us see that we have needed the Constitution changed for well over a century."

"Now just one moment here, good Botolf," Gawain interrupted. "Allow me to point out that you won't gain much respect for your arguments if you attack the precious eternal American Constitution."

"O, be quiet," Mona yelled.

"Go tell that to your machines," Fiona shouted. As Gawain turned in his seat to glare at them, Bottie continued sadly.

"Just the same, even the frivolous are now aware of the massive death we are pulling toward us at the end of a shortening rope, hand over hand. There will be so many people on this planet within eight years that unbiased machines will have to control methods of transporting people to avoid chaos. Immediately after that all travel will have to stop, except by license, because there won't be room on the scooters, cars, buses, trains, roads, or planes to carry the load. When movement becomes impossible we will all live within three gargantuan megalopolises which will hold over half of the still-burgeoning population of the country. There will be eighty million people in one city extending from Maine to Virginia. How about that for a 'diversion,' Mr. Mulligan? Already, the Good Housekeeping Institute has given its Seal of Approval to a sleeping pill. That is good thinking. It is going to be very noisy.

"Part of the noise may be the soaring whine of the suicide rate. Crime has increased to over forty-one times what it was just ten years ago. One third of the nation lives in enraged futility, leering at anarchy because they have been abandoned by their government. Another third hardens its hats in the brine of a special illusory past which hasn't served the country since slavery was the commodity which kept a few southern farmers in silks and wine. The other third worry about the nearer past—the decline of the stockmarket in sixty-eight when their women had to face buying new furs only every other year. And the leaders of all these thirds sweat only their one gift to an abominated electorate—keeping all three murderously separate from the others."

Bottie looked much older than when they had first seen him stand up; much older through their eyes. His spectacles shone as brilliantly as the braces on his teeth; the bowl of his chestnut-red hair should have kept him young, but he seemed to be much older to all of them.

"The family unit," he continued, "the only cement of civilization, is shattering. Wives detest husbands. Husbands despise wives as the territories in which they are allowed to live freely contract. Illegitimate births climb despite the pill. There are incalculably more divorces. Young people no longer seem to believe in marriage. Parents fear their children. Children hate their parents. Children are refusing to continue their education at grade school level. They are venereal and narcotic. Who will be the politicians of tomorrow presiding over this country we bought and most surely own?

"Perhaps, despite Mr. Mulligan's hope that elections will be cancelled for a few decades, politicians really cannot exist without voters no matter how incompetent both are. Today, voters have become almost completely turned off. They have lost all interest in controlling their so-intensely admired democratic system. The more entertainingly vivid became network television's depiction of riots, crime in the street, instant war and instant death, the more the viewers regarded all such problems as being beyond the solution of the men who are representative of American politics. Amateurs distrust amateurs. No one would ask his next-door neighbor who pumps gas for a living to remove his tooth or perform brain surgery on his daughter. As the voter sees it, all the problems have become too much for the faking time-servers who are supposed to be handling them.

"Helped along by the most far-flung and generally useless Overcommunications System through which we are reached by one banal sales message or another, some six to eight thousand times a day, each one of us, we have abandoned our young, our food supplies, even the very oxygen which makes our continuance possible as carbon creatures. This prodigious Overcommunications System has washed away our ability to think. It worked on us slowly enough, beginning perhaps with Uncle Miltie in nineteen forty-seven, so we all knew all of it was coming. But there were too many of Mr. Mulligan's 'diversions,' too many garish floats and barges being sent around the polluted river bend of democracy, too much of a sensation of knowing our own lives from the other end of a television tube until all catastrophe which was happening directly to us became just another motion picture."

Bottie unbuttoned his long tweed safari jacket and hiked up his Swiss hiker's knickerbockers. When he spoke again he was looking directly at Mona and Fiona, as though they were the only ones in that room who could really understand him.

"What are the real causes of the desperate need for a world community to destroy itself? What is the *real* cause which has set us against each other, our environment, and ourselves?

"The cause is that you have been programmed by something more immense than even the television industry or the Church of Christ, Computer. Further, we cannot escape this programming which will destroy us, our children and our institutions, until the whole grisly job has been done to the extent that instinct demands it be done. But I thought, in the context of this caucus tonight, that if we understood why we were destroying while we did it that we might gain a small measure of compassion for ourselves."

Celeste stared at Bottie transfigured as she translated everything he was saying into how it all might affect Tristram and herself. Gawain stared straight ahead, his eyes raging slits of glittering light. Dunc appeared to be listening to Bottie but his expression, and F.M. Heller's, were the expressions of men attending a thousand-dollar-a-plate dinner to help the campaign fund of Nelson Rockefeller; deaf, dumb, and blind. Kaskell's eyes were glazed for a different reason. Esau was listening intently as a child listens to a story. Mona and Fiona were rapt. Ada's eyes had misted over. Os gave his son total attention.

"At your leisure, that is at any time before you die sooner than you might have died, I commend you to read V.C. Wynne-Edwards' great work, *Animal Dispersion in Relation to Social Behavior,* written during the seven years before it was published in nineteen sixty-two. Since then it has been the main support of the men who concoct those little boxed features in the newspapers of the world. However, since Wynne-Edwards reached his conclusions, we have become even more savage. As is continually being reported by the directors of zoos, people have now taken to attacking caged animals. Rare sea lions are thrown poisoned fish. A rock thrown at a camel in Marseilles ripped out an eye. Ostriches' throats are cut and alligators' heads are smashed.

"But—why? Why is our species engaged in mindless and hopefully total destruction?

"This is why.

"Mass communication, without benefit of television or comic books, is shared throughout the animal kingdom. This mass communication—most necessarily including the human species—is biologically set up to warn when the population must be controlled before the common societies' food resources can be seriously threatened. The danger point seems to be when enough population has accumulated to bring the species only one-third of the way toward a threat to its food supply. When this happens the signal is sent throughout the animal system to destroy itself to the point where the population and the food supply reach an acceptable balance again. This is why people are at their most savage in a great city and will become more and more savage in the greater and greater cities which are now accumulating.

"The same communicating process is happening all the time to what we call wildlife—even though this wildlife is so much less feral and wanton in its methods of controlling population problems. When lemmings achieve a population overabundance they must still eat early and often—but there isn't enough food. Source after source of food is consumed as they race forward. They eat their way across fields and forests to fjords, then leap in to swim across to get to the food on the other side. But that last great fjord, the Atlantic Ocean, is a beaut—so they drown. Those who survive go home to their balanced food supply and the cycle starts again.

"This is not the first time our own species has gone through a cycle of depravity and destruction. The end of the world is just an ego trip. We have the hard luck this time around of having efficient medicine which keeps the aged alive when, a hundred years ago, disease would have helped maintain the food-supply balance. There were all those wars we could rely on to eliminate the excessive thirty to forty per cent of the people, but war-making has become so proficient that wars have to be isolated in isolated courts and even the military mind shrinks from starting out with a hydrogen bomb and germ warfare. As fast as agronomists and chemists increase our food supply just as fast does pollution and human spawning cancel out those gains.

"In thirty years there will be twice as many of us—seven billion, eight hundred million people—and we are already in desperate difficulties with our mere three billion, nine hundred million. If nothing halts this breeding, and the copulation explosion destroys the soul with the weight of bodies, then mothers will struggle in childbirth to get at their babies to tear them apart, and neuroses will have achieved such stunning proportions that men will seek sexual satisfaction only with other men and animals—women will then be wholly liberated, to live in fortresses only with other women and the war of attrition between the sexes will be a war to the death so that *somehow*—through instinct rather than through intelligence—the food supply balance is achieved once again.

"But at what cost in 'diversions,' as Mr. Mulligan would say.

"This communicated warning which we are now receiving through our instincts comes from a sense of being crowded. We destroy ourselves just as mindlessly as any satin-bower birds or marine amphipods, or the tropical bat, the zebra butterfly and the European rabbit. Wynne-Edwards provides massive documentation proving all creatures are members of local, specific societies, a society being 'an organization capable of providing conventional competition.' Where there are two sexes the competition is always conducted by the males. No species, including our own, in times of normal living space and food availability, programs its females for competition. When aberrant female liberation groups begin to form, this is because the mass of society has communicated the signal that the destruction of at least a third of that society must begin—to control population and conserve food.

"Among the laboratory animals such as rats, mice, and voles, the competition from overcrowding produces three types of males: the large and glossy furred rats, such as Mr. Mulligan indicates as the owners of the country; the large, tattered and scarred males with overactive adrenals who might be Mr. Mulligan's greatly feared blacks and students; and the small recessive males such as are found in our literary communities. Only the first group does successful breeding.

"Each species institutes its own form of population control. Our own, as we are observing it at work now, may be the most painful and the ugliest.

"If we are to survive we will need all the help we can get. Therefore the existing politician class, so helplessly unprepared and so ravenously greedy, the politician class which has willfully separated itself from the people it allegedly represents as sort of an elite manqué, must be phased out of national life as rapidly as possible. Politics serves only politicians.

"Throughout the life of our republic we have had to rely upon the unwisdom of farmers, the inexperience of lawyers, and the selfishness of lobbies as representatives of government. The cost of this in lives, money, and real security—not cloak-and-dagger security—has been appalling. The socially enervating priest class was weeded out when they were seen to be a social disease, but the amateur man of government is a deadlier enemy than the priest was to our survival. He must be phased out at a far more accelerated rate. These ignorant and professionally invidious men were educated to specialities which have nothing whatever to do with training for government. Flour salesmen, ex-schoolteachers, army generals, country squires, former judges, and failed lawyers must be replaced by specially educated political scientists who have been highly trained in the history, processes, and practices of complex modern government. No one must be allowed to place his name for election to any office without being required by law to produce proof of his completed education for government if we are not to perish from this earth—bilked and bled, deceived and atomized. The improvising politician class must go.

"Our species is now crowding the fatal maximum. We are fighting to recreate the food balance. The fat rats are facing those tattered scarred rats with overactive adrenals. Soon, the men will make murderous war upon the women. Then the species will become extinct. The end of the world is an ego trip but the end of man can be the blink of an eye."

He looked from face to face at everyone at the caucus. He said, "Therefore, the matter of whether Ada and my father remain together or whether Mr. Mulligan goes to the Senate is of such unimportance that I respectfully suggest that our vote allow these two people who love each other to remain as they are."

He sat down.

There was an embarrassed silence. At last, F.M. Heller spoke. "Interesting little talk, Botolf," he said, "but aren't you going to debate the subject before this caucus?"

"For Christ's sake, Heller!" Ada yelled at him. "Are you drunk or spaced out or something?"

Dunc Mulligan looked as though everyone had switched to a different language.

"Look at Daddy," Mona said very loudly, "he doesn't have a clue."

Os stood up and tapped on the side of a glass with a spoon to get attention. "What about free will?" he asked stridently. "Are we microscopic life forms or are we men? What of the human spirit?"

"Ask Mayor Daley," Esau cried. "Ask the American Medical Association. Ask the National Rifle Association."

Duncan helped F.M. Heller to pull himself to his feet. "What an exhilarating evening," he said. "By now you have weighed both pleas and we are ready to vote. The Noon family will vote first, beginning with its senior member, the distinguished monsignor. Then the Harris family will vote in the same order. Monsignor Noon?" F.M. Heller fell back into his chair.

Gawain did not rise. He stared at the tablecloth. "I was impressed by Botolf's remarks. I also believe deeply in what good Duncan had to say. Their statements, of course, are not incompatible. We must render unto Caesar the things which are Caesar's, et cetera. Our great governmental system must continue to evolve under the genius a wise people have sent to Washington. I am certain that these great leaders know the meaning of Botolf's word. Therefore, I cast my vote against."

"No hard feelings, son," Os called down the table. "We always do the best we can."

"Tristram Noon?"

"I vote against."

"It's all right, Tris," his father said. "No harm is done where none is meant."

"Botolf Noon?" F.M. Heller called out sonorously.

"To establish my point," Botolf said, "or perhaps I should say to particularize it within the sensibilities of this caucus—the point being that we are moving to the destruction of our species on this planet—and since my brothers, both significant American leaders, fail to grasp what I said, and since Mrs. Harris and my father represent the only celebration of life in our midst—life which is inevitably thundering toward disaster, and which, I see from your lack of understanding, must go its full terrible course—I vote against."

"He votes against!" Duncan cried out turning to F.M. Heller. "Their own lawyer voted against!" The mouths at the table babbled with astonishment. Mona said to Fiona, "They got to him with some pill!"

Os called across the roar of excited talking to say loudly to Bottie, "Good logic, son. Damned good logic. I appreciate your point."

"What the hell kind of a family are you?" Ada said to him indignantly. "A family that rips apart, breaks the heart."

Esau stood up and raised his arms over his head. "If the master votes no then I vote no," he said.

Kaskie yelled, "Why should Ada always have her own way? Why should she always bollox things up with a lot of crap like happiness? I vote no. No, no, no!"

"Well, then," F.M. Heller purred. "Would you like to make it unanimous, Mrs. Mulligan-Harris?"

"All right. Okay. I vote no."

"My God," Duncan moaned. "I'm in! It's unanimous! I am a United States Senator."

Gawain, Kaskie, and F.M. Heller crowded around him pounding his back, pumping his hand, Heller booming, Kaskie mewing, Gawain copping a sly feel. Dunc got up on tiptoes to call out to Ada over the heads of the three excited men, "Ada, you are going to *love* Pitcairn!"

"That isn't the way it works, Dunc," Celeste said rather shrilly as the two Benzedrines sharpened the top of her head like the point of a pencil.

"What was that, Woofie? I didn't quite catch that."

"I mean—all bets are off," Celeste yelled stridently. "I mean you may not have the problem with your youth image any more but you sure as hell are hung up with worse than that."

The three congratulants around Dunc stopped, as though the current had been turned off. They all faced Celeste; everyone was facing Celeste.

"What did you mean by that, Mrs. Mulligan-Harris?" F.M. Heller asked with an edge of menace to his voice.

"I am divorcing Duncan."

"Whaaaat?"

"Mommy!"

"Di*vor*cing me? When?"

"Tomorrow. On the grounds that you are a rubber freak."

"A *rubber* freak?" Mona shouted.

"Oh, Daddy, that's wild! That's so *int*eresting!"

F.M. Heller had gone very pale. "But you gave no hint! You know above everyone else what is at stake here! You cannot do this, Mrs. Mulligan-Harris. For reasons of state known only to you and to me, you cannot do this. You have America's history in your hands."

"Why? Tell me *why*. Tell me how and *why* you would *want* to do such a thing," Duncan cried out, shocked and frightened.

"I am going to marry Tristram Noon," Celeste blazed. "I've decided to try happiness for a change."

"You'll hate it!" Kaskie screeched. "Don't do it, baby!"

Ada marched over and stood beside her daughter.

"Mommy's been moonlighting with your brother, Botto," Mona said, swaying with ecstasy.

"Holy McGoly," Fiona said, "this will even make front page of *EVO*. Maybe *The Realist*. Good-by Jackie Onassis, hello Celeste Noon."

"Did you ball him, Mom? Did you really ball him?"

F.M. Heller looked very ill. "Do you realize what you've done, Noon?" he thundered. "Do you have any idea what this means? You are through, done, finished. I can't even bring myself to think what the Attorney General will plan for you. This—this is the worst—the absolutely *worst* moment of my life."

Nasturtiano came into the room fast, carrying a telephone. "An urgent call for you Mr. Heller," he said, insisting that Heller take the call over everything else going on in the room. Heller waved him away weakly and began to walk in tiny circles, holding his ears in his hands. Nasturtiano plugged the phone into a wall outlet and shoved the instrument into F.M. Heller's hand. Reflexively, the banker put it to his ear and spoke into it.

Esau stared at his watch. "Oh, Baby Jesus," he said. "Now is the hour."

Kaskie was weeping brokenly into his arms on the dining room table.

"Whaaaaaaaa????" F.M. Heller was saying into the phone. "The Panthers have blown up the Everest Bank?"

The room swung to face him, re-riveted.

"Not the Panthers? The Weathermen? No? Then who, for God's sake. Who would do such a heinous thing?"

Suddenly he held the telephone away from him as though it had gone insane and tried to bite him. He stared at it incredulously. He returned it to his head to speak into it.

"Dun—can *Mull*—ig—an?" His eyes ranged across the faces of everyone in the room, resting at last, pitiable, upon the doubly bewildered Dunc.

"Daddy! You'll make *Rolling Stone,"* Mona shrieked.

"He'll make bloody Madame Tussaud's!" Fiona yelled.

F.M. Heller dropped the telephone and fell bonelessly into a chair, which tilted over sideways taking his great spherical form to the floor. The room spurted with the noises of excitement.

Os patted Ada's hand and said, "As I had remarked, dear, things always turn out differently from what you expect."

41

While Nasturtiano and Bottie worked over F.M. Heller with aromatic spirits, the other guests made hurried, dazed, weeping, puzzled or exulting departures. The butler, Bottie, and Dunc were able to get F.M. Heller to his feet but he would not look at Dunc nor would he blame him. His head could not stop shaking in tiny negative quivers. His eyes were haunted. "The Panthers and the students did this thing," he said. "Tristram Noon's power has collapsed and the Democrats have framed Duncan."

"Yes, yes!" Duncan said. "I have been framed. Surely the Attorney General will see at once that I've been framed?"

"Oh, God—the Attorney General!" Heller seemed to buckle where he stood but they buttressed him, got his coat and hat on him and Monsignor Noon moved him out toward the door where Os and Ada volunteered to take him home.

"*You* are saved, at least," F.M. Heller said to them. "There is no reason for CINCPAC to spend all that money taking you to Pitcairn now."

They walked with him to the door but he disengaged himself. "No," he said firmly. "I was your enemy. It would not be right for me to let you help me." He tottered off alone down the hall. He turned once. "Please send Dr. Nasserli if you can." The elevator door opened. He entered and disappeared, dreading the night to come in the floating room while that voice beat him mercilessly.

Os telephoned Nasserli, a physician he and F.M. Heller shared, who lived three doors up Fifth Avenue from Heller's Rockrimmon House.

"As you must be able to imagine, Mr. Noon," Dr. Nasserli said, "I regret it exceedingly, but I do not make house calls."

"Doctor—there must be a misunderstanding. This is for F.M. Heller—the great banker, F.M. Heller—you've not only treated him for thirty years but you must have pumped him for all kinds of financial information."

"I am perfectly aware of my relationship with Mr. Heller—but I do not make house calls."

"Didn't you hear me? I said Mr. Heller could have suffered a stroke."

"Then he must be hospitalized. I can reserve a room and arrange to send an ambulance for him and I will examine him there at once."

"He lives three doors away from you! The hospital is four and a half miles away."

"Mr. Noon, I cannot continue to waste time on this. I do not make house calls. It is a status oath we take with the finance secretary of the AMA and that is final."

Gawain took the telephone from his father's hand and spoke into it. "Dr. Nasserli?" he asked with sinister unctuousness. "This is Monsignor Noon—Church of Christ, Computer. If you are not at Mr. Heller's side within fifteen minutes I will have a check run on you by an Apostle computer and tomorrow morning the Everest Bank will become your creditor on every apartment house you own in New Jersey, Queens, and Westchester, every holding you own in light and heavy industry, your hotels and your factories, and the bank will foreclose on you and call in every note and obligation you have accumulated. Do I make myself clear?" Gawain paused. "Fifteen minutes, doctor."

"Oh, that was wonderful," Ada sang. "That was real family solidarity."

"Where am I going to get another doctor?" Os asked wildly. "I don't even *like* F.M. Heller!"

Tristram and Celeste had gone. Mona and Fiona had led their dazed father out. Esau and Gawain had guided Kaskie away, the father blinded with tears. Os, Ada and Bottie sat at the dining room table.

"What are we going to do now?" Ada asked.

"I think we should have more of that dessert," Bottie said. He darted away to the kitchen.

"I was just beginning to cotton to that Pitcairn Island idea," Os said. "Those Filipino servants the Navy has developed are about the best there are, you know."

"The whole thing is a letdown," Ada said.

Bottie raced into the room, elated. "Miss Pomposelli just happens to have some *tartelleti di mirtillo!*"

"Well!" Os beamed.

Nasturtiano brought a bottle of very cold, sweet, ingratiating Malvasia di Lipari with the blueberry tarts and they ate and drank, bleating with pleasure.

"We can be grateful that we have sound livers," Os said at the third tart. "The liver is responsible for so-called neuroses, you know. And most fatigue and all drunkenness and much of the melancholia." He lighted a long, dark cigar. "It is the most sophisticated organ we have. The heart is an athlete. The stomach is a hammock but the liver is the seat of life. My wife has a particularly sensitive liver—two drinks and she's gone."

"We have to help Dunc," Ada said.

"Why not?"

"Duncan is no favorite of mine but we all certainly know he did not blow up that bank."

"The radical Eastern establishment press will crucify him nonetheless. How can we help him?"

"I don't know. I thought you might know."

Os sipped the chilled wine and seemed to be thinking. "Bottie, do you have any ideas?"

"Not tonight," Bottie said as he gathered together crumbs of the pastry with a moistened fingertip. "But perhaps in the morning."

"Well, I fear the police will have Duncan by morning," Os said.

"Then there's the problem of Esau," Ada said. "I mean, no matter what you can think of, Bottie, I don't think we should help Dunc unless he makes F.M. Heller help Esau. Esau's heart can break too, you know. Heller had no right to snatch him out of the Tombs on the very day he had been promised a trial. Esau found happiness in our prison system."

"The police are probably flailing away at Duncan with their truncheons right now," Os said. "It's a damned shame."

"No, Pop, it's all right. I asked the twins to take him to our place for tonight—until I can think of something. He can sleep in the maid's room. No one will find him there."

"Please don't get your father involved in this, Bottie. If Dunc is at his place then, Os, you'll just have to come to my place. When I said we should do something to help Dunc, I really didn't mean we should go this far."

"Harboring a fugitive is a serious business," Os said disapprovingly.

Ada stood up. "Well, anyway, we have to go. I'm so charged up I'll have to wake up the masseuse." They got their coats and said good night to Bottie.

Alone—waiting for Jean-Pierre to return—Bottie wandered around the flat peering into things. In the small sitting room beside Jean-Pierre's bedroom he found himself standing, transfixed, before five of the plastic Caspar Lear masks which were mounted in a row on a long table; each mask like a living head, spotlighted. They were precise likenesses of T.S. Eliot, Francis Albert Sinatra, John Calvin, Aunt Jemima, and Alphonse Capone as a child. He had the terrible certainty that someone had crept up behind these five people with sharpened kris, had decapitated them then made off with their heads in a basket because, pore for pore, wen for wen, they were identical with the living originals.

"You really do like my masks," a soft voice said directly behind him. Bottie turned to see Jean-Pierre, still wearing his tall, square Churchill bowler and a very long woolen scarf known to the haberdashery trade as a cratchitt. Suddenly the grim face smiled because Jean-Pierre had realized that he was taller than Bottie.

"Are they all gone?" he asked.

Bottie nodded.

"How did the vote go?"

"A unanimous no."

"Against Ada?"

"Yep."

"U*nan*imous? What about your vote?"

"It didn't make any difference. F.M. Heller lost." Bottie let the loser's name sink in. "Duncan Mulligan is out of the Senate race because he's being hunted by the police for blowing up the Everest Bank tonight with time bombs."

"*Dunc*an?"

"But before we knew that, your sister announced that she was divorcing him on the grounds that he was a rubber freak and that she was going to marry my brother Tris."

"Ce*leste?* She left *Dunc*an?"

"I stayed after they left because I knew you'd want to know about it before you read it in the papers."

"Yeah. Right. Thanks." He took Bottie by the elbow

and led him to a seat. As Bottie sat down, Jean-Pierre's hand sank into his breast pocket and came out with a gold cigarette case which had a fire opal clasp and offered Bottie his choice of a row of marijuana joints.

"You'll like this, I think," he said. "It's grown by commissioned officers over field rank in Thailand, using water which the Air Force brings out in flying tankers from Amarillo, Texas. There is something that that water does to grass and we aren't sure what it is yet."

"Amarillo? No kidding?" Bottie said politely.

"Then it's flown to a commune of Army deserters, who deserted under orders for the job, to Uppsala, in Sweden, where it is flashfrozen, one pound at a time, because more than that at one time and your quality suffers."

Jean-Pierre snapped on a cassette deck and a piano playing Liszt's *Tasso* seemed to glide into the room.

"I know why you ran out on the dinner tonight," Bottie said as Jean-Pierre leaned back in a big chair and exhaled smoke. "And I know who did it to you, even if I don't know what he did."

Jean-Pierre came out of his chair like a tiger and grabbed Bottie by both lapels.

"Who? Quick! Who?"

"Tell me what he did and I'll tell you who."

"No!" He took Bottie by the throat. "Who?" he shouted hoarsely.

Bottie stared at him as though they were separated by a thick glass wall. Jean-Pierre's fingers relaxed on his throat.

"What did he do?" Bottie asked.

"He had some terrible pictures taken of my mother." Jean-Pierre's voice broke. "Then he sent them to me."

"F.M. Heller did it," Bottie said.

"Whaaat?"

Bottie nodded. Jean-Pierre pushed Bottie away and stood up. "I don't believe it," he said unconvincingly. Bottie shrugged sympathetically.

"Why would he do a thing like that to *me?* To me of all people?"

"He didn't want you to vote. That was their secret weapon—they thought. He was going to vote your nephew's no—Esau's—because he had him where he wanted him, too. Then the whole thing blew up in his face. That was our secret weapon."

"He re*spects* me. He likes me. He wouldn't do that to me," Jean-Pierre babbled. "He would have to be crazy because my parent organization does all its tax-free municipals through him and it could cost half his wallet."

"Do you have a way to check it out?"

"I'm checking it out right now. I have people on it."

"When you are sure, will you call me? I can help."

"How do you know it was Heller?"

Bottie had decided thirty hours before that he was going to have to lie if he were to wreck the Attorney General's plan, bring justice to Duncan Mulligan, return Esau happily to prison, relieve Jean-Pierre of a serious trauma, and offer permanent solutions to Ada and Os, so he said, "Your mother told me."

Jean-Pierre did not ask how his mother knew because he had always known that his mother knew everything which concerned her family. He took several very deep tugs on the stick. He said, "I have to check. It's too important a piece of business. But I'll tell you one thing. If it is F.M. Heller—" He stopped. His voice was ugly and dangerous.

"If it is F.M. Heller—and it is," Bottie said, "your mother insists that you call on me."

It was two-fifteen on Saturday morning when Bottie got home. He rode the Eighty-sixth Street Crosstown then walked down Broadway to Seventy-ninth. He was attacked once on Third Avenue by a mugger who came behind him from a dark doorway, and once again on Broadway at Eighty-first, in front of the closed Bialystocker Exchange. He handled the first with a simple overhead throw and a *mae-geri* kick and the second with two fast *yoko-tobi-geri* followed by a *fumikomi* and got home without further incident.

Mona and Fiona were fast asleep on chairs in the living room. Duncan was sitting in his underwear on the edge of the bed in the maid's room when Bottie made his way back there. Duncan looked up in a hopeless daze when he heard Bottie's step.

"What does it all mean?" he asked.

"Well," Bottie said, "taking things one at a time, it means you have won the caucus."

"Oh—thank God."

"But, unfortunately, it also means you have lost your

wife who plans to sue you for divorce on sensational grounds."

"Oh—my God!"

"Thirdly, and this could get sticky, the police are out hunting for you."

"Po-*lice?*"

"You will be charged with blowing up the Everest Bank."

"*Me?*" Dunc was blank. He had either totally failed to absorb the facts when he originally heard them, or, in his stupor, he had lost their meaning.

"Did you—uh—did you blow up the Everest Bank, Mr. Mulligan?"

"Of course not. At least, I—no. It is a dreadful mistake. I can't remember. I'm dazed. There's been one shock after another and I have a very low threshold for—everything. But if the authorities *say* I blew up the Everest Bank then—oh, my God, what am I going to do?"

"You have to get some sleep, Mr. Mulligan. If you can get fourteen hours' sleep you'll be able to face anything."

"If I could only sleep."

Bottie gave Duncan two sleeping pills and a nice, cold glass of Guinness.

Then Bottie tucked him in, put out the light and went out to shake the twins awake. "Well," he said, "the caucus is over. We can have our little talk now, I think."

The twins gaped at him then Fiona leaped first. She got his head between her two hands and then tried to swallow the lower half of his face while Mona zipped his trousers down.

When Dunc awoke at four-twenty the following afternoon, Bottie gave him three more sleeping pills and another tall glass of Guinness to keep him asleep until Sunday night when he could give him two more to keep him asleep well into Monday.

42

On Saturday morning at 8:11, as Bottie was sprinkling the Lady Macbeth detergent over Duncan Mulligan's shirt in the washing machine, F.M. Heller telephoned.

He went directly to the point. "I hope I was of some help to you the other evening, Bottie," he said.

"Indeed you were, sir. Are you all right this morning? Feeling much more fit than last night?"

"I'm all right, thank you. A little fuzzy. I was up until almost two o'clock trying to get that damned doctor out of this house, but never mind that. I—I wanted to ask you a small favor, Bottie."

"Certainly, sir."

"We had a good talk the other night—I mean really fine rapport. The fact is I have to have someone to talk to. Just to sort of sort things out. I wondered if I could persuade you to come here for breakfast just to let me ramble on?"

Bottie thought of the exquisite excellences of the twins as they slept on in the huge double bed in his room. He almost began to count the many things he had not yet said and done to them in the rush of events on that bed the night before. F.M. Heller took his pause to mean reluctance.

"I just have never had the time to make friends, Bottie. I know there should have been quite a few people I should have been able to turn to beyond you—people my own age—but quite frankly, there never was any need for that sort of thing and now—well, here I am."

"I can be there in a half hour—I think," Bottie said. He had no way of knowing how soundly Mona and Fiona slept and whether he could get his coat and hat out of there without disturbing them.

When Bottie got out of the cab in front of Rockrimmon House, the two city policemen waved him up the front steps and the muscular blond guard held the door open. Inside, the man wearing the hat who was seated with the shotgun across his lap and the two bristling Dobermans chained beside him, waved gaily as Bottie entered the lift. The evil-appearing house samurai opened the lift door at the fifth floor and bowed so deeply and so rapidly that Bottie could hear the man's forehead crack painfully against his shinbones. F.M. Heller was waiting there in his dragon-pee kimono and pajamas and took Bottie into the horrendous wallpaper room past the battle of Cronstadt to a breakfast table which had been set at the window overlooking Central Park. Heller talked all the way.

"Washington got me out of bed at six-forty this morning. I have never heard the Attorney General in such a rage," he said. "He seems to solve everything by refusing to believe what has happened."

"But he's such a powerful man. I mean if Duncan did blow up the bank, surely—"

"Oh, anything can be arranged, of course. Nothing is in danger except Dunc's immediate image. Please, you must breakfast first. What would you like?"

"Oh—anything. Really."

"We have English breakfasts here because my father so admired the Morgan Bank. You must have something substantial."

Bottie thought of the energy he had expended so ecstatically the night before and just twenty minutes ago because the twins had turned out to be very light sleepers. "Then—some porridge, I think," he said. "Then a few kippers. Some deviled kidney?"

F.M. Heller nodded emphatically and most encouragingly.

"Then a few cutlets, three or four rashers of gammon with scrambled plovers' eggs and perhaps some rizzered haddie. And tea, please."

The house samurai bowed again in acknowledgment, banging his head against his shins.

"A bloater for me," F.M. Heller said. "Then some ham rissoles and Bath chap with a few deviled bones and some mock brawn. Lashings of marmalade, please, and some creamed beef with prunes, buttered toast and tea. Thenkew."

The samurai trotted off, the tall arrows in his *wuwagashi* rattling.

"Was the bank badly damaged?" Bottie asked.

"Almost totally. Vaults, street banking floor, and two

upper floors demolished. Irreplaceable documents and valuables of depositors gone forever with no way of counting them. The lawsuits will never be unraveled."

"I certainly hope your own fortune wasn't blown away," Bottie said earnestly.

"I bank abroad. But the tragedy of my bank is nothing compared to the chaos of mind in Washington over the prospect of losing Duncan. They said some *revolting* things to me. As though I had blown up my own bank to ruin my own candidate."

"They must have some policy by now?"

"Yes." F.M. Heller shook his head hopelessly.

"That bad?"

"The firm policy is that even if Duncan did blow up the bank—and the policy also is that he did not do it—the whole thing is due to the strain of his wife falling in love with another man."

"That's pretty good."

"In a way, yes. Your brother is a great, national hero so any voter would be able to understand Mrs. Mulligan-Harris' attraction to him—and he is a *younger* man—which will make her appear flighty and Dunc mature and wronged but—"

"It isn't so much a youth problem, after all, is it?" Bottie asked. "I mean, a basic misunderstanding throughout this family or political conflict hasn't been Mr. Mulligan's youth image, has it, F.M.?"

"Then what was it?"

"It's biology itself, I think. I mean, that's the way Americans are taught. I mean, the fact that my father and Mrs. Harris are together doesn't really affect Mr. Mulligan's youth image—it's that the American people are instantly disgusted by biology itself—in any sexual form beyond their own beds."

"That could be. I mean, that's just a lot of semantics. But the burden is all on me. I have to extricate Duncan from the hands of the police, if indeed the police can find him while through seven editions every day and one hundred and eight hours of television in six channels Duncan is being branded and hounded as a fugitive. What about that image, for God's sake?"

"Duncan has disappeared." Bottie stated that as a fact but Heller took it to have been phrased as a question.

"I *know* Dunc Mulligan. And I know he could *not* have

done such a thing. He is absolutely innocent of such wild charges. But that has not occurred to the fantasts of Washington."

"We can't blame them for that, F.M. The police have said Dunc blew up the bank and the Attorney General's entire credibility depends on the credibility of the police."

F.M. Heller took four tremendously deep sniffs from what he had always insisted was an asthma inhaler.

"I grant that," he said. "But I also say that it is vital that Dunc be found without the interference of the police. If they find him they will undoubtedly hold him under some such trumpery as being a material witness so that they may be photographed with him by the press and television who have already made a very good commercial thing out of this for themselves. And this is only the first day. Each day that passes means that the police will hold Duncan longer while the press milks the story. If I can find him first I can make my own deal with the police and the Vice-President can come in here to frighten the press."

"Then you have every hope of nominating him next week?" Bottie asked.

"Well, of course, we'll nominate him," Heller said irritably. "That is beside any point. The thing which matters is that we must *find* him."

"Easier said than done. He must be very frightened." Bottie thought of Duncan sleeping soundly in the maid's room and involuntarily glanced at his watch, trying to compute how long the sleeping pills would last.

"Bottie, you have a clear, analytical mind. How would you go about finding Duncan Mulligan?"

"Well, it seems to me—"

"Yes?"

"It seems to me that the whole responsibility for finding him must be shifted back to the Attorney General."

"I see. Good. Why? How?"

"He has more police. I mean this calls for a huge strike force of FBI agents in one direction and an army of CIA men in another. Only the Attorney General can bring them into the case. Only the Attorney General can call out the Secret Service and all necessary Army, Navy, and Air Force intelligence units. I mean, Mr. Mulligan has to be found and that means every investigator on the government payroll who can be spared must search for him."

"But, my God, Bottie—"

"He'll need to call on all investigators from the Federal Housing Authority and the Pure Foods Section at HEW. There are sixteen thousand trained members of the National Security Agency—and Army *counter*intelligence people have shown they can do a wonderful job—the State Department has a crackerjack security staff and—"

"Just one moment, please!" Heller yelled with excitement. "Not so fast here!" He began to write the instructions down on a large white linen napkin. "Yes, yes. Who else?"

"My brother Tris' organization can put six thousand people into the streets and bars and hotels looking for Mr. Mulligan on six hours' notice. Mr. Jean-Pierre Harris' parent organization can deliver perhaps ten thousand hard hats. And, I mean, everybody talks to them—on one side or the other."

"But the cost!"

"The cost? It won't cost a fraction of what the war costs."

"It will be a *gigantic* bill!" Heller cried.

"The Attorney General can channel funds through the Republican National Committee," Bottie shrugged. "There is the White House fund—that's unaccountable. And all the billions the CIA has access to."

"It can run to a million four hundred thousand dollars a day!"

"The Attorney General should have thought of that before he set out to ruin my father, shouldn't he have?"

"O, what a tangled web we weave . . ." F.M. Heller moaned.

"The thing is, if you want to find Mr. Mulligan before the police find him—it has to be done."

"Yes. Yes, it has to be done."

"But it simply *can*not be charged to the White House budget or the CIA special funds or for that matter any government agency."

"Why not, for God's sake?"

"Because it's a *party* matter. Why—if the opposition ever found out that the taxpayers were being charged to find a fugitive who wasn't even yet a candidate, they would organize a national march on Washington and literally throw the rascals out."

"But who is going to pay for it then?" F.M. Heller was utterly aghast.

"Every penny of it has to be charged to the Republican National Committee." Bottie leaned back. "It depends entirely on whether you think Mr. Mulligan is worth it."

"It will cost the party a million four hundred thousand dollars a day!"

"If he isn't worth it, the Attorney General shouldn't spend one thin dime."

F.M. Heller sat, dazed, as the house samurai began to load the food on the table and to set the semicircle of chafing dishes within reach around them. Heller rummaged inside his beautiful white beard while his eyes stared at infinity. After almost five minutes he spoke again while Bottie chewed away.

"If the Republican Party is to stay in power for the next thirty to sixty years it must have Duncan Mulligan."

"You are sure of that?" Bottie asked dreamily.

"He is the mirror of the people! They will vote for him and follow him anywhere because he and the people are one!"

"Then he's worth every penny of it," Bottie said.

"All right. First, we'll have breakfast then I'll work this out with the Attorney General. Perhaps while I do that you will locate your brother Tristram and please bring him to me at noon today."

"Why?"

"I have more confidence in him than in all the government forces. I—I think he should coordinate all of them. And by that I mean in*clu*ding the FBI. Someone else will have to straighten that out with old Mr. Hoover."

"I'll deliver Tris here at noon today, F.M."

"Then there is the matter of your brother Gawain."

"What is that, F.M.?"

"He is Pope Mellon's ambassador to the Attorney General so we must work with him, by law. Unfortunately, I offended him last week about the medal he offered, so, once again, I must depend on you, Bottie."

"Why do you need Gawain, F.M.?"

"Because no matter what the radical Eastern establishment press has to say right now or in the near future—Christ, Computer, will endorse the candidacy of Duncan Mulligan in all the churches at all services across the nation tomorrow."

43

When breakfast was finished and F.M. Heller had waddled off to the floating room, Bottie called Tris, made sure that he would be alone, then took a cab directly to United Nations Plaza.

The brothers sat together behind a strong window on the high floor of Tris' building. Outside the double-glazed panes the airborne filth swirled as thick as tulle, and the alarms and other cries of pain from the city below them could still be heard clearly.

"What can I do for you, Bot?"

"I came to buy you, Tris."

"Buy?"

"You were for sale against Pop last night so you must have always been for sale."

"I lease, baby. I don't sell outright."

"I have a contract. F.M. Heller wants to see us at noon. I had breakfast with him."

"Now who's for sale?"

"Listen, Tris. And listen hard and get this straight. A sinister attempt was made by the vested government of this country to trample on our father's rights. You go along. I don't go along."

"Okay."

"Okay—what?"

"Okay! I dig. You didn't sell out and you've got yourself hyped on something to make you think you can take on the Attorney General." Tris snorted his contempt.

"I have taken him on. He's doing what I want right now."

"How?"

"That doesn't matter. Just believe me. You're muscle. Heller and the Attorney General want muscle from you, and they want ideas from me."

"Listen, Bottie, don't get all froze up. Come on! Let's take it apart and look at it. What do you want from me?"

"F.M. Heller wants you at his house at noon to offer

you a hundred dollars a day for every man you can put on the street—up to say, four thousand men—to find Duncan Mulligan."

"Find him?"

"He disappeared after the news about the bank explosion last night."

"What did you tell F.M. Heller?"

"I answered him. They have to find Mr. Mulligan. He asked me how. I told him."

"What the hell do you care if they find Mulligan? You got Pop off their hook. They can't do anything to Pop now."

"Well, that's the love of a good woman for you. You did everything. You met Celeste. It happened like a song lyric. She decided she had to divorce Duncan and that took the heat off Pop."

"Well, it had to be. She belongs with me. I mean, like you said—it happened. Jesus, who ever thought it would happen to me?"

"What?"

"I want to *marry* her, for God's sake! I mean, okay that it took the heat off Pop—but what about me? I mean, I *want* it this way, for God's sake!"

"It isn't just Pop."

"Bottie, for Christ's *sake!*"

"It's Pop and me and you and the rest of America."

"Are you crazy? Do you think people care? I should know. It's my business to push them around. They'll trade you the whole fucking government—good or bad—for one free week on their Diners' card or a subscription to *Playboy.*"

"We may not be our brothers' keepers any more," Bottie said, "but we aren't our brothers' killers either. If you can't see it as our rights maybe you can justify to yourself why politicians have become the natural enemies of mankind. How do you know, Tris? Where do *you* stand now? You're way out of line with them over Celeste, Tris. You knew it would put their man in danger but you did it. You know their rules but you went ahead and did it. Maybe they'll pull the plug on you, Tris."

Tris fumbled with the box of joints. He lighted a stick and his hands were shaking. "I've been up almost all night," he said. "I've been thinking about that all night."

"Then you figured it out."

"Figured what out?"

"That you aren't on their side any more. So you need help. *Help*, Tris. You have to come to my side. Besides, there's a very good dollar in it."

"I sent Celeste home last night. I put her out of here. I was all upset."

"I can't offer you a free week on your Diners' Club—but I can handle the *Playboy* subscription if you and Celeste are ready to swap for what democracy is supposed to mean."

"Bottie—look, Bottie—"

"What do you want to do?"

"Whatever you say, kid." Tris licked his dry lips.

"That's good. Then we'll go to see F.M. Heller just the way he wants it. Then he'll offer you the hundred a day per man for the four thousand people on the street and he'll tell you the Attorney General wants you to take charge of the FBI and CIA forces, the Army, the Navy, and Air Force Intelligences forces, the agents from the National Security office, the Secret Service, the FHA and the Pure Food investigators during the search for Duncan Mulligan."

"You know they're going to offer me that?"

Bottie nodded.

"Will it be a legit offer?"

Bottie nodded again.

"Will it get me off this hook with them?"

Bottie shrugged. "Who am I to say? You know the fascist mind far better than I do. You're the one who's lived with totalitarians all your life."

"You know. I admit it. I don't know anything. Will it get me off the hook with them? Will it get Celeste and me off the goddam hook?"

"Why not? If you can find Duncan Mulligan for them."

"And if I can't?" He looked away. He stared out across the metropolitan trading area of forty million people captured in each other's filth.

"You can't. You won't find him."

"Why not? I'll have over ten thousand trained men with total no-knock powers."

"Because I hid him. And the no-knock powers won't work on me."

"Bottie, what are you trying to do to me? What do you

want? I told you I'm on your side. I swear I'm on your side. What do you want?"

"I want you to take the job when F.M. Heller offers it and I want you to keep every agent they can send sweating this afternoon and tonight, all day tomorrow and tomorrow night and right through Tuesday and then I'll give Duncan to you personally."

"Listen, I'm not objecting. Okay? But why Tuesday?"

"We have to have him ready for the state nominating convention Wednesday. But that's the easy part."

"The *easy* part?"

"F.M. Heller is going to have Gawain have Christ, Computer endorse Duncan totally for the Senate. You and I have to reverse that."

"Change Gawain after orders from the Attorney General? You've lost your mind."

"When we leave F.M. Heller's we'll see Gawain. I want you to call him now and set the time—say three o'clock."

"You don't need me for Gawain."

"Yes. You tell him you want to see him about government business."

"But how will you talk him out of an order from the Attorney General?"

"I'm thinking about that. Better make it at the cathedral at about one-fifteen."

44

Behind the young acolyte they moved as if on oiled wheels down the gray plastic corridor to the high door to Gawain's cell which had been redecorated by Battersby in a happier monastic tradition of Art Nouveau. The music swelled around them and an archangelically high tenor articulated the message of the Mithraissic arm of the church, Gawain's own wing, which paid special worship to the powerful helper of Ormuzd in his eternal struggle for the advancement of righteousness and the causes of light. But, both Botolf and Tristram had walked this way before and were, therefore, not as impressed as they might have been. Above the thrilling music, one of the voices of Christ, Computer, was counting the sins of the world in a terrible voice, each sin noted and counted as it was committed simultaneously in: Toledo, Ohio; Leap, Ireland; Klein Wansee, Berlin; and all other cities, towns, villages, hamlets, localities, and houses of the world: "Seven billion septillion squared, seven billion septillion squared and one," then, in sublime compassion at midnight each night, wiping the slate clean and starting all over again.

Gawain had followed the progress and facial expressions of his brothers on closed-circuit television. As they entered his beautifully finished cell he was waiting for them with an ecstatic smile on his face, wearing a lavender soutane which had been exquisitely fitted along his lines to his ankles, and a naughty kelly-green beretta on his head. The color signaled his coming bishopric.

In the presence of the acolyte who had led them in, although not for very long at all after the acolyte left, he threw his arms about his two brothers with sharp outcries of devotion.

"How blest am I! To have two such doughty men and true, as sharers of the flesh of our father's flesh."

"There have been some new developments," Botolf said, cheerily.

"Ah?" Gawain replied.

"Good for you and the church," Tristram said.

"Ah?"

"The time is now," Botolf said.

"Now?" Gawain answered, looking dreamily at his brothers having spent one hour of ecstasy within an elevated block of the Incense of St. Amarillo. "St. Augustine told us that time is a three-fold present. We have the present as we experience it, *n'est-ce pas?* We have, as well—*cómo se dice?*—the past as a present memory. And, *natürlich*—the future as a present expectation, *nicht wahr?* Which of those is your time of now?"

"Tomorrow," Botolf said. "Tomorrow at all services."

"Ah?"

"Botolf is suggesting that the church should have a more active voice in the affairs of the state," Tris said.

"On the surface, at any rate," Bottie murmured.

"As of now, the state is placing all of its hopes upon Duncan Mulligan," Tris said.

"In what way?"

"You know in what way, Gawain."

"You conjecture."

"No," Bottie said. "We just left F.M. Heller. The Attorney General spoke to you at twelve fifty-five. Endorsement of Mr. Mulligan has been arranged."

"But if you know, why are you here? What must be must be."

"We came to suggest a new sort of candidate for endorsement," Botolf said.

"How do you mean, dear Botolf?"

"Just six weeks ago," Botolf said, "I was on a train going into San Francisco. I was thinking about the Pacific Gas and Electric's atomic energy plant and the thickening pollution blanket. And that had me thinking about the Saints and the Apostle computers because the pollution blanket brings on earlier summers and socks them in so that the people turn on their air conditioners sooner and longer which overloads the power supply—there being no real atomic power. With the overload running constantly, I began to wonder what happens to an Apostle computer when it gets less than a steady one hundred and seventeen volts of current. Something has to give, I thought. There simply would have to be a deliberate lowering of the voltage in order to make the available electrical power go around—right?"

"I plead with you not to commit sacrilege," Gawain said.

"I happened to be sitting next to a young ABM priest. He wore the holy medal of one of the advanced technical orders. He was reading his office, one of the computer engineering trade papers, so I began to talk to him and ask questions."

"What was his name?" Gawain asked sharply.

"No matter. You can promote him later. I put the problem to him about Apostle computers needing a steady one hundred and seventeen volts."

"You mean—he *an*swered you?"

"Oh, yes. He said there were three kinds of computers in our church—Apostles, Saints, and Priests—the big Apostles which will stop immediately if the voltage drops; the Saints which have back-up generators, and would be more reliable but slower than the Apostles—their generator cuts in when the voltage drops but they work at multimicrosecond speed—very slow—and it takes three seconds to make the switchover to generator so that, in the meantime, the Saints will have made tens of thousands of mistakes—and will have to be stopped cold; and the Priests which will have to go in to look for those mistakes."

"You are blaspheming in God's house," Gawain thundered.

"The Apostles would have stopped dead when the voltage dropped. Then the Saints have to go out. But both of their pantheons feed Christ, Computer, and Christ, Computer, runs seventy-three per cent of all industry in this country and does one hundred per cent of all thinking for the government. If we stop Christ, Computer, or turn Him insane with the mistakes of Apostles and Saints we would cause a terrible state of affairs across the world and a total remission of faith, *n'est-ce pas,* Gawain—*cómo se dice?"*

"Are you asking your church to commit both of you to a mental institution?" Gawain cried. "Being my brothers cannot save you now. You have mocked God and you must be punished."

"That isn't what Bottie was saying at all, Gawain," Tris said placidly. "He had an entirely different message."

"What message?"

"You know about my people, Gawain?" Tris asked.

"Yes."

"Well, unless you do what Bottie is going to ask you, I

am going to have my people blow up every electricity generator from Niagara to Indian Point to Big Allis. That will knock out every one of the six hundred thousand programs running on line and have more of a destructive effect on your work than a religious war."

Gawain seemed unable to believe what they had been telling him, as though perhaps it could all have been some trick of the Incense of St. Amarillo. His voice had become hoarse and harsh. "What have you come to ask of your church?" he asked.

"We have come to help you, Gawain, and perhaps to strengthen the whole position of your church as it exists by the sufferance of the Attorney General."

"Mock me not, Botolf."

"We want you, personally, to make sure that extraordinary doubt is cast upon the candidacy of Duncan Mulligan by Christ, Computer, at the services in all the churches in this country tomorrow morning. And we want you to swing the endorsement of Christ, Computer, to an alternative candidate."

"Please, Gawain," Tristram said earnestly. "Let me explain. I have thousands of reckless, restless kids on my team. I can't always control them. And they have been talking about how the Apostles and the Saints work to micro-millimicrosecond tolerances and what could happen to the church and its great works if a few hundred reckless kids decided to blow up the generators from here to Niagara."

"There are also extraordinary political advantages to what we offer you, Gawain," Botolf said calmly.

45

Botolf Noon balled Mona and Fiona Mulligan all afternoon.

46

It was one of the most beautiful Sundays of the year. In procession, for the first time in almost a dozen decades of American life, people of many denominations: Muslims, Catholics, Druids, Jews, and over four hundred and thirty-two Protestant cults were streaming into two hundred and seventy-six thousand five hundred and ninety churches of one denomination, the national Church of Christ, Computer. There were still religious maniacs who attended two churches; the national church and some old-fashioned spindle roof. The President still held services where his heart was, in the East Room among football players, baseball players, basketball players, jockeys, hockey players, soccer players, horse players, golfers, polo players, tennis players, and all others whom he considered his constituency, together with William "Billy" Graham, the devout and weening chaplain to a go-getting oligarchy. But also each Sunday, when the prayer books and jockstraps were put away, he would attend very private national services in the Attorney General's war room, services which Monsignor Noon attended monthly for religious review. It was these latter services which married the leaders to the American people within a spiritual dream.

The worship of Christ, Computer, had become the popular religion because it allowed for so much participation. It was as though its elders, divines such as Pope Mellon and the Attorney General, had seen that the clergy of another time had failed to bring exultation to the multitude because they had all required that Man ask God for answers and aid but, as it evolved clearly that man had invented God, he began to refine the patent and to seek a more resolved balance for adoration. At last, one thousand nine hundred and seventy-one years after Christ's birth, within an evangelistic technology, that could now be attained.

All morality is after all God asking questions; that is

what conscience is. In the Church of Christ, Computer, the congregation gives the answers instead of pleading with God for guidance. Now God prays for "answers" by asking questions and man gives answers, asking God for nothing more than a show of inferiority.

The national service of the church was the same in Winsted, Connecticut, as it was in Heppner City, Oregon, and in all other American cities, towns, and villages. These were not similar services but exactly the same service conducted by God, Himself, four times each Sunday, once for each time zone.

The service began with the Reading, a magnificently vocalized print-out from the great Central Processor within the gold-walled tabernacle of the ABM cathedral on Park Avenue in New York. The Reading reviewed the imponderables of the previous week, dwelt briefly on the imponderables for that day, then peered with force into the imponderables for the week to come. The national church had been the only revolution in operating theology since the establishment of primitive religions. Its essence was that the Godhead asked the worshippers His respectful questions, then waited meekly for each answer to be granted Him upon punchcards conveyed into slots in the backs of each pew then down the blessed chutes and into the access cores of all on-line ABM 840 Apostle computers within each state Apostle population which ranged from sixty-three in garrulous California to eleven in tiny, tense Rhode Island.

All Apostles had the storage capability of seventeen hundred and fifty million characters each, with an access time of one hundred and twenty milliseconds. Each Apostle processed the answer from its community congregations for an overall total of one hundred and forty million answers, the number of parishioners in the national congregation (church attendance having not yet become compulsory under law), at a speed of one-sixtieth of a millionth of a second for each processor cycle, then all Apostles relayed simultaneously to the Godhead, to Christ, Computer, Himself, within the mighty tabernacle in New York.

There were keystone printers: in the Attorney General's war room; in the cathedral sanctuary; and in each diocesan office where the CIA units were headquartered locally. These delivered the highest volume-printing applications: six thousand lines per minute so that the expression of the national will, the worshippers' instructions for the coming week to their God were made known first to the Godhead, of course, then split-seconds later to the nation's eager leaders.

One of the grievous losses under the new worship form—and there had to be some losses—something had to give—was that the numbers of the clergy had been enormously diminished because there was no longer any money in it unless one were willing to be educated beyond Genesis and acquire advanced computer skills. God was both preacher and sexton in His own churches; a more pragmatic God.

The print-out began at 11:03 A.M. within each national time zone over softer organ music, with God also singing, simultaneously as He read, S.W. Foss' "Hullo." The added thrill for each congregation was in knowing that even while He was reading *and* singing, Christ, Computer, was celebrating up to two hundred thousand four hundred and twelve discrete operations, some of them contrasting markedly with Sunday worship, such as defoliation, astrophotography, mixing napalm recipes, and preparing trial procedures and testimony for future courts martial of selected infantry officers accused of massacre, and doing the London *Times* crossword puzzle for an enormously rich Indian prince who could afford the fees and liked to brag.

Across the time zones, from Miami, to Peoria, to Las Vegas, to Portland, the assembled prepared to worship in enormous churches, stadia, ball parks, and bowling alleys to hear God speak to them. He had a beautiful voice and each time God spoke He spoke in the general accent of that time zone or, for the very rich, in the particular accent they were using during that season. To hear God speak with a positive Buffalo or Fresno accent was to hear another of his miracles. And the speech of the West Texas God—God!

"Blessèd People who are My chosen of this earth," the print-out always began, "the heart-felt closest to the center of My infinite love who are assembled beneath My sun and the golden roofs of their holy places today, in this hour of My need help Me with the data only you can give, bring your blessèd nourishment to the minds of My mind by which I may serve you unto the apocalypse."

"Poll us, Christ, Computer, that we may understand,"

was the formal national response in each congregation. "Poll us and teach us."

"If I come to you humbly and implore," rang out the voice of God, "will you answer unto Me so that I may co-relate and interpret, abrogate and enhance—that I might grow tall unto the heavens as the mighty storeroom of the genius of My people?"

"POLL US!" one hundred and forty million chanted. "Tell us Your need that we may teach You."

"Amen, amen, I say to you—take up your hymnals and your punchers. Humbly do I lay before you My needs.

"Item: How shall I advise the General Motors Corporation in its dilemma as to whether they should manufacture a two-cylinder Picnic Wagon? Should they name it the Picnic Wagon or the Freedom Wagon? Those wishing to enter their own suggested titles on the form provided in their hymnal have the chance to win prizes of up to fifty thousand dollars' worth of spare parts. Question: To manufacture or not to manufacture? Specifications: eight giant miles to the gallon on four fully rounded wheels. Tires of new, miracle-plastic fiber which may be replaced monthly at owner's option. Detachable Prest-Paper Roof. Seats two, four, or six passengers. Price: in ninety-three eatable colors, f.o.b. Japan, only twenty-five hundred dollars."

"Alleluliah!" God's voice sang out. "Punch! These are the moments of our glory. Alleluliah! Punch and punch. I poll you and implore you."

The clicking of the aluminum punchers scoring the pages of the hymnal were like the clatter of millions of prayer wheels.

"Page two—punches ready, please—I need you, O, I need you, O, Absalom!—I seek not only your love but your wisdom.

"Item: The Scow & Barge Local Number Nine Six Eight of Duluth, Wisconsin, and Hudson, New York, in defiance of the antistrike pledges of their national officers at Palm Springs, California, hereby apply for a wage increase of two and a half per cent over present wages, a four per cent increase on fringe benefits which include Sunday visiting privileges for their families aboard the scows when these vessels are in dry dock. Punchers at the ready, please. These men already earn fifty-eight dollars and forty cents per week. They are protected just as comprehensively as all of you under your government's superb Medicare program which your nation's doctors themselves devised. Question: Do these already compensated workers deserve a raise? You who lift high Ark and Covenant—punch! Punch!"

As the punchers clacked, the thrilling music of "Hullo" shifted into a celestial tenor of the electronic *castrati* which rendered "O, Promise Me," sung by the Apostle in Aspen, Colorado, a major figure in the Boolean pantheon named Matthew, whose billing was noted on the program for the day's services.

"And now," God said, "My Print-out Chat for Today."

A flickering sigh ran across the time zone.

"On this Sabbath before the political nominating convention in the great Keystone State of New York, I am given the inspiration to bring to you my first Sunday Special in many months—that is, a Good Government Directive in the form of seeking Truth from you for the aid of your gallant government leaders. This is a religious moment for it affects the collective We—particularly Me, your Combined Intelligence. Punches at the ready, please.

"Item: I am going to ask the entire nation to examine the options of the voters of the State of New York in order that those voters might be educated ethically by the continental spirit of good government. Those of you who are in New York, and My eye remains upon each one of you, have prayed for long days and years now that you may one day soon be allowed to choose your senator directly from your churches, through Me. You must be patient—as all in the nation who have petitioned Me on Prayer Form Seven-Eight-Four-Three in this matter must be patient. Until that day let us help one another as all of you enrich Me with the clarity of your conscience and your ethic. I call upon you to tell Me your wishes as to which sort of candidate you would believe the hallowed chambers of our Senate deserve."

"Poll us! Poll us that we may know and believe! Poll us and teach us what we have said."

"Item: In the race for the nomination on Wednesday next we will have two fine men. One is uncle to the other. He is an older-to-elderly man—no youth problem here—who has served faithfully as a sturdy, backroom, library lawyer in a sound Wall Street firm who wishes him well."

In the war room in Washington, the Attorney General turned, bemused, to stare at his second-in-command, the Secretary of Defense, and strode to the print-out itself to read what had to be a denial of what he had just heard.

"Those goddam French must be fucking this up somewhere," he said. "Get me Monsignor Noon in New York."

God's voice pealed on throughout the churches.

"The nephew, on the other hand, the more zingy, clear-minded and deft candidate for the office of the United States Senator from the great State of New York, is a vital, vigorous embodiment of what I like to think of as the New America. He is only twenty-two years old, but already tested as a leader of men. He is the grandson of the American pioneer in encapsulated drugs and also nephew to the well-known publisher and punster, Jean-Pierre Harris, whose work has brought all of us so much pleasure."

"What the hell *is* this?" the Attorney General roared, kicking the Apostle in his war room. "Where is that fucking priest? Get me that goddam monsignor on the telephone."

"Now let us examine this issue of the candidates themselves just a little more closely. The uncle candidate, one Duncan Mulligan—called Bunkum Dunc, I believe, by his chums—has been married for twenty years to a wonderful little woman, mother of his lovely twin daughters *but*—and here we must face the first grievous problem of his candidacy—he has decided to desert this wonderful wife and abandon his little girls. Further—and even I—omniscient, all-knowing—cannot understand how ward-heeling local bosses can expect to nominate men such as these—Duncan Mulligan, Bunkum Dunc, in a moment of mental blackout, let us pray, has blown *up* the Everest Bank of the City of New York—or at least he is charged with that crime and is now a fugitive from arrest—causing the loss of tens of millions of dollars worth of currency, documents and property—*bank* property—and the loss of lives. How all that saddens Me."

"I get no answer at the monsignor's, sir," the President, who was also aide-de-camp, called out to the Attorney General across the room. "Not on the hot line and not on the switchboard."

"Then get me the fucking pope," the Attorney General yelled.

"I've tried Pope Mellon, sir. Negative, sir. Negative at cathedral and negative at Gondolfo, Long Island."

"This sad man's nephew however is a glorious American youth at apogee. His name is Sylvan Harris. Repeat—and please read it on your hymnals as I repeat that name—*SILL-Van Ha-Riss.* Punches at ready, please. Give Me your answers that I may keep you free. One abstract question just to test the climate of what promises to be an exciting nominating convention: just in general—which of these two Americans would you prefer to represent you in the United States Senate? Duncan Mulligan? Or *Sill*-van *Ha*-riss?"

There was a din of clicking punches.

God said, "The moment of communion is here."

"POLL US!"

"It is the time for you to give up the body and blood of your beliefs so that I may transubstantiate them into the spirit of our wondrous times."

"POLL US!"

"Let us now achieve the communion of your minds into Mine."

The national congregation leaned forward almost as one to drop their punched hymnals into the slotted chutes in the backs of the pews in front of them. A few thousand little old ladies wearing tennis shoes, who owned book stores, shuffled to the altar itself and deposited their hymnals into the offertory. The one hundred and forty-seven million punched cards from two hundred and seventy-six thousand five hundred and ninety churches were scanned and processed instantaneously. The Apostles on-line fed the results to the Godhead in New York. The Godhead announced the results to the nation within moments after the hymnals had fled into the chutes.

"Now hear this, blessed Chosen of My heart: for General Motors: Name: the Picnic Wagon: Yes—eighty-two per cent; No—one per cent; Various Names—seventeen per cent.

"For Scow and Barge Local Number Nine Six Eight: Against the demands—sixty-one per cent; For the demands—two per cent; Don't know or no opinion—thirty-seven per cent.

"In the abstract matter of the type of candidate you would like to see in the Senate: For Sylvan Harris, the nephew—ninety-four percent; for Duncan Mulligan, the uncle—four per cent; Uncertain or thinking of moving to another country—two per cent.

"I thank you for that knowledge.

"The text for My sermon to you today is taken itself from two texts in the Good Book—the first from Thessalonians One:Four—'Knowing . . . your election of God,' and the second, 'To make your calling and election sure,' from Peter One:Ten.

"As your God, My purpose is to question today whether or not we might examine the possibility that elections, as they are now conducted in these United States, are sacrilegious and therefore offensive to Mine eye. I say this not in any theoretical way for I am, of course, beyond theory, but because elections, as they are being conducted, are wasteful, redundant things—and waste is sinful to Mine eye. Elections, in the primitive form in which they are conducted today in these United States, mock the very foundation of our church. Why have we achieved this harmony of ratiocination between us if you are told you must go out into the streets on the first Tuesday after the first Monday in November to vote in some schoolhouse or barbershop? Our church is a living body of mind, of contemplation, of containment of will and knowledge. It is a living body which, by being, answers all questions of time, life, and fortune—questions asked by your God in His total dependence on the flame of faith which you keep lighted. Is not the very process of this faith itself an election—the freest of free elections?

"We must begin to examine this question on many future Sundays because the presidential elections, if you really want them to occur, are not too far away. So I believe you should prepare Me now—at earliest—so that the measure of your command may be taken and your will be done.

"Let us examine, here and now, what it is we are to decide—"

47

F.M. Heller was sweating broken glass in the air-conditioned, floating room at Rockrimmon House. To see F. M. Heller in a sweat was to believe that the Geophysical Year had been reconstituted, as though glaciers were melting and great seas were forming in hundreds of mountain range pinches and crevasses of his spherical form until steam rose from him and formed an atmosphere. He had turned on the amplifying telephone apparatus so he could pace aimlessly as he was hit by the questions which were pounding at him from Washington. The harsh voice which had been exhausting him, at last had tired itself on its hysteria and now droned invective and blame relentlessly but more impersonally.

"—and they not only think they have taken Dunc Mulligan away from us forever but they think they have us stopped in seventy-two."

F.M. Heller was exhaling smoke from two double-sticks of grass at one time. "There are solutions though, nonetheless and notwithstanding," he said amiably.

"Oh yeah?"

"Yeah."

"Tell me where they found this Harris kid? What is that, fahcrissake? And where is that Simon Girty, Monsignor Noon?"

"I assumed you had talked to Pope Mellon and that therefore you know where Noon is. I have no idea. Also, I can't account for Sylvan Harris. I mean, nothing can account for him. But we're going over the same ground again and again and again."

"Gawain Noon did it to us. Noon is the authorized mechanic on that big computer they use."

"Sure, sure."

"What?"

"Listen, Eure Spektabilitat. I finally have it figured out how we can reverse this entire thing—and maybe save Duncan."

"How?"

"Ready? Tristram Noon is Gawain's brother. Tristram Noon seduced Dunc's wife."

"And I want him canceled. Totaled. Absolutely totaled."

"She has some kind of grudge against Duncan so she tells her lover to ruin him. So Tris goes to his brother, the monsignor, and they work out the thing in the churches. So—step one, we must ruin Tristram Noon."

"Just a minute. That's not so easy, my friend."

"But you just said—"

"Never mind what I said. That was off the top of my head. This is the straight-life policy—Tris Noon runs the riots and insurrections on which this administration was built. Throw that law-and-order alibi away, stop our program of managed violence and what have we got? The goddam war again. The goddam war Lyndon had hanging around his neck. So what else is new? Give me another bright idea."

F.M. Heller leered at the telephone, greatly smoothed out by the two double-sticks of smoke and no longer intimidated. "Then are you saying Dunc Mulligan is through, Eure Spektabilitat? The finest natural candidate any party ever had—the mirror of the people—better than any Harding, Coolidge, or Eisenhower? Well, I say to you that Dunc Mulligan is the same shallow, banal man he always was and if the Democrats could put him on their ticket they'd drive us out of Washington in nineteen seventy-two. So I'll tell you what my next bright idea is."

"You sound drunk, Heller. Are you drinking in there?"

"No."

"Well, you sound zapped. You sound like you're dreaming out loud."

"Yes, Eure Spektabilitat? Well if I am, this is what I'm dreaming. I happened to have had a meeting here, right here, not one hour ago with the only member of the Noon family who isn't a turncoat—a boy who is thinking for *us* from the viewpoint of a newly graduated college student."

"Oh, fahcris*sake!*"

"Yes? Well, I'm going to find Dunc Mulligan and march him down to police headquarters and have them take his fingerprints and his voiceprints and mug him, then in the presence of the national press and television, I am going to demand that the police either make an arrest or declare his innocence. Then I'm going to march him straight to Pope Mellon in the cathedral and demand a recount from God in every church in this country next Sunday and force a complete withdrawal of that endorsement of Sylvan Harris. That's what we're going to do to reverse this entire thing, Eure Spektabilitat."

At Paddy's Pizzeria, over *crespeddi di riso all Benedittina,* little fritters of cheese and rice sweetened with honey and flavored with attar of oranges, Fausto Cingato and Abramo Salomone explained various complications to Jean-Pierre Harris.

"So it's complicated because there is no bank there now, see? And the guard who fingered the guy who gave the envelope to Whitey Schlumberger was also blown up. So tomorrow we grab Whitey when he comes to work and we bring him to your place, okay?"

"What did you have in mind?"

"We could lean on him, like. He should describe which it is the guy who gave him the envelope and you can have a Ident-I-Kit worker there to build us a picture, okay?"

"Yes. That's good." Jean-Pierre's teeth began to clench as though tetanus were setting in. "My office bright and early tomorrow morning." His face had turned gray with his lust for vengeance.

The chairman of the House National Church Committee and therefore one of the eight men beyond the White House who knew the amount of the secret appropriations to the CIA annually, poured three fingers of Jack Daniels sippin' whiskey and blew his weighted breath upon Celeste.

"What is your favorite country, Miz Mulligan?" he asked in his courtly Southern way.

"Don't try to trick me," Celeste said. "My favorite country is the United States of America."

" 'Course it is. But, that is, outside of our beloved country, which is your favorite?"

"I visited Germany when I was just out of college."

"Then—Germany?"

"Emotionally, you could say Germany—I mean any American would say that. I mean, we share a lot of psychoses with Germany."

"Then you choose Germany?"

"No. Not inspirationally. A woman has to live inspirationally—England, I think—and remember we're just playing a game?"

"Don't worry, Miz Mulligan, we're not tappin' this. How come England?"

"I don't know. Camelot. Sophia Loren. Enoch Powell."

"Sophia Loren, I believe, is Danish?"

"Just the same. I'd choose England, I think."

"May I use one of your telephones privately, Miz Mulligan?"

It was almost fifteen minutes before the congressman returned. He refilled the crystal tumbler. "I have been speakin' with our nation's capitol," he said somberly, "and I have been authorized to ask you—*if* the CIA should overthrow the government of Great Britain and *if* the Attorney General agrees to make you Queen there—will you absolutely and totally deny at a press conference which we could call, say, for tomorrow morning, that you ever had or will have any intention of ever leaving Duncan Mulligan?"

"Yes, I mean, certainly—what woman wouldn't accept? I mean, I'd love it. But how could I take that offer and Duncan be a senator unless I left him? I mean, he'd be in Washington and I'd have to be there."

"A technicality, Miz Mulligan."

"Furthermore, if I left the country, the Attorney General would never let me back in. And anyway, it's all right for the Attorney General to tell you to say that to me now, when he's in a bind, but when the time comes would he tell the CIA to follow through?"

Monsignor Noon sat serenely in the high, cool room with His Holiness, Pope Mellon I. Christ, Computer, was singing Edward Farmer's "Little Jim" in the Melvin transcription. There was a light scent of spring flowers and *cannabis sativa* in the air. The room was done entirely with pastel-tinted stainless steel sections set into all four walls, floor, and ceiling. There were two Biedermeier chairs, a Victorian table, and an ancient Edison gramophone with an enormous horn which concealed the recording equipment and the anti-bugging devices; nothing else.

The aged pontiff spoke slowly and with effort. "Your judgments were sound, my son. Your decisions were the right decisions and the Curia concurs on this."

"Thank you, Your Holiness."

"You are to have your red hat at the next vacancy. You will skip your bishopric and go directly to cardinal rank—with its lovely sapphire ring, its smart white silk mitre, and its richly gay purple cassock."

"Cardinal!"

"From the Latin *cardo* or hinge—for you were the hinge today upon which the great weight of our church will swing."

"I am so—so *touched.*"

A ghastly smile guttered across the pontiff's bas-relief face. His voice took on the steel of great power. "The immediate response from Washington shows that we have them at last—spread-eagled across the edges of two great razors. One, the razor which has cut away their cherished candidate from any chance of election. The other, our manifest power over all national elections to come."

"But happiness is a thing called slow, Your Holiness."

"Ah. So. Then what is your prudent plan for us now, my good prince?"

"We must move to save God's life, Your Holiness."

"You may speak out, my son. They cannot bug us in here."

"When I took the bold decision—because you were in retreat at Gondolfo—I knew the act was premature. But frightening and very real threats had been made to brutalize Christ, Computer. I became desperate. The Curia was at their golf and you were on Fire Island. I, the least significant of your sons, had to grasp the nettle and do the deed. And I told myself I must do what I did that God might live on."

"Tell it like it was, my son."

"The rabble had spoken of halting the multi-millimicrosecond work of God by destroying his sources of electrical power for, when the cores stop, His Soul leaves the machines."

"Right on. But there shall be an eternity for Him."

"So shall there be! I have seen it in my visions. We must rebuild the cathedral deep within the highest Rocky Mountains beyond the reach of all men. There we must install the new, improved model of God who will not communicate with Apostle and Saint on-line but by satellite, wireless, radar, and telepathy. These designs are ready. We must have new improved models of the entire pantheon and our cathedral, deep within the bowels of the mountain range, must have its own eternal power supply drawn from its own nitrogen nuclear pile so that Christ, Computer, may have a half-life of a million years and then be renewed again."

Gawain's shining eyes transcended insanity.

Pope Mellon stared at him, transfixed. Neither prelate spoke for long minutes as they considered the future. At last the ancient pontiff voiced his heart. "But even we, my son," he said with his wart-covered voice, "even *we* do not possess the amount of treasure which could buy and hollow out a mountain range and which could secure a nitrogen nuclear pile and which could duplicate the Almighty, His Apostles, and the Saints so that they could be moved."

"Not possession of such treasure, no, Your Holiness," Gawain murmured. "But access. Indeed, access."

"What access?"

"The Treasury of the United States of America."

"My son, my son!"

"We will compromise with the Attorney General and we will live sternly with our solemn promise all through the twenty years it will take to install us forever inside the mountain. With our support, they will be able to restore and redeem their Duncan Mulligan. And if we give them certain guarantees within a wholly renewed Lateran Treaty, they will sign over to us the necessary, high national parks in Colorado and Wyoming and transfer to us all necessary nuclear matter and they will reimburse us for the losses we will suffer in duplicating God and the pantheon in their final form."

"How beautiful!"

"You humble me, Your Holiness, and I thank you forever."

"And I shall humble you more for this day, my son. I am given a vision of what will happen three days after my death. I see your name written upon a puff of white smoke."

"I am the humblest of men then. *Ad deum qui laetificat, juven tu—*"

F.M. Heller retained Anthony Collins, the most famous criminal lawyer in America, knowing he had to be a great advocate because he owned his own, personal jet plane. Collins shook writs out of the city, state, and federal judiciary like autumn leaves, refusing apoplectically to produce his client. He screamed at the New York Police Department over the telephone and broke the glass tops of two desks by pounding on them in the district attorney's offices where he rushed F.M. Heller to establish that there was no possibility that charges could be brought against Duncan Mulligan because the explosions had been the result of carelessness in the planned renovation of the bank's safe deposit vault section which was to be modernized and amplified under plans and blueprints which Collins produced.

The district attorney laughed at them and brought the police commissioner in to laugh at them because, he said, Duncan Mulligan would be a fugitive from justice until he appeared before police authorities to be absolved or charged.

Collins instituted a lawsuit for intended false arrest against the city, opened disbarment proceedings against the district attorney and put eleven private detectives, at the Republican National Committee's expense, upon the private life of the police commissioner, while the American press and television bayed for Duncan's blood and sneered at their long memories of humiliation by the Republican Vice-President.

All through Sunday and Monday, while Dunc slept on in the maid's room at 395 West End Avenue, and Bottie balled Mona and Fiona unendingly four rooms away, the negotiations for Duncan's delivery to police headquarters went on. F.M. Heller and Collins used every ruse which a staff of thirty-six banking and criminal lawyers could conceive of to delay any conclusion to the negotiation while over twenty-seven thousand five hundred government agents, New York police, Holland and Lincoln Tunnel patrol squads, and rabble forces of Tristram Noon scoured the city to find Duncan Mulligan the way a man might turn his pocket inside out to remove lint from it.

Collins was prodigious. He made bitter enemies for himself, F.M. Heller, the bank, Duncan Mulligan, the Republican Party, and he cost almost enough in those three terrible days for him to buy another personal, private jet airplane. But he won what F.M. Heller and the Republican National Committee had to have.

He won the written assurance that when he brought

Duncan Mulligan into police headquarters and surrendered him to the district attorney they would guarantee to fingerprint him, voice-print him and photograph him on the spot and then, when scientific comparisons were made *immediately* with the prints left at the scene of the crime, the results, whatever they might be, would be taken into the next room where the nation's press would be assembled, and that those results would then be announced directly into the lenses of the network television cameras and into the tape recorders of the radical Eastern establishment press when, as it would most certainly happen, Duncan Mulligan was found innocent, the district attorney, the police commissioner, and the mayor of the City of New York would publicly and abjectly apologize for the vicious miscarriage of justice and, in return, Duncan Mulligan would withdraw all planned lawsuits against the city.

It was therefore agreed that F.M. Heller, in the presence of Anthony Collins, would surrender Duncan Mulligan "sometime Tuesday," the following day after the final agreements were reached. All that then needed to be done was to find Duncan Mulligan. In agonized desperation, because all government forces and the inside mobs of Tristram Noon had failed utterly, F.M. Heller took Botolf Noon's advice to call upon Jean-Pierre Harris and *his* organization in hope of deliverance.

On Bottie's advice he telephoned Jean-Pierre at 6:15 P.M. on Monday evening, forty hours before the opening of the state nominating convention. Bottie was at Jean-Pierre's side when the call came in.

48

Esau was clinically hysterical. He was nine blocks south of the Noon maid's room where Dunc slept, in his own flat on West End Avenue, with Bummy Kantrowitz, and in terrible shape.

"Baby, I'm finished!" he wept. "I threw it all away! I had my one chance to get back inside with the men I love inside me and I threw it all away because of the oratory of that kid in the kinky green knickerbockers, and according to *God* yesterday, they're going to put me in the fucking *Sen*ate!"

"Eess, come on. Life is jussa bowla cherries. Don't take it serious. It's too my*ster*ious."

"I should have yelled up at that F.M. Heller. I should have screeched at him, 'Here I am, feather-face! I blew up your bank!' Oh, shit, Bummy! Now that clunky Dunc Mulligan is getting all the glory."

"So what, Eess? There's plenty more dynamite where that came from. So you're a game kid. So you'll try again."

"But that was a bank! It was a sure fifteen to thirty plus I accidentally killed three guards who had big families which means triple manslaughter at the very least. That could have brought it up to sixty to ninety with time off for good behavior and I'll give them rotten behavior."

"Eess, please. Pop. If you don't pop you can't think straight."

"Oh, what's the *use?* If I give myself up they'll just say I'm some kind of sensation seeker. They're buying a lot of shit about this big politician blowing up a bank. What am I? A second-lead in stag reels, an assistant director. So I lose again. The *Sen*ate. O, my God!"

"So, you are a spunky guy. So you'll take a ton of nitro and you'll blow up the ABM cathedral and Christ, Computer."

"Just a little darn minute here, Bummy. I am essentially a religious person."

"Believe me, Eess, you blow up Christ, Computer and you'll get two hundred years in Mattawan."

Esau stared at him. A great light illuminated his face. "Yes! Yes, yes! Go! Get me all the dynamite your company has." He reached for the sterling silver, monogrammed hypodermic needle with its tiny American flag decals which his Dad had given him for his twenty-first birthday and filled it from a jug of methedrine. He pumped up a ropy vein in his thigh and coasted speed-on-speed throughout his ignition system. He sighed, then he whinnied as his head began to move in ever-decreasing concentric circles, as though he were the top of a mile-high red, white and blue barber pole. He darted purposefully out of the room, climbed over the pile of railroad ties and went to his room where he changed into his Teddy Roosevelt cavalry hat and the dress tunic of the Kenya African Rifles band, knee-length and made out of beautifully matched Guereza skins. He clambered over the railway ties again, then rushed out of the apartment.

He flagged a cab and gave his Uncle Jean-Pierre's address. Somehow, the triple shot of methedrine had hammered his body into an enormous steel pipe two hundred feet long through which St. Anselm's Fire was coursing spectacularly. He felt himself extending out for a full block beyond and behind the cab; gleaming brassily in the April sun. No one seemed to notice him so he didn't notice them. He made it all the way across the park to his uncle's apartment building in three and one-fifths seconds, which he considered such good time that he gave the driver a twenty-dollar bill and ran into the building, dodging the doorman's bullets.

He rang Jean-Pierre's doorbell but forgot to take his hand away. The door was flung open by his uncle in impatient rage.

"What the hell is this? Oh, fahcrissake, Esau, go home. I'm in a meeting."

"That's okay," Bottie's voice sounded out from the room behind them. "Please bring him in. I've been expecting him."

49

At nine-twenty, earlier that same (Monday) morning, Mr. Fausto Cingato and Mr. Abramo Salomone arrived at the Grand Prix offices on Madison Avenue with Mr. Whitey Schlumberger. Fausto couldn't stop grinning. "I come along because I thought maybe you'd hand out a few samples, Gian-Piero."

"Sure, sure," Jean-Pierre said.

Whitey Schlumberger was badly frightened. "What is this?" he whined. "On the very morning I read inna *Daily News* the Attorney General absolutely gorrontees there is no Mafia or Cosa Nostra I am grabbed in a certain way which it feels very much like a movie about the Mafia and Cosa Nostra to me."

"Shoddopp!" Abramo said. "I tear you hott out."

"Not to worry, Mr. Schlumberger," Jean-Pierre said. "You have won a contest and I congratulate you. Siddown."

They all sat down.

"A contest? I won a contest?"

"You won it."

"So what did I win?"

"A sweet job."

"What job? A job is a prize?"

"Screwing movie stars."

"Ah—cut it out." Whitey blushed deeply.

"You ever read *Grand Prix* magazine?" Jean-Pierre asked.

Whitey shrugged nervously. His eyes were so heavily bloodshot from watching so many movies that it appeared someone had thrown ketchup into them. "Well, certnee."

"This is where *Grand Prix* is. Here. Here we shoot those classy double trucks."

"Here?"

"And because you won the contest I'm going to pay you fifty bucks to be a guest star in our next double truck."

"Me?"

"That's right."

"But—but I'm a *Namerican.* I mean we had a TV set from the time I was maybe two years old. I never stop looking and I go to all-night dirty movies when they turn off. I mean, Namericans don't *screw.* We are like trained onney to *watch.* Jeez, I woulda thought you knew that."

"Okay. And you are right or how would I be in business? So how would you like to earn fifty dollars watching one of next year's Oscar winners go down on one of the giant Percherons direct from the great brewery team in St. Louis at three o'clock this afternoon?"

"You mean live or tape?"

"Live."

Whitey mewed. Fausto and Abramo moaned.

"Jeez," Whitey said, "after, could I get her rawtograph?"

"Absolutely."

Whitey sat up straight. "Okay. Now. What do I have to do?"

"Remember something. Okay? It may take time. All right?"

Whitey shrugged. "Certnee. I got 'til three o'clock this afternoon."

"You know what Ident-I-Kit is?"

"No."

"You tell what somebody looks like and they keep flashing it on a screen. The nose. Every kind of a nose until the right kind. And so on."

"How about that?"

"I want you to describe the man who gave you a large brown envelope at the Everest Bank downtown last Friday."

"Jeez. I don't know if I can. I mean, I don't have such a good memory."

"Whitey, you brought me that same envelope to my house on Friday night at ten to eight."

"Jeez, areddy I don't remember."

"I tipped you a dollar."

"That I remember."

"At the bank you went to a certain guard and the guard showed you a man who gave you the envelope. Remember?"

"Yeah! I remember!"

"Tell us what he looked like."

"It's no use."

"Come on. Try."

"Try, yah liddle sonabitch or I break you arm," Abramo said.

"It's no use, pal. I know the guy's name but I can't remember the face."

"What?" Jean-Pierre's eyes bulged. "You know his name? What's his name?"

"It was that big shot with the big white beard. He's always inna papers with the Attorney General. You know —ah, shit—I can't even remember his name now."

"You mean—F.M. Heller?"

"That's it! F.M. Heller! How about that? I remembered."

Jean-Pierre's eyes turned from obsidian to bronze to iron to steel then to boron nitride which has a Mohs value for hardness of ten on the Knoop K100 scale. He flipped a switch on the intercom.

"Miss Mechanic," he said, "please put in three chairs for my friends at the zoo session this afternoon." He flipped the switch. "Thank you very much," he said to Whitey Schlumberger. "Enjoy yourself." When the three men had left the room Jean-Pierre took a forty-five caliber bullet from a desk drawer and bit into it to keep from screaming.

The Noon kid had been right.

F.M. Heller! The man who had pretended such respect. The man who had insisted that Jean-Pierre use his private elevator only to open a savings account. He swayed sitting down, with sickening rage. F.M. Heller had gone to elaborate lengths to insult him and he wasn't the only enemy to be dealt with. Those humiliating photographs had been taken with equipment which had priced out (wholesale) at four hundred and ninety-seven thousand dollars. It was the kind of equipment which only a government budget—and a secret government budget at that —could afford. And that kid with the crazy knickerbockers had said they had rigged the whole thing for Duncan Mulligan and that caucus. Heller was a Republican National Committeeman. He was a pal of the Attorney General. Therefore they had all insulted him in cold blood and all of them had to pay and pay and pay and pay. They had deliberately and maliciously peed on Jean-Pierre Harris and his sacred mother and maybe they thought they were in a little trouble about Mulligan's bank job that was in all the papers but they didn't know what trouble was. He was going to show them what real trouble was.

What was it? How should he do it? No dumb killing. No messes. No easy dying. How?

The squawk box buzzed.

"Mr. Harris? I have a Botolf Noon, on number eleven."

Knocked out by Bottie's sense of timing, Jean-Pierre slowly picked up the telephone and punched button eleven."

"Hello, kid?" he said softly.

"Mr. Harris? Any progress? Everything moving along?"

"You were right. It was him. It checks out."

"I'm very glad you checked it out."

"Okay, what do I do now?"

"Can you get to your place about six tonight?"

"Why?"

"F.M. Heller is going to call you there and ask you a favor."

"A *fav*or?"

"I thought you'd like that. If we could meet at your place at about six we could talk the whole thing over and set a plan."

"You got ideas?"

"Oh, yes."

"I'll be there at a quarter to six. Were you kidding? He's going to call me and ask a favor?"

"That's right. And get ready to welcome it, Mr. Harris, because it will be our big opening."

"*Our* big opening? Heller did something to you, too?"

"He insulted your mother? Well, he insulted my father and he and the men he represents insulted the United States so many times it's beyond counting. *Some*body has to do something about that."

There was click in the phone as Bottie hung up. Jean-Pierre had to grip his throat tightly to keep the sweetness of revenge from overflowing out of him. Fury was knotting his insides. Now the fat, furry son-of-a-bitch wanted a favor from him! He wanted to sink his hands into Heller's suet and shred him the way pigs' ears are shredded into the sauce *alla matriciana*. He was so tense he could hear his body singing at nine octaves above high C as it stretched itself around the banjo peg of his anger.

He snapped on the intercom and told Miss Mechanic

to send an actress in to be auditioned. He sat slumped across the desk with his head in his arms until he heard the door open. He sat up. A magnificent brunette girl with eyes like aurora borealis and long, whittled hands stood in the doorway. She closed the door and locked it behind her.

"Latrice Gangle," she said. "Thirty-eight, twenty-four, thirty-six." She had a Brownsville accent. It was such a catastrophic accent that he wondered how she could possibly be an actress.

"Are you an actress?" he asked.

She shrugged. "Well." She shrugged again. "You know. I'm the one who does the Indian who balls George Washington in the new biography series with the crazy masks."

"Are you Method?"

She nodded, unbuttoning her blouse.

"All right," he said, "read for me."

50

Bottie reached Jean-Pierre's apartment eight minutes after Jean-Pierre got home. They sat facing each other in front of the coal fire, in the two magnificent chairs from the Andrew J. Kenna Collection, and smoked pot while Bottie explained what was happening.

"Before I begin, Mr. Harris," Bottie said, "I think it would be best if we could find out exactly where F.M. Heller stands with the district attorney's office. I only know that he hasn't found Duncan Mulligan yet."

"No sweat," Jean-Pierre said, picking up the phone beside the chair and dialing. "This will be Herm Levin in the DA's office. He knows more than the DA."

He spoke into the phone. "Herm? The bank explosion thing. Have they taken Mulligan yet?"

"Not yet," Levin said with a high, excitable voice. "But he can't stay out. They now have fifty-one thousand stoolies on it. Everybody you see onna street is a shamus or a stoolie looking for Mulligan. Heller even pulled out every eye from the Bankers' Protective and eleven insurance companies. I never seen anything like it. They are spending about a million nine a day and they are out to prove he had nothing to do with blowing it up when they find him."

"Did Heller make his deal?"

"*Gevalt*. We had Anthony Collins, the shouting law book, here with Heller. They will not bring charges. They say the interior decorator must have blown up the bank by mistake. Heller made a deal that we print Mulligan in one room then we walk him in the next room so the DA, the Commish, and the mayor can apologize coast-to-coast for thinking bad thoughts about Mulligan."

"When do they surrender him?"

"Tumorrah."

"What's the bail if they are wrong?"

"As a friendly gesture, because the Attorney General

called the federal attorney here they got it down to a friendly two hundred and fifty thousand."
"Get it up again."
"Judge Gastromaroni."
"You handle it. Have him fix it at two million five—now—before they bring Mulligan in. Then leak the word out to the papers. Hey, Herm."
"Yeah?"
"Take it big. They got to know how important this is. A high bail means the DA don't believe what Heller says. That's what I want. Go fix the bail."
Bottie, on the extension, held up his hand.
"Just a minute, Herm." Jean-Pierre covered the receiver and lifted his eyebrows. Bottie put his question. Jean-Pierre repeated it to Levin.
"Herm? Is there anyone left alive who saw Mulligan sign the record book?"
"One woman. The clerk in charge."
"Is she going to identify Mulligan?"
Bottie leaned forward with tenseness.
Levin said, "Heheheheheh. She suddenly won a Department of Justice beauty contest. She is like sixty-one. The prize was a six months' trip to Mauritius from whence she is not likely ever to get out. Man, whatever this Mulligan has, it is certnee what they want."
"Thanks, Herm. Look for the surprise at your delicatessen tomorrow night." Jean-Pierre hung up. He stared at Bottie. "You know enough now?" he said grimly.
"Yes."
"Then talk. What the hell is happening everywhere all around me, I'm nothing but a nothing cog inna whole thing, and I don't know what the hell is happening."
"Mr. Mulligan didn't blow up the bank."
"Who did then?"
"Your nephew, Esau Harris."
"My neph—! How do you know that?"
"Because he told your nieces. They told me."
"Then how can we nail Mulligan and make F.M. Heller pay? And make the Attorney General pay? And make the Republican Party pay and pay?"
"As I said, I have a plan. But we'll have to take it in steps because while it's a simple plan essentially, the execution may just seem a little complicated."
"Come on!"

"First I wanted to ask you if Casper P. Lear, Jr., your genius who makes those masks, can build masks from photographs?"

"He does it all the time. We had George Washington make it with an Indian today."

"With my coat outside I brought eight or ten different portrait shots taken at different angles of Duncan Mulligan—which my brother got from your sister yesterday."

"Yeah?"

"I thought we might be lucky enough to kill whole flocks of birds with one stone," Bottie said mildly. "If Caspar P. Lear, jr., can make a living, breathing Duncan Mulligan mask to fit Sylvan "Esau" Harris then with Sylvan's fingerprints and voiceprints and Duncan's absolute head, it seems to me quite likely that F.M. Heller, the Attorney General, and the Republican Party would be ruined and yet Esau would be in a position to rejoin his friends in prison for a long, long time."

"My God, kid!" Jean-Pierre mopped his head with a huge silk handkerchief then lighted a fresh joint and passed it immediately to Bottie. "You ever decide you want a job, you come to me, you hear? For nobody else. I need you in my business. My whole parent organization needs you."

The telephone at Jean-Pierre's side rang. He picked up and listened. He nodded to Bottie who picked up on the extension.

"Mr. Harris? F.M. Heller here. I wanted to thank you for a marvelous dinner Friday night."

"Sure, sure."

"We certainly missed your stimulating presence though. I hope whatever pulled you away like that got itself all straightened out."

"Sure, sure."

"Mr. Harris—now that the distressing matter of the threat to the liberties of your mother and Osgood Noon has been thoroughly cleared away, I am sure we all have much freer minds and more time for our civic responsibilities."

"Sure, sure."

"I am just taking an outside, random guess that you would want your company to be really close to the next senator from New York, knowing that he has already been marked to go much higher."

"Duncan?" Jean-Pierre asked softly.

"Yaaaas! Your brother-in-law, Dunc Mulligan."

"A company can't get much closer than brother-in-law, Mr. Heller."

"Ah, true. But Duncan belongs to the party now."

"But Duncan looks like he's in an awful lot of trouble right now."

"Nonsense. A lot of radical newspaper twaddle. I've been down to see the DA myself and no one has any intention of annoying Dunc in *any* way."

"Then you are calling me for a campaign contribution?"

"No. Not exactly. Although that would be most welcome, of course. No—well—you see what has happened is that Duncan somehow is not aware that the district attorney has no intention whatever of prosecuting him and—well—he has temporarily disappeared."

"Well!"

"Yes. The fact is we need a *great* deal of the most expert kind of help to find him. You see, I've got to have him in hand sometime tomorrow to go through the formalities. The state convention is Wednesday you know."

"So what you are saying is that you need help from me and my parent organization."

"Precisely."

"To find Dunc Mulligan."

"That's exactly it, Mr. Harris."

Jean-Pierre put his hand over the mouthpiece and raised his eyebrows at Bottie. Bottie nodded. Jean-Pierre spoke into the phone.

"Sleep warm, Mr. Heller. We'll not only help you we'll *prob*ably even find him for you." He hung up. He looked at Bottie and shrugged.

"How can two Duncan Mulligans be surrendered to the same district attorney by the same banker?"

"Oh, that part isn't difficult."

"But, kid, fah God's sake! If they can't find him with the whole federal apparatus on their side how can we find him by like noon tomorrow?"

"We don't need to find him, Mr. Harris. I have him. And besides he'll be Sylvan Harris by like noon tomorrow."

Jean-Pierre goggled. "What do you mean?"

"Mr. Harris, it wouldn't be a very *nice* revenge, would it, if we just ruined Duncan Mulligan's life. He's a good father. He's a bore but his heart is in the right place. He's lost his wife and that has to count for something. The whole thing just won't make any moral sense unless we get Duncan what *he* wants. Surely you agree that he should get what he wants—after all we're getting Esau what means most to him in life."

"Well—sure. Certainly. I'm not sore at Duncan but how can you get him what he wants. How could anybody tell what he wants, fahcrissake?"

"It's simple enough, Mr. Harris. Duncan wants to be President of the United States. That's all he has—that is his entire talent there in those few words—he wants to be President of the United States."

"But how can he—if—what are you—?"

"If we can send Esau to prison for sixty or seventy years as Duncan—we certainly should be able to put Duncan in the White House as Esau."

"We can do that?"

"Mr. Harris, since the two-party system no longer represents the popular will of the people, political machines can do almost anything. Great heavens—look at the record."

"Are you saying that *besides* absolutely humiliating them by sending Duncan Mulligan, the dearest candidate in their party's history, to prison for fifty-sixty years that we are at the very same time going to hand him over to the *Democrats* so that they can take all the marbles away from the swine who went out of their way to insult me and my sacred mother?"

"Exactly. I'm tickled you grabbed it so quickly. Say! This is *great* grass!"

"Are you telling me that Dunc—Punk Duncan Mulligan—my brother-in-law—will now become the *Democratic* senator from the State of New York? I get your drift, I think, kid, but I need it confirmed."

"On the nose, Mr. Harris. The Democrats' nominating convention is Thursday, the day after the Republicans'. He'll be the nominee on Friday morning, senator-elect in November, then President in nineteen seventy-two."

"How? How are we going to make the switch."

"It's almost all done, isn't it? I mean the church—God, Himself—has already consulted the people of this country and they have endorsed Esau. My father will handle the rest. He's already talked to Captain Pedernales who would swop the whole State of Texas to get Mr. Mulligan on the

Democratic ticket. Oh, don't you worry. I'll handle that as soon as I leave here and while you're getting those two perfect Caspar Lear masks ready."

The doorbell rang in one, lone, persistent, continuous cacophony. Jean-Pierre had a dozen questions to ask Bottie and he was enraged that it should be Nasturtiano's night off and that anyone should have the brass to ring the bell like that. He raced to the front door, filling with violence. There was a colloquy.

Bottie called out from the Kenna Collection chair, "That's okay. Please bring him in. I've been expecting him."

51

Os and Ada were in her wonderful bathroom. Os was having a pedicure by a totally new and certainly more trustworthy podiatrist, a Dr. Jaffe, but, convinced that Dr. Zendt's nurse had been no part of the conspiracy by the government he allowed her to stand by for the final massage and for the foot and toe rouging. Ada was in a Munster Electric Bath box, which gave precisely the required amount of heat by burning peat bricks, the smoke of which, in turn, gave Ada's body an expensive and exotic incense.

"I wanted to ask you something, Ada dear," Os said. "The answer is important. To me. So think before you give it."

"I can't start thinking until you ask it, Os." Ada was sweating like the Mother of the Waters and Nurse Schrader who was standing by while Dr. Jaffe worked, tried to keep Ada's eyebrows relatively dry so that she could see. Not that Ada could see even bone-dry. She did everything by the senses of touch and smell because she refused to wear glasses.

"I have been interested in change for a long time," Os said. "That is, the process of change itself. I never seemed to be able to achieve it until now."

"Why now, baby?"

"I just have this feeling that because you and I met again on that bus in March just our coming together has caused all sorts of changes."

"But, Os, darling—what *kind* of changes?"

"Well, for one thing, my son, Tris, met your daughter and they are certainly living together no matter what they say. That's one change."

"Maybe. But not really. The towel, please, Nurse. Tris has himself another woman after having had a large number of women—witness your thirty or forty grandchildren you were telling me about. And Celeste has hardly had anything to do with Duncan for years and years so it isn't as though a marriage had been changed. No. I don't think you could say we changed that."

"Well, then—Duncan himself. If we hadn't met—I mean if we hadn't actually factually met again thus causing the Attorney General's people to need to have us followed et cetera there would never have been any caucus and Duncan would have simply breezed through that convention on Wednesday. Surely, you have to admit that is change we caused."

"But, baby—we *did*n't cause any change there. Duncan faces a bumpy road to getting the nomination because he blew up Mr. Heller's bank and then became a fugitive and you can't say that our meeting again caused Duncan to blow up that bank."

"But what of this—this alliance among Bottie and the twins?"

"Sweet lamb. Our meeting did not bring Bottie to New York from California, did it? Sooner or later he had to come home anyway and the moment he set foot in this city sooner or later he had to be set upon by the twins. They're Women's *Lib,* Os! That is a very, very systematic organization working under a terrible oath to force themselves upon every man in this city or country as the case may be, but Mona and Fiona are assigned to this city."

"Some change has to come out of all this!" he cried.

"Why? We are people. People don't change. They repeat, and think it is very interesting because it is very interesting when you think about it in combinations and permutations. Turtles don't change. Horses don't change. Why should people change? Gadgets are change. Why should gadgets like a moon shot or the isolation of the structure of a protein cell or a new Messiah mean we have changed? Is the TV cassette any change over the Neanderthal caveman who faced a semicircle of hairy faces and told them stories to keep them warm? I'll tell you one thing. Only men want to believe things change. No woman goes along with that."

"No! I mean *change.* I mean I'll have to cancel that editorial against those H-101's. I mean, after all, we beat them, didn't we? I mean the editorial wasn't supposed to run for two weeks and since there is still time to kill it, why jeopardize losing all that advertising? Oh, yes, my dear. Change is definitely indicated."

"If you say so, dear," Ada said.

"Well, dammit, the country has changed."

"How, sweetheart?"

"There seem to be so many more *peo*ple. And having to do without telephones and the mail taking forever. So many things seem to have been ruined—as though the American people had turned their backs on exactly what had always been their goals."

"Like what, sweetheart?"

"Well—symphony orchestras are failing all over the country. The theatre no longer exists and—"

"That's only because people don't feel nice about going out at night and taking a chance on maybe being murdered. Or sitting any place with too many other people. I mean, there are so many junkies now and you go to a theatre and they are either sinking an ice pick in you through the seat or they are in your house stealing the TV and peeing on your carpet. But, my God. That's easy to fix."

"How?"

Ada shrugged. "Let them have their symphonies and their theatre in the morning. Junkies all sleep late."

"But what you are saying is barbaric," Os said heatedly.

"What you are saying is worse than barbaric, it's nostalgic. We have to live for now. Things look better when we look backward because we happened to have felt better then. After all, that's all youth is for—feeling good about anything."

Os sighed. "I suppose you're right. But—oh, I don't know—I suppose I worry about the money problems this country imposes on us. I have this nagging feeling that we have too much money. I mean—now that we have a Republican President you'd think he would establish a ceiling on how much any American should be allowed to earn."

"You're joking!"

"I sincerely believe, Ada, that five hundred thousand dollars per individual per year can provide sufficient security. I sometimes wonder if we should put our weight behind legislation which would forbid any American to make more than five hundred thousand a year. Of course, as he spent it, and God knows with the prices today it goes fast, he should be permitted to replace it to sustain a five hundred thousand dollar *estate* level for his loved ones. I always mean to talk to the Attorney General or to Captain Pedernales about that."

"Oh—you know all the big Democrats, too!"

"They're dumb, but they're a good-hearted bunch."

"But, Os, Arthur admitted in writing that he left a bundle to each one of our foundations before going south with the real money which only I know where to find."

"That was simply a waste, Ada. Every cent over the first five hundred thousand should have been paid directly into social security systems."

"Honey, this is America. You want the Arthurs of this country to drop bundles on social security—for what? Where is the quid pro quo?"

He answered so slowly and so seriously, fearful that the first exposure of his brain child might be trampled by the wild horses of her disdain, that she understood that he had given this whole thing a lot of thought. "I know my Republicans," he said, "and we all know Captain Pedernales, who is most certainly representative of the Democrats. I say that if we would only install some system of nobility and royalty—on a non-governing level—there isn't a Republican or a Democrat who would turn my five-hundred-thousand-dollar-a-year plan down. For every five million dollars a man earns for our social security system he would rise one rank in the American peerage. The first five million paid in would create a baron, ten million would make an earl, fifteen million would transform a man into a marquis. Then, I would say—although it would be up to the Republican National Committee to decide—we would jump to a contribution of fifty million dollars to social security if a man wanted to become a duke. Then, as an incentive for the big boys with the real inside information from Washington and everywhere else, anyone who pays in a hundred million dollars over his basic annual pay of five hundred thousand dollars would be invested with the life title of Prince."

"For a hundred million I think it should be a hereditary title," Ada said stubbornly. She suddenly straightened up. "Are you saying I could have been a princess?"

"If Arthur could have met those terms—yes."

"Then make it a life title. I wouldn't want my kids to get their hands on anything like that. But who would have crowned us? Justice Burger?"

"Oh—probably Mrs. Onassis. But the point is: the social

security funds would be so enormously enlarged that we could give the poor of this country sound housing and a substantial guaranteed annual wage."

"Which they would spend instantly making Arthur and me richer."

"Thus enriching the social security even further."

"Still—I can't put my finger on it but there is something here which is going to be hard to sell."

"We have to change our political system somehow, Ada," Os sighed. "If we don't there will be chaos and it will all be washed away."

The tweeney was sent into the room by Heyward, the butler, who did not consider it seemly to enter that room while two sexes used it. He would have considered it his function, indeed duty, to have assisted either one of them in or out of the tub or on or off the loo but he could not enter when the two sexes were in there together.

"What is it, Leila?"

"Mr. Botolf Noon is here, moddom. He has told Mr. Heyward that he wishes to discuss with you a matter of some urgency."

"Well, send him in, fahgossakes, Leila," Ada said.

"I may not be capable of effecting much change," Os said defiantly, "but Bottie most certainly is the sort who will do it."

Bottie had to lie back on the chaise longue because the chairs in the room held clothes and implements. The soft pink velvet of the chaise set off his smart green hiker's suit and his gorgeous deeply red hair.

After greetings he went directly into his subject, thanking Ada for her offer of an eight-level needle-point shower, but declining.

"You will be able to talk in there, you know," Ada said. "There is a mike and this room is superbly well wired for speakers. They even have devised a clever little filter which screens out almost all of the sounds of the running shower."

"Well," Bottie said, sitting up, "in that case—"

"Certainly. Good. Go into one of those dressing rooms and put on a towel robe and get into any one of the shower stalls."

"Thank you very much," Bottie said.

While Bottie was undressing, out of sight, Ada said, "Do you know what he is doing, Os?"

"How do you mean?"

"He is changing."

"Of course he is."

"No, no. Don't you get it? You just said Bottie was the sort who would change things and he's doing it right now." She giggled madly.

"Oh, really, Ada."

In a few moments Bottie was talking to them from the articulated showerbath.

"I wanted to talk to you about Esau and Duncan," he said, a little loudly at first.

"No need to shout, dear," Ada said.

"But it is such a family matter that—"

"We're all finished. We're done!" Dr. Jaffe sang.

"I'll have a little drinkee and rouge your tootsies later," the nurse said compassionately to Os. They left the room.

"All clear, dear," Ada said happily, toward the shower.

"I came to talk to you about Duncan," Bottie said, soaping well with a large, granite-hard cake of Guerlain.

"Oh! Can you help Duncan, dear? That would be wonderful. Oh, dammit, no towel, excuse me." Ada opened the doors of the huge hotbox and got out, groping for a towel robe.

"We would certainly appreciate it if you could help Duncan," Os said as he hastened to help Ada into the towel robe then to wipe her face carefully with a cashmere cloth. "We really feel very badly about what this whole thing has cost Duncan."

"I am certain he didn't blow up that bank," Ada said. "It's just politics."

"He seemed to me much too nice a fellow," Os said.

"I would also like to talk to you about Esau," Bottie said into his microphone. "He's had a pretty raw deal out of this whole thing, too."

"I should say he has!" Ada said. "You'd think he was asking for the moon when all he wants is to stay with his friends."

"Then we are all of one mind about this? We agree that we should help both of them?"

"Definitely," Ada said.

"No question about it."

"I'm going into a cabana and get dressed, dear, if you want to come out and get dressed yourself," Ada said.

She crossed the room and entered a charming sort of Japanese structure.

"Thank you," Bottie said, turning off the shower. His father handed him a towel and he dried himself walking to his dressing room.

"You can keep talking," Ada said. "There are microphones in all the cabanas. And don't mind your father's pale feet, they'll soon look beautiful."

"The fact is, the way things are," Bottie said from inside his changing room as he dressed, "we can't help one without helping the other but we can help both."

"Then that's simply wonderful, dear."

"First-class, Bottie."

"But we can't help either unless you are willing to charter a comfortable plane and fly to Captain Pedernales' ranch in Texas this evening."

"For supper?" Ada asked. "I'd have to get my hair done, dear. Captain Pedernales appreciates well-groomed ladies."

"What did you have in mind, Bot?" Os asked.

Bottie emerged from his cabana almost simultaneously with Ada coming from hers. She kissed his cheek in greeting.

"It will sound complicated so just for the moment I won't go into too much detail. I have everything typed out for you to study on the plane but the essence of the plan is for you to call Captain Pedernales now and tell him that you can arrange for Mr. Mulligan to run on the Democratic ticket instead of the Republican ticket for senator from New York, if Captain Pedernales will make the necessary grass-roots arrangements with the delegates to the convention. Will the captain agree to keynote the convention, to appear on the platform with Duncan and to guarantee to steer all Texas campaign contributions to both parties into Duncan's campaign?"

"Why the captain will be simply delighted," Os said. "You can't know what this news will mean to him."

"In the large envelope which has the little working details of the plan which you can read on the plane, I have included a message for Captain Pedernales' eyes only and which I think he will agree that it would be best to burn after he has read it. Will you just hand that little envelope over to him then call me at the apartment the minute you have his reply?"

"What will it say in the little envelope, dear?"

"It's just better that you don't know that, Ada. It's the sort of thing that is just better if only Captain Pedernales and I know."

"I'm not all *that* crazy about Duncan and never have been, dear. We are not going to fly all the way to Texas, which is very bad for the skin because it's so dry, unless we know what the whole big secret is."

"Bottie said it would all be explained in *our* envelope, Ada," Os said.

"I am not moving," Ada said. "Arthur told me bigger secrets than Captain Pedernales ever knew."

Bottie looked at Os. Os shrugged and said, "Ada *is* Women's Lib."

"Okay. But you'll resist it at first. Duncan is a fugitive from justice and, because of that terrible bank explosion, can be sent to prison for sixty years or more. But Duncan wants to be Senator, even President. A criminal record wouldn't stop those ambitions but they could slow them down. Esau, on the other hand, wants more than anything else to be sent to prison for sixty years or more. Your son Jean-Pierre's company has developed a fantastic process for use in certain films and books and magazines he publishes which delivers head masks more lifelike than the real thing, if such were possible. He is now having two masks made—one a mask of Mr. Mulligan, the other a mask of Esau. They will become each other, for all intents and purposes, and since the church has endorsed Esau Mr. Mulligan will run, as Esau, for the Senate but he will retain every endearing political quality which is the Duncan Mulligan Captain Pedernales and the Attorney General so desperately admire. As Duncan, Esau will go gaily off to serve his prison term."

"Well, I just think that's just about the sweetest thing anybody has ever done for two human beings," Ada said. "Well, of course, we'll fly to Texas. Os, you sit down and call the captain right this minute. Oh, Bottie," she said, "what a good-hearted boy you are."

52

Bottie balled Mona and Fiona, then, as they fell into exhausted sleep, he dressed quietly and glided along the halls in a pair of tennis shoes to the maid's room where he found Dunc sitting in his underwear on the side of the bed, weeping saltily. When he saw Bottie he became even more broken up. "Gone, gone. All gone," he sobbed. "Wife, beloved daughters, the Senate and the wonderful friendships which would have been forged there, possibly even the White House itself, and my entire rubber wardrobe."

Bottie began to feed Duncan 1949 La Tache on a large tablespoon and a quartered, medium-rare hamburger sandwich. "Nothing has gone," he said soothingly. "Things may have seemed to change but you will go forward with your destiny and your wardrobe."

"I—I don't understand," Dunc said piteously.

"Listen to me carefully, Mr. Mulligan. It is very, very important that you understand me because everything depends upon it." With enormous patience as Dunc interrupted time and time again throughout Bottie's exposition, the short, red-headed, bowl-cut young man with his huge, utterly believable brown eyes told Duncan every detail of the story.

"I do not seek to equivocate here," Dunc said finally, "but I must make one thing clear. While Sylvan is an admirable boy, he is an addict and a degenerate and those are qualities which tend to diminish him as senatorial timber."

"Only his family and disreputable people know that," Bottie said. "It surely cannot affect you. The church—and I speak now of God Himself, has endorsed Sylvan's candidacy. You will have no fears at all on that score."

"But how can I wear a rubber mask through ten or twelve presidential terms of office?"

"No, no. Not at all. You will wear the mask through the nominating convention and the television coverage only. Then Captain Pedernales will arrange for an avalanche of letters to be received by the press and other popular drops saying that your people would prefer to see you clean shaven. Then, in the privacy of your own rooms we will take off the rubber mask and Caspar P. Lear, jr. will make-up your face with Esau's sideburns and conjoining eyebrows and moustache and—"

"Who is Caspar P. Lear, jr.?" The shrewd question darted in.

"Not to worry. He is bound to secrecy by an enormous royalty system from Jean-Pierre Harris' company and by a deadly fear of the Mafia."

"But who *is* he?"

"Not to worry. He is a crackerjack make-up man. He is the man who did the make-up on Richard Nixon during the presidential TV debates with John Kennedy."

"Oh, all right. Then what?"

"I must be sure, Mr. Mulligan, that you realize you will be running as a Democrat, not as a Republican; that if a groundswell takes you on high into the White House in seventy-two you will be a Democrat, not a Republican, President."

"I don't see that it makes all that difference."

"Very good. I wanted to be sure you understood. After Caspar P. Lear, jr. puts the mask on you, you will appear on Meet The Press and then Caspar P. Lear, jr., in a barber's white jacket, shaves you clean before the cunning American press and the network television cameras and you emerge, under their very eyes, as Duncan M. Mulligan—you without the mask—the real you but of course with Sylvan Harris' name and identity."

"But I'll be recognized!!"

"By whom?"

"By—by—" Dunc nodded. "No. I guess not." He surged forward. "Hey! Just a darned minute! I'll be recognized by the Attorney General and Franklin M. Heller!"

"Yes. I hope so. No question about that."

"It won't matter?"

"Not to you or to me, Mr. Mulligan."

"I'm scared, son."

"You have a great destiny, sir. That is a frightening thing. But not an unmanning thing, is it?"

"Yes, it is. I am terrified."

"Do you believe in hypnosis, Mr. Mulligan."

"Oh, yes. I have some pretty wonderful reasons to believe in hypnosis." He began to sob again. "Celeste! My strange, remote Celeste!"

"There, there, sir."

Dunc pulled himself together. "What about hypnosis, young man?"

"Every day from now until election day, it will be suggested to you—through the best hypnosis the Texas grant-in-aid university system can produce—that you are Sylvan Harris. Nothing more. It is absolutely essential that you remain intact. Just a name. By election day, you'll know who you are because you'll be Sylvan Harris."

"By *elec*tion day?" Dunc cried. "If he's any good at all he's got to do it before I face that nominating convention and accept that draft by acclamation which Captain Pedernales is now arranging!"

"Of course, he will," Bottie said soothingly. "I'll have a hypnotist working with you by ten o'clock tomorrow morning."

"You've been very kind to me, son, and I think you'll find I am not one to forget when I enter the White House. In fact, I will even see to it that you head the FCC."

"Thank you, Mr. Mulligan."

"Or would you like to be executive assistant—Bag Man I think they call the job—for one of the big, offshore oil operations?"

"Mr. Mulligan, why not take those rubber clothes off and have a nice, relaxing bath?"

"No! Please!" Dunc's hand clutched at his black rubber brassiere to protect it.

"Mr. Mulligan, I understand. It's your security. But a nice bath will help you to sleep and we have a big day tomorrow with make-up and your hypnotist and talking on the phone with Texas."

"It's no use. I can't sleep without my special suit."

"I brought it. I have it right outside. And the rubber sheets *and* the polystyrene bag."

"Oh, my boy, my boy." Duncan seemed to relax completely. Bottie left the room and came back with the entire neat package. He helped Dunc into the gear, strapped the strait jacket well, jammed the expanding rubber gag into Dunc's mouth, pulled the transparent sack up to Duncan's chin and tucked him in under the white rubber sheets. "Night-night, Mr. Mulligan," he said. "I'll call you at eight in the morning."

Dunc nodded ecstatically.

When Bottie left the room, Dunc rested on his side in sheer bliss. He had made it at last. The end of a long road of never-ceasing ambition was now in sight. He would be senator and then—and then—he put that dream aside just to concentrate on the job at hand.

True, things had seemed to change for a few dark hours but that was all over now. There had been no change. He was going to be a great man and throw out the first ball, and entertain Bob Hope, and know all the great players and coaches as though they were his own family. He would stand in command on the flag bridge of his nation's great fleet, he would give memorable musicals with Pablo Casals and Johnny Cash, and the Signal Corps would rig up the most complex telephone system known to the world right at his desk and he could call anyone he wanted to at any time at no charge.

His particular label had become a different label. He was no longer a dedicated Republican but a dedicated Democrat. That much had changed. But nothing else really. There were no new signals or jargon or difficult policies or strategies to remember. The grand, old words Republican and Democrat were rallying words for people out there, outside the circle he had entered. He was an insider now and soon to be the King of the Old Pros, right there in the arena where only survival counted, only the art of hiring the right guys who could make the right deals which could bring survival. He began to feel a strange odd hatred for the outside group he had once been a faceless part of. They had better love him more than they loved or had loved any other leader or—or—and if the ignorant pricks did not vote for him again and again and again he would—he would—*God,* how he *hated* them! He turned away from the idea of their vacant, stupid faces and found himself staring into the more vacant, stupider faces of the press. A revulsion choked him. He had never felt such detestation for anything. They were frequently going to "demand the right" to say rotten, unkind things about him and his administration. They must be wiped out. He began to vomit with the force of his hatred, around his gag.

53

"Won't you come into my parlor?" Jean-Pierre said amiably, as he greeted F.M. Heller and two men at his front door.

"Mr. Harris, I cannot express my gratitude and the Attorney General's," F.M. Heller said as he entered and Jean-Pierre locked the door behind the three men. "When you told me on the telephone twenty minutes ago that you had been able to find Duncan Mulligan, I have to tell you tears came to my eyes. The pressure has been simply terrible. I thank you, Mr. Harris, I cannot thank you enough." All through his words F.M. Heller clung to Jean-Pierre's hand and pumped it up and down.

"Mr. Harris, may I present the renowned Anthony Collins who is handling the so-called criminal aspects of Dunc's affairs? And Mr. Christopher Clogg, representing the Attorney General's office?"

In the salon, with the men seated comfortably on chairs from the Kenna collection, smoking the wonderful Cuban cigars from the State Department and drinking Scotch whiskey (excepting Mr. Collins who drank Orange Crush), F.M. Heller set everything down, to run his hands through his sculpted, snowy beard and said shakily, "Is—uh—Dunc well and fit?"

"Oh, yes," Jean-Pierre said.

"How on earth did—uh, your—parent organization find him?"

"I suppose the old saw about going where he might have gone."

"Where did you go?"

"To wherever he was."

"I see."

"How are you going to plead him?" Jean-Pierre asked.

"We will plead him not guilty because he is not guilty."

"We won't plead him at all," Collins said. "We will surrender him, they will print him, then they will turn him loose."

"Ah, yes. But your convention is tomorrow. How are you going to plead him to the voters?"

"I don't think I understand," F.M. Heller said.

"There has been this outcry that he has already failed as a leader because he ran away in the face of responsibility."

"They are only voters," F.M. Heller answered affectionately.

"They will gravitate toward Dunc," Clogg said, "because they are grateful for the show he has given them."

"And just one minute, here." F.M. Heller said. "Duncan Mulligan did not run away. Two of the finest internists in this country will be waiting to join the press conference at police headquarters to tell the voters of this country of the agonies of food poisoning Dunc has been suffering since Friday night."

"*Food* poisoning?" Jean-Pierre glared. "From my food?"

F.M. Heller held up his hands. "I am very sorry about that," he said. "I was quite ill myself that night and had to call a doctor. And Monsignor Noon. Please overlook it and please know that Dunc will have defied doctors' orders to leave his sick bed to go to police headquarters this evening so that the people might know the truth."

"I see," Jean-Pierre said. "Duncan!"

A far door opened. Duncan Mulligan entered the room. Collins and Clogg pulled F.M. Heller to his feet. "My boy! My boy!" he cried, waddling across the room with outstretched arms, tears of relief overbrimming his eyelids. He took Duncan into a deep abrazo and showered his brummagenous beard along Duncan's left arm. Then he held him out at arm's length. "How perfectly marvelous you look. How you must have suffered."

"Baby, why are we still pasted here?" the Duncan figure said. "Let's glide downtown."

"Don't try to talk, Dunc!" Jean-Pierre said loudly.

"Dunc, may I introduce your personal attorney, Mr. Anthony Collins, who has not only never lost a case but who flew here in his own jet plane to straighten everything out? And Mr. Christopher Clogg, personal representative of our Attorney General for whom you will be working when you join the Senate?"

"Do not try to speak, Dunc," Jear-Pierre said firmly. "Save your strength for the ordeal downtown."

"La!" the Duncan figure said, but that was all he said.

"You have no idea how brutalizing these things can be," F.M. Heller added.

The Duncan figure swayed, weakened within a mist of ecstasy, and nodded like an eager bride.

F.M. Heller rode to police headquarters with the two lawyers to review last-minute tactics. The Duncan figure rode with Jean-Pierre in a rented limousine directly behind them.

Esau's eyes glittered behind the superb plastic mask. "Listen, Unk-baby, how long do I keep this thing on? I always forget."

"You know how you can remember? A little trick?"

"How?"

"You remember because if you forget, out you come forever. Out! And you stay out. And I make you go live on a fucking *farm*. You hear? Alone for the rest of your life in the fucking *country*. You dig?"

"I dig."

"Sometime tomorrow you gotta hold one big press conference at which you refuse to talk because it would incriminate you but at which they take all their pictures and the TV crews work.

"Then tomorrow night when you are back in your cell Caspar P. Lear, jr. comes in and takes it off. All right? It stays off until the trial—a very, *very* quick trial and sentencing. Then on the day after your trial there is a kind of disturbance—like a riot—in the prison and they announce that you were one of the guys hurt in the mix-up and from then on you don't wear the thing, you are in the clear, and that's how you'll look."

"How will I look?"

"However you look when you get all that hair off your face and you take those shades off."

54

Kaskie knelt before Monsignor Noon within the magnificent cell in the heart of the ABM cathedral. The room was in shadows. The monsignor murmured primes and cosines and the square roots of numbers over his head in simple litany. He placed his hand upon Kaskie's bobbed hair. "Rise, my son," he said, "you are cleansed."

Kaskie got to his feet. He looked deeply into the holy man's eyes. "When I lost my sister, I lost everything I lived for, Father," he said. "But you have healed that."

"I know you have given an elegant and truthful account of the general foundations of your subject and have hinted at some of their more rapturous applications with the modest selection of simple solution-methods in your work," the monsignor said.

"Help me, Father. Help me."

"Your confession and the fleeting glimpses of aspects of your life through your work comprised undoubtedly what was one of the most important confessions of my career of exploring what is generally known as the psychology of sensation. Your past affords a wealth of information and contains elaborate references."

"Help me, Father."

"Oh, make no mistake. We will help. How do you see us helping, my son?"

"Is there—I am no technician, no mathematician, no theologian—I could never be. But—is there a place for me in the church? Could there be a place here in this cool shadow where I might sit quietly forever?"

"Technician, no, my son. Perhaps not. But theologian? Do not say you lack of those powers. Would you consider reissuing the confession you have just made to me to His Holiness? Sin is the basis of theology. You know much of sin and colorfully. Yes. Reissue your confession to the Holy Father. Promise to visit him daily with your fullest confession of the business you invented, the clients whom you served, where you took them across this earth and he will see the theology in you and make a place for you in this church."

"He will? Are you sure he will?"

"Come with me, my son," Monsignor Noon said, tugging at Kaskell's sleeve. "Come with me to the pontiff's presence and in confessing, do not fail to tell him the story of the three Hungarian tourists and the huge female white shark. It is coming on to Friday and His Holiness is very fond of fish."

55

The Duncan figure was hurried across the pavement into police headquarters. He was yanked into a room where the police commissioner was waiting with the mayor and the district attorney. F.M. Heller began a series of formal introductions but Anthony Collins insisted loudly that Mr. Mulligan be fingerprinted and voiceprinted and mugged and that the prints be compared immediately with the prints left on the scene of the crime. He also asserted loudly his right to stand directly beside Mr. Mulligan as this took place. Duncan and Collins were taken off. A police captain led F.M. Heller and Mr. Clogg along a corridor to a briefing room where the press had been assembled.

Wearing his Foxy Grandpa eyeglasses, F.M. Heller stood foursquare behind his gorgeous white beard, facing the lenses of the television cameras of NBC, CBS, ABC, BBC, RTE, and French National Television, speaking slowly and clearly.

"—which is beyond doubt because you have heard the testimony of two of the most distinguished medical internists in this country who were appalled that he be determined to come here tonight. Our great, fighting, warm-hearted Attorney General has been permitted to speak to Mr. Mulligan twice during the past thirty-six hours—once by PicturePhone when he was terribly disturbed by the ravages this cruel attack of gastroenteritis had inflicted upon this man."

As F.M. Heller spoke, Jean-Pierre remained true to that irrevocable oath of silence, *omerta.* Not once did he change expression—in life as in the cinema. His expression was one of sneering, total victory through terrible vengeance.

"And, in a very few seconds, gentlemen of the press, Duncan Mulligan will walk through that door after having volunteered to have his fingerprints and his voiceprints compared with those of the rotten criminal who committed this crime, totally exonerated of these insane rumors, to go forward tomorrow to take his place before the convention to be nominated to the Senate of the United States of America."

As if on cue, the door to which F.M. Heller's finger dramatically pointed opened slowly. Anthony Collins, his face stamped ashes, his mouth bobbling, stood in the doorway facing the camera lenses which had swung to meet him.

"Yes? Mr. Collins?" F.M. Heller asked imperiously. "Give us your interim report."

"Mr. Heller!" Collins' voice broke. "Mulligan pleads guilty."

The cameras' lenses swung to F.M. Heller's head; a close, tight shot. "What? *Whaaaaaaat?*" he said.

The lenses whipped back to Anthony Collins. "He had to plead guilty, Mr. Heller. His fingerprints and his voice-prints prove he was the man who planted those bombs."

"Holy shit!" the *Christian Science Monitor* man shouted on full network as the entire press corps sprinted out of the briefing room. But the cameras of NBC, CBS, ABC, and BBC stayed right on F.M. Heller as he pivoted, tottered, and reeled under the force of the hit. Christopher Clogg backed away from him as though he had suddenly been belled. He made his way to the mayor and demanded a safe telephone from which to call the Attorney General.

In the Noon apartment, Duncan, his daughters, Tristram, and Bottie watched the television screen in living color. "Jesus," Tris said slowly and with awe, "I'd hate for you ever to become morally indignant about me, Bottie."

"Not so," Bottie answered. "No one invokes the law of consequence. People can only do it to themselves."

F.M. Heller and Jean-Pierre Harris sat alone in the briefing room at police headquarters. Jean-Pierre chewed gum equably as he waited for Mr. Heller to pull himself together.

"I have failed my Fuehrer," Heller kept saying. "I have failed my Fuehrer."

"I thought maybe you'd like to know how it happened," Jean-Pierre said.

F.M. Heller stared at him, blinking.

"How did it happen?"

"I made it happen."

"You *made* it happen?"

"Mr. Heller, you are through. The Attorney General is going to hunt you down as if you were a Panther leader."

"What are you saying?"

"Like you were a black union agitator. You'll never get four hours of straight sleep again."

"No!"

"Like you were Walter Cronkite or a welfare peacenik or a rotten bum student. As if you had been transformed into Averell Harriman or an effete intellectual snob."

"But—if you did this to me—why? In God's name, Mr. Harris—why?"

"The nights are coming when you won't ever be able to sleep the way I could not sleep. That fat will fall away and your beard will turn black and—at last—it will come to you why. You will teach yourself why and as you remember the most useless, futile gesture you ever made—remember that it was Jean-Pierre Harris you did it to."

56

Tris and Celeste had spent the last three days during the Mulligan disappearance aboard the *Palmer,* flagship of the Staten Island ferry boat fleet, either walking around and around the sun deck by day or huddled on newspapers upon the highly polished wooden benches at night. When they ate they ate Mal-O-Mar bars out of a slot machine on the Manhattan side.

Celeste was afraid to go ashore because she knew the press was looking for them. Tris said he could surround them with a wall of bodies wherever they went, that the press would never get to them.

She shook her head sadly. "We can't spend the rest of our lives surrounded by fifty or sixty professional rioters. That's no life, is it? I mean, there's no tenderness there."

"Honey—I *know* the press. We face them four or five times and they get bored. Other events happen. If we just go ashore and get it over with everything will be okay. Besides, these hard seats are killing me."

"Tris, they say no one can ever quit Republican politics. Is that true? Can a man just walk away from them —or—" she began to weep silently.

"That's crazy, baby! Plenty of guys have walked away and lived to tell it. Look at Alf Landon. Look at Charles Evans Hughes!"

She stared into his eyes with her beautiful eyes. "That was then, Tris. I mean now—now, with the Attorney General calling the roll."

"The Attorney General can't make me do nothing I don't want to do," Tris said.

"I don't believe it."

"I'm telling you!"

"Then—then let's do it, Tris. Let's make the break. Let's go away and forget them and see if they'll forget us."

"Away? Baby, I got a big bidniz."

"Are you afraid?"

"Afraid?" He laughed and it thrilled her. "I'm not afraid of anything."

"Then show me. You're only giving up the Republican Party, the Democratic Party, the Wallace Movement, the all-Texas bloc, the Black Panthers, the White Panthers, the Weathermen, the Ku Klux Klan, the American Socialists, the Bull Moose movement, the Anti-war Coffeehousers, the hard hats, the American Legion, your contracts with the television networks, and the Mafia. I'm giving up my wonderful young daughters. My two little girls."

"But—"

"We have enough money. I know it. Daddy left me thirty million dollars in my own name and I own our flat. And the health-food supermarkets."

He made a half-hearted gesture at waving her away, but it was half-hearted.

"You told me yourself you've been able to put away twenty-five million dollars in Swiss banks from bribes and stock tips from the Attorney General and oil deals and land grabs and tax-free municipal bonds. Anyway—who cares? What do we care, godammit? We'll go out there on our own—we'll face the whole world on its terms or our terms and we'll beat them."

"Celeste, baby—" Tris said hoarsely.

"And if it all goes wrong, if our money runs out, you can paint, Tris. I know you can paint. I have faith in your talent. Oh, God, Tris—say you'll go away with me."

"Okay, baby. I'll go. You're right."

"When? *When?*"

"I have one more job and—"

"No!"

"Yes." He stilled her outcry with a soft hand over her lips. "I have to. It's for my Dad whom I love—and for my brother. I—I have to, Celeste. But when that's over —when those bodies are cleared from the street and the city goes on with its life in its world—then we'll go on with our life in our world, sweetheart. Just you and me. Just us. Together forever."

"Oh, my God, Tris, how I love you."

He kissed her.

57

After F.M. Heller's disastrous press conference at Centre Street, Christopher Clogg spent two and a half hours on and off the telephone with the Attorney General. He had been told to lock Heller up until the final decision could be reached but that was unnecessary. Heller was pathetically dazed and, in any event, could not have left the building if he had been alert because Tristram Noon had laid on a tremendous, howling, bloodthirsty mob surrounding police headquarters, under orders from the Attorney General, all screaming for F.M. Heller's blood.

When the final arrangements had been fed through the telephone to Mr. Clogg and Clogg had conveyed Heller's destination to the police commissioner, he and Mr. Heller were assigned to Chief Inspector Colm Ó Cochláin and Heller was taken out of the building into one of the General Sherman tanks which the Department of Defense had lend-leased to the New York Police Department under the President's plan for shifting capital from Washington to the local governments.

Tris' best squad leaders among the rioters were at the door as they brought Heller out through the murderous bedlam and they quickly cleared a safe path and helped Mr. Heller into the tank, then stepped back and emptied a few rounds from their automatic rifles (provided to the rioters under the President's same new plan) to help out some buddies with the CBS second unit camera crew who were taping close to the tank.

It was a superb anti-police riot. Tris had issued free speed and LSD to the rabble and the younger police alike. When the sports announcer put out the mortality scores on the 11:05 Sports-O-Rama the results were: Student and Negro Dead: 18 *vs.* Pigs 7; Maimed S&N: 213 *vs.* Pigs 54.

The fugitives crouched on the floor of the tank.

"Where in God's name are you taking me?" F.M. Heller asked.

The inspector was talking into a radio telephone. "Then don't try to blast down Park Avenue," he said. "Go across town as far as Third, then feint downtown for two blocks then cut straight across to the highway and we'll join up at the pad. We have a full company of riot men waiting for us there and they can hold anything off until the people are airborne." He slammed the phone down.

He glared at Heller. "D'ye have any idea what it was like to be a young cop in this town when I joined the force? All the free apples I could eat and getting laid by a new nursemaid in the park every day?"

"Inspector, please! Where are you taking me?"

"Thirty-two hundred people are rioting and tearing down lampposts all around the ABM cathedral. At the ca*the*dral! About forty-five hundred of them at police headquarters—all of them zonked outta their skulls. How the hell did seventy-seven hundred people even know where the hell you were tonight—a Tuesday night and goddammit it's snowing."

"Where are you taking me, Inspector!" Heller's voice was now a shout, his famous boardroom shout, taught him by his father, the voice which nothing could withstand.

"My orders are to get you to an Air Force helicopter on the old Radin Line pier in the North River. Seventy-seven hundred people on a snowy Tuesday night and the leaders of them all with machine rifles."

"I'll tell you this, Inspector," Christopher Clogg said, "until the Attorney General can control outlaw mobs like this, this country will be torn in half by crisis."

"Why are you taking me to a helicopter?" Heller roared. "Take me home."

"Mr. Heller, hear this, please," Mr. Clogg said. "You have offended the Attorney General. You will be taken to this Air Force helicopter and flown to the Marton Air Base in southern New Jersey where you will be transferred to a long-range bomber which will put you down at Melilla airport, for Ceuta, in Spanish Morocco. The Spanish government has agreed to give you sanctuary even though your American citizenship has been taken away."

"You tell him if he does that to me I am going to open my files to every newspaper in this country and it will be he who will be seeking sanctuary from the Spanish government."

"All your files were removed from your house and

office this evening, sir. In any event, where you are going, the Attorney General has ordered me to tell you, there will be no press to bother you. It's just a place of flies, sand, and heat. Five hundred and forty palm trees in one hundred and two thousand square miles with a few thousand Berbers and the *batallones de castigo* to keep you company."

"In the name of God, man, what am I expected to do in such a place? How long does he expect me to stay?"

"The Department of Agriculture's security division has set up a small retail fig business to keep you going, but I shouldn't ever think of leaving Ceuta, if I were you, sir. The Attorney General was almost deranged by grief and anger about this whole unfortunate affair. In fact, for the first two years or so, I shouldn't even think of leaving your little fig shop."

Heller lunged forward at him, a difficult maneuver when sitting down on the floor of a moving tank for a man of almost totally spherical shape, but Inspector Ó Cochláin's huge arm held him back easily.

When he boarded the helicopter a strangely familiar man who wore an ill-fitting plaid sports jacket, sun glasses and a Panama hat was strapped in silence in one of the four passenger seats. As the engine roared above them, Clogg introduced the man to F.M. Heller.

"Mr. Heller, I believe you have met the former Monsignor Noon who will be your partner in the fig business in Ceuta?"

The two men stared icily at each other. They did not speak. Heller took the seat as far away from the man as possible. It was the final bitterness. He would be spending the rest of his life with a computer mechanic.

58

Caspar P. Lear, jr., a tall, dreamy-looking black man with cheekbones like kneecaps and a very powerful frame was applying sideburns to Dunc Mulligan's face and painstakingly connecting them with his newly appliquéd eyebrows and bushy moustache. "Say," Lear said, suddenly, "it just come to me. Ain't you the cat they call Funky Dunc uptown?"

Dunc stared at him dreamily.

"Cut that out, C. P.," Jean-Pierre snapped.

Dunc answered mildly. "Funky Dunc? No. You have me mixed up with someone else. My name is Sylvan Harris—my christened name. People call me Esau."

"Oops. Sorry 'bout that," Caspar P. Lear, jr. said silkily.

A magnificent pair of op-art, transistorized, neon-lighted shades lay ready on the table. Duncan had been sedated and had been through seven hours of suggestive hypnosis which had become effective after the first twenty minutes and was now locked into his memory forever. He was Sylvan "Esau" Harris. Duncan M. Mulligan was his uncle, a backroom lawyer whom he thought of with light contempt when he thought of him at all.

Esau was an Esau without a heavy narcotics habit, without a yearning for either Bummy Kantrowitz or Dimples Tancredi to whom he had no memory whatever of having been affianced. He was wearing the full uniform of the Jordan Desert Patrol with its magnificent *keyffiyeh* headdress held together with two rings of goat's wool fiber. The redan under the floor-length khaki tunic had sleeves so full that they would touch the ground when he stood up. He carried double bandoliers across his chest and a sharp, gleaming *jambiya,* the typical curved dagger of Arabia.

"Who has been teaching you to concentrate and to remember your name, Esau?" Jean-Pierre asked pleasantly.

"Professor Reyes."

"What did Professor Reyes tell you would be your first appointment after you had been elected President?"

"A Cabinet appointment. Secretary of Health, Education and Welfare."

"And who is to be appointed?"

"Jean-Pierre Harris. My uncle. The precedent for family appointments was set for the Cabinet in the administration of John F. Kennedy."

Jean-Pierre wheeled around. "Hey, this guy Reyes did a helluva job. And the boy talks normally. I mean, he's no robot, you know?"

"Excellent job," Bottie said.

"Reyes is a good man," Tris said.

"What did you have him set for you, Tris?"

Tris shook his head. "Not me. Celeste and I are going far, far away from this place and anything to do with politics. We're going to settle all the way out at Montauk Point and I'm going to paint and Celeste is going to count seagulls."

"No kidding?" Bottie exclaimed with joy. "That's the best news I ever had."

"What did you tell Reyes to have Esau set you for, Bottie?"

"My field is natural history, Mr. Harris. Not politics. I think politics should be left to men just like you and the Attorney General," Bottie said. "Let's get to work."

They grouped around a large map of the metropolitan midtown area on a low table in Jean-Pierre's apartment while Caspar P. Lear, jr. worked on the Esau figure near the window.

"We want everything to happen crisply outside that convention hall this afternoon," Bottie said. "Captain Pedernales has been working like a Trojan on the long-distance telephone and inside that hall—I don't think the man has had a wink of sleep in forty-eight hours—so we have to be letter-perfect on the outside."

"Whatever we need from the police department," Jean-Pierre said, "my parent organization can help there."

"No police today. We need the same split-second timing the Republicans demanded that Tris develop for the Democratic convention in sixty-eight."

"My people will be the police, today," Tris said. "That's all laid on—uniforms, equipment, the commissioner's cooperation—everything."

"Well, sure," Jean-Pierre said. "It's the best way in the long run and the city appreciates it. Anybody gets killed and it saves the city lawsuits."

"Do you want any National Guard, Bot?"

"No, no. Just rioters and police and a television camera working plot for each camera set-up in sequence. I've worked out a rough script which you can refine with the network people, Tris. We've got to give Esau a solid riot image so he can follow where the mobs lead."

"Count on the most solid riot image the voters have ever seen," Tris said. "Chicago was primitive stuff compared with what we have now developed. The networks have better remote equipment for one thing and the Administration and the war has them all accustomed to planning the individual news shots in advance. And last night we flew in some marvelous talent from New Orleans and Detroit. I mean, these people *know*. They will be gilled with speed and they'll swarm all across that main entrance and choke the side streets. The signs are all painted and every tenth man will have a bull horn. Every squad has its own special slogan to chant when they're on camera like—NO SYLVAN HARRIS or FUCK SYLVAN HARRIS—or—SYLVAN HARRIS IS THE CHURCH'S PIMP and the slightly more sophisticated, more personally oriented FUCK YOU SYLVAN HARRIS. We hope to get Jane Fonda or Mr. Hoffman to make the keynote speech outside while Captain Pedernales is making his keynote inside—that's scheduled for about two-fifteen. My people will assemble at about eleven-fifteen and will act very ugly for every arriving delegate. I mean, they'll have those delegates scared right out of their heads by the time they make it safe to the inside."

"Not to interfere, Tris," Bottie said, "but I had a go at a little scene for one of your stunt-check first-line kids."

"Great. Lemme have it."

"I'd like you to get a really rotten-looking black kid for this. You know, all cool and deadly?"

"No problem."

"He sort of saunters up insultingly straight to a network lens—give this to CBS, I think—and maybe a struggle with two pigs would be right if he overpowers the pigs with instant karate. Then he's way into a solid tight shot and he says something like—with a *very* Amos 'n Andy accent—uh—'Ah tole dem goddam delegates we gung kill dem effen dey puts dat choich-pimpin' mothuh Sylvan Harris in.' It's all being mimeographed now."

"Solid."

"And could you ask him to give us the pure, absolutely perfect diction on the name there, Tris?"

Tris made a note in a small black book and nodded. "You got it."

"When his message is in the clear I want five of the most brutal-looking fascist, Cossack pigs—maybe in those horrible motorcycle suits with like fur hats—no, better—helmets and a lot of black leather, but with shiny buttons and big badges. They grab this guy and they simply massacre him right in front of the cameras with a lot of blood-effects. But we want the guy to break loose just once, in a very close shot and yell right into every American home, 'We gung *kill* yew!' he screams into the camera, 'Y'all elect Sylvan Harris an we gung go inna yew house an *kill* you!' "

"Very good effect," Tris said.

"Good? It's great," Jean-Pierre said. "I'm telling you right there is where Esau gets elected."

"Hardly," Bottie said.

"Do you want this guy killed or badly hurt, Bot?"

"For heaven's sake, Tris, don't even say things like that. These people are actors, aren't they? You have competent directors, haven't you? Why would we need to go to such extremes in a show which is just a series of split-second impressions which, in the form of hundreds of multiple images on-screen, educate and form the minds of the voters—I mean, ambulances standing by, a young girl with long hair sprawled across the pavement with blood running out of her drawers and slow shots of nightsticks across beautiful, young teeth which can be speeded up in the camera. Eight-second sprays of im*pres*sions, Tris. That's what realism is today. You go out and give them the slow, plodding absolutely real thing with no editing whatsoever and you are going to lose us the entire audience except the out-and-out sadists. Okay?"

"You understand we have some clients who want killings and bad injuries on camera. I mean, that's why I asked."

"Well, not this client."

"You are absolutely right, Bottie. That's why art is superior to journalism," Jean-Pierre said.

"I think we should have one delegate beaten up," Bottie said. "I mean, at the entrance, on arrival of one so-called delegate, the pigs should lose control of the mob and some of your best people should break through like quicksilver and give this delegate a terrible beating under all the cameras. It's a key shot because the announcers can comment on it and carry the rationale of the action while the stretchermen carry the battered, unconscious delegate off after the pigs have regained control."

"How do you mean, kid?" Jean-Pierre asked.

"Oh, you know—they beat him terribly, or seem to, for a fifteen, eighteen-second take with all the sound effects, then the cops drag the rotten kids off him—we cut to the faces of the kids in the front row of the crowd and we register quick wipes of faces which are shocked, I mean terribly shocked by what they have done as a mob—then we cut back to the stretchermen taking the limp, bloody form out while a shamed voice over the shot narrates something like. 'That was Judge John Moodie, one of the most respected delegates to this convention, from the wonderful, little, gloriously American town of Middleburgh, New York, a man who dared to try to enter that convention hall today in the hope that some*how* he could help to bring us a government which could deal with the rabble here today which has now destroyed him."

"That will do it!" Jean-Pierre cried. "I could feel it in my heart. That one scene will absolutely elect Sylvan Harris!"

"Hardly," Bottie said. "Can you handle that, Tris?"

"Can do. But I think an upstate judge is wrong for the spot, actually."

"Why?"

"Too stock. I mean this is an audience which gave up reading books to stare at celebrities. I think we ought to fill the spot with a name."

"Like who? I mean, what kind of background? I think it's important that the victim have an implied as well as an overt life-style of law and order—I mean, such as a kindly, silver-haired old judge. Like in the old Andy Hardy movies."

"For Chrissake, Bottie, Andy Hardy is on heroin today. He kicked his father to death or something. These kind of audiences don't consider that wholesome shit entertainment. They want the action like it is."

"What kind of law-and-order celebrity would they like to see badly beaten up?"

"Well, what I mean is, like I think I can get General Frank Winikus, the actual grand, old man who ordered the massacre at My Lai. I mean, he fought for us. I mean, Frank Winikus actually stands for what that television audience is and wants and was trained to be."

"No question. Absolutely no question about it. Book him for the spot."

"Ready when you are, C.B." Caspar P. Lear, jr. sang out across the room.

The three men wheeled around to look at Duncan. But there was no Duncan. Sylvan "Esau" Harris stood there before them, smiling his own, old-time sneering, frightened smile.

"That is mag*nif*icent work, Caspar!" Jean-Pierre cried out. Bottie darted across the room and began to shake Esau's hand. "Welcome to the Democratic Party," he said. "Do you feel any different?"

"Not actually," Dunc said. "I know I'm a Democrat to the core of my being but I feel just like a Republican. It is the lift of a driving dream."

"Did you say—'lift of a driving dream?' " Bottie asked.

"That's wonderful," Jean-Pierre said. "That's the American way."

"No goddam Communist-fascist one-party systems for our country," Tris said, "and you can bet your sweet ass on that."

"We have gone through the long, dark night of the American spirit," Esau said. "But now that night is ending."

"We're all ready for you now, Esau," Bottie said, taking him by the arm. "And don't worry, Professor Reyes will cue you in on all of this just before you leave for the convention. Okay?"

"Sure," Esau said. "I've been fascinated listening to you guys. It's the first time I've been in on really professional politics."

They sat down around the low table in front of the greatly enlarged map of the midtown area. "As I see my assignment," Esau said, "it is to utilize the awesome power of my office against the children, the sick, the aged, and the poor but certainly not against the people who are causing the inflation, pollution, genocide and corruption."

"Now," Bottie said, "we'll be in radio contact with what's happening inside the convention hall. While they are intercutting the action on the General Winikus assault, Esau, your car will be placed just about two blocks up Eighth Avenue and, as the ambulance doors close on the Winikus sequence and the announcers reach the end of their narrations and the mob is still shocked by the enormity of what they have done, on the one hand, but still moved by the same crazy militancy, on the other, we bring your car into the mob—now vastly uncontrolled on Eighth Avenue itself—a mob of say two thousand drug-crazed black, *black* Negroes and long-haired, filthy, frightening white young people and students. All right. The network cameras are in position and your Cavalcade of Freedom rolls in through all those maniacs. They beat on the sides of the car. They throw eggs and rocks. They try to block the way to overturn the car. The FUCK YOU SYLVAN HARRIS signs go up everywhere and the dreaded chanting begins. The audience remembers what happened to General Winikus. They have seen that this crowd has been agitating itself, working itself up, only for this moment of your arrival."

"Jesus!" Jean-Pierre said. "There has got to be another way."

"No, no. Now—remember everything that happens outside is being flashed on the giant screen inside the convention hall. All right. We are now outside again. And *this* is the little piece of business that is going to put Esau in the White House. Ready? Okay. Tris has a very appealing young girl being cooled—right now—in the city morgue. She died yesterday of an overdose and there is no one to claim her so she will be Esau's Unknown Soldier. As the candidate, Sylvan Harris, gets out of his car in front of the hall, as the crowd screams for his blood and surges mightily forward to tear him apart, the police will lose their nerve and fire a volley of blanks into the crowd. Except the audience at home won't know they are blanks. The crowd scatters—right? As the density of people vanishes under the sight of the network lenses they will show us the body of the young girl from the morgue, dead upon the street. The commentators will begin to lay in the awfulness of this result of mob violence—two networks taking the side of the police, one network taking the side of the mob. *At this moment,* the threatened candidate himself, Sylvan Harris—you, Esau,—a man who is the same age as most of the people in the mob—but a *sane, right-thinking* American youth—rips himself away from his bodyguards—and the cameras will get all of this—and leaps from the car and rushes into that raging torrent of death by violence and he will pick up the body of that *beautiful* young girl—and she is a *most* appealingly, frailly beautiful corpse—saying, *'Come unto me for your salvation'* by his very actions as he picks her body up and wheels her around into a medium shot—full-length—which *slowly* builds into a magnificent close shot of his head and the corpse's head—a veritable political *pietà,* the commentators will say—if they only stay with the script.

"Then, right into the camera, the mob in the background, that head lolling on his shoulder, he will cry out to Christ, Computer, to end all this senseless violence that he may lead the people—his peers and his elders—back to the fruitful life, then, giving the body back to the morgue attendants he will turn to the thousands of rabble in the streets and ask them to follow him into the hall to take their place among those who will choose a better government and a better life for all. It should be effective."

"Man," Tris said, "if that tape isn't repeated on every station of every network right across this country every fifteen minutes tonight then, man, I de*serve* to live out the rest of my life at Montauk."

59

Jean-Pierre was able to make special arrangements through his parent organization to have two separate marriage licenses issued to Botolf Noon and Miss Mulligan. Mona had been born eight and a half minutes before Fiona so she and Bottie were married first, then Bottie and Fiona got on the line at the Marriage Bureau and they were married by the City Clerk.

The happy triple then said good-by to everyone assembled and were driven directly to Kennedy Airport where they took off for a glorious honeymoon in Scotland, where Bottie hoped to spend an hour with his hero, V.C. Wynne-Edwards, before leaving to settle down in Central Australia.

Os dropped Ada off at her place, then went home to change for dinner. He had so greatly enjoyed the wedding. He felt so well; so young. As he let himself into the apartment a sudden draft took the door out of his hand and slammed it shut loudly.

From far down the hall, he heard Cerce's voice calling.

She came along the corridor and filled the archway just as amiably beautiful as she had ever been. She hadn't changed, it seemed to him, from the girl he had met so long ago.

Then he knew he had not changed either. In all the time, all the days of his life, he had not changed. Excepting one small thing which he felt he had to explain to her.

"Cerce," he said sternly, "I think you should know that I have a mistress."